IVORY ASHES

NOVIKOV BRATVA
BOOK 1

NICOLE FOX

Copyright © 2024 by Nicole Fox

All rights reserved.

No part of this book may be reproduced in any form or by any electronic or mechanical means, including information storage and retrieval systems, without written permission from the author, except for the use of brief quotations in a book review.

❦ Created with Vellum

ALSO BY NICOLE FOX

Egorov Bratva
Tangled Innocence
Tangled Decadence

Zakrevsky Bratva
Requiem of Sin
Sonata of Lies
Rhapsody of Pain

Bugrov Bratva
Midnight Purgatory
Midnight Sanctuary

Oryolov Bratva
Cruel Paradise
Cruel Promise

Pushkin Bratva
Cognac Villain
Cognac Vixen

Viktorov Bratva
Whiskey Poison
Whiskey Pain

Orlov Bratva
Champagne Venom
Champagne Wrath

Uvarov Bratva
Sapphire Scars
Sapphire Tears

Vlasov Bratva
Arrogant Monster
Arrogant Mistake

Zhukova Bratva
Tarnished Tyrant
Tarnished Queen

Stepanov Bratva
Satin Sinner
Satin Princess

Makarova Bratva
Shattered Altar
Shattered Cradle

Solovev Bratva
Ravaged Crown
Ravaged Throne

Vorobev Bratva
Velvet Devil
Velvet Angel

Romanoff Bratva
Immaculate Deception
Immaculate Corruption

Kovalyov Bratva

Gilded Cage

Gilded Tears

Jaded Soul

Jaded Devil

Ripped Veil

Ripped Lace

Mazzeo Mafia Duet

Liar's Lullaby (Book 1)

Sinner's Lullaby (Book 2)

Bratva Crime Syndicate

Can be read in any order!

Lies He Told Me

Scars He Gave Me

Sins He Taught Me

Belluci Mafia Trilogy

Corrupted Angel (Book 1)

Corrupted Queen (Book 2)

Corrupted Empire (Book 3)

De Maggio Mafia Duet

Devil in a Suit (Book 1)

Devil at the Altar (Book 2)

Kornilov Bratva Duet

Married to the Don (Book 1)

Til Death Do Us Part (Book 2)

Heirs to the Bratva Empire

Can be read in any order!

Kostya

Maksim

Andrei

Princes of Ravenlake Academy (Bully Romance)

Can be read as standalones!

Cruel Prep

Cruel Academy

Cruel Elite

Tsezar Bratva

Nightfall (Book 1)

Daybreak (Book 2)

Russian Crime Brotherhood

Can be read in any order!

Owned by the Mob Boss

Unprotected with the Mob Boss

Knocked Up by the Mob Boss

Sold to the Mob Boss

Stolen by the Mob Boss

Trapped with the Mob Boss

Volkov Bratva

Broken Vows (Book 1)

Broken Hope (Book 2)

Broken Sins *(standalone)*

Other Standalones

Vin: A Mafia Romance

Box Sets

Bratva Mob Bosses (Russian Crime Brotherhood Books 1-6)

Tsezar Bratva (Tsezar Bratva Duet Books 1-2)

Heirs to the Bratva Empire

The Mafia Dons Collection

The Don's Corruption

MAILING LIST

Sign up to my mailing list!
New subscribers receive a FREE steamy bad boy romance novel.

Click the link below to join.
https://sendfox.com/nicolefox

IVORY ASHES

My new boss is gorgeous, arrogant, and filthy rich.

The only problem?

He doesn't know he's also *the father of my baby*.

Six years ago, I was supposed to get married.

But the night before the wedding, my groom-to-be showed me sides of himself I'd never seen before.

I might've died in that hotel room...

If Mikhail Novikov hadn't burst in to save me.

Handsome, strong, capable knight in shining armor—sign me up, right?

WRONG.

Because Mikhail wasn't just the hero I never knew I needed...

He was also way more dangerous than I ever could've known.

But for one night, I let myself do something I never should've done.

It was worth it—several times over, if you catch my drift.

In the morning, though, I did the reasonable thing:

I RAN.

For six years, I keep running.

Until I walk into work one day, and find my new boss waiting in my office.

Guess who?

And guess what he does when finds out about **our baby**?

IVORY ASHES is Book 1 of the Novikov Bratva duet. The story concludes in Book 2, IVORY OATH.

1

VIVIANA

"Touch her again and I'll kill you."

The unfamiliar voice echoes through my bridal suite. I might be concussed, courtesy of my soon-to-be husband's strong backhand across the face just a second ago, but *is that the rumbling baritone of God?* If so, excellent timing. The Big Man Upstairs hasn't done jack shit for me up until now, so I'd say some divine intervention in my shitshow of a life is long overdue.

I want to crack a swollen eye open and chance a peek at my savior, but lifting my face is what got me slapped for the third time this weekend, so I don't.

The first was for not holding Trofim's hand during the rehearsal dinner. Then, when I mentioned that surely he'd hate to bruise my face the day before our wedding, he slapped me again for presuming to know what he does and doesn't hate.

This third time was for… well, shits and giggles, I presume.

Nothing says "can't wait to get hitched" like wearing the gaudiest signet ring in existence and slapping your fiancée around 'til kingdom come. I probably have the Novikov Bratva crest indented in my left cheek by now. It's fitting, since I'm being offered up to Trofim Novikov himself bright and early tomorrow morning. Might as well brand me like cattle tonight, before we make vows before God when the sun rises.

Not that Trofim gives a shit about vows before God. When we went to his cousin's brother's hairdresser's… niece's— well, hell if I know who it was for, but we went to *someone's* baptism together a few months ago, and I was positive Trofim would recoil in fear when the priest sprinkled holy water on the baby's head and accidentally splashed some in our general direction.

I expected sulfurous smoke to pour out of his mouth. Maybe some *Exorcist*-style head spinning. Unfortunately, his head stayed facing forward, but I've been holding out hope he'll burst into flames when we step up to the altar tomorrow.

Based on the booming voice coming from the doorway of my bridal suite, God might be a little ahead of schedule.

"Get away from her," that voice snarls. "Now."

The words vibrate through my bones.

"The fuck…? Get the hell out of our room." Trofim's voice is whiskey-slurred, but his grip on the back of my robe is immovably solid.

That's the real cause of all of this. Trofim is a heartless bastard when he's sober. When he drinks, though, he's straight-up *soul*less. And right now, he's probably more alcohol than blood.

Maybe this new god of vengeance should be careful.

"This isn't *your* room," the deep voice corrects angrily. "It's *hers*."

I cringe and duck my head further. *Don't bring* me *into this!* Maybe, if I make myself small enough, Trofim will forget I'm here.

Neck bowed, I look down at the floor and catch a glimpse of my reflection in the mirrored coffee table.

It's enough to make me suck in a sharp breath. My eye is swollen. My cheek is as red as the parade of flags that have lined every inch of the road from the moment I met Trofim to now.

First, he's a Taurus. I should have run for the hills the moment I made *that* little discovery.

Second, my *father* approved of Trofim. That in itself is the biggest red flag of them all.

As much as I wish it was because Daddy Dearest just didn't know the horrible truth of my intended's cruel and unusual ways, that's not the case. My father was literally in the room for slap number one. He was actually, physically standing in the doorway right where Potential Savior #2 is standing now.

Except, instead of telling Trofim to back off and leave me alone in a soul-shuddering baritone, my father whispered in my ear—which was still ringing from Trofim's slap, might I add—to "keep your head down and *make him happy.*"

In my father's eyes, that's all I am: a tool for others' happiness.

Not mine. No, no, don't be ridiculous—*never* mine.

I, Viviana Giordano, exist for *his* happiness. Whoever "he" may be in any given scenario. My father's. Trofim's. Any other man whose alliance might be of some value.

To my father, I'm a bartering chip who just so happens to have the blood of the Giordano mafia running through my veins.

And Trofim, by very specific design on my father's part, *just so happens* to be the eldest son of the Novikov Bratva's *pakhan*.

Tomorrow is the crime world's equivalent of a royal wedding. Lighter on the fascinators, heavier on the bloodshed.

But if Trofim gets his way, the bloodshed portion of the event is going to start tonight.

Trofim laughs. The sharp, grating sound skitters down my spine. I flinch away from him, but he fists his hand in the back of my robe again. The sleeves are halfway down my arms now. I'm one gentle tug away from standing here in nothing but my silk and lace nightie. And Trofim is anything but gentle.

"What's hers is mine," he sneers.

"Not until tomorrow," the deep voice barks again. "And not ever, unless you let her go. *Now.*"

"Or what?" Trofim challenges.

He's the son of a *pakhan*. Unless it's his father standing in front of us—which I know it isn't, since the elder Novikov is just as bad as Trofim—there's nothing anyone can say to scare Trofim. He always has the upper hand. And the *back*hand, as my poor cheek can attest.

There's a brief pause. "Or I'll have no choice but to kill you, brother."

Brother?

Before I can stop myself, I look up.

Trofim has two brothers, and if you'd asked me three seconds ago, I would have put all of my money on it being Anatoly in the doorway. The man is a golden retriever in human form. If anyone would have a soft spot for a battered woman, it would be him.

But it's not Anatoly in the doorway.

It's the brooding, mysterious, never-met-a-smile-he-wanted-to-try-on youngest brother standing in the doorway.

It's Mikhail Novikov.

Mikhail hasn't so much as glanced in my direction since I first saw him at mine and Trofim's engagement party, and now, he's standing *here*. In my bridal suite. Threatening to murder his own blood brother to save me.

What in the ever-loving fuck is going on?

"You'd kill *me* over *her?*" Trofim shoves me forward, but his hand is still fisted in my robe, so the material slides off my arms and I flop onto the floor between the brothers like a dead fish. A dead fish in very tiny, very revealing pajamas.

I glance up at Mikhail Novikov from my knees. He's staring down at me, face as unreadable as ever. It's the same blank expression he gave me the first day we met.

It was my engagement party. As the bride-to-be, I was the reluctant star of the show. Terrible as my groom was, I'm a Sagittarius through and through. I love a good party and the

Novikovs throw great parties. Incredible parties, truthfully. Ice sculptures, champagne fountains, and canapés abounded.

With a smoked salmon cracker in one hand and three flutes worth of champagne fizzing in my veins, I marched up to Mikhail in the corner and hit him with my most dazzling smile.

Hello there. I'm Viviana, your new sister. Pause for polite laughter.

But… crickets.

Mikhail didn't smile. Didn't smirk. He didn't even bother giving me a disapproving once-over. No, he simply took a sip of his drink… and walked away.

Like I was nothing. No one.

Like I didn't matter.

Now, I'm sprawled half-naked on the floor in front of him— *while he is trying to save me from his abusive older brother,* no less —and I still get absolutely nothing from him.

Mikhail sighs and meets his brother's eyes. "I'd kill you for almost anyone, Trofim. Fucking give me a reason."

I start to lift myself up. Maybe I can slink away while the brothers duke it out. But Trofim's foot lands in the middle of my back. He presses me down to the floor, stealing the air from my lungs.

Mikhail takes a half-step towards us, but he stops. I can't see his face from my new vantage point literally under Trofim's heel, but his voice shakes with rage when he says, "Final warning."

Trofim laughs. "I gave you a reason the moment I was born, little brother. Do you think marrying Giordano's daughter will secure you the Bratva? I'll inherit the title of *pakhan* whether I marry this bitch or not."

"This isn't about her," Mikhail snarls. "This is about *you*. You're unfit."

"Unfit to what?" Trofim slurs.

Mikhail moves closer. "Unfit to lead *and* to marry Viviana."

I should be fighting for breath, but I'm too busy being shocked Mikhail even knows my name.

Why does he care who I marry? What does it matter to him if his brother is an abusive asshole?

"Oh, wait. Wait a minute. Is this—Are you trying to make up for past mistakes?" Trofim chuckles. "Holy fuck. I mean, come on, Mikhail, it's funny, isn't it? You standing here talking about *me* being unfit. If anyone is unfit to marry, it's you. Look at what happened to—"

Air whooshes out of Trofim's lungs at the same time it returns to mine.

Because, between one second and the next, Mikhail launches himself at Trofim and knocks him off of me.

I scramble across the floor as the glass coffee table shatters under their weight. Shards of glass skitter across the hardwood floor.

The door is right in front of me. It's unlocked. I could run.

But run where?

I'm in a nightgown that barely covers my ass and my father is right down the hall. He'll never let me escape.

I know all too well what happens when I poke that bear. Daddy doesn't like when his pawns talk back.

So I just stand here, stranded between one nightmare and the next. I press myself against the wall and watch Mikhail pummel his older brother into the floor.

Trofim doesn't stand a chance. He can hold his own against a woman half his size, sure, but he can't keep up with the speed of Mikhail's punches.

Blood and spit and broken teeth fly as Trofim's neck snaps one way and then the other.

Mikhail is going to win. He's going to overpower Trofim, and then…

Before I can sort through the stew of terrible options in front of me, Mikhail wraps his hand around his brother's throat and drives a knee into his chest. He pins him to the floor.

"Stop fighting if you want to live," he growls.

It isn't much of a choice. Trofim is panting, exhausted from just that little bit of fighting. He couldn't throw Mikhail off if he wanted to. And he really, *really* wants to.

"What?" he pants. "You want her? Fucking take her, then."

I shrink back against the wall, but Mikhail doesn't look at me. Instead, he snatches Trofim's hand off the floor. The two thrash around for just a moment before Mikhail gets whatever he's after and lets his brother's wrist flop back down.

"Leave." He stands back, power rippling off of him like a forcefield. Goosebumps bloom across my chest. "You so much as set foot on the same continent as me ever again, you're dead."

Trofim works his jaw back and forth. "Exile."

"It's a better option than death. Take it."

I think he might lunge at Mikhail again. Argue.

Instead, Trofim stands up, wipes blood from his split bottom lip, and stomps out of the room without even looking at me.

I don't move. Don't breathe. Everything is happening so fast and I don't have time to think about where it leaves me…

Until Mikhail turns to me.

Whatever he's feeling, it's still elusive. But slowly, he lifts his hand and slides something onto his finger.

The gaudy ring that cracked across my face less than ten minutes ago settles on his right hand like it's always been there. Like it belongs.

I look from the family signet ring to its new owner.

The Novikov Bratva just got a new heir. And his sights are set on me.

2

VIVIANA

"What are you still doing here?" Mikhail asks.

The words of my savior, everyone.

"I'm naked," I blurt.

The words of the socially illiterate, everyone.

I'm usually much more eloquent, but word vomit must be a nasty side effect of cranial and/or emotional whiplash.

Not to mention, Mikhail is handsome. Stunningly, stomach-twistingly handsome.

It's the reason I walked over to him at my engagement party in the first place. Sure, I was there to marry his brother, but being betrothed didn't make me blind. Mikhail was leaning against the wall with a diamond-cut jaw and a curl of golden brown hair that fell perfectly across his forehead. I wanted to see what he was about. Could the inside possibly match the outside?

I thought the answer was a definite no, but now… He saved me. Does that change things?

Now, I'm seeing him up close and in better lighting. Does *that* change things?

The same strand of hair sweeps slightly lower over one of his cold blue eyes now. Eyes that are wholly fixed on me.

I shake my head to clear away the lusty cobwebs. "Well, not naked," I correct quickly. "I'm almost naked. Barely clothed. I'm in pajamas."

Mikhail looks pointedly at the skewed scrap of lace covering my lady bits and little else. "You wore that for him?" Mikhail's upper lip curls in disgust. It's the first easily-readable emotion I've seen on him.

"I didn't wear anything for him. It's for me." I cross my arms over my chest, which only serves to put my cleavage even more on display. I quickly uncross them. "I think it's pretty."

Trofim may have been a monster, but he had great taste in lingerie. Well, really, whatever poor maid he got to order me the present had great taste, is more like it.

Silk triangles cover my breasts, but the rest of the nightie is intricate lace. It flutters over my midsection and brushes against the very tops of my thighs. If I turned around, Mikhail would get an eyeful of the matching silk thong.

I press my bare ass more firmly against the wallpaper so that doesn't happen.

"You should leave while you still can."

I frown. "I didn't realize my salvation came with an expiration date."

Mikhail roots through the mini-bar fridge, grumbling when there's nothing but champagne inside. He pops the bottle and crunches over the remains of a shattered vase and haphazardly spread rose petals to find a glass.

The fact that we're in what would have been mine and Trofim's honeymoon suite tomorrow night is becoming hard to ignore.

For me, at least. Mikhail still won't look at me.

"Why are you here?" I demand.

His throat bobs as he swallows down champagne before pouring himself another glass. "Were you not listening? I already explained myself. My brother was unfit."

Unfit to lead and *to marry Viviana.* I'm about to hand over the last of my dignity to ask which one he's referring to now.

Instead, I nod. "He was. But he was unfit yesterday. Last week. Six months ago. Why did you decide to finally do something about it tonight?"

I didn't ask the question with an answer in mind, but I suddenly find myself hoping Mikhail will turn and look at me. I let myself imagine his icy blue eyes burning with passion… *for me.*

You, Viviana. Since the moment we met, I've wanted you. I couldn't stand it for another second.

Or, y'know… something along those lines.

Mikhail does turn to me, but there's nothing but an icy chill when he looks at me. His eyes scrape over my skin. I swear he can read every thought bouncing around my funhouse of a brain.

It's confirmed when he tilts his head to the side. "Do you think I'm here for you?"

"Wha—No!" I cross my arms again. Mikhail's eyes drop to my chest.

I don't uncross my arms this time.

He takes a step closer. "This has nothing to do with you, Viviana."

Heat coils low in my belly at the way he says my name. "Why should I believe that? I'm the woman promised to the heir of the Novikov Bratva." I gesture to the ring on his finger. "That's you now, isn't it? Some people would argue we still have a binding agreement."

My father would be among the loudest of those people.

I, however, should probably have shut my big, dumb mouth. In a flash, Mikhail crosses the distance between us and cages me in.

His palm is flat against the wall next to my head. He holds his body stubbornly away from mine, but he might as well be smothering me. I feel him everywhere. Heat pours off of him and tingles across my skin.

He smells like mint and champagne as he dips his chin and whispers in my ear. "Do you want me to make good on that agreement, Viviana? Is that why you're still here?"

Truth be told, I don't know why I'm still here.

Fear? Habit? Curiosity?

I wrote Mikhail Novikov off the first night we met. I assumed he was a pompous asshole and never thought of him again, no matter how much I enjoyed the sight of him at functions Trofim dragged me along to.

No women dared get close to him. Mikhail didn't deign to talk to anyone else. He was a shadow on the edge of the room.

But now, he's revealing himself to be something else entirely.

I want to find out what.

"I'm still here because…" I duck under his arm and walk across the suite. "I'm still here because helping clean up some of this mess is the least I can do for the man who saved me."

I bend over and scoop a handful of glass shards into my palm. It's only when I turn around to find the trash can that I remember what I'm wearing. Or what I'm *not* wearing. Full coverage underwear, for one.

Mikhail is standing rigid against the wall. And he isn't the only one. There's a noticeable bulge at the front of his pants. A *large,* noticeable bulge.

My gaze drops down, back up, down again, and finally back up to the dark holes where his eyes once were. His pupils are blown wide.

Mikhail Novikov may be difficult to read, but I know desire when I see it.

He blinks a few times and seems to snap himself out of it. His mouth twists down into a scowl. "Me being here has nothing to do with saving you."

"Really? You had me fooled. *'Touch her again and I'll kill you,'*" I say in a terrible impression of his voice. "Seems like it had at least a little to do with saving me."

"You think I came to save you? Is that why you're putting on this little show for me?" He crosses the distance between us and swats the glass shards out of my hand. They rain down over my bare feet, but I barely feel it. Not when Mikhail is staring into my soul. "Am I to collect my reward now?"

My cheeks burn. "I'm not putting on a show! I'm cleaning up the mess you and your brother made."

"This is why you're not the right fit for this world," he says almost to himself. "Someone does one nice thing for you and you're throwing away your chance at freedom. You don't owe me anything, Viviana. *I didn't come here to save you.*"

If he keeps saying that, I might start to believe him.

Maybe that wouldn't be such a bad thing, though. As it is, my heart is doing an interesting little dubstep in my chest.

"You said Trofim wasn't a good fit for this world."

"He wasn't."

"But now, I'm not a good fit, either? Why not?" It doesn't matter. I shouldn't care. I don't care, actually. Still, I find myself adding, "Is that why I've never seen you with a woman before? Because no one is good enough for you?"

He's silent for a moment. His breath rasps in his chest, his throat, past his lips in plumes of mint and champagne. Then he sighs.

"Leave," he snarls even as he shifts closer to me. My hip brushes against his leg.

I stretch onto my toes. "You don't want to honor the deal our fathers made because you think you're better than me."

The words are barely out of my mouth when Mikhail's hand grips my neck. His thumb works into my pulse point as he tilts my head back so he's towering over me. "This has nothing to do with me being better than you."

I swallow, my neck bobbing against his fingers. "Then what's it about?"

He dips his head. More mint and sweet champagne wash over me as he whispers, "It's about me being the worst possible thing for you."

Who could be worse than Trofim?

Mikhail seems to see the question in my frown. He slides closer. His erection pushes against the lace of my nightgown and my eyes flare wide.

"My brother wanted you for a wife. He wanted an alliance. I couldn't care less about that. Fuck the deal our fathers made." His thumb strokes possessively along the column of my neck. "There is only one thing I want from you, Viviana."

"Take it," I breathe.

It's out of me before I can stop myself.

Mikhail shakes his head and walks me backwards. His long legs brush against mine until I fall back onto the bed.

"You shouldn't let yourself be someone's pawn. Not in this world." He looks down at me for a second before he wraps his big hands around my hips and jerks me to the edge of the bed. "I'm going to teach you why."

3

VIVIANA

"Trofim didn't deserve this," he muses as he strokes the outer curve of my ass, discovering an erogenous zone I didn't know existed five seconds ago.

Didn't deserve me?

No, he must mean sex in general.

I tend to agree. For the sake of the human race and future generations, Trofim and his evil seed shouldn't be allowed near any vaginas.

"Trofim and I never... We didn't... It was part of the arrangement. He never even came to my apartment."

I don't know why I feel the need to explain, but I do.

As soon as Iakov Novikov informed his son he couldn't touch me until we were married, I expected Trofim to throw a temper tantrum. Our engagement was planned by our respective paternal overlords to be just over six months long. That kind of celibacy was a lot to ask, even for me. Not that I had any desire to do the dirty with Trofim.

But the only desire Trofim had was to knock me around.

"You were together for six months." Mikhail sounds confused. Like that math isn't even close to mathing. *Six months with no sex? Impossible.*

I can practically hear his thoughts now. *What's the point of living if I can't rip off my shirt and ravage maidens on the daily?*

To be fair, as a maiden about to be ravaged, I get it. The promise of seeing what's going on beneath Mikhail's shirt is the current singular focus of my life.

"I'm sure six months without sex is like a lifetime for you," I drawl.

"Only the last six months."

I don't have time to understand what that means before he strokes his thumb over the soaked front of my panties. He groans a single time. Just one deep sound, low in his throat, before he slips his thumb under the lace. He plays in my wetness, dragging it up and down until I'm covered in myself. When the calloused pad of his thumb brushes over my clit, I jerk off the bed.

Mikhail arches a brow like I'm an interesting puzzle and does it again.

I want him to say something. I want him to talk dirty. Tell me I'm beautiful. Hell, call me a dirty slut. Just give me *something*.

But he is the same stoic, detached Mikhail I've seen only in passing for the last six months. Except now, he's sliding his thick middle finger inside of me.

"Oh my God." I arch my back, my head lolling against the mattress.

Mikhail is working his finger into me with an aloof professionalism that I am not in any way matching. He's calm, cool, and collected—I'm an absolute fucking mess.

I moan, rolling my hips to take more of him. I *need* more. I reach down and grab his wrist. I'm prepared to fuck myself with his finger if I have to.

But before I can, he pulls out of me.

I start to sit up, my body pulsing helplessly around nothing, my mind whirring as I try to come up with the world's least-prepared, most-convincing argument for why he should *always* be inside of me, starting, like, *rightfuckingnow*. Then Mikhail takes my wrist and pins my arm to the mattress above my head.

Belatedly, I register that he has unzipped his pants. That's probably why he let go of my wrist. To get himself ready.

Then my logistical thoughts burn up like space junk entering the atmosphere as Mikhail enters me. He presses his cock to my throbbing pussy and slides in.

"Big," I gasp. Sometime in the last six months, I must have lost my filter. Sometime in the last six seconds, I lost the power of speech.

But I'm not wrong. Just the head of him feels like too much.

Also, weirdly, not enough.

His fingers dig into the soft curves of my hips as he braces me. He holds me still as he fills me in a relentless, heady stroke.

"Better than I imagined," he rasps, sliding deeper inside of me.

Somewhere in the distance, a record scratches. Mikhail *imagined* this? Me? *Us?*

I don't have the neurons to process that. Not when I'm already at the brink of physical overwhelm processing the way he's stretching me. The way I've never been this full. The way people write songs about sex like this and here I am, having it, with Mikhail Novikov.

The brother of the man I was supposed to marry.

This is not the way I thought tonight was going to go.

I lift my hips and we fall together at a new angle. I clamp down around him. And Mikhail grunts.

My vision is blurring, but I look up at him. He's over top of me, granite jaw clenched. His lower lip is curled between his teeth. His brow is furrowed.

Testing a theory, I tighten around Mikhail again.

He growls and drives into me harder. His hand is wrapped so tightly around my wrist that my fingers are going numb. I send a silent thanks out to the editors of *Cosmo* for being a girl's best friend and encouraging me to add in a few sets of Kegels after yoga. Then I do it again.

"Don't," he warns.

He's looking at me. The ice in his eyes is everywhere now. It's spreading. His entire expression is frigid despite how hot he is between my legs.

My body flutters around him. Seeing Mikhail Novikov hovering over top of me is almost enough to push me over the edge.

"Don't what?" I gasp.

He slams into me, his weight pressing against my clit. "Don't move."

"I'm not."

He fixes me with a look that says he knows better. He knows what I'm up to.

Mikhail is a man who likes to be in control. Color me shocked.

"You're the one who told me I shouldn't be anyone's pawn," I remind him. Then I clench around him again.

I'm still holding tight when he jerks out of me. Before I can react or beg for forgiveness, Mikhail shoves my thighs wide and *drops to his knees.*

The moment his tongue delves into me, I realize the dangerous position I'm in. He could leave me like this, aching and needy. I'd probably go mad with wanting him. God, I bet he'd love that. Sick, cruel bastard.

"Is this your kink?" I rasp, grabbing a fistful of his hair. "Are you into edging until I combust?"

He doesn't respond. It's probably hard to talk with his lips wrapped around my clit, his tongue flicking at every sensitive part of me until I'm grinding against his mouth.

This sure doesn't feel like edging.

He drives a finger into me again and I cry out. "Mikhail!"

He growls in response and that vibration is all it takes. I explode in a mess of gushing tremors that I'm way too far gone to be embarrassed about. I pull on his hair and drive my heels into his back as an orgasm more powerful than anything I've ever felt tilts my planet off its axis.

His tongue slows, lapping at me as my legs tremble over his shoulders.

When he pulls back, his lips are slick. His hair is sticking up where I dug my fingers in. He is gloriously disheveled and I can't even bear to look at him.

I stare at the ceiling instead. "Was that my punishment?"

"No." He pushes my legs aside and they fall open around his waist. His erection pushes against my opening. "I wanted to know what you taste like *before* I fill you with my cum."

I'm drained. Spent. Used up and discarded.

Then he slides in me to the hilt and I'm back.

When he presses his thumb to my clit, I might as well be one of those emergency flashlights with the hand cranks. Every time Mikhail touches me, I light up. My lust could power a lighthouse. A beacon. One of those spotlights outside of the circus.

Come one and all, and witness never-before-seen heights of sexual arousal!

"This can't be real." I lift my arms over my head because I'm not sure what to do with them otherwise. I'm fully out of my body.

Until Mikhail uses his other hand to gather up my wrists. He holds them firmly while he fucks me.

"Please…" I whimper. I don't even know what I'm asking for.

He shakes his head. "Not yet."

Tears are forming in the corners of my eyes. I need to come right now. What could he possibly be waiting for? What could feel better than this?

I'm not sure if I said all of that out loud or if Mikhail is as deep in my head as he is my pussy, but he responds.

"I want to finish on your chest. Your stomach. Your ass. I want to paint you like you're mine." He growls again, slams home in me again and again. "But you're so fucking tight…"

I clench around him, the rumblings of another orgasm taking hold. I drag my hand down the flat plane of his stomach. "Later. Do it later. Next time."

We'll do this again, won't we? Several more times. We have to. This can't be it.

Even if this is it, I want what he promised. I want him to finish inside of me.

I don't want him to pull away.

He tips his head back, the long column of his throat strained as he drives in and out of me again and again.

I fist the front of his shirt. I'm lowkey dying a little bit at the fact that this is the best sex I've ever had in my life and he didn't even take off his shirt. "There, Mikhail. Right—Don't stop."

He looks down at me and for one fleeting second, I see him. The *real* him. The heat in his eyes. The fire burning beneath the surface.

The iceman has an inferno raging inside of him.

In a flash, it consumes us both.

I cry out as Mikhail roars, twitching out a release deep inside of me. Distantly, I recognize what he's saying. The name he's calling out again and again. *My* name.

Viviana.

We come down together, panting and slicked with sweat. Mikhail collapses on top of me, his heavy weight pressing me comfortably into the mattress. Then he rolls away, tucks himself back into his pants, and stares up at the ceiling.

I want to know if he's thinking the same things I am, but I actually don't know what I'm thinking. My mind is a mess.

Will Trofim come back for me?

Am I going to marry Mikhail?

If I do, will my father approve? I know far too well what happens when he doesn't.

Questions and possibilities chase each other around my head, circling until the warmth has leached out of my limbs and I'm shivering and sore.

I look over and Mikhail is still next to me, his eyes closed. His breathing is deep and even… sleeping.

Fuck knows he earned a nap.

So have I—but what happens when we wake up?

I hear Mikhail's voice in my head. *You should leave while you still can.*

Carefully, I slide off of the bed. Evidence of what we did is sticky between my legs, sliding down my inner thighs, as I tug on a pair of jeans.

There's no time to clean up. No time to make myself presentable.

If I want to go, I have to go *now*.

So why do I stop in the doorway and look back?

Mikhail's long legs are draped over the side of the bed. One hand is resting across his stomach. Regret pangs through me so painfully my breath catches.

This—*this* is the danger of Mikhail Novikov. There's a reason he lurks on the edges. There's a reason he shields himself with an icy, indifferent mask. He reveals nothing because all it takes is one tiny sliver of him… and you're hooked.

I close my eyes before I turn away.

Then, without looking back, I slip into the hallway and run like hell.

4

MIKHAIL

I should feel like a piece of shit.

Not for fucking my brother's girl—I would have gladly busted into the suite in the middle of Trofim's wedding night and fucked his new bride first just to spite him.

But Viviana never belonged to him. Not in any way that mattered.

No, I should feel like a piece of shit because I *wanted* her at all.

Since the day we met, actually.

The only reason I was at their engagement party is because my father demanded it. "Family unity is important, Mikhail," he snarled when I suggested staying home. "You need to show your loyalty to your brother. You need to remind people that you're still here."

Still here after my world shattered. Still here after they took everything from me.

"Plus," he added, "Helen will be there."

It would have been physically impossible for me to care any less about Helen Drakos, the Greek mafia princess. My father didn't care about her, either. Not really.

Then and always, my father's goal was to make sure everyone knew the full might of the Novikov Bratva. He didn't want there to be any more questions about whose horse the family name was being hitched to.

Before my father announced Trofim as his official heir, there were whispers it would be me. That it *should* be me.

I don't mind answering those questions with an obvious truth: *It should have been.*

But I played the dutiful spare and watched Trofim parade his new pet around their engagement party without ever really looking at the spectacle. She was a nameless, faceless woman in a green dress. My sadistic brother's trophy.

Then Viviana came over to me.

I felt her watching me as the party dragged on. It was a prickling awareness. An itch down my neck. The same kind I feel when I'm being approached from behind. A vulnerability I can't ignore.

She hadn't tried to talk to me all night. There was no time, not when Trofim needed everyone to see the woman he would impregnate and then spend the next lifetime cheating on with a revolving door of mistresses.

I couldn't even blame him—well, not for that, anyway. It's what our father did. His father before him. A real noble lineage of Novikov *pakhans* fucking anything with a heartbeat, wedding vows be damned.

I was the freak who broke the mold. Alyona and I were only twenty-three when we got married, and I never once even thought of straying from her.

But during a break in the parade, Viviana slipped away. Trofim was caught up in a financial circle jerk with a group of businessmen desperate to strike deals with our family and too afraid to approach our father. He didn't see his little wifey-to-be cross the room. He didn't see her walk towards me.

But *I* saw.

I noticed all of it without noticing the one thing that was truly important.

I wanted her.

That realization rang loud and clear only once she was standing in front of me. The moment she curled her honey gold hair behind her ear and smiled.

It wasn't some fate bullshit or love at first sight. Life has kicked me when I'm down enough times for me to know that there's no reason to roll over and show it your soft underbelly. No, it was that my brother's fiancée had fuck-me lips and an ass I wanted to take a bite out of.

The second thought quickly chased the tail of the first: *I should feel like a piece of shit.*

But I didn't.

I still don't.

Viviana Giordano is the first woman I've wanted—the first woman I've fucked—since I lost Alyona three years ago. And I still don't feel one shred of guilt.

I spread my arms out across the bed in a long stretch. It's empty, thank fuck. Viviana must have made the right choice and ran.

No matter how glad I am I finally got to feel her tighten around my cock, it wouldn't have been worth it if she'd tried to stick around afterward. The last thing I need is some lovesick damsel in distress pining after me.

I meant what I told her last night: I didn't walk into this suite last night to save her.

I was on this path long before she made her dirty deal with my brother.

The moment I lost Alyona and our daughter, I knew I was done being the spare to my brother's heir. I was done waiting in the shadows while someone else called the shots. I was never going to let anyone else have the power to hold my family's fate in their hands.

I swore that much as I stood over my family's graves. Even as I swore I'd never have another family again.

Add "sworn bachelorhood" to the long list of reasons why I have no interest in taking Trofim's place at the altar today. I pledged my love, 'til death do us part.

Then death parted us and took my wife and daughter with it.

One pretty woman moaning my name is not going to change my mind about the things I vowed while I stood over the corpses of my wife and daughter. Even if I go to my grave thinking about the way Viviana milked my orgasm out of me.

I'm sure six months without sex is like a lifetime for you.

It wasn't. I did just fine for two and a half years.

The last six months, however, have dragged.

Hell, maybe I solved two problems last night. Trofim is out of the line of succession and Viviana should be out of my system.

I told her I only wanted one thing from her. The only thing I've wanted for six months. The thing I imagined every time I wrapped my hand around my cock.

So I took it.

Now, it's time to claim the rest of what is mine.

~

My father is sitting behind his desk when I walk through the door. It's barely dawn, but he's in a white button-down and an undone tuxedo tie. The suit jacket he's planning to wear to the wedding I just canceled is hanging from a hook behind him.

He doesn't look up from the letter he's writing as I enter. Someone probably warned him I was heading this way already. He knows it's me. He just doesn't care.

Until I drop Trofim's signet ring on his desk.

He stops mid-sentence. Stares down at it. Sits back.

Then he carefully picks up the ring with liver-spotted fingers that have grown shakier over the years and holds it to the lamplight. A spot of blood I didn't notice is dried into the grooves of the Novikov family crest. It was hard to inspect the ring too closely while it was deep inside of Viviana.

I bite back a rare smile when I realize I finger-fucked my

brother's fiancée with the ring I won from him. It's almost poetic.

My father leans back in his chair and looks at me for the first time. He sighs, tired. "Is he dead?"

"As far as you're concerned, he might as well be. You're never going to see him again."

Iakov rolls his lips together and places the ring in the center of his desk. "What's the plan now?"

Are you going to kill me, too? The question is layered there, unspoken.

I could. It's been done before. A hostile takeover from within is the kind of patricidal shit that happens when power is passed to the person who happened to be born first rather than the person who is more qualified to wear the crown.

I overpowered Trofim. I stripped the ring off of his finger.

His position is mine.

"I'm going to wear that ring and become the next *pakhan*."

He nods. "And when will that be? My death?"

He's speaking evenly, staying calm. He's hiding it well, but he's terrified. Yet another sign that the sun is setting on his leadership.

The bloodstained legend who has run this Bratva for the last three decades wouldn't sit there and ask when he was going to die. He'd stand up and fight. But my father doesn't even bother calling for the guards I know are stationed nearby. He sees the writing on the wall, clear as day.

"I'm not going to kill you unless I have to."

His shoulders ease down from around his ears. If he's sad about his oldest son's fate, he doesn't show it. For thirty-one years, my father prepared the way for Trofim. He poured everything he had into making him a great leader. Now, he doesn't even shed a tear.

I never expected him to. Death is a cruel fact of our world. If you're powerful enough to avoid it yourself, then you'll live long enough to see everyone you care about die. One way or another, it takes everything from you.

"I didn't even have to fight him," I add. "He was too busy beating his fiancée to see me coming and too drunk to resist. I exiled him. With the promise to kill him if he ever returns."

He arches a graying brow. "I'm surprised you didn't kill him for hitting Viviana. You've always had a tender spot for that kind of thing."

"You're confusing me with Anatoly."

My father snorts. "I wouldn't insult you like that. It's always been you and Trofim. Now… I suppose it's just you."

That's what it takes to earn my father's respect: don't be born a bastard like Anatoly and don't be overthrown like Trofim. Who knew a father's love could be so fickle?

"You're right. It *is* just me. Which is why you are going to begin the process of handing over power to me."

"You think you're ready." It's a statement, not a question. But I hear the doubt in his voice.

"I'm ready to take the Bratva to new heights. I'm ready to demand respect."

"That's what we've been doing for—"

"Not with fucking pageantry and politics, but with strength. Raw power."

He leans back in his chair, hands folded over his stomach. "How will you do that?"

If there was any chance my father could wrench power away from me and keep control, I wouldn't say a word. But he knows it's already over.

I've won.

"I'm going to consolidate the entire North American gunrunning market under our control."

His cool mask cracks under his surprise. "How?"

"I'll worry about how," I snap. "The only thing you need to know is that I'm going to make our family richer than you ever have. If you keep things peaceful, I'll make sure you're taken care of. If not…"

I don't need to finish the rest. This is his best option. He knows it. I know it. The only alternative is that I kill him now.

So he nods. "Things will need to be arranged. Plans unmade. I assume I'm not going to a wedding this afternoon."

"It's been canceled," I confirm.

He starts to unbutton his sleeves. "What happened to the girl, then? The bride?"

Does he even know her name? My father was ready to sign Viviana up for a lifetime of suffering with Trofim and he doesn't even bother with her name.

The realization chafes, but I ignore it. It doesn't matter. *She* doesn't matter.

"She's dead."

In every way that matters, Viviana is dead. That's all my father needs to know.

"That's just as well." He sighs. "One less thing."

Exactly.

One less thing.

∼

"Is there a body to dispose of?" Raoul asks the moment I step out of my father's office. He isn't smiling—he never is—but I see the hopeful gleam in his dark eyes.

"Don't be ridiculous. Mikhail wouldn't have killed Dad without me." Anatoly elbows him in the side. Then doubt flickers across his face. He turns to me. "Right? Please tell me you didn't kill him, Mikhail."

"Not yet."

He sighs. "Good. I want to watch."

I'd hate my father a lot more for acting like Anatoly isn't his son if Anatoly didn't hate him so much. The only thing he ever felt towards the man who fathered us both is resigned loyalty. The kind of loyalty that bides its time. Waiting for the moment it can turn. When that day comes, all the training Anatoly has gathered will be aimed directly at our father.

It'll be well earned. Our father all but fed Anatoly's mother to Trofim. He let Trofim kill her to secure his own ascendency.

Those kind of twisted family dynamics can really fuck a guy up. I'm just glad that guy in question is on my side.

The moment Trofim killed Anatoly's mom, my allegiances were set.

For my father, there is only me.

For me, there is Anatoly and Raoul.

I walk past them down the hall and they fall into line behind me. "Where is Trofim?" I ask over my shoulder.

"Airport, last time we saw him," Raoul says. "He booked the first flight out to Moscow."

Anatoly snorts. "Our guards saw him arguing with the desk to upgrade him to first class. Poor baby is exiled to the tundra for the rest of his days, but God forbid he fly coach."

"I would have lent him the private jet. So long as he's gone, I don't care."

"He's gone. Dad is out of the way." Anatoly slings an arm over my shoulders. "Who would've thought a bastard like me would be the right-hand man to the *pakhan*?"

"I'm not the *pakhan* yet."

"Good as," Raoul says quietly. "You've always been *pakhan* to me."

Not always. But since the moment Raoul and I met three years ago, he's looked up to me.

It has a lot to do with me not killing him on sight.

Like Anatoly, Raoul was born a bastard, but he hails from the Falcao cartel in Colombia. He was never supposed to be in the line of succession—bastards being barred from inheriting the family name and all that—but when the war between my family and his escalated, Raoul was the only surviving offspring. His father offered him up as a sacrifice. A peace offering to save his own life and assure us the cartel had no plans to continue operating in our territory.

My father then gave Raoul to me as some kind of twisted consolation. As if killing Raoul might erase the fact that his family killed mine.

But one death would never satisfy my rage. Anyway, it felt like a waste of his talents.

Instead of killing him, I gave him a job.

I fall back a step so I'm walking between Raoul and Anatoly. "Good. Then your new position as my second shouldn't chafe too badly."

Raoul's mouth twitches. It's the closest I've ever seen him to a smile.

Anatoly reaches around me to clap Raoul on the back. "Look at us! Who woulda thought a bastard and a slave would be the *two* right-hand men to the *pakhan*?"

If Raoul doesn't like being called a slave, he doesn't show it. He just mutters, "He can't have two right hands."

Anatoly hums thoughtfully. "You're right. Someone's gotta be left. Should we solve this in the ring? I was hoping for a bit more of a fight from Trofim. I have some energy to burn off."

I wave at them to stand down. "No fighting. I need you conscious and walking."

"*I'll* be conscious and walking," Anatoly mutters.

"Both of you," I amend. "You all don't know when to quit. We don't have time for a hospital stay."

"Boo. You're no fun now that you're the boss," Anatoly complains.

Ivory Ashes

Raoul ignores him and steers us back to business. "Did you tell your father about the plan?"

"As much as he needs to know."

"Does he know you're planning to ally with the Greeks?"

Anatoly whistles. "If you were sick of Helen before... She's going to be all over you now. Maybe she'll convince you to break this pious monk act of yours."

I scowl at Anatoly, who has the good sense to look apologetic.

We don't talk about Alyona. Directly, indirectly—it doesn't matter. Anatoly knows that and he holds up his hands in surrender. As a nice bonus, his guilt keeps him from looking directly at me and noticing the half-mast hard-on tenting my pants at the thought of just how thoroughly I broke my "pious monk act" last night.

I readjust discreetly. "Helen can't convince me of anything. Least of all that."

Viviana, on the other hand...

The way her lips wrapped around my name when she came. Fuck... those lips would have looked good around my cock. *I should have stayed. Should've dragged the night into the morning.*

No one would be calling me a monk if they knew the thoughts swirling around my head.

"Where is Viviana?" Raoul asks suddenly.

It jerks me out of my regrets. For a second, I think he knows about what we did last night.

Then he adds softly, "I heard you tell your father... Is she really dead?"

"She might as well be." I shove every thought of her down deep. If I don't give them air, they'll suffocate. They'll disappear and she'll be gone for good. "We're never going to see her again."

5

VIVIANA
SIX YEARS LATER

"I don't sound frazzled because I'm *not* frazzled," I insist, phone wedged between my ear and my shoulder. I slide a pair of socks and a sticky bowl of half-eaten yogurt to the end of the counter, but still no keys.

If this shoebox-sized apartment had an entryway, I'd have a little table by the door to keep my keys. I guess I could install a hook, but that would require knowing how to install a hook. Better yet, I'll have my keys surgically stapled to my hand. Maybe then I wouldn't lose them *every single day*.

"I can call you later if you're busy. We don't have to do this now."

"I'm not busy, Bianca. I'm just—*Fuck!*" My pinky toe makes direct contact with the wooden leg of a barstool and, call me dramatic, but I swear there has never been pain this intense in all of human history.

I kick out at the barstool again with my other foot. More pain is worth teaching it a lesson.

"You can call me later when you—"

"I'm—*ow*—fine." I shove the chair into the counter more aggressively than necessary for an inanimate object and take a deep breath. "I stubbed my toe, but I'm fine. I'm fine and everything is fine and I can chat right now."

I'm running late for work, I can't find the keys to my front door, and there's a pile of dishes in my sink that, given another day or two, could become a biohazard. But I'm fine. Everything is fine.

It has to be.

"Are you sure?" Bianca asks. I can imagine her chewing her nail polish off right about now. She hates conflict, which is making this phone call absolute hell for her, I'm sure. I decide if I can't ease my own burdens, I can at least ease hers.

"This is about Friday, right?" I ask. "You're busy and that's totally fine. Don't worry about it."

"But you have that gala for work."

"I know and I'll figure something else out."

Like staying home and watching *Gilmore Girls* until I pass out on the couch in a sugared-up coma. That sounds better than squeezing into a fancy dress just so I can still be the Administrative Assistant to the CEO of Cerberus Industries, but in much less comfortable shoes.

These kinds of industry-wide, "networking" events inevitably have me sprinting all over the ballroom, passing notes from my boss to people stationed in every far corner of the room.

Have a drink, they say. *Enjoy yourself,* they say. But they don't mean it. I'm never off the clock. Unless I call in sick.

Really, calling in sick is the superior option, anyway. Bianca is doing me a favor.

"Did you already have a date?" Bianca asks. "Because I can reschedule my thing if—"

"Yes!" I snatch my keys out of the pantry where they are wedged between a box of off-brand Lucky Charms and a half-eaten Rice Crispy Treat.

"So you do want me to reschedule?" Bianca asks.

"Wha—No! I found my keys." I do a small victory dance and then place the keys securely in the absurdly-small pocket of my trousers. "You can't reschedule your *thing*. Your *thing* is emergency wisdom tooth surgery."

"Yeah, but it's not a real emergency. I'm on pain meds. I can push it to Monday if you have plans."

I snort. "I haven't had *plans* in six years, Bianca."

Mikhail Novikov's face rises up in my mind—the Ghost of Unbelievable, Life-Changing Sex. He pops up a lot more than I wish he did. But for good reason.

He changed my life that night.

I drop down into the traitorous barstool. "Six years. I can't believe it's been six years. Is that too long to go without a date? It feels like too long."

"Oh, um… I don't know," Bianca stammers. "I haven't really —I'm not—"

I groan. "Ignore me, Bianca. It's early and apparently, I'm inappropriate before I've had coffee."

I'd stop at the coffee stand down the block, but there won't be time. Toxic brown sludge from the break room at work, it is.

"It's okay."

"I wish it was, but it's not. I pay you to be my babysitter, not my therapist."

Suddenly, a golden brown head of hair pops around the corner, a red-and-blue felt superhero mask strapped to his eyes. Terrible morning aside, I can't help but smile. Dante has that effect on people. Me most of all.

"Is that Bianca?" he asks.

I nod and hold out my phone.

"Hi, Bianca!" he shrieks.

Bianca laughs and says hi, but Dante is already darting off back to his bedroom, making *vroom* noises like he's flying through the air. *Five-year-olds are a trip, I'm tellin' ya.*

"You sure it's okay that I cancel on you tomorrow?" she asks again.

"Unless you want to chase Dante around the apartment while you have ice packs strapped to your swollen cheeks, then yes, it is absolutely okay for you to cancel."

"Well, I mean, I *could* do that. Maybe if I put on a movie for him, I could stay on the couch and—"

"No! Rest up, eat boatloads of ice cream, and I'll see you when you're four teeth less wise, okay?"

Bianca chuckles. "Okay. Thanks, Margaret."

I wince. It's been six years, but the fake name still stings. I should have gone for something more original. Like, I dunno… Athena. Or Aphrodite.

Then again, being the goddess of warfare or love would definitely stand out in a crowd, which would have made the name change counterproductive.

I'm in hiding, after all. A life lived undercover is one where you attract as little attention as possible. No social media, no friends, and definitely no dates.

No matter how many times I'm forced to replace the vibrator in my bedside drawer.

The closest thing I have to a friend is Bianca, and she only comes around when I pay her. So we aren't close and I definitely shouldn't be confessing to her that I haven't been out with a man since the night I got pregnant.

I've been too busy running to be with anyone else. Even if I wasn't, I'd never be able to relax enough to trust them anyway.

No matter how many years pass, I always catch myself looking over my shoulder. I expect to see Mikhail Novikov walking right towards me. *I've been looking for you, Viviana,* he'd purr in that darkly delicious voice of his.

Some days, it's a nightmare.

Other days—mostly nights—it's a fantasy.

But this morning, I look over my shoulder and see Dante padding down the hall in bright yellow rain boots, a fuzzy bear sweatshirt, and a superhero mask. He grins. "I picked out my own clothes."

"You're kidding. You put together this fabulous outfit?" I

reach for his hand and twirl him around until he giggles. "This look could be on a runway somewhere."

"What's a runway?" he asks, adorable face squished in a frown.

I hustle him towards the door. "I'll tell you on the walk. We're late."

He forgets the question the moment we're in the hall because he's too absorbed in racing me down the four flights of stairs to our apartment lobby. His boots clomp gracelessly down the steps while I lock up.

"Don't open the front door!" I yell after him. "Wait for me at the mailboxes."

When we first moved to New York, Dante was an infant. I kept him strapped to my chest, tucked away neatly in the stroller I got secondhand from some hooded man in a back alley. For months and months, he was never out of arm's reach.

Now, the only time he wants to be within arm's reach of me is when I'm pretending to be Mrs. Ticklepus, an eight-armed octopus who likes to tickle him before bedtime.

I've had to learn to give him his space. To let him explore. It wasn't an easy process.

It helps that even my father doesn't know where we live. In a city of over eight million people, we might as well be invisible. I can afford to loosen his leash.

A little.

"There she is," a deep voice says from behind me.

I jolt in surprise, dropping my keys to the cracked tile floor.

My neighbor Tommy hurries across our narrow landing to pick it up for me. "Sorry, neighbor. I was just happy to see you. It's been a hot minute."

"A few hot minutes," I say, smiling as he hands me my key. "How's it going?"

His hand lingers on the other end of the key a bit longer than necessary. "Better now."

Tommy is nice. Cute, too, in a buttoned-up, door-to-door Bible salesman kind of way. He has bright blonde hair, a friendly face, and the personality to match. The day he moved in three years ago, he gave everyone in the building a plate of cookies.

"Mama, I'm going to beat you!" Dante's voice echoes up the stairwell.

Tommy shoves his hands in his pockets. "Sounds like I interrupted your race."

"You did. I would have absolutely crushed him if you hadn't gotten in my way."

Tommy laughs and runs a nervous hand through his hair. I know what's coming next. "So—"

"I better—" I hitch a thumb towards the stairs. "Before he escapes."

"Oh, right. Yeah, I'll walk you down."

Shoot. A stairwell is not the best place to ditch someone. Unless he's headed to the rooftop at 7:30 in the morning, there's only one direction Tommy could be going.

We walk in silence for three floors. Silent, that is, except for the sound of Dante playing drums on the metal mailboxes in the lobby. *God, my neighbors must love me.*

But as we approach the second floor landing, Tommy grabs my arm.

"Just real quick, Margaret." He gives me a tight smile and blows out a breath. "I was wondering if you—I know you said it wasn't a good time, but that was six months ago. Not that I've been counting. I mean, I have but—so I thought I'd try again. That is, I thought I'd ask you out. So that's what I'm doing… Asking you out. Do you want to go out?" He grimaces before I can even respond. "That wasn't as smooth as I hoped it would be."

"I thought it was great," I lie. It wasn't great. But it *was* endearing. I almost feel bad for turning him down over and over and over again for the last three years.

"Yeah?" he asks, hopeful. "Because as much as I love our meetings in the stairwell and that one time I ran into you at the bodega, I'd love to actually sit down and talk to you. Over a bottle of wine, maybe."

"That would be nice."

His eyes go wide. "Really?"

"Of course it would, but…"

His face falls and I hate myself for doing this to him.

It's not you; it's me, I want to say. But it's too cliché, no matter how true it is.

This is *my* fault. The reason I can't have friends or take Dante on play dates or go on dates myself is because it isn't safe.

Sure, it's been six years without incident. Mikhail hasn't even sent us a mysterious letter, let alone shown up on our doorstep demanding to know his son.

But it could happen.

Dante could also fall through a subway grate and be kidnapped by mole people, I argue with myself. *That's no reason to hide in your apartment all day. It's no reason to stop living.*

You can't live like this forever, Viviana.

Tommy sighs. "It's okay. I knew it was a longshot. I just thought—"

"I think I'm free next week," I blurt before I can think better of it.

Tommy's mouth falls open. "Y-You're free? To see me? Next week?"

"Or the week after. If you're busy, then—"

"Then I'll clear my schedule and make space for you," he says, a wide smile spreading across his face. "I'll make myself free."

He's nice. He's cute.

Does he send flutters of sexual awakening straight to my lady bits? No.

Does just the *memory* of the sound of his voice have my hand slipping between my sheets late at night? Definitely no.

But men who cause reactions like that are why women like me end up as single mothers under assumed names. They scramble your brains. They force you to think of them every day for the rest of your life when you see the light of your world toddling towards you in rain boots and a superhero mask.

So Tommy and I part with him promising to pull together some options and get back to me. I wave and pray I'm not making a mistake.

"I beat you," Dante proclaims, wrapping his little arms around my legs. "I'm the fastest in the whole world."

I scan the sidewalk outside the building before I hold open the door. "Is that right?"

Dante tromps out in his boots. "Uh-huh. The fastest, strongest, smartest… biggest in the world."

He deserves everything. Not just this little life I can give him. He deserves two parents and a world of opportunities and real friends that can come to his house for birthday parties and playdates.

"I agree," I say, "but I'd add cutest, sweetest, and funniest."

Dante wrinkles his nose. "None of that helps in a race."

I bend down and kiss his rumpled hair. "No, but it still makes you pretty cool."

He seems pleased with that and spins like a top down the sidewalk.

I can't just step out of my comfort zone; I'll have to inch out of it. If we're doing metaphors, then my comfort zone is a hammock and I'm wearing one of those inflatable sumo suits, but I'm prepared to wrestle my way out of it so we can have some semblance of a community.

I'll do anything for that boy. Absolutely anything.

I'll even forget about Mikhail.

6

VIVIANA

I practice my speech to Mr. Fredrickson on my walk from the train to work, but I don't get any further than "I know I'm late again, but please don't fire me. Think of the children!" before I walk through the front doors.

Cerberus Industries shares the building with three other businesses. I have no idea what the other ones are, but the first floor is a catch-all lobby space. Jackie waves from behind the front desk.

She's been the main lobby receptionist as long as I've worked here. She technically doesn't work for any of the companies that lease space. She's also on the building's payroll as a member of "security" even though she's five-foot-nothing and can barely see over her own desk. Not exactly reassuring to the paranoid amongst us—a.k.a., me.

I wave back, but Jackie stands up and flags me down. Her eyes are wide. My boss must have called down to ask if I was in the lobby yet.

"I know, I'm late," I say before she can. "I'm going to appeal to Mr. Fredrickson's compassion. If that doesn't work, I'll appeal to his laziness. No way he wants to find a new personal assistant right now."

"Based on what I'm hearing, he doesn't need a personal assistant anymore," she whispers. "He's gone."

"Like… dead?" I gasp.

I'm definitely going straight to hell because a small part of me thinks, *At least he'll never find out I was late again.*

Jackie shakes her head, leaning in closer. "He's out as CEO. All the executives are out. The entire board of directors has been replaced."

I look around the lobby and notice that there are a lot more worried faces down here than usual. The men in suits typically march through the lobby straight for the elevators. They're too important to waste time smiling or waving. *No, business must be done. Industrial metals must be sold.*

But today, they're huddled together talking in low voices.

"Cerberus?" I double-check. "That's where I work. That's what you're talking about?"

"I know where you work, Margaret. Five years you've been here. You think I don't know you better than that?"

You'd be surprised.

"That can't be right," I insist anyway. "They would have sent an email or something."

"There was no one left to send an email. They were all fired." She says it slowly like it might help me process what is happening. "Security had to drag the CFO away from the doors at midnight last night. He was trying to get in to clean up his office, but he doesn't have access."

"Paul?" I wrinkle my nose. "God only knows what he kept on his desktop. Losing his job will be the least of his worries if they decide to go through his search history."

Jackie snorts with laughter and then quickly swallows it down when she gets a nasty look from a passing suit. Today is a somber day.

"I'm sure your job will be safe," she whispers. "There's no reason to fire everyone. It would make too much work. They need people who know how this place actually runs. That's definitely you."

"Yeah. I'm sure you're right," I say, smiling weakly.

But by the time the elevator doors close, my smile is gone and a full-on panic has set in.

I can't afford to lose this job. Financially, obviously. I have bills to pay and a growing mouth to feed. Dante goes through snacks like a bear bulking up for winter. The amount of food he can put in his forty-pound body is shocking.

But also, I got this job under a false name. A false name I legitimized with very expensive fake documents that I only got by making a deal with the devil himself: my dad.

But that was under duress.

After I left Mikhail asleep in that hotel suite six years ago, I went on the run. Which mostly meant I stayed in motels that didn't charge my card until *after* I was checked out. It was a simple plan that made it hard to track me.

It also fell apart the moment the exhaustion and morning sickness set in.

One day a couple months after my great escape, I was too busy hurling my guts into a barely-sanitized motel toilet to pack up and hustle off before checkout time. The motel charged my card and dear old Dad was on my doorstep within a half-hour.

He saw me hunched over the toilet. He saw the pregnancy test in the trash. I literally watched my worth dwindle in his eyes as he understood what was happening.

I was pregnant.

No one would touch me now. He couldn't marry me off to the highest bidder if I was knocked up with someone else's baby.

"You're getting an abortion," he announced. "Now. Get up. We're leaving."

"I can't."

He grabbed me hard around the elbow. "Then don't stand. I'll drag you if I have to."

I shook him off. "I can stand. But I can't get an abortion."

"Why not?" he growled.

In that split second, I had a decision to make. The most important decision of my life.

Also the easiest.

I was going to do whatever it took to save my baby.

"Trofim may be exiled, but I have another connection to the Novikov Bratva." I wiped my mouth with the back of my hand and then pointed down to my stomach. "This baby belongs to Mikhail Novikov."

Just like that, I was in my father's good graces again.

Mikhail was still young. Untested. His takeover of the Novikov Bratva was anything but certain. Iakov seemed to be rolling over for his son, but there was no way to be sure Mikhail's mini-mutiny would finish successfully. Not yet.

Besides, my father was happy to have me up his sleeve. A trick card he could whip out when he needed it.

At least, that's what he muttered as he paced back and forth across my room while I tried to keep some water down.

"You said Trofim is exiled?" he asked, changing trains of thought too fast for me to follow.

"Yeah. Mikhail gave him an out. He didn't kill him."

My father resumed his pacing, muttering something about liabilities and assurances.

Then he turned to me, a wicked smile on his face. "How much is your freedom worth, Viviana?"

I can tell you right now: it was worth enough that I don't want to pay that price again. If I lose this job and have to start over, I don't know what I'll do.

The ghosts of my past are swirling around my foggy head as the elevator doors open and I step into the office proper of Cerberus Industries. Twisted metal sculptures line the main hallway, showcasing the kind of quality metals you can expect from Cerberus.

No one likes when you point out that we rarely receive quotes for art installations. Our money comes from the perpetual construction all over the city that everyone always complains about.

Stainless steel for new builds is our primary money maker. Then there's aluminum for vehicle manufacturing, magnesium alloy for aerospace, and copper for—*Oh God, what am I going to do with all of this useless information once I'm laid off?*

There's an unnatural hush in the hallways.

No footsteps clicking across the tile floors. No catching up on last night's shows while people wait for the machine to spew out their single cup of burnt instant coffee.

I'm too deep in my own head to think about where everyone else is. I'm too busy wondering if I'm going to turn the corner and find my desk packed into a box with my name scribbled on the side. I've never been fired before, but I've seen it in movies. That's how it usually goes.

I'm so worried about what's ahead of me that, for the first time in years, I'm not thinking about what's behind me.

Until a voice I'll never forget calls down the hall.

"Finally. I've been waiting for you."

No.

This is a nightmare. A waking nightmare. I'm hallucinating under the stress. That's the only explanation why *he* would be *here*.

"You're the P.A., aren't you? You're late."

I don't move. The wall of windows in front of me looks tempting. I'll throw myself out of them.

Dante.

Oh, shit. Dante.

I can't jump. I can't run. There's no way out. No escape. I don't have a choice.

Slowly, I turn around. I already know who I'm going to see, but the sight of him still knocks me back.

His name rushes out of me in a single breath. "Mikhail."

7

MIKHAIL

"Finally," I say down the long hallway. "I've been waiting for you."

This entire fucking building is full of people who don't know a damn thing. Every employee I've spoken to all morning has pointed a trembling finger in the direction of the empty desk outside my new office.

"Margaret will be able to help when she gets here," they said before fleeing into nearby offices and locking the doors behind them.

As if I couldn't get in by myself if I wanted to. I own them all now. Cerberus Industries. This building. All of it.

The problem is, this Margaret, who is apparently the only useful person in this entire company, is also the only person in the office who hadn't shown her face yet.

Until now.

If her coworkers are to be believed, *Margaret* runs this place. *Margaret* knows where the keys to the conference room are;

Margaret is the holder of the passwords and the keeper of the schedule. By the looks of it, there isn't a single thing that takes place under this roof that doesn't go through Margaret.

Maybe that's why *Margaret,* my new personal assistant, feels fine rolling into work twenty-five minutes late.

Her heels click down the hallway in front of me, a pair of high-waisted trousers hugging the generous swell of her ass. It crosses my mind that Margaret might get away with showing up late because she looks so fucking good doing it.

"You're the P.A., aren't you?" I call.

She stops dead in the center of the hallway. Her hips go still, but her wavy, honey blonde hair swishes back and forth across her stiffened spine.

I can't stop myself from tracing the curve of her hips. From noting the cinch of her waist.

I catalog her the way I cataged the rest of Cerberus Industries assets. I may only be taking over the business as a way to launder money from my much more profitable gunrunning ventures, but that doesn't mean I won't trim the fat around here.

Or, in the case of Queen fucking Margaret, tear it off with my teeth.

It's been a long time since I've been even vaguely interested in a woman. There hasn't been time. But now that I'm finalizing things, there's no reason I couldn't have a little fun before I fire her.

"You're late." I'm only a few steps behind her when she finally turns around.

Her eyes are emerald green in the fluorescents. I have a good view of them because they are as wide as saucers. Her skin is pale white. She wobbles on her heels like she might fall backward.

I want her. The familiar thought pangs through me the same way it has only two other times in my life.

Both times, as it turns out, for the exact same woman.

Viviana Giordano.

She exhales a single word. "Mikhail." Her full lips wrap around my name exactly the way I remember.

She shouldn't be here. She's gone. I know because I've paid a fuck ton of money to make sure of it. I've had a private investigator on my personal payroll for the last six years trying to track down where this woman went and they found nothing.

Part of me was proud. I told Viviana to leave while she had the chance and she actually listened.

Another part of me has always wondered if the fact that I couldn't find her is why she pops up in my thoughts so often. I'm used to getting exactly what I want in life. Not being able to find her was unusual.

Humans long for what they can't have. That's all it is. That's what I told myself on those endless, sleepless nights.

But here she is in front of me.

And I still want her.

"What are you doing here?"

Her eyes dart around like she's looking for the eject button. Her hands are knotted into fists at her side.

The last time we saw each other was a little unconventional, but she shouldn't be this nervous. I never hurt her. Quite the opposite, actually.

I take a step closer. "Viviana, what—"

Suddenly, she shoves her hand at me, a paper-thin smile plastered on her face. "Margaret. I'm Margaret. Nice to meet you."

My gaze flicks from her hand to her face. There's a sheen of sweat on her forehead and her hand is shaking.

She's lying. I know she's lying.

But I don't know *why*.

Trofim is gone. She isn't in any danger from me. What does she have to hide?

I grab her hand and hold it, running my thumb over the soft inside of her wrist. Her throat bobs and I remember what it felt like under my palm. The way her pulse fluttered in my hand. I bet her heart is pounding just as hard now as it did the last time I touched her six years ago.

I know who you really are, Viviana, my thumb says, stroking over her silky skin. *You can't hide from me.*

"Good. You've met Margaret." Viviana jerks her hand away as a dumpy man in a wrinkled suit walks over. He steps too close to her, the tip of his scuffed dress shoe covering the toe of her heel. "Mr. Novikov is looking for the keys to the kingdom, Marge. Passwords, keys, all that good stuff."

"Marge"? Give me a fucking break.

I slide closer, forcing the imbecile back and wedging myself between them.

Viviana doesn't want to look at me, but she doesn't have a choice. Not unless she wants to raise more eyebrows than mine.

"I've been looking for you for a long time," I murmur.

She swallows and spins away. "I have a file with all of the security information on my laptop, sir. I'll get it for you."

I wave Rumpled Suit away and drum my fingers on Viviana's desk. She mistypes her password three times before her computer dings with recognition.

"You're a hard woman to find."

She looks around, but we're alone. My new office is at the back of the third floor. Her desk is stationed just outside my door. Close enough to touch.

"Sorry. I was running late this morning. I would have been on time if I'd known I was going to see—*meet* my new boss."

I have a feeling she wouldn't be here at all if she knew I would be waiting for her inside. Which begs the question: *why?*

Why have I been looking for her while she wants nothing more than to sprint in the opposite direction?

I lean on my elbows, only a few inches away. She smells like vanilla and honey, sweet and warm. The same way she tastes. "Are we going to pretend we haven't met before?"

She turns her hazel eyes on me. She's fighting to stay calm, but she's practically buzzing out of her skin. "What's your email? Is it the same as Mr. Fredrickson's old account or do you have a new one set up?"

"How long have you been here?" I ask.

If she's been here this entire time, I'm going to make sure Kenan never works another day as a P.I. He'll be strip-mining glaciers in Siberia by the time I'm done with him.

Alternatively, I could send him a thank-you bonus for being absolute shit at his job. Viviana has been back in my life for five minutes and she's already proving to be a distraction. Tracking her down could have thrown everything off-course.

A distraction like her is the last thing I need as I'm finalizing things I set in motion six fucking years ago.

She tugs on her lower lip and turns back to the screen. "I can set up a new account for you. I'll send the file there. Then you'll have everything you need."

"Don't bother. I already have what I want."

"You're being inappropriate." Viviana jerks her hand away and spins her chair to face me.

There she is.

"Then maybe I shouldn't tell you that you look fucking delicious."

"Maybe not." Her jaw twitches. "I don't know how things usually operate under your control, but—"

"Actually, I think you have an intimate understanding of what it's like to be under my control... *Viviana.*"

Her face flushes red before she stands up. Her rolling chair slams back against the wall. "Mr. Novikov, I don't know who you think I am—or who you think *you* are, for that matter—but you can't talk to your employees like this."

"Mik—Mr. Novikov." Raoul looks sorry to have interrupted, but that doesn't stop him from surveying the scene. How close we're standing. Her eyes narrowed in defiance.

"What, Raoul?" I growl, turning back to Viviana. I feel like she'll disappear if I look away.

"The shareholders are here to sign the final documents," he reminds me. "They're in the boardroom."

Ten minutes ago, we didn't have a key for the boardroom, which is why I went looking for *Margaret* in the first place. I'm guessing Anatoly got bored with waiting and put a shoulder through the door.

I'll be annoyed with him for that later. Right now, I'm too busy paying attention to the flash of recognition in *Margaret's* eyes.

She knows these people. Their names. She's met them all before.

"Alright." I wave Raoul off. "Go ahead. I'll follow you."

If it was Anatoly, he'd resist. He'd want to stay and watch the show. But Raoul strides away without hesitation, leaving us alone again.

I turn towards the door and Viviana sags in relief. Only to go rigid again once I snap my fingers.

"Come along, *Margaret*. I've waited long enough for you. Don't waste any more of my time."

She blinks. "But I don't—I don't go to these meetings."

The disappointment on her face tells me all I need to know: Viviana wants to escape.

But until I understand why the sight of me has her running for the hills, I'm not letting her out of my sight.

"You do now." I swipe her purse off of her desk and offer her an elbow. "I want to keep you *close*."

8

VIVIANA

I have to get out of here.

Years ago, when I first brought Dante to the city, I had an escape plan. There was a Go Bag permanently stationed by the front door and a roll of cash in the freezer.

Then Dante learned to crawl and his favorite activity was unpacking the Go Bag and wedging the contents between the cushions of the couch.

The roll of money in the freezer lasted a little longer, but last year, he needed tubes in his ears to stop the onslaught of nonstop ear infections and I had to buy a new window A/C when the landlord refused to replace our old one during a heat wave.

Now, I have nothing except a deep-seated instinct to run and a five-year-old who loves his school and his friends and the glow-in-the-dark stars on his ceiling. He's going to hate me for ripping us away from his life.

My horoscope today told me to "be decisive and confident." What it failed to mention is that a person from my past was coming to royally fuck my shit up.

A sharp elbow in my side sends me jolting like I've been electrocuted. Water glasses around the table slosh and every single set of eyes are locked on me. I grimace my apology to the shareholders, avoiding eye contact with the broad-shouldered devil stationed next to the door. Mikhail's position right by the only exit is not an accident, I'm sure.

Instead of looking his way, I force my attention to Steve, the owner of the elbow.

"Yes?" I whisper, glaring at him.

How dare he and his halitosis draw attention to me. As if a set of ice blue eyes haven't already been drilling into my skull for the last hour.

"Um…" he draws out. His onion breath might as well be a green cloud between us. "Mr. Novikov is talking to you."

I frown. "What?"

"Mr. Novikov," he repeats slowly. "He said your name."

No, he didn't. I know what it sounds like when he says my name. I've had countless dirty dreams of nothing but him saying my name. I would know if he'd said—

"Margaret?" Mikhail taps his pen on the table like he's trying to get the attention of an easily-distracted cat. "Can you hear me, Margaret?"

Oh. He didn't buy the fake name before. He definitely won't buy it now.

I smile politely at him, my cheeks practically cracking under the strain. "Yes?"

"Do these valuations look right to you?"

God, he's gorgeous. Mikhail arches a brow, highlighting the angular slant of his cheekbones and the square line of his jaw. This man might as well be carved from marble. How am I supposed to think about any numbers with this face in front of me?

How am I supposed to think about *these* numbers when the only number running through my head is the very small one in my bank account?

I can't afford to run, but I don't have a choice. I have to—

"Margaret." He cracks the fake name like a whip and I jump to my feet.

"I'm not feeling well," I blurt.

Then I sprint out of the room.

As far as exits go, no one would call that smooth. But once I'm in the hallway, I don't care. I can breathe again.

I fill and empty my lungs in deep, even breaths. *Decisive and confident. I need to be decisive and confident.*

I decisively, confidently swipe my phone off of my desk and make a confident decision to flee this building. The rest of the decisions, I'll make on the train. Confidently.

But I'm only halfway to the bank of elevators when the door to the boardroom opens. Mikhail thunders towards me like a storm cloud. A force of nature. He doesn't hesitate, doesn't falter. Before I can even consider dodging him, he grabs my arm and yanks me into his office.

It still smells like Mr. Fredrickson. Like cheap aftershave and the honey mustard pretzels he kept stashed in his bottom drawer for a mid-afternoon snack.

Then the door closes and Mikhail is in front of me, close enough that all I smell is cedar and mint. All I can see is the broad expanse of his chest.

And all I can think is, *I'll never be free of him.*

"Where were you going?" he demands coolly.

"I told you: I don't feel well."

"We were in a meeting."

"If you'd like me to go back and throw up on the shareholders, say the word," I snap. "I'll be sure to make note of 'violent puking' in the minutes."

Mikhail almost looks amused, but his face is incapable of joy. There is only scrutiny and self-assuredness.

"You don't look like you're going to be sick. How do I know you're not lying about this, too?"

"Mr. Fredrickson trusted me." That's not true. He demanded a different doctor's note every single day when I had the flu last year.

"That's because he didn't know who you really are." Mikhail towers over me. "*Viviana.*"

My stomach flutters. I might actually be sick. My body isn't sure how to handle my worst nightmare and most frequent fantasy coming true at the same time.

"My name is Margaret."

He growls low in his chest. "I know who you are. I could never forget."

He barely even spoke to me that night. I don't know this man. And yet… he's right. I never forgot the sound of his voice. His smell. This thing between us was—*is*—primal. It's pheromones or chemistry. Every time I see Mikhail, my body goes into fight, flight, or fuck mode.

I turn away from him long enough to see a large bouquet on his desk. Two dozen red roses. A card with a heart scribbled in the corner is tied to the neck of the vase.

"Who are the flowers from?" I blurt.

"Don't change the subject."

"I'm not. I'm just curious." Yes, curiosity. That's what this pit yawning open in the bottom of my stomach is. Simple, innocent curiosity. "Are they from your wife?"

He snorts. "Jealous, Viviana?"

I wish he'd stop saying my name. It's been too long since I heard it. It's doing things to me.

"My name is Margaret," I repeat with as much conviction as I can muster. "I have no reason to be jealous of my boss's wife sending him flowers. I think it's sweet."

He takes another step towards me. "I think you're lying."

"I'm not."

I meant it. I think it's sweet that some woman out there has seen him without his shirt on and gets to kiss his mouth whenever she wants. Maybe he even has kids with her by now and I'm happy for them, too. I'm thrilled that they get a father while Dante just has me.

I'm over the moon about it. Super fucking thrilled. Couldn't be happier if I tried.

"I can see it written all over your face. The lies. The fear." He dips his head low, his breath hot on my cheek. "I can fucking *smell* it on you, Viviana."

I swallow and stare at some point just past his ear. I can't bring myself to look at him. "I don't know what you're talking about."

He hooks a finger under my chin and lifts my face to his. "Look at me."

Hell no. Looking at you is how I got into this mess in the first place.

"No."

"Why not?" he grits out.

"Because you keep calling me by someone else's name! And because you're my boss. It's inappropriate for us to—"

Mikhail's hand bands around my neck and he's kissing me.

Between one second and the next, I'm transported. Back to that bridal suite. To the night Mikhail saved me from a lifetime of being someone else's pawn.

To the night he gave me the greatest gift I've ever received.

I should push him away, but six years' worth of unspoken gratitude and pent-up sexual frustration pour out of me instead.

Between fight, flight, or fuck, I've made my choice.

I hook my hands over his shoulders and hold him close.

Everything about Mikhail is hard, but his lips are soft. His tongue slips confidently between my teeth. He tilts my jaw and claims my mouth in hot strokes. I moan when his hand slips around my thigh, hooking my knee over his hip.

Holy hell, it's been a long time. Too long.

When Mikhail pulls away, I chase after him, my lips parted.

He presses his forehead to mine, breathing heavily. "I'd never forget that taste. I know it's you, Viviana."

His words are the equivalent of an ice-cold shower. They snap me out of my lust-filled delirium and I slam my palms against his chest.

He doesn't even flinch, so I slide away from him, edging around the office towards the door. "Don't touch me."

"Is that what the moan meant?"

My legs are trembling. I really would have let him take me on Mr. Fredrickson's desk.

What in the hell is wrong with me?

"Stay away from me," I warn again, a little redundantly.

Then I yank the office door open and run.

9

MIKHAIL

Anatoly and Raoul pop their heads into the doorway Viviana just sprinted through. "Nice reunion?" Anatoly smirks, glancing down at my painfully obvious erection.

I scowl at him and adjust my pants.

Raoul at least has the decency to hide his amusement and focus on the task at hand. "Should I follow her?"

"Don't let her out of your sight," I order.

Raoul nods and disappears down the hall.

I balance on the edge of the desk while Anatoly crosses his arms and pouts. "I could have followed her."

"I thought it might be hard to do your job when you're so busy being a smug bastard."

"You're right. I *am* busy being a smug bastard." He drops into the chair in the corner. "Am I right to assume the flowers from your Greek princess aren't what has your tent pitched?"

The roses from Helen are sitting on the corner of my desk. I don't need to reread the card to remember what it said. ***All the pieces are falling into place. Congratulations. XO, Helen.***

Helen is right. All of the pieces are falling into place.

My alliance with the Greeks will be solidified soon, giving me access to their ports all along the Eastern seaboard. I'll control imports of millions of dollars' worth of illegal weapons, utilize the Bratva's already robust cross-country shipping infrastructure, and then launder the profits through Cerberus.

I'm going to own every part of the process from top to bottom. The puzzle is almost complete.

But now, there's Viviana. A rogue puzzle piece I didn't expect and can't seem to place.

"She's lying about her name," I tell him. "She's calling herself Margaret now."

Anatoly frowns. "Sounds like a cat lady. Doesn't suit her."

"No, it doesn't. It also doesn't make any sense. Trofim hasn't poked his head out even once since I exiled him. She has no reason to be afraid."

"Maybe she's not running from Trofim."

"Me?" I ask in shock.

"Or maybe this has nothing to do with you. Maybe she's running from her father," he guesses. "Don Giordano is a hard-ass. I mean, he did sign her up to marry Trofim in the first place. He's not winning any Dad of the Year awards. Maybe she's trying to hide from him."

"If it had nothing to do with me, then why wouldn't she just tell me that? She knows I know who she is, but she's still lying."

Why do I even fucking care? That's the real question.

"Why do you even fucking care?" Anatoly asks, reading my mind.

"Because it's my job to know what is going on around here. If someone is lying to me, there's probably a good reason. I want to know what it is."

He holds up his hands in surrender. "You haven't seen this girl in, what? Four? Five years?"

"Six."

"Okay, six years," he amends. "I just don't see how she could be relevant to anything we have going on."

That's what I've told myself for the last six years. *Viviana doesn't matter. I fucked her out of my system. I dealt with her.*

Except, I didn't. She's still lodged in my chest like a piece of shrapnel I can't claw out. I want to know why.

Anatoly leans forward, elbows on his knees. "Is this about Helen?"

"What does Helen have to do with anything?" I snap.

"Well, she's your fiancée, but your balls are blue over some other woman. Call me crazy, but that doesn't sound like things are healthy at home."

"Helen and I don't live together."

"Yet," he agrees. "But you will. Soon."

All the pieces are falling into place.

For me, that's the ports and Cerberus.

For Helen, it's the engagement ring that fell onto her finger last week.

"It's a political move. The Greeks have the ports. I need the ports. Marrying Helen gets me the ports."

"But you hate her," he fills in.

"I don't hate her."

I'd have to feel something for Helen in order to hate her. Unless someone else brings her up or she's standing in front of me, I don't think about her.

"I feel nothing for her," I clarify. "It's a good thing. No feelings means things don't get messy."

Suddenly, Anatoly gasps and jerks around. I drop my hand to the holster at my hip, ready to take on whatever threat is coming for us.

Then Anatoly presses a hand to his heart and eases back in his chair. "Sorry, bro. For a second there, I thought Trofim was in the room. You sounded just like him."

I drop my hand and scowl in disgust. "Watch your fucking mouth."

He isn't wrong, though. I've caught myself wondering if I'm doing the right thing.

I'd never hurt Helen the way Trofim hurt Viviana. But I'm never going to love her, either. I'm not going to give her the dream of a happy marriage I see in her glazed-over eyes every time she looks at me.

I'm not going to give her even a sliver of what I had with Alyona and Anzhelina.

If Helen hasn't figured out what I'm offering by now, that's her problem. As *pakhan*, I have bigger shit to worry about than feelings: hers *or* mine.

My phone rings and Raoul's name lights up my screen. "You have eyes on her?" I ask as soon as I answer.

"Yeah. I see her."

"Is she running?"

"I don't..." Raoul hesitates. "I don't know."

Anatoly leans in, frowning. "What does that mean? How does he not know?"

I turn the speakerphone on and balance my phone on my knee. "Is she packing bags? Heading to a train station? Booking an airline ticket? For fuck's sake, Raoul, give me something."

"She's at an elementary school."

"Maybe it's like a sanctuary situation," Anatoly shrugs. "You know, like, when people escape the law by hiding out in a church."

I don't have the patience for Anatoly today. Or any day, honestly. "Last I checked, I'm not the law and an elementary school isn't a fucking church."

"Just an idea," he mumbles.

I roll my eyes. "Can you see what she's doing, Raoul?"

Viviana asked if I was married. It's not crazy to think she might be. Sometime in the last six years, she settled down. Maybe her sweet, non-criminal husband is an elementary school teacher.

I remember the way her leg felt wrapped around my hip and decide I'll fight a teacher if I have to. No way he deserves all of that.

No one does.

No one but me.

"She went in a few minutes ago. I haven't seen anything else yet. I can go inside if you—Shit, there she is," he hisses.

"Is she wearing a disguise?" Anatoly asks. "Don't let her escape!"

I swat my brother away and grab the phone, pacing back and forth across the office. "What's happening, Raoul?"

"She almost saw me. But she… She's with…"

He takes a deep breath. I hear car horns blaring. Scattered voices on the sidewalk.

"Raoul?" I bark. "What the fuck is going on?"

"Sorry, but she's with a kid."

Anatoly stands up. "Like a hostage situation?"

"No. They're holding hands. The kid is smiling. I think… I think she's his mom."

Anatoly turns to me, eyes wide.

I never told him Viviana and I had sex, but he's always suspected. It's why I know exactly what inane theory is going to pour out of his mouth next.

"How old is the kid?" Anatoly steals my phone away, talking directly into the speaker.

"How should I know?"

"If you had to guess!" Anatoly pushes.

Raoul sighs. "Probably five. Maybe six."

Anatoly points at me, eyes wide. "Holy shit. Holy *shit*!"

I snatch my phone out of my brother's hand and turn off the speakerphone. "Stay on them, Raoul. Let me know where they're headed and I'll meet you there."

I pocket my phone, but Anatoly is still pointing at me.

"What? What could you possibly be thinking, Anatoly. There's no way I could ever guess what you're going to—"

"It's your kid!" he interrupts, grinning like a devil. "That is your *bastard* kid."

"Shut the fuck up. No, it's not." I grab my wallet and head for the door. "Stay here. Make sure all the necessary paperwork gets filed before the shareholders leave."

"Sure, yeah, don't worry about it," he calls after me. "I'll hold down the fort here…"

For a second, I think he's going to leave it there. For a second, I have faith in my brother.

Then he finishes the sentence.

"While you're gone meeting your son!"

10

VIVIANA

"Mama, where are we going?"

Dante is literally vibrating with excitement, probably because I've never picked him up in the middle of the day before. His class was heading to lunch when he saw me walking down the hallway. He grinned ear to ear and I had to bite back a sob.

I need to get him something to eat before his good mood spirals into a hangry meltdown for the ages, but there isn't time.

We have to leave. Now. Yesterday. Last week.

At one point, I considered hiring an ex-detective or an investigator to keep an eye on Mikhail and the Novikov family. If they were coming for me, I wanted to know. Then I realized that Mikhail probably has a fleet of detectives who exist to catch people looking too closely at what their family is doing. Hiring someone to watch him would have put an even bigger target on my back.

Worse, on Dante's back.

Now, Mikhail is here and there isn't time to rehash the past or figure out what I should have done differently. I need to get Dante the hell out of Dodge.

Dante shakes my arm. "Mama? You're not listening to me."

"I know, buddy. I'm sorry." I squeeze his hand as we walk through the double front doors of the school.

There's no one waiting outside on the sidewalk, but I still expect Mikhail to pop out of a bush or parachute down from the sky and yank Dante from my arms. Heirs are important to men like him. Even if Mikhail has kids of his own—maybe with the woman who sent him the flowers?—Dante will always have a blood connection to the Novikov Bratva. If they know Dante exists, they'll come for him.

I scan the street, but no one seems to be paying any extra attention to us. Still, I eye them all suspiciously. Every dogwalker, every stooped Hasidic grandmother, every hot dog vendor and pirated DVD salesman hawking their wares from the corners. When I came for enrollment in the spring, I liked that the school was close to a green space and the Hudson. I imagined picking Dante up and going for walks, buying ice cream.

Now, everyone in Battery Park is a threat.

Suddenly, Dante's hand tugs out of my grip. I spin around, heart in my throat and stomach on the ground.

"Mama!" he shrieks, arms crossed and feet planted. "Where are we going?"

I blow out a breath that does nothing to loosen the knot in

my chest and kneel in front of him. "Sorry. I-I'm sorry, baby. Mama is distracted right now."

"Where are we going?" he whines, his lower lip pouting out.

We are entering the hangry danger zone faster than I expected.

I paste on a smile. "We're going to grab lunch at a deli—"

"The one with the special drinks?" His ice-blue eyes light up. I have to blink away the image of the man he shares them with.

"The one with the special drinks," I confirm. It's amazing what a cardboard box of apple juice will do to a kid's mood. "Then we're going to go home and pack for an adventure."

He gasps. "What adventure?"

My heart cracks open. I look down, half-expecting to see it puddling on the ground at my feet.

He doesn't deserve this.

I gently tap the end of his nose. "You'll find out when we get there."

Five-year-olds aren't known for their patience, but the ham, egg, and cheese sandwich from the deli keeps him busy for most of the train ride and half of the walk back to our apartment. I pick at a bag of chips and try to keep up with his conversation, but it's hard to focus on anything except the way the walls are closing in.

The adventure I'm currently hyping up to my child? Homelessness.

My grand plan involves getting home, packing the

necessities, and then… The future stretches out in front of me like a black hole.

Is there something on the other side? Will we be swallowed up forever? Only time will tell.

"What kind of adventure will it be?" Dante bounces from one foot to the other while I unlock our apartment door.

"You'll have to see."

"Swimming?" he guesses. "Can I wear goggles?"

"It's too cold for swimming. Grab your favorite jackets. And your stuffies." I think about navigating the subway with Dante and multiple suitcases and correct myself. "One stuffy. Your favorite."

He frowns. "I don't have favorites. They're all my favorite."

"We don't have space for more than one," I say as calmly as I can. "Pick the one you want to take with you. Do it fast. We need to leave."

I'll grab the folder of important documents out of the kitchen junk drawer, pack some snacks and water bottles, and then a few changes of clothes. I'd like to get everything in one suitcase if I can.

Pictures of Dante line the walls. Dressed as an elephant for his first Halloween, squeezing my neck while he's riding a rainbow-colored unicorn on a carousel. They're glimpses of the life we've built. It's small and a little shabby and not nearly as much as he deserves, but right now, it's all I want.

I don't want to start over.

I don't want to keep running.

"I'm not going!" Dante declares. His eyes are watery.

I reach for his hair, but he pulls away and crosses his arms.

"I'm sorry," I breathe. "I wish we didn't have to go, but we do. We have to—"

"You said it was an adventure."

"It is. It is an adventure. But it's an adventure we *have* to go on. So I need you to—"

"I'm not going!" he yells again, diving for the coat closet by the front door. "I'm staying here."

The closet door slams closed and I drop my face in my hands. It's not even noon and this has already been the longest day of my life.

I take a deep breath before I cross the room and lightly rap on the closet door. "I'm coming in, okay?"

I crack the closet open and Dante is curled in the very back. For a New York City apartment, the closet is surprisingly deep. I'd love to sit in the entryway and still be able to reach him, but he's too far back. I don't have a choice but to duck my head and crawl inside.

Instantly, my chest tightens. Coats and rain jackets brush against my skin and I can't breathe. It's the same ache I've felt in my chest all day, but worse, somehow. More imminent.

Get out of here before you suffocate, it says.

I breathe through the claustrophobia and squeeze my son's knee. "Honey, I wish we didn't have to leave. I wish we could stay here and you could have all of your stuffies with you all the time."

"Then let's do it," he whimpers, swiping at his nose.

"We can't. I'm sorry."

"This isn't an adventure! Adventures are s'posed to be fun."

My throat is tight. My thoughts are scattered. I'm doing everything through a haze of panic I can't shove away. "You're right. I wanted you to be excited, so I might have fibbed a little bit."

"You lied?" he says in shock, eyes wide.

I give him a tight smile. "Mamas make mistakes, too."

This Mama's mistakes, in particular, are starting to pile up. We're drowning in them.

"Are you sorry?" he asks.

I swallow down the lump in my throat. "So, *so* sorry."

Dante thinks about it for half a second and then wraps his arms around me. "I forgive you."

Instantly, the weight on my chest lessens. I take a deep breath for the first time since I stepped through the door.

What did I do to deserve this kid?

I squeeze him back until he complains he can't breathe. Then I kiss his hair. "I love you, D. You're my favorite person in the world."

"I know," he says without an ounce of doubt in his voice. "Do we still have to go?"

"Yeah. I'm sorry. I wish we didn't have to, but—"

"Clifford," he says, cutting me off. "I've had him the longest and he's the fluffiest. I'll take Clifford with me."

I crush him in another hug, plant a barrage of kisses on his cheeks, and finally let him go once he's giggling and squealing.

He runs off to take care of Clifford while I throw anything I can't bear to part with in a bag.

During a last sweep of the apartment, I pluck the picture of Dante and me at the carousel off of the wall and throw it on top of the bag. Then Dante meets me at the front door, his T-rex backpack strapped to his shoulders and Clifford tucked under his arm.

"You ready, bud?" I ask, tousling his hair.

He ducks under my hand and grabs the doorknob. "I'm going to beat you down the stairs!"

He doesn't know this is our last race down the stairs. He doesn't know we aren't coming back. That the landlord is going to put the rest of our stuff out on the curb for scavengers.

I want to hug him in the doorway and weep, but that won't help anything. Dante needs me to be strong for him. He needs me to keep it together.

I chuckle as he darts out the door onto the landing. "Okay, but make sure you wait for me at the mailb—"

I see the figure out of the corner of my eye and reach for the tiny arm of Dante's T-rex backpack. But I miss.

Dante runs out of my reach and straight into the person standing at the top of our stairs.

"Oh," Dante squeaks, stumbling back.

I grab my son and shove him behind me, but it's too late.

It was too late the moment I heard Mikhail's voice coming towards me down the hallway this morning. The last few hours have been nothing but a delusion.

Mikhail looks past me to the little boy peeking from behind my back. The boy with the same ice blue eyes and golden brown hair.

Mikhail looks past me to his son. And I see the truth light up in his eyes: *he knows.*

Now, there is no place left to run.

11

VIVIANA

"That's my son," Mikhail breathes.

He says it softly like he's trying to convince himself. But it doesn't take much convincing. Not once you see Dante and Mikhail in the same room.

"Mama…" Dante grabs onto my leg. He's always been shy around new people. Mostly because he hasn't met very many of them. I keep our circle small on purpose.

I squat down next to him. He's taller than me like this, so I have to look up to see his eyes, though he keeps sneaking glances at Mikhail.

Does Dante see the resemblance, too? Does he know?

"Go back inside, okay?" I wrinkle my nose in a smile. "I'll come get you in a minute."

"Can I watch a show?"

I wordlessly swipe to his favorite show on my phone and

hand it to him. Strict screen time rules can take a back seat, seeing as how life as we know it is on the brink of collapse.

Dante sinks into the far end of the couch, Clifford sitting next to him. He smiles as the theme song plays. I pull the door closed behind me.

Mikhail is still standing at the top of the stairs. He's staring at the place where, a second ago, Dante was fidgeting next to me. If it's possible, he looks stunned.

"Listen, Mikhail, I don't know what you want, but I just want to—"

"My son." His gaze shifts to mine. Hardens into steel. "That's my son."

Yes. Of course it is.

"No." I shake my head. "He's mine. We just want to leave. Whatever is happening here, I don't want any part in it."

I've gotten good at hiding over the years. At giving people tiny snippets of me, but never the whole. Even with my own father, I had to hide. What I wanted—*who I loved*—was never good enough for him. I'm a pro at shapeshifting into who I need to be in any given situation.

But with Mikhail, there is no hiding.

He stares at me, peeling me apart layer by layer until I'm flayed open in front of him. "He is why you lied about your name. He is why you disappeared."

"*You* are why I disappeared," I snap. "You told me to run while I had the chance. You told me I shouldn't let myself be anyone's pawn."

"That's before I knew you were pregnant with my son!" He's in front of me in a second, pinning me against the door, roaring in my face.

I want to go inside, but I don't want Dante to see this. I've hidden him from this world for five years. I'm not going to throw him into the middle of it now.

"Lower your voice. My kid is in there," I hiss.

Mikhail dips his head. We're in the same position we were back in Mr. Fredrickson's office, but this time, I'm ready to fight. I'll do anything to shield my son from this.

"Are you trying to protect him from me, Viviana?" His voice is low and even, but there's a dangerous edge to it. Trofim had to yell and scream to show me how big and scary he was. Mikhail simply needs to exist. He breathes and I quiver, simple as that.

"This has nothing to do with you," I lie. "I'm protecting him from that entire world—yours and mine."

"That's right. You have a foothold here, too. Does your son know his mom is a mafia princess?" Mikhail starts to smirk, but a thought occurs to him. "Your father... He knows about your son."

It isn't a question, but I seal my lips together anyway.

Mikhail laughs bitterly. "I knew there was something strange about the way he supported me becoming *pakhan*. I mean, I fucked over your little arrangement with Trofim. Agostino should have hated me. Turns out, he had a good reason to want me in charge. A baby is even better than a marriage when it comes to alliances."

"My son isn't some bartering chip." I jab him in the chest. "Stay the hell away from him."

Mikhail snatches my wrist and pins it over my head. It thuds against the door, and I hear Dante inside. The show he's watching pauses.

"Mama?"

Mikhail's breath is hot on my neck. I look into his cold eyes and try to keep my voice even as I talk through the door. "Sorry, bud. That was me. I'll be inside in a second."

Dante's show starts back up and Mikhail leans in closer. "He's mine, Viviana. Admit it."

I shake my head.

He traces my jawline with his thumb. I feel like I'm being circled by a predator. "Don't lie," he drawls. "I'm sure you've noticed the resemblance."

Only every day for the last five years.

I shrug. "I don't see it. Maybe it's because the sight of Dante doesn't make me want to punch him in the face."

Mikhail leans away and sighs. "If you aren't going to cooperate, I don't have much choice. You know how these things are. I can't have my offspring running around the streets unaccounted for. If you won't give up what I need to know, I'll get it myself."

"How?"

He starts to push me to the side, reaching for the doorknob. "I'll take the kid and get a paternity test done. It'll only take a couple hours. I'll bring him back when I'm done... probably."

"No!" I slide between Mikhail and the door. "Don't touch him."

"Then tell me the truth," he snarls.

Everything I've done since Dante was born has been to avoid this moment. Every sacrifice, every lonely night, every scraped-together bill paid to keep the lights on and food in our fridge—all of it was to keep Dante a secret from the man in front of me.

Now, I don't have a choice. No matter what I do, I could lose Dante.

Tears well in my eyes. When I look up at Mikhail, they roll down my cheeks. "Please don't take him away from me. Please."

It's as much confirmation as he's going to get. Turns out, it's as much as he needs.

Mikhail watches my tears with an unreadable expression. Then he tips his head towards the door. "I want to meet him."

My instinct to shield Dante from the world rises up. I block the door. "He isn't ready. Give him time. Let me ease him into the idea and then—"

"If you think I'm going to walk away and give you a chance to run again, you're wrong," he breathes in a low rumble. "The only reason I didn't find you for the last six years is because I wasn't looking very hard."

I didn't know he was looking for me at all. That's news.

"But," Mikhail continues, "if you run again, I'll raise heaven and hell to track you down and take my son back. You've stolen five years from me; I'm not going to give you another day. Open the door and introduce me to my son. Now."

"Okay, but—"

"You're not in a position to barter." He looms large over me to highlight exactly which position I'm in. As if I need reminding. It's hard to forget you're in a snare while you're being dangled upside down by your ankle.

"I'm not bartering for me," I argue. "It's for *him*. Being a father is a lot more than genetics. If you barge in there and announce yourself as his dad, you'll terrify him and scar him forever."

"What have you told him about his dad? Does he think I'm a flake? Dead?"

"He doesn't think anything," I admit. "I told him… I told him our family was complete. Just the two of us."

It was a lie then and it's a lie now. There was always something missing.

I'm just not convinced that the missing piece is Mikhail. But it's too late now.

"Tell him your name and say you're my friend," I advise. "Don't overcomplicate it. He has a good eye for liars."

As I open the door, Mikhail mutters behind me. "Apparently not."

Dante has one leg crossed over the other on the couch. Clifford has slipped sideways, his stuffed head resting against Dante's shoulder. He doesn't look up as we enter, too entranced by the crime-fighting dogs on the screen.

But when Mikhail clears his throat, Dante's eyes snap up.

"Who is that?" he asks, not waiting for Mikhail to introduce himself.

The male role models in his life are slim pickings. I didn't even officially introduce him to Tommy until he'd lived in the building for six months. I didn't want Dante getting attached if he wasn't going to be a long-term tenant.

Now, I'm introducing him to his actual biological father. A man I've spoken to for no more than one hour total in my life.

"Dante, this is Mikhail."

Dante eyes him up and down.

My stomach twists. I feel nauseous. My instincts are screaming at me to wrap my arms around my son and shield him from what's coming next. It's like a bomb is about to go off, except I'm the one pushing the button.

"Is he going on our adventure, too?" Dante asks.

"Oh. Um… Well, I don't know if—"

"I'm taking you on your adventure," Mikhail interrupts.

"You are?" Dante looks at me to confirm, but I don't have the words.

Mikhail nods. "Pack whatever you want. We're leaving soon."

He holds up Clifford. "I already did. Mama said only one stuffy could come with us. I chose Clifford."

Mikhail takes a step forward and I trail silently behind him, a ghost. "Well, things have changed. Now, you can take as many stuffed animals as you want."

Dante's eyes light up. This time, he doesn't look at me as he asks, "I can?"

"You can. Just do it fast. I need to get back to my castle."

If it was possible for a little boy's jaw to unhinge, Dante's would be on the floor right now. "You live in a *castle*?"

"Of course I do. All kings live in a castle."

"You're a *king*?!" Dante jumps up, a wide grin on his perfect face. "I didn't know kings were real life!"

Mikhail slides his hands in his pockets casually. He doesn't need them to rip my life up by the root. It comes easily for him. The same as everything else in his life.

"I'm real life, aren't I?"

Dante looks him over like he wants to pinch him to check. I share the instinct. "Yeah."

"So, there you go. Kings are real." Mikhail waves him off. "Go finish packing and you can come live in my castle."

Dante is halfway down the hallway before he turns back. "If I live in your castle, what does that make me?"

"I believe that would make you a prince, Dante." Mikhail looks at me, amusement written in every line of his face. "Wouldn't you agree?"

I'm going to be sick.

Dante bounces to his room and I slump back against the door. My six-year-long detour was for nothing. I'm right back where I started.

Except, this time, I took Dante down with me.

12

MIKHAIL

Dante takes one look at the mansion and yanks on his mother's arm. He whispers in Viviana's ear loudly enough that I can still hear him, "Is magic real life?"

"Mostly, no—but it's complicated."

Everything is complicated. The sooner Dante learns that, the sooner my world will make sense to him.

Viviana is still wearing the clothes she showed up to work in six hours ago. *Six hours? Is that all it's been?*

Six years of searching for Viviana without a single hit. No sign of her, nothing. Now, she's been back in my life for six hours and she's moving into my house with our son.

Life can really come at you fast.

"Castles are from movies. Maybe other things from movies are real, too. Like…" Dante squishes up his face in thought. "Can dogs talk?"

"No," Viviana answers patiently, "dogs can't talk."

"What about cats?" he fires back.

She shakes her head. "Nope. Not them, either."

"Birds?"

God, this woman has the patience of a saint.

I've never been around kids. I was barely a kid myself. Something about his innocence, his pursed lips, the seriousness on his face… it makes a dormant part of me stir. I shake it off and leave them behind.

Stella is waiting in the entryway. "Mr. Novikov." Fifteen years of service to our family and Stella still bows deeply when she greets me. I asked her once why she always bows and she said that every time she sees me, she realizes she could be looking at Trofim instead. It leaves her overflowing with gratitude.

Fair enough.

"I'm leaving them to you, Stella. Get them settled and give them whatever they need."

"We weren't expecting guests, so the guest wing hasn't been aired out yet. I can have the maids speed up the process if you—"

"They'll stay in the family wing," I say dismissively.

The last time this house was regularly occupied, every room in the family wing was full. The master bedroom and all three of the bedrooms—one for each of us boys. Now, my son is going to occupy one of those rooms.

Only so I can keep an eye on them, I remind myself coldly.

"Whichever room they want," I continue. "But make sure they don't leave."

Stella nods. "Understood."

I don't offer an explanation for why Viviana and Dante are coming to stay with me and can't leave, but Stella knows better than to ask for one.

Viviana is still inching Dante up the stairs while answering every question he peppers her with. The conversation has shifted from magic to every crazy thing he's ever seen in a cartoon.

"If a piano lands on your head, do you get squished flat like a pancake?" He glances up at the facade of the house like there might be a Steinway baby grand dangling from the balcony with ropes.

Before Viviana can respond, I hear a soft gasp behind me.

Stella is frozen in place, staring through the open door. She's watching Dante like he's impossible. Like he's—

"*Yours*," she breathes, turning to me. "Is he—"

"Help them get settled and mind your own business," I snarl.

My tone is a little overly aggressive, but it's been less than an hour since I learned he existed. I'm not ready to talk about it with anyone else. I don't even know what to say. Based on Stella's reaction, denying Dante won't be an option.

"I'm sorry, sir. I shouldn't have…" She dips her chin. "Understood."

Viviana and Dante step into the entryway, necks craned back to take in the dual marble staircase that leads to the second-floor landing.

"I have work to do," I explain without meeting either of their gazes, "but Stella will show you to your rooms."

"I get my own room?" Dante asks in disbelief.

At the same time, Viviana takes a step closer. "You're leaving?"

"I have work to do," I repeat.

She frowns.

Disappointment? I wonder. *Frustration?* Not that it matters. The only reason she's in my house is because of Dante. Because she kept my son from me for five years. If anyone has good reason to be disappointed or frustrated, it's me.

What does she expect? A guided tour? After everything she's done, she should be grateful she's here at all. I could have grabbed Dante and ran.

I pivot and toss back over my shoulder, "Make yourselves at home."

Dante doesn't hear. He's too busy asking his mom if he gets to wear a crown now that he's a prince.

I walk straight to my office for five minutes of peace, but Raoul is waiting outside the door for me. No peace to be found here today, it seems.

"Not now," I tell him as I turn the key. "I need five fucking minutes to myself before you and Anatoly jump on me."

"Anatoly is in the dungeon."

"Because he's smart enough to send you to do his dirty work," I surmise. "If he wants to know more about Viviana, he's going to have to wait."

Anatoly is going to lose his mind when he realizes he was right. He's unbearable enough as it is. The last thing he needs is a reason to gloat.

"Mikhail, this isn't about Viviana."

His tone is solemn enough that I turn to face him. "Then what is it about?"

He takes a breath before he says, "It's about Trofim."

13

MIKHAIL

As I follow Raoul down to the dungeon, I don't ask the question burning through my mind: *Where is Trofim?*

I can't. I don't have the energy for half-baked theories and possibilities. As a leader, they aren't useful.

Questioning whether Trofim and Viviana showing back up on the same day after almost six years of radio silence is connected in any way isn't helpful.

Wondering whether the mother of my child is in cahoots with the ex-fiancé I saved her from is a waste of energy.

So I shove the thoughts deep down inside and descend the stairs into the dungeon.

In reality, it's a glorified basement. Despite everything I said to Dante, I don't really think I'm a king who lives in a castle. But when you hold prisoners in your basement, calling it "the dungeon" is the natural next step. What can you do?

Raoul unlocks a second door at the bottom of the staircase and lets me into the first soundproof interrogation room. A middle-aged man with a paunch is tied to a metal chair in the middle of the floor. His hands are bound behind his back.

Definitely not Trofim.

"I told you everything I know," the man whines through a thick Russian accent. His bottom lip is split and blood dribbles down his chin.

Anatoly wraps a length of tape around his bloody knuckles as he paces the concrete floor. "I wish I could believe you, but you've said that already. Twice now. And each time, a little knockaround shook some things loose."

The man is trembling. "I swear, I don't have anything else! I'm out of the game. It's why I moved here. Whoever you think I'm going to tell, I'm not. I don't have any more connections."

"Lucky you," Anatoly muses. "If you did, I might have to kill you. As it is, you only managed to run your mouth to a few old drunks at the bar."

"Run his mouth about what?" I ask.

Anatoly turns to me, a wide grin on his face. "I hear congratulations are—"

"What did he run his mouth about?" I repeat with a warning glare for my brother.

He closes his mouth, but the amusement is hard to miss. After a few seconds of silence, Anatoly kicks the shaking man's chair. "Well, my *pakhan* asked you a question. Tell him what you ran your mouth about."

"I didn't run my mouth!" the man starts. "Some men at the bar started asking questions about my work. I'm retired now.

I haven't practiced in four years. But I told them about my work as a coroner. People find it interesting. They have questions! These guys, they, they, they wanted to know if I'd ever cremated anyone they would know and I remember a case from a few years ago. There was a guy who—"

Suddenly, Anatoly's fist connects with the man's jaw. His head snaps to the side, blood spraying out of his mouth.

"Anatoly," Raoul complains with a sigh, "he was talking."

"It was boring. Besides, I should be the one to deliver the news." Anatoly shakes out his fist and walks closer. He meets my eyes and, for the first time in a long time, there is no joke. "Trofim is dead."

I thought Trofim might be plotting something. I half-expected to find him strapped to a chair in the dungeon.

But… dead?

"How?" I ask.

Anatoly hitches a thumb over his shoulder to the bleeding man. "Long story short, I overheard this asshole running his mouth at a rival bar. He was talking about cremating the son of the Novikov Bratva in Moscow. I figured he was full of shit and just trying to get some clout with the bartender for free drinks, but… he had a lot of information."

"Description, tattoos, and where Trofim was staying," Raoul lists off. "It seems legit."

Trofim is dead. It's not so hard to wrap my head around. I haven't seen him since that night in the bridal suite. In a lot of ways, he's been dead to me since the moment I exiled him.

"That's not all." Anatoly spins around, kicking the man's chair again. The coroner is slumped down, but he blinks back to full awareness as we all stare at him. "Tell him the rest."

"I got the call to take care of Trofim Novikov's body in the middle of the night. Usually, these kinds of things can wait until morning, but there was a rush. Someone with more power than I have wanted the body cremated immediately. But when I got there, I noticed—"

"He was murdered," Anatoly blurts. After a few seconds, he waves his hand at the coroner. "Go on. Keep going."

The man sighs and carries on. "Someone suggested it was suicide, but it wasn't like any suicide I've ever seen. There were cuts and bruises all over his body. Most people don't brutalize themselves like that before they pull the trigger. It didn't make sense."

"That's because you didn't know him," Anatoly drawls. "To know Trofim was to want to kill him. I'm not surprised it happened; I'm just surprised we're only finding out about it now."

"Did you hear anything about this, Raoul?"

He shakes his head. "Nothing. Trofim was staying in some tiny little town outside of Dzerzhinsk. I had eyes in the surrounding areas in case he ventured out, but he never did."

Because he was dead.

I counted it a luxury that my older brother at least knew when to call it quits. I exiled him and he didn't fight back. He took his defeat on the chin.

Or, maybe not.

Maybe someone killed him before he could scrabble together a comeback attempt.

"Is that all the information we have?" I ask.

"So far," Anatoly confirms. "I'd like a few more minutes with our witness here, though. He doesn't like to cough it all up in one go."

The man whimpers, rightfully so, and Raoul and I head back upstairs to my office.

Unlike Anatoly, Raoul knows when to give me space. He stands quietly against the wall as I pace the room back and forth, repeating these new facts in my head.

Viviana is back.

Dante is my son.

And Trofim is dead.

I don't believe in coincidences. Especially not when I'm this fucking close to controlling the vast majority of shipping ports on the East Coast.

I'm still pacing when Anatoly shoves through my office door. He drops into the leather chair across from my desk, panting and sticky with sweat. "The guy didn't know anything else."

"It could be a distraction," Raoul suggests now that the silence has been broken. "Someone wants to pull your mind away from finalizing the deal with the Greeks."

"Trofim is dead. That's nothing but good news in my books." Anatoly shrugs. "The son of a bitch got what he deserved. The only thing that's sad about it is that I wasn't there to witness it."

Anatoly never forgave Trofim for what he did to his mother. I don't blame him. If someone slaughtered my mother, I wouldn't have been able to breathe knowing they were still alive. Especially if it was over some fucking Bratva title I never wanted. Yet Anatoly *lived with* Trofim. For years.

If Helen and I have other children someday, will Dante live the way Anatoly did? Will he be relegated to the sidelines simply because I'm not married to his mother?

Will someone go after Viviana to make sure there's no chance Dante can ever be legitimate?

My fists tighten into balls at the thought. Mental images of Viviana in her lacy bridal lingerie flicker through my head and something else tightens, as well.

I shake my head to clear it all away. "The problem isn't that Trofim is dead. The problem is that someone found him while he was exiled and murdered him. We need to know who it was to make sure they aren't a threat to what we're doing here."

"I already have men looking into it," Raoul assures me. "Should I alert Iakov to the development?"

On one hand, my father deserves to know his eldest son is dead.

On the other hand, knowledge is power.

"No," I decide. "I don't want this getting out until we know more."

"Which development are we talking about? Trofim's death? Or the new addition to the family?" A shit-eating grin spreads across my half-brother's face. Any chance at peace is gone now.

"Who told you?" I growl.

Anatoly hitches a thumb towards Raoul, who has the decency to duck down in shame.

"And who the fuck told *you*?"

"No one had to. I knew the second I saw him. He looks just like you, Mikhail."

I drop my head in my hands with a sigh.

"Bastard or not, the Novikov genetics are strong with that one," Anatoly chimes in.

I snap my gaze back to his. "Watch your fucking mouth."

"Mea culpa." He holds his hands up in surrender. "Where are they now?"

"Stella is getting them settled."

Anatoly's eyebrows shoot up. "'Settled'? How long are they staying?"

"As long as I want them to stay,"

"Helen might have a few thoughts about that."

"Hard to have thoughts about something she doesn't know exists," I fire back angrily. "I don't want anyone breathing a word of this to anyone. I want a total information blackout until I understand what happened to Trofim."

"You think it has something to do with Viviana?" Raoul asks.

I throw up my hands. "I don't know. What I do know is, Trofim or not, Viviana and the kid are going to be targets the moment this information gets out." I turn to Anatoly. "You know I'm right."

A shadow crosses over his face. Memories he's never been

able to fight or drink or fuck away rising to the surface. "Yeah. They'll be targets."

"So we keep them close and don't say a word." I pinch the bridge of my nose. "The boy is in school, so he'll need a tutor. We can have them sign an NDA. Money is no object, obviously."

"What about Viviana?" Raoul asks.

"What about her?"

He shrinks back slightly. "She's his mother. I assume she'll have feelings about his education and your plans. Does she know you're planning to keep them here long-term?"

"Considering I didn't know my son existed until an hour ago, I don't give a fuck about what she knows," I growl. "She's going to do whatever I tell her to do."

An image of Viviana lying beneath me fills my head. Her legs spread wide. She looks exactly the same, but I want to see all of her. I want to see her body now that she's carried my child. I want to see the ways I changed her.

"She might try to run again," Raoul says.

"She's in even more danger now than she was before. She won't run. I won't let her."

I push away from my desk and move to the bar cart. I pour myself a shot of vodka and toss it back.

Viviana can't leave. I won't let Dante end up like Anatoly. He's going to have an inheritance. He's going to have a mother *and* a father. I'm going to do for him what my father should have done for Anatoly.

When I turn back around, Raoul and Anatoly are looking at each other. They'll gossip about me later, I'm sure. Right now, I don't fucking care.

"Boys," I announce, "I have a job for you."

14

VIVIANA

Mikhail may have lured Dante in with talk of castles and kings, but I know this world of shiny objects and dark underbellies too well to be fooled by it. I grew up in it.

There aren't enough crystal chandeliers in the world to make me want to raise my child here.

The plush carpets alone are sending me into a PTSD flare-up. Let me tell you, priceless pieces of art and designer sofas don't make up for your parents leaving you alone on your birthday. Marble floors and fancy gardens don't make up for being made to play the piano for their rich friends again and again and again until your fingers cramp and bleed. Luxury can't replace love.

But for Dante, it's all new and wonderful.

It takes an extra hour to get him to bed, thanks in no small part to him gorging himself on Mikhail's endless pantry. Even after bathing him in a tub big enough to require goggles and a snorkel, I swear he still has an orange smudge of chip dust behind his ear.

But eventually, all the excitement dries up and he falls asleep in my arms as I towel him dry. I put him in pajamas and tuck him into bed. He's softly snoring when I pull the door closed.

Being away from him, even for a few minutes, leaves an ache in my chest. I'm used to him being just on the other side of a paper-thin wall. In this mansion, I could take a wrong turn and be several football fields away from him.

"Is he asleep?" Stella is leaning against the wall next to the door. Her hands are tucked behind her back. She looks relaxed. But I know better.

She's on patrol.

"Out like a light." I yawn, stretching my arms over my head for effect. "I think I'm headed that way, too."

"Already?"

"Are you telling me every thirty-something you know doesn't have a strict eight o'clock bedtime?" I joke.

She laughs. "Not unless I'm gearing up for a night out. Then I might take a power nap to recharge."

Stella looks to be about my age, wearing a pair of wide-legged trousers and a gray tee with a French tuck. She is young and fashionable and, based on the way she has been Dante's personal wish-granting genie all day, friendly.

She doesn't look like Mikhail's secret police... but I know better.

"Well, no big night out for me. I'm going to need a solid eight hours to recharge before the wild child is ready to raid the snack drawers again."

Stella's smile doesn't falter, but her eyes narrow. "Was today a big day?"

Oh, gee, let's see: There was a hostile takeover at my job, I ran into a one-night stand I thought I'd left in the dust (see also: ex-fiancé's brother and father of my child), and now, I've been kidnapped. So, yeah, you could say it has been a big day.

"Something like that."

She nods and gestures to the room across the hall. "I've put your things in here. I can take you in and show you how to run the bath. It's great when you need to unwind. Don't tell on me, but I've used it a few times."

"Your secret's safe with me." I zip my finger across my lips. "Thanks, but I can manage."

Stella was already moving towards the door when I refused, so she has to pull back. "The faucets in that bathroom are finicky. They're backwards and really touchy. It goes from boiling lava to glacial in half a second. I'll just go in and show you—"

"That's okay," I say firmly. I tack on a smile at the end for good measure. "I don't need to wash up tonight anyway. I'm going to go straight to sleep. I'm exhausted."

Stella chews on her bottom lip like her religious beliefs involve showing me how to run a bath for myself. Like me refusing to let her teach me about shower faucets is blasphemy.

"Thanks for everything you did for us today." I edge towards the door, never turning my back on her. "You made Dante feel right at home."

"He's such a sweet boy. You've done a great job with him. I can tell you two have a very special bond."

Oh, yeah, she's definitely Mikhail's secret police. Probably the head of his secret police. This woman is responsible for war crimes somewhere, I'm sure.

Only someone truly diabolical would say something like that to a mother.

Stella wants to make me cry? She wants to soften me up and lower my guard? She'll have to try harder than that.

"You are so sweet. Thank you." I yawn again. I don't want to oversell it, but Stella has got to go.

"You're sure you don't need me to help you get settled?" she asks one final time.

"I'm sure. You've done enough already. You're off tour guide duty for the day." I open the door and Stella looks past me into the room. I have no idea what she's looking for. Maybe a rope ladder and grappling hook on the bed? But I give her one final wave and slip into the room.

Alone at last.

I stand in the middle of the room, facing the door, for a full ninety seconds. When I don't hear any sounds coming from the hallway, I start throwing everything Stella unpacked for me into a pile on the bed.

I'm not sure what Mikhail's staff did with our suitcases. Probably mistook them for garbage and threw them away. I don't blame them. The wheels were all broken off and mine was more duct tape than fabric. I actually found them originally propped up next to a dumpster.

From trash they came; to trash they shall return.

Unfortunately, that means my only option is to strip the queen-sized bed of its luxury sheets. I pile all of my things into the center and tie up the four Egyptian-cotton corners around one of the wooden rods I ripped out of the walk-in closet.

I give the rod a test swing. It could be a weapon in a pinch. But what I wouldn't give for the Taser in my bedside table right about now.

Once I have everything packed, I sit on the floor, the makeshift pack in my lap, and wait.

Minutes crawl by. One, two, ten, sixty. And then sixty more.

I'm actually starting to see some of the upsides to meditation. My mind is empty and I am all that is Zen.

Or at least, as Zen as I can be while planning to flee into the night with my son and our scant belongings balanced on a stick bundle over my shoulder like a cartoon hobo. But I'll take it.

Finally, just after midnight, I tip-toe to my door and crack it open.

The hallway is dim, but not full dark. Most importantly, it's empty. From here, it's all simple.

Grab Dante. Run for the front door. Don't stop running.

It's a full moon tonight. It will make it harder to hide, but at least I won't be navigating my way around in the dark.

Grab Dante. Run for the front door. Don't stop running.

Chanting those words to myself, I step out of my room and creep across the hall. I grab his doorknob and start to turn it…

Just as a hand wraps around my elbow.

I yelp and spin around, simultaneously throwing myself off-balance and sending my closet rod/only weapon skittering off of my shoulder and thunking to the floor.

Before I can even think about grabbing it, a large shape rises up in front of me.

"Where do you think you're going?"

15

VIVIANA

"Where do you think you're going?"

The overwhelming smell of mint and cedar hits me before my eyes adjust. Mikhail is only a few inches away from my face, so I have to tip my head back to see all of him.

He's wearing a black shirt that hugs his large biceps and gray sweatpants that somehow fit him better than the suit he's been wearing all day. And his face is... sparkly? I might be hallucinating.

Before my mind can spin off in some *Twilight*-esque vampire fantasy, I realize Mikhail is sweating.

"Were you working out?" I blurt.

"I was... until I saw a hobo lurking in the hallway outside Dante's room." He kicks at my makeshift stick-and-bedsheet suitcase. "What in the hell is this?"

"Someone hid my actual suitcase."

"Because you don't need it," he growls. "You aren't going anywhere."

Before I can argue, Mikhail throws me over his shoulder and carries me back into my room. I pound his annoyingly muscular back with my fists.

"Put me down!"

No sooner than the words are out of my mouth, he drops me on the bed.

I flop and flail like a fish for a few seconds before I get my land legs and scramble to the edge of the mattress—only to find a wall of hard, sweaty flesh there blocking my path.

"You can't keep us here," I snap, knowing full well he absolutely can and will. "This is kidnapping."

"I think it's actually abduction."

"Same thing."

"Not in the eyes of the law," he says, his own eyes chilling me to the bone.

I cross my arms. "What kind of person knows those legal definitions?"

"The kind who can get away with them," he retorts. "You aren't going anywhere."

I shove against his chest. "You smug, cocky—"

In one move, Mikhail grabs my arms, spins me onto my stomach, and—

The sound of his hand cracking against my ass steals the breath from my lungs, the thoughts from my head, and the "what the hell" from my "are you doing"?

I snap my head around, eyes so wide I'm sure my face will be stuck like this forever. Permanent shock and horror for the rest of my days, like a gargoyle with a messy bun.

"Did you just *spank* me?!" I scream.

Instead of answering my rhetorical question, he does it again. Pushes me down with the flat of one hand between my shoulder blades. Rears back. *CRACK.*

Hand, meet ass. Ass, meet hand.

Pain, meet pleasure. Pleasure, meet pain.

"Get off of me!" I wiggle to get free, but Mikhail silently bends me over the edge of the mattress and spanks me a third time.

The force drives me into the bed, grinding me against the edge of the mattress. Heat that has nothing at all to do with how much it stings blooms low in my belly. My back arches all on its own, that traitorous little bitch.

When his palm slaps against me the next time, a soft moan forces its way out of my lips.

Suddenly, Mikhail backs away, panting. In an effort to look like I'm not the world's horniest masochist, I flip over and slide to a human puddle on the floor. Only to find myself eye level with Mikhail's gray sweatpants, which are doing absolutely nothing to hide the significant erection he's sporting.

I gasp and look up at him. "You *liked* that!"

Even from down here, his dark eyes shine with a light all their own. "Am I supposed to deny it?"

"You're supposed to pretend you're not a fucking psychopath," I hiss. "You kidnapped—No, I'm sorry, *abducted* me—and now you're getting your rocks off by spanking me. Red fucking flag, Mikhail. I guess I should have known. It runs in the family."

In the blink of an eye, Mikhail rips me off the floor and back on the bed. He stands between my spread legs, his hands on my thighs. His thumbs trace up my inner leg slowly, inching towards the pulsing ache at my center.

God, it's been a long, long time.

"I could check and see if you liked it, Viviana." He spends time saying my name. He savors it like a decadent dessert. "I'm sure I'll find you dripping for me. Don't think I didn't hear the way you moaned."

I want to deny it. I want to stick my tongue out at him like a tantruming child and tell him I'm as dry as the fucking Dust Bowl.

But there's no point. If I push him, he'll check. I know he will. Then he'll find the evidence of how much I liked him touching me.

None of that is the problem. *The problem* is that he'll assume wanting him is the same as wanting to be with him. He'll assume I want this house and this world and this life.

I don't.

Not for me or sure as hell not for my son.

"Sue me; I moaned," I admit. "But touching isn't something we ever had trouble with. It's how we got into this mess in the first place, actually. It's everything else we struggle with."

"There is nothing else."

I snort. "Of course you'd say that. The man who kidnapped a woman and her child with less than five words spoken is bad at communicating? Who would have guessed?!"

"I didn't kidnap *your* child. I kidnapped *mine*."

I sit up, my legs tightening around Mikhail's hips, and jab him in the chest. "He's mine. And nothing you can say is ever going to convince me to lie down and let you destroy his life. I'm not going to let you use him like some bartering chip. I'll never stop running and I'll never stop fighting and I'll—"

"Get yourself killed," he snarls, interrupting. "You want me to communicate? Fine. You are the mother of the one and only heir to the Novikov Bratva. It can be a position of power if you accept it. If not, it's a liability."

I know how this world works, so I know just how right he is. Women have been killed for getting in the way of their children inheriting their birthright. I've heard stories about it. Girls who ran off with their secret heirs only to turn up dead once the father found out. Those stories have been haunting me to sleep every night for the last five years.

"You'll kill me?" I challenge.

Mikhail's jaw clicks. "Dante loves you. You're his whole world. I would never do anything to harm him."

"Except rip him out of his school and his house and his routine," I fire back. "Sorry, but you've been in his life for an afternoon and your track record is already shit."

"I'm his father. I want to take care of him."

"That's what my father said before he literally sold me to a madman. But you already know how that ended up."

He knows parts of it. Not all of it.

Ivory Ashes

Mikhail doesn't know exactly how deep my father's control ran. If he thinks selling me off to Trofim for a reputation boost is the worst of it, he needs to get a hell of a lot more creative.

No matter what, I won't let anyone treat my son the way I was treated. Not while I'm alive to stop them.

So I need to stay alive.

"Promise me..." I lick my lips, trying to think of the right words to say. What concessions could possibly make this situation livable? "Promise me that you won't hurt him."

"Done," Mikhail says without even pausing to think about it.

"Don't just say that. I need to know that you actually mean it."

Mikhail tips his chin down to meet my eyes. A strand of dark hair falls over his forehead and my stomach flips. But I ignore it and focus on the words coming out of his mouth... which is very close to mine. Too close, probably.

"Dante is my heir, Viviana. He will have the full protection of the Novikov Bratva and *my* full protection."

"Isn't that the same thing?" I breathe, staring at his lips while I wait for a response.

He shakes his head slowly. "The Bratva is an extension of me. But it isn't *me*." His voice softens and I swear it's almost musical. "So I give you my word as *pakhan* and as Dante's father that I'll keep him safe."

What would it be like to be with Dante's father? To be with the version of Mikhail who loves my son and gets off on spanking me without all of the fucking baggage attached?

I fist my hands in my lap before I do something stupid like run my fingers through his hair. It's just hard to think about anything else when he's standing between my legs.

"Fine," I croak, clearing my throat. "I won't run. We'll stay, but… But I'm his primary parent. I'm the only parent he's ever had and I should be the default. You get him for Bratva stuff, but I get him for everything else. And I don't want you to be alone with him."

"No."

The response is so fast and so final that I almost think I imagined it. But when I look up into his face, I know I didn't.

"What do you mean, 'no'? You're going to refuse everything I said just like that? Do you take a second to consider literally anything or do you always shoot straight from the hip?"

"I don't need a second to consider a bullshit offer. You want me to interact with my son under your supervision and only when it concerns the Bratva. I say no. Fuck no, actually. Hell fucking no."

It's not lost on me that I'm disappointed that the father of my child *wants* to be involved. The world feels upside down right now.

"Well, I can't promise you any more than that. That's all I'm willing to give."

"Whether you approve of it or not, Dante is *my* son. He's going to live here in this house with me as *my* son. He's going to inherit the Bratva I build for him as *my* son."

"And where does that leave me?" I try to push Mikhail away, but he doesn't give me an inch. I'm forced to face off with him while my legs are still wrapped around his hips. "I know what it's like for mistresses in this world. I saw the flowers in your office; I'm sure you have an army of ass on the side if you aren't already married. I'm not going to sit on the bench in your harem while you steal my son from me."

His nostrils flare. His eyes are black. There's desire written all over his face, but I'm positive it has more to do with the desire to spank me than anything else. Poor Mikhail probably isn't used to his stable of women pushing back.

"There is no harem. I don't want you to be my mistress."

"Then what do you want?" I snap.

"I want you to be my wife!" he roars.

I fall back, catching myself on my elbows, jaw flopping open in sheer shock.

Mikhail jerks away from me and runs a hand through his hair. His jaw flexes as he grinds his teeth together.

"I'm sorry, you... you want me to be your wife?"

He can't be serious. He isn't.

He turns to face me, his expression wiped clean. His eyes are cold and distant. "I want my son with me. Dante is staying here no matter what. Either you can marry me and stay, too, or you leave."

"Leave?" I reach for the escape hatch. "We can leave? You'll let us—"

"*You* can leave," he clarifies. "Dante is staying."

I can leave—without my son. Either I live here with Mikhail as his wife or I leave my son behind.

That isn't an option. There is no future for me without Dante. There's no life without him. I can't leave him here alone. I won't.

"I'll give you the night to think it over," Mikhail says, as if he hasn't already sealed my fate.

Then he walks away, leaving my bedroom door wide open behind him.

16

VIVIANA

I don't know how long I've been crying when someone knocks on my door. All I know is my eyes burn, my cheeks are sticky with dried tears, and I absolutely do not want to see Mikhail. Not now. Not ever.

"Go away!" I try to yell, but it comes out in a croak. My throat is raw from crying.

The door opens. "Come again?"

The deep voice doesn't belong to Mikhail, but that doesn't matter. Everyone in this house is loyal to him. That's how Bratvas and mafias and all of these messed-up criminal organizations work. The sun shines out of Mikhail's ass and everyone is dying for a tan. I don't want Mikhail or any extension of him in my room right now.

The room sways as I sit up, but I turn to the massive mountain of a man peeking through my doorway. He looks familiar, but my vision is blurred from the many hours of weeping. "I said, 'Go away.'"

"That's what I thought you said." Then he walks into my room like his comprehension skills aren't quite up to snuff, the door snicking closed behind him. "I thought I'd come see how badly my brother fucked things up."

Brother? Jesus Christ, how many Novikov men are there?

I look the man over, taking in his tree trunk legs and barrel chest. Then I make it to his face, which is split in a wide grin. He wags a brow at me.

"Anatoly," I say, the name and flirting tactics clicking into place. I watched him woo and win many a woman over the six months I was engaged to Trofim. It was like his mission at every event was to leave with a different sexual conquest. In the case of the christening, two sexual conquests.

"You remember me? I'm flattered." He toes at the curtain rod and sheet bundle still laying on the floor where Mikhail left it. "Is this some weird sex thing?"

"Ew! No! It's—" I run my hands over my face. "Go away, please. It's the middle of the night and I'm exhausted. Too exhausted to hash out my current situation with one of the many people responsible for keeping me and my son trapped here."

"I'm also one of the people responsible for keeping you alive."

These Novikov men and their over-inflated egos. I want to take a needle and pop each of their swelled heads like a balloon.

"I've kept myself alive for twenty-five years without the Novikov family's involvement just fine, thank you very much," I spit. "Actually, I've kept myself alive *despite* your family's involvement."

"Up to now," he agrees with a shrug. "But you know that would have changed the second someone found out who Dante is. Who his father is. He would have been a target."

I stare down at the comforter, picking at the delicate embroidered flowers along the edge. "That's why I wasn't going to let anyone find out."

Easier said than done, I know. But at least out there we were free.

"It would have come out sooner or later. He won't be a five-year-old kid forever. He would have grown up. Had questions. Even someone as stubborn as you couldn't have kept Dante from looking for answers."

"You don't know me or what I'm capable of."

He hums a surprisingly high-pitched, unconvinced sound. "Both of my brothers have been engaged to you at one point. I know enough."

"Mikhail and I are not engaged," I growl. "I don't care what he told you, but—"

"You think Mikhail tells me things?" He snorts. "I'm sure you've noticed, but Mikhail isn't exactly a chatterbox. The only thing I've noticed is that every time he walks out of a room you're in, he's in a mood."

I roll my eyes. "I don't know why he wants to marry me if he hates me so much."

"He doesn't hate you," Anatoly says almost too softly to hear. Before I can ask what he means, he pushes on. "Besides, marriage is about a lot more than love."

"Of course you think so. Because this world is a toxic stew of violence and status and bloodrights. It's medieval. I'm the daughter of a don and I couldn't even make my own choices about who I got to marry."

"You mean with Trofim?"

"Yeah. But even before that."

Anatoly leans in closer. "Who did you want to marry before?"

I don't owe him an explanation. I don't owe anyone my life story. But having someone in Mikhail's inner circle who has some sympathy towards me can't be a bad thing, right?

"His name was Matteo." I swallow down the emotion that bubbles up every time I think of my first love. "He was the son of one of my father's maids. He picked her up from work a few days every week. While he was waiting for her, we would talk."

Matteo had big brown eyes and an even bigger heart. He talked about the world like it was full of possibility. Anything he wanted, he could have if he worked towards it: a college education, enough money that he could take care of his mom… and me.

"Matteo and I weren't stupid. We knew that my father wouldn't like us being together. Even his mom tried to warn him against it. She was afraid she would lose her job, but…" I shake my head, blinking away a fresh wave of tears. "I don't think either of us really understood the risks we were taking."

Anatoly moves to sit on the end of the bed. He curls one massive leg up on the mattress to face me. "What did your father do?"

"He told me to stop seeing him, but I refused. When he forced me into agreeing, I kept seeing Matteo secretly. We were going to elope." I chuckle humorlessly, remembering the night I crawled out of my window with a white dress tucked under my arm and ran to Matteo's car to meet him.

Except he wasn't in the driver's seat.

My father was.

The next minutes and hours are a black spot in my mind. The memories are locked away and I've never tried to access them. I don't want to relive what I know happened.

"Your father killed him," Anatoly guesses.

I swipe my sleeve across my cheek. "In front of me. Yeah. 'My duty was to the family,' he said. What I wanted didn't matter. *Who* I wanted didn't matter. I wasn't my own person; I belonged to the Giordano name. And I... I don't want that for Dante."

A new wave of tears burns at the backs of my eyes. Hopelessness crushes my chest worse than any claustrophobia attack I've ever experienced. Because now, I can't just open a door and leave.

I'm trapped here.

"Yeah," he sighs. "This life is no walk in the park, that's for fucking sure."

The words pull me out of my self-pity spiral. I glare at him. "Yes, what a hard life you lead," I sneer. "I saw you at enough fundraisers and parties to know all about your many burdens. Being the son of a *pakhan* has been horrible for you. Is all that meaningless sex with people who only care about your last name becoming tedious? It must be so hard."

Anatoly's face hardens for the first time. I'm aware of exactly how big he is and exactly how alone we are. If he wanted to crack me in half like a glowstick, he could.

"Keeping the Novikov family name and a place in the Bratva is the prize Iakov awarded to me after he let your ex-fiancé slaughter my mother in her bed," he snarls.

I gasp. "Mikhail?"

"I thought he wasn't your fiancé?" Anatoly taunts with a raised brow. He shakes his head, blowing out a long breath. "No, Trofim."

"Trofim killed his own mother?" I whisper.

"He killed *my* mother. Iakov's mistress. One of them, anyway," he mutters. "She got pregnant while Iakov was only courting Trofim's mother. Trofim wasn't even a fetus yet. But Iakov didn't offer to marry my mom. He was interested enough in a waitress to get her pregnant, but not interested enough to marry her and protect her from this fucked-up world."

"Why?" I breathe, too horrified to speak above a whisper. "Why did Trofim kill her?"

"To make sure Iakov wouldn't change his mind and marry my mother. It had been decades. Iakov was never going to change his mind, but Trofim was too power-hungry to see it. He wanted to make sure I'd never have a direct line to the leadership he was born into."

Anatoly isn't a legitimate Novikov. Not in the ways that count.

Like Dante.

"This world is dark and brutal and fucked up at times." Anatoly turns to me, sympathy etched into every line of his face. "But not all of us are that way. Some of us try to do the right thing."

"Like you?" I ask.

"Like Mikhail," he corrects. "You might be pissed at him right now, but Mikhail could have abandoned you and Dante to your fates. He could have taken Dante and left you with nothing. But he's offering you the key to the kingdom."

Too bad it feels like the key to my own prison cell.

I'm exhausted and off-balance. I entertained this conversation to try to endear Anatoly to me, but now, I'm sitting here feeling sympathetic for him *and* Mikhail.

It's too much for one day. It's too much for one lifetime.

I shake my head. "Please leave."

This time, Anatoly listens. He stands and walks to the door. But he stops, his hand on the knob, and looks back at me.

"You thought you knew me when I walked through this door, but you didn't," he says softly. "Give my brother the same benefit of the doubt. You think you know him, but you don't."

"I know enough," I fire back, doubting the words before they're even out of my mouth.

I know Mikhail is offering me something a lot of men wouldn't. Again and again, he has taken care of me when he didn't have to.

But he said it himself: the Bratva is an extension of him. No matter what kind of man Mikhail is, I can't separate him from the world I hate.

Anatoly sighs. "He saved you once before when he didn't have to—when you didn't ask him to. Think about the life you'd be living right now if Mikhail hadn't done that."

With thoughts of a Dante-less, Trofim-filled life bouncing around my head, Anatoly finally leaves me alone.

17

MIKHAIL

I keep my distance the next day.

It's not hard. Viviana and Dante spend most of the day in the pool. I hear the splashing and Dante's excited shouting through the walls, but I stay in my office.

I told Viviana I'd give her time to consider my offer, and I meant it. I laid out her options and now, it's up to her to decide.

But also, the last thing I need right now is to see her dripping wet in a bathing suit.

The image of her bent over the edge of the bed, my hand curling perfectly around her ass, is enough of a distraction. Not to mention the low moan my spanking dragged out of her.

I readjust my aching dick and try to focus on the contracts in front of me. My lawyers have summarized everything I need to know about the Cerberus Industries takeover, but the words refuse to lodge in my brain. There's already too much other shit lodged in there.

Like, *I proposed to Viviana.* And *I have a son.* Also, *Trofim was murdered.*

But mostly, *I proposed to Viviana.*

It makes sense. Logical. Undeniable. We already have a child and, no matter how much she might hate her father, Viviana is well-connected, by virtue of the blood in her veins if nothing else. There's a reason my father agreed to her marriage to Trofim in the first place. It's a good match.

So why do those words make me want to punch through walls?

Good match. Like Viviana is some pocket square I'm trying to accessorize with my tie.

It doesn't matter. The proposal wasn't about her anyway. It had absolutely nothing to do with how I was on my way to see Viviana for no reason at all last night when I found her trying to sneak away. It definitely has nothing to do with the way I wanted to rip through her panties to feel how wet she was for me.

No, this is about the Bratva and my son.

That's what I'm still telling myself hours later as someone knocks softly on my office door. A second later, it opens and Viviana lets herself in.

"Can we talk?"

Her hair is damp, twisted into a loose braid over one shoulder. She's changed out of the swimsuit she must have been wearing, but the long-sleeved shirt she tugged on clings to her damp skin. I can make out the pucker of her nipple through the pale pink material.

Talking is the last thing I want to do.

But I nod and wave her in.

Viviana closes my office door and then stops a few feet away from my desk, her hands folded behind her back. She trains her hazel eyes on me and declares, "I'm not going to have sex with you."

I'm tempted to glance down and see if there's any possible way she can see the hard-on I've been wrestling almost nonstop since last night. But I resist.

"I don't remember offering," I drawl.

Her cheeks flush, but she lifts her chin. "We aren't going to have sex, but you also can't have any mistresses. I don't want Dante to see his father treating his mother like she's worthless the way Anatoly did."

How does she know anything about Anatoly's mother? That question slips through the cracks of the much larger thought in my mind.

"You're accepting my offer."

"I'm making my desires known before I accept," she corrects, voice oddly formal.

"And do you have any other desires, Viviana?"

I don't miss the way her neck flushes to match her cheeks. Her teeth tug on her full lower lip. "I don't—I don't think so. I think that's it."

"Okay. Then I agree."

She frowns. "You do?"

She probably expected me to fight. To argue for my right to stick my dick in any woman I want. Little does Viviana know, that list is incredibly small. One name. The only woman who might tempt me to break my vow of celibacy is standing in front of me right now.

"I've already told you: I'm going to protect Dante. Marrying you and keeping you safe is a good thing for him. So, yes, I agree."

Her mouth falls open. It might be the first time I've ever seen her too stunned for words.

"Anything else?" I ask.

She shakes her head slowly. "No, I mean… I guess that was… You really don't mind not having sex? I thought that was going to be a sticking point for you."

"I can control myself if you can."

She ignores my insinuation and charges ahead. "And this is all for Dante? You're willing to do all of this for him?"

I nod.

"Why?"

I know what happens when I don't sacrifice everything for the safety of my family. I've lost one child; I won't lose another.

"Because he's my son," I say flatly. "And you're his mother. What other reasons do I need?"

Viviana studies me for a long time. I have the sense I'm being assessed for any signs of deception. Like she's strapped me to an invisible lie detector test and is reading my responses.

Our eyes catch and hold.

There's a physical weight to the tension between us. I have to fight against the force of it. If I don't, I'll end up across the room and between Viviana's legs.

Where I belong.

"Also, I'm going to continue working at Cerberus," she says in a rush.

"You want to be my assistant *and* my wife?"

She flips the end of her golden braid over her shoulder. "I earned that position on my own and I'm good at it. I don't want to give up everything in my life just to play house with you."

"You can be on the board of directors. No wife of mine is going to work as a—"

"Then get another wife," she snaps.

I'm up and around the desk before I know it. Viviana's gaze doesn't waver, even as her throat bobs nervously and I crowd into her, pressing her back against the closed door. "You know, I could if I wanted," I breathe in her face. "It would be easy to replace you."

Technically speaking, I already have a fiancée on deck.

"If you wanted to," she admits with a nod. Her tongue sweeps across her lower lip slowly. I'm not even sure she knows what she's doing. If she does, she's too good at it. "But you don't want to replace me."

No. No, I don't.

But why the fuck not?

"Why should I care who takes my last name? It's not like I'll get any of the benefits out of you." I scrape my eyes down her curves to highlight exactly which benefits I'm talking about.

"Is that all marriage is to you? Sex?"

"Not this marriage. No, this marriage is business. And I can make this same arrangement with any woman I choose."

"How charming."

"It's just a fact," I tell her. "I could have any woman I wanted, but I'm vowing to give your son a father and an inheritance while also taking care of you. You won't get another offer like this."

She works her jaw back and forth as she thinks. Finally, she narrows her eyes. "I don't want to be on the board of directors. You're going to scare them all to death so they just agree with you anyway. I want to keep my job."

So fucking stubborn.

I could refuse and promote her anyway. It's not as if she'd really be able to refuse. But the idea of her sitting directly outside my office every day isn't completely unappealing.

Because I'll be able to keep an eye on her, of course. It's logical. Undeniable.

"You have a deal."

I hold out my hand and Viviana takes it.

Her fingers are warm and soft. Before I can stop myself, I tighten my hold and pull her close.

She slams against my chest with a yelp and I bend her back, my lips against the shell of her ear.

"Just don't fall in love with me, Viviana."

"No danger of that." She shoves against my chest and scrambles away. Her face is flushed and her hands are shaking. "So, what now?"

I smirk. "We get married."

18

MIKHAIL

"Now?" Viviana looks from me to the priest and back again. "You want to get married *right now?*"

"I don't see the need to wait."

Anatoly and Raoul are standing in the back corner of the sitting room. The two of them wrangled a priest and got City Hall to fast-track a marriage certificate in the last twelve hours. Their job is done here, but Anatoly will never forgive me if I don't let him stand in the room as my best man.

Raoul would deny it to his dying day, but he feels the same way.

"I'm wearing a pair of ripped jeans and smell like chlorine," Viviana points out. "That could be a reason to wait."

"Unless you've changed your mind about the consummation, I don't see why your appearance should make any difference at all to me."

It doesn't make any difference to me either way. Bending her over the sofa and taking her from behind would be easier in what she's wearing now. Some fancy dress with layers of tulle and lace would just get in my way.

"You—" She glances at the priest and then lowers her voice. "You asshole. Can we at least pretend that this is official instead of some under-the-table, backdoor deal?"

Anatoly snorts at the buffet of potential dirty jokes sitting in front of him and Viviana tosses him a glare. When she turns back to me, she's composed, but barely. "When I was engaged to Trofim, there was an engagement party. I had six months to prepare for a wedding."

"Was six months enough? Were you ready to marry him?"

"That's not the point," she huffs. "This is happening too fast. I haven't had enough time to—"

"You've had six fucking years, Viviana," I growl, cutting her off. "Tonight, we're doing things at my pace."

Her hazel eyes flare, but she doesn't panic. She doesn't beg.

Instead, I see the mafia princess in her as Viviana presses her shoulders back, lifts her chin, and turns to the priest. "Forget whatever speech you have prepared and skip to the vows. I want to get this over with."

My father really had no idea exactly how good of a match Viviana was.

Not for Trofim. He would have beat this defiance out of Viviana until there was nothing left of her. He never would have let this stand. But it's only because my brother would have looked weak standing next to a woman like Viviana. A terrible *pakhan* would only look worse next to a proper queen.

And that's exactly what Viviana is.

The feeling settles over me as the priest skips straight to the vows, just as Viviana ordered.

And when I stand in front of the woman who has weaseled her way into my thoughts for the last six fucking years and call her "my wife," some primal urge I've never felt before rises up in me.

When I vow to protect her and cherish her, I'm not lying.

Viviana is *mine*.

"This is my solemn vow," I recite at the end, holding her delicate fingers against my calloused palm.

Viviana rolls her eyes and repeats her own vows through gritted teeth.

A large part of me wishes sex was on the table. The only thing that would make her defiance better is knowing the way she'd melt beneath me later. It's been six years and I can still feel the way she pulsed around me. Hear the way she moaned my name.

"I now pronounce you man and wife," the priest says, clapping his book closed like he has an Uber to catch. "You may now kiss the bride."

I want to do a whole lot more to the bride than kiss.

Which is a problem.

This marriage is a business arrangement. Just like it was going to be with Helen. I stood over my first wife's grave and swore I'd never have another family.

So I won't. Not like that. When Viviana isn't around, I won't think about her. I'm not going to fuck her or fantasize about her. She's here only so I can keep my son close. So I can have an heir without being a monster about it the way my father was, the way Trofim would have been.

She doesn't mean anything to me.

Viviana licks her lips and I force my eyes away.

"A kiss isn't legally binding, is it?" I ask.

The man frowns. "No. Not strictly. It's a matter of tradition, but most people—"

"We are not most people." I offer Viviana my arm and she takes it. "We're done here."

As we walk out together, I hear Anatoly dramatically fake-sniffling behind us. "What a beautiful wedding."

∼

As soon as we make it into the hallway, Viviana rips her arm away from me. "Don't touch me."

"I take it you don't want a first dance as husband and wife?"

"No first dance," she confirms with a scowl. "But if there's cake, I'd love to shove some in your smug face."

"No cake. Sorry to disappoint."

"Yeah, right." She turns and walks away, her golden braid flipping over her shoulder. "Disappointing me is probably how you get it up. I bet you're hard as a rock knowing how much I hate being married to you."

I shouldn't let her talk to me like this. I *should* hate the way she pushes and fights and resists.

I should turn around and go back to my office and let my new wife live out the rest of our marriage in her own wing of the house. Preferably with a brick wall between the two of us.

Instead, I shift into place behind her, whispering into her ear. "Me being hard as a rock has nothing to do with how you feel about our marriage. You just look that good walking away from me."

I watch a blush spread to the tips of her ears even as she refuses to slow down or turn around to face me. "Are you going to follow me all the way back to my room?"

"Just giving you a chance to reconsider your decision about not having sex. Personally, I have a lot of frustration I could burn off."

"You should try bottling it up way deep down inside," she says flippantly. "I hear that's great for your health."

She's only steps away from the door to her room when I grab her around the waist and flatten her against the wall. "For your sake, you better hope I live a long, healthy life. Otherwise, Dante is going to inherit the Bratva sooner than anyone expected. Do you think he's ready to fend off attacks on his life between recess and lunch?"

She tries to push me away, but I pin her wrists to the wall. "That's not funny."

"It wasn't meant to be," I growl. "Hate me all you want; I don't fucking care. But if you really think I'm not doing you and your son a favor, you're not as smart as I thought you were."

Her hazel eyes burn through me. By the looks of it, she has a good deal of frustration she could stand to work off, too.

Her pupils expand when I press my hard frustration against her stomach, but she schools her face into a frown. "Careful, Mikhail. I think you almost gave me a compliment."

"Not a compliment—a warning. If you play this wrong, Viviana, you aren't the only one who will suffer. You have Dante to think about."

She strains away from the wall, her body arched against me even while her wrists stay firmly against the wainscoting. "I know I have Dante to think about! He's all I've thought about for the last six years. *You're* the one who isn't thinking about him! Ripping him out of school and turning his life upside down doesn't scream 'stability.'"

She smells like vanilla and chlorine. Strands of blonde hair curl against her heaving chest.

I lean my weight into her, forcing her flat against the wall again. My erection is pinned between us, throbbing against the heat of her skin.

"What exactly is 'stable' about living in an apartment you can't afford under a fake name?"

"*Love*," she fires back. "I love him, which is more stability than I ever got growing up. Having someone who cares about you is better than any big, lonely mansion."

I hate Agostino Giordano for what he did to his daughter, but I can't help but admire the way Viviana rose from those ashes. I thought she was fiery before, but the way she is ready to go to the mat for our child? I've never seen anything like it.

"Lucky for you, Dante will have both here. A big mansion *and* two parents who want what's best for him."

Viviana tries to pull back, but there's nowhere to go. Instead, she fidgets, effectively grinding her body against me. If she realizes what she's doing, it doesn't show. She's too busy trying to kill me with her eyes to know she's actually killing me with her hips. "You don't know what's best for him. He needs to be back in school. He needs to see his friends—his peers."

"The only reason he was in that school to begin with is because you stole him away from the world he was born into. Those civilians will never be his 'peers.'"

"Spoken like a typical, haughty Novikov," she mutters.

I ignore her for her own sake. "Until things settle down, I'm hiring a tutor for him. He'll be more comfortable here."

He'll be safer here, at least. Until I know who the fuck killed Trofim, I'm not going to put Dante at risk by sending him out into the world.

"You can't take him out of school. He has friends. Socialization is important at his age."

So is his life, but Viviana either doesn't understand the risks she took keeping Dante away from me for so long or she's in deep denial.

"There are plenty of people to talk to here."

"Maids don't count."

"Who's haughty now?" My fingers tighten around her wrists. I can feel her pulse thundering against my hand. "Between the two of us, the maids, his tutor, and Raoul and Anatoly—"

"Just what he needs: more chauvinistic assholes as role models."

"He'll have plenty of people to talk to," I growl, ignoring her in an effort to keep hold of my control that is slipping away a little more every time she opens her mouth. "And when he's ready, we'll send him to a private academy."

"When *you* are ready, you mean," she challenges, dragging her body against mine again. My cock twitches as she stretches to her toes, her lips less than an inch from mine. "Because this has nothing to do with me or Dante. This is all about you, Mikhail. It's all about what *you* want."

"If this was about what I wanted, we wouldn't be standing here having this conversation!" I shove away from the wall before I do something stupid.

For all Viviana's talk, I see hurt flicker across her face.

She thinks I don't want her—as my wife, here in my house. Maybe she even thinks I regret Dante. That I wish I'd never touched her that night in the bridal suite.

But if I had what I wanted, we'd be in Viviana's room right now. Her clothes would be in shreds on the floor and that pouty mouth of hers would be wrapped around my cock.

Instead, Viviana's lips flatten together. "Fine. Go to bed on your wedding night alone, Mikhail. Since that's what you want."

She storms into her room and slams the door in my face. A second later, she slides the lock home.

Good.

It's for the best that we keep a locked door between us. Out of sight, out of mind.

I don't have to think about the soft curve of her hips or the warmth of her thighs. If I can't see her, there's no reason to imagine her neck arching as I fill her. The way I know she can moan my name…

For both our sakes, I hope the lock is strong enough to keep me out.

19

VIVIANA

"I want to go swimming," Dante pouts, lagging behind as I try to pull him down the hallway.

Stella greeted us this morning with the news that we have plans, but she is under strict orders not to "spoil the fun," apparently.

Exactly how much "fun" we're going to have remains to be seen.

So far, convincing Dante to get dressed in anything other than his swimsuit is proving to be approximately negative fun for me.

"I know, but we can't go swimming every day."

"Yes, we can!" he chirps back. "The pool is inside. It's climack patrolled."

Dante's little chin is raised. He's clearly proud of his argument, but I have no idea what he's talking about. "What?"

"*Climate controlled*," Stella chuckles. "I taught him that last night while you were… busy."

Busy getting married, she means.

Busy getting married and then having the first of many fights with my husband less than five minutes after we walked down the aisle.

Such a promising start.

What is *actually* promising is the fact that Mikhail is nowhere in sight this morning.

Maybe, just maybe, he's going to keep his distance. Dante and I will live in this house, but we won't have to deal with him much. He may be a raging control freak, but he can't keep tabs on everyone all the time, right?

Then we turn the corner and find Anatoly grinning in the entrance hall. "You all ready to go?"

"Where are we going?" I ask while Dante repeats "climate controlled" under his breath, trying to make sure he's got it down.

Anatoly winks. "You'll find out."

He leads our party onto the porch where a large SUV is idling in the driveway. A middle-aged man with a buzzed head is standing next to the open backseat.

"Viviana, meet Pyotr," Anatoly says, gesturing at the driver. "Pyotr, Viviana."

Pyotr looks like a boulder disguised as a driver, his broad chest nearly popping the buttons of his black suit. He reaches to shake my hand just as Dante wiggles between us.

"And Dante!" he adds, squinting up at Pyotr against the bright morning sun.

Pyotr squats down to one knee, grinning. "*Especially* Dante. We could never forget you. It's lovely to meet you."

Being nice to Dante has always been the fastest way to my good side, but these people are going to have to work a lot harder than this. Working for Mikhail puts them at a disadvantage.

"Where are we going?" I ask again.

Stella opens her mouth to answer, but Anatoly interrupts. "We'll tell you on the way."

The secrecy has me imagining underground bunkers. Maybe some compound outside of the city where Mikhail keeps his harem of women. He said he didn't have one, but do I really want to take his word for it? No. No, I don't.

Anatoly slips a rainbow-colored lollipop to Dante as he helps him into the backseat and Stella gets Dante strapped into his booster.

If they're taking us to our doom, they're being awfully cheery about it.

I climb up to slide in next to Dante, but he waves me off with his lollipop like it's a baton. "I want to sit next to *him*."

I follow the point of his lollipop and find Anatoly beaming through the open door. "Absolutely, little man." He squeezes his muscular body through the second row seats and into the third row. His knees are in his chest when he sits down, but he's never looked happier. "It's cozy back here."

"It's just because you gave him candy," I grumble under my breath to no one in particular.

The entire car shifts as Anatoly leans forward to whisper, "That was the point."

I roll my eyes, but can't quite keep from smiling.

Anatoly wants to make a good impression on Dante. That can't be a bad thing. Plus, our little confessional the other night did, unfortunately, leave me with a pang of sympathy for Anatoly and everything he's been through. He understands better than anyone else what Dante might face in this world. I like the idea of him taking Dante under his very massive wings.

"Okay. Someone tell me where we're going," I demand once I'm strapped in and Pyotr is pulling down the drive.

Stella grins. "Shopping spree!"

"Shopping spree?" I ask. "Is that code for something?"

"It's code for a shopping spree. Mikhail wants you and Dante to look the part now that you're—"

"Living here," I interrupt, eyes wide.

Dante doesn't know about the wedding yet and this isn't how I want him to find out.

"Right," Stella says slowly, nodding in understanding. "Now that you're *living here*, Mikhail wants you to have everything you need. You didn't bring much with you when you moved, so now, you get to go shopping."

Admittedly, the mall is better than a nuclear fallout shelter or churning my own butter with all the other sister-wives Mikhail has abducted and impregnated… but not by much.

"No."

"What do you mean?"

"I mean that we aren't going." I slap the roof twice. "Pyotr, take this ginormous armored SUV back to the mansion. I'm not going."

"This is why we didn't tell you." Anatoly leans forward, one elbow on my seat and his other arm splayed across the back of Stella's. His hand rests casually on the maid's shoulder. "You're going to go buy a few things on Mikhail's dime and not make a big deal about it, Viv. It'll be fun."

"I don't want anything from him," I hiss quietly enough that Dante can't hear.

"Too late for that. Mikhail has given you plenty already." Anatoly hitches a thumb in my son's direction and wags his brows suggestively.

I slap his chest and he falls into the back seat laughing, giving Stella's shoulder a tender pat as he pulls away.

Stella's smile is shaky when she turns to me. "You really are going to need more clothes. There are a lot of responsibilities now that you're... *living with Mikhail*. You'll need dresses, at the very least."

"It's not like he's going to take me anywhere. This is all some power play on his part. He doesn't actually care what I look like."

"Of course he does," Stella says, looking genuinely offended I'd suggest otherwise. "You are his—" She glances back at Dante and huffs in frustration. "You are *living* with him now. That means something to Mikhail."

Bless Stella's heart for having so much faith in her employer. It would be sweet if it wasn't so annoying.

"It's really not that serious, Stella."

"It is," she insists. "To Mikhail, family is the most important thing in the world. He wouldn't ask you to step into this role if he didn't mean it."

She's wrong. Mikhail asked me to marry him because he wants access to Dante. It has nothing to do with me. I'm still not convinced the mission today isn't for his henchmen to lose me at the mall and kidnap Dante.

But I don't have the energy to un-brainwash everyone in this car. So I sit back and try to enjoy the ride.

∼

"My legs are tired." Dante sags forward, his knuckles dragging on the pavement like the little chimp he is.

I can't blame him. We've been shopping for three hours. Two and a half of which have been spent in the children's dressing rooms of designer clothing stores all up and down Fifth Avenue. Dante has never tried on so many clothes in his life.

I've never been able to *buy him* so many clothes in his life.

"I know, but we're almost done. What if we go across the street and look for a new coat before we call it quits?" I ask, trying to make it sound exciting.

"He already has eight bags of stuff," Anatoly points out.

Tired of being the pack mule, he asked a woman at the dress shop Stella all but forced me into to have all of our bags shipped to the mansion. I don't even want to know how much of Mikhail's money he paid for that luxury courier service.

"And I'm hungry," Dante groans. "This is boring. My legs are—"

Before he can finish, Pyotr sweeps in from behind and scoops Dante up. He does it easily, settling Dante on his shoulders like it's a circus sideshow they've trained for.

"You don't have to do that, Pyotr. He can walk."

"My job is transportation," Pyotr says with a grin. "Wherever you two need to go, I'll get you there."

Dante doesn't have any reservations. He giggles and grabs the lapels of Pyotr's suit and pretends to steer him like a horse down the pavement.

"I want a hot dog!" Dante declares, pointing at a cart on the corner. Without hesitating, Pyotr gallops on.

"He doesn't need a—" I save my breath and let them go. Two days of living with Mikhail and my son is already spoiled absolutely rotten.

I can't even be mad. All I've ever wanted is to get Dante everything he wants. Now, I can… so long as I can swallow my pride long enough to do it.

Stella glances nervously up at the quickly darkening sky. "I think it's going to rain."

"Sounds like we're done here, then. Let's pack it in and go home—er, back to the mansion."

Stella winks and I think maybe she caught my slip. "We can't leave yet. You only bought five dresses."

"And a new pair of jeans," I add.

She frowns. "My job wasn't to buy you more jeans. You're supposed to have a whole wardrobe. We still need to get—"

"I don't need anything else."

"But Mr. Novikov wanted me to get you everything you would need. He'll be upset with me if I don't—"

"Order it," I interrupt. "Whatever is left on the list, order it. I trust you. You have a good sense of style."

"While I agree that Stella always looks marvelous," Anatoly says, seemingly unaware of the way his attention sends Stella into a near-conniption, "there are some things you need to pick out for yourself, Viv."

"Don't call me that," I mumble as Anatoly grabs my shoulders and turns me towards a limestone building on the closest corner.

Warm light shines out of the windows into the overcast day. *"Cartier"* is written in gold script on a red awning above the front doors.

"Jewelry?"

Anatoly grabs my left hand. When I stare up at him blankly, he grabs my bare ring finger and shakes it in front of my face.

"He wants me to pick out my own wedding ring?" I gasp. "Should I get down on one knee and pop the question to myself, too?"

"A little late for that, since you're already hitched," Anatoly points out.

I cross my arms over my chest. "If he wants me to wear a ring, he can pick it out himself."

"You might not like what he chooses."

"What do I care?" I snap.

"You'll care when he decides to forego a wedding ring and get your finger—or other delicate parts of your body—tattooed with his name."

Anatoly looks a little too pleased with that suggestion. I'm not convinced he wouldn't offer up the idea to Mikhail himself. It would probably earn him a pat on the head and a treat from his master.

Stella swoops in, tossing a disapproving glare at Anatoly. "He won't tattoo you! But it would make Mr. Novikov happy if you did this for him. He wants you to pick it out yourself to make sure you'll like it, that's all."

"He doesn't care if I like it."

"Of course he does," she insists. "You're going to have to wear it every day for the rest of your life. He wants you to like it."

The rest of my life. I look down at my left hand and try to imagine a ring there. A ring that symbolizes this sham of a marriage we've entered into. That I've been *forced* into, more or less.

If I have to wear a diamond shackle, it only seems fair that Mikhail should wear a ring, too.

"Fine, I'll do it," I relent. "But only if I can select a ring for him as well."

"What are you doing?" Anatoly asks, eyes narrowed and no small amount of suspicion in his voice.

I shrug innocently. "I want Mikhail to have a daily reminder of our eternal love."

Stella claps her hands, thrilled. "That's so sweet."

Pyotr and Dante gallop back to us, a hot dog clutched in Dante's little fist.

Anatoly just shakes his head. "This should be interesting."

20

MIKHAIL

It's late when the front door opens. Soft voices float down the hall to the kitchen.

"He's exhausted," Viviana whispers. "I think the pizza for dinner did him in."

Anatoly texted me a picture of Dante a few minutes ago. He was asleep in the backseat, his head lolled to one side. The red marinara smudge on the corner of his mouth makes a lot more sense now.

"I don't mind putting him to bed," Stella offers. "I saw him eat your slice, too. I'm sure you're hungry."

"A little," Viviana admits. I can hear the hesitation in her voice. "Are you sure you don't mind?"

I don't hear anything else, but they must have come to some silent arrangement because a few seconds later, Viviana pads into the dark kitchen.

She doesn't see me leaning against the counter in front of the sink. She drops a handful of bags on the floor and turns to the fridge.

For a second, I get to take in Viviana's halo of blonde hair backlit by the hallway light. Her cinched waist and flared hips. I get to admire her without the layer of hostility that seems to come default. At least when she's looking at me.

I shift, crossing one ankle over the other, and Viviana jolts.

"God, I didn't realize I was living with Dracula. Ever heard of turning on a light?" she snaps.

I reach over and flip on the under-cabinet lights. "Your good mood tells me you must have had a nice day spending my money."

She rolls her eyes. "I didn't ask you for that. I was actually tricked into it. Kind of a common occurrence around here."

"Looks like someone tricked you over and over again. That's a lot of bags you carried in."

"It's not even half of them," she retorts. "Anatoly is having the rest of them delivered."

Willing or not, the thought of Viviana spending my money—wearing nice things because I bought them for her—satisfies some dark place inside of me. I want her to be marked as mine from head to fucking toe.

"Did you get anything good?"

Her eyebrows jump like she just remembered something. A smile spreads across her face. It's so rare that I almost catch my breath.

"I bought something for you," she says, digging into the pile of bags and coming up with two burgundy jewelry boxes. "For both of us, actually."

Viviana slides both boxes across the counter to me.

I already know what it is. I told Anatoly to make sure she came home with a ring. Right now, her finger is still bare.

"You were supposed to wear it out of the store."

"If you were serious about the rules, you would have been there to make sure I followed them." There's a sultry quality to her voice that she's turning on just for me. I know her well enough to be suspicious.

What has she done now?

I open the first box and stare down at the ugliest ring I've ever seen. It's as big as a flotation device and covered in a rainbow of tiny stones. Yellow, pink, green, and blue gems reflect and catch the light like some toy from a kid's fast food meal.

"Do you like it?" Her brow arches in a challenge. "I wanted you to see it before anyone else."

"No one will be able to ignore," I admit.

She grins. "My thoughts exactly. Which is why I got you one to match."

I grit my teeth and yank open the second box. Just like she said, the same obnoxiously-colored stones are arranged in concentric squares and set in a thick yellow-gold band.

"Look inside," she says, leaning across the island. Her shirt gaps open. I can see the lace of her bra against her skin. "There's another surprise."

I assume she means inside the ring and not down her shirt. I lift the ring up to the light and notice ridges on the inside of the band.

Carved out of the gold like a stamp is one word: **Viviana.**

"Even when you take it off, my name will be imprinted on your skin," she says, obviously amused with herself. "Isn't that sweet?"

I close the rings in my fist until I feel the cut of the stones in my palm. Then I shove them in my pocket.

"Do you like them?" she asks, knowing full well I don't.

"Remind me to come along next time you go shopping. Apparently, it's true what they say: you can't buy class."

Her smile vanishes. "I guess not. If you could, I'm sure you'd have some by now."

"I never would have bought these rings, so it's a start."

"Maybe you should have picked them out to begin with," she snaps. "Real class act, by the way, having your wife pick out her own wedding ring."

There wasn't time to buy her a ring. Everything happened so fast. Even if there had been time, I still wouldn't have done it.

The last time I bought a ring for a woman, I buried her in it. I have no interest in repeating history.

"I figured a roof over your head and a closet full of new clothes for you and your son was enough of a gift."

Viviana's jaw clenches. Then she whips around and kicks the pile of bags. They go flying across the kitchen floor. "I don't want any of this shit!"

"Then what do you want?"

Her eyes scrape over me, the truth tucked away inside them.

"From you? Nothing." She overturns the bags, silk and lace spilling across the tile floor. "Maybe you're used to women you can pay off with pretty clothes and diamonds, but I'm not fucking interested. None of this makes up for what you've done."

I ease around the island, aware of every inch of space I'm closing between us. "What is it I've done, Viviana?"

She's breathing heavily, her shoulders rising and falling with each breath. I watch her scan me, scan the room. She's looking for an exit as if there's any chance she can escape. As if I won't cut her off at every pass.

"You forced me to marry you."

"You had a choice," I counter.

She drags her hand through her hair, tugging at the roots. "You command me around your house like you own me. Like I'll just go and do your bidding. *Buy this; wear that; go here, not there.*"

"I do own you," I growl. "In every way that counts, you're mine."

"You've taken away everything. Everything I *worked* for." She blows out a breath, a strand of hair fluttering around her forehead. "Maybe you don't know what that's like, but I had to build a life from nothing. When I walked out of that bridal suite, I didn't have anything. No money. No connections. No —" She looks up at me, something like guilt flashing in her eyes before it's gone. "I had to sacrifice more than you know for the *pitiful, classless* life you think I was living. Now, it's gone."

"It was going to get snatched away from you either way," I growl. "One way or another, someone was going to destroy your fantasy. You should be grateful it was me instead of someone who would have left you both dead."

"As far as I can tell, *you* are the threat, Mikhail. You're the one who kidnapped me and my son. *You're* the one I've been running from for the last six years."

"You weren't running because of me."

She was running from Trofim. From her father. I never threatened her.

"Tell yourself whatever you need to justify what you're doing. I don't need to stick around for it." She spins around to leave.

I spent the last six years looking for her. Not because of Dante. Not because of an heir or because she was in danger.

But because I wanted her.

I still do.

All the while, she was running in the opposite direction.

She still is.

I catch her arm and pull her against me. We slam together, chest to chest. My hand fits perfectly around her throat. My fingers curl into her hair. She smells like sweet vanilla.

I have no fucking idea what I'm going to do to her right now, but she can't leave. Not yet. Not until I understand why she can get under my skin when no one else ever has.

Then I see the tears pouring down her face.

"Viviana."

She twists her face away and shoves against my chest, but I don't let go.

"You're crying."

"I'm surprised a robot like you recognizes human emotions." The words come out watery and weak. There's no real punch behind them.

"What's wrong?" I brush my thumb over her wet cheek and it sets off a new wave of tears.

"This is a new low," she chokes out. "*You're* what's wrong. You know that, right? You're the reason I'm crying. I'm trapped here and I have no idea what's going to happen. But for some reason—"

I can't remember the last time I held someone while they cried. Usually, if someone is crying, it's because I'm standing on their broken femur or my thumb is in their eye socket.

"What?" I press.

Viviana looks up at me, her hazel eyes green through the tears. Then she rests her weight against me, her cheek against my chest. "This feels nice."

My hand finds the curve at the small of her back. I stroke my thumb down her spine. We stand like that for a long time. Until her breathing evens out and the tears stop falling.

"Are you done freaking out?" I ask softly.

She rolls her eyes. "Almost definitely not. Being married to you, expect it to happen a lot."

I laugh and Viviana looks up at me. Her lips are full and pink.

They part as she exhales. We're so close. All it would take is the tilt of my head.

"I should go to bed," she breathes. But I can tell by the way she says it that she doesn't want to.

She *should* go to bed. Instead, she might stay here with me… depending on what I do next.

Viviana's hand is still on my chest. I reach for it, curling my fingers around hers. "One more thing before you go."

Her lashes flutter against her cheekbones, expectant. "Yeah?"

I slide the gaudy ring onto her finger. "I never want to see you without this on."

I watch the moment shatter in her eyes.

Viviana pulls away from me and grabs the bags from the kitchen floor. She's halfway into the hall before she calls back, "Don't forget to wear your ring, too, *hubby*. Otherwise, I'll superglue it on while you're sleeping."

I'd love to see her try.

21

VIVIANA

This feels nice.

"This feels nice?!" I mutter, jabbing two fingers into my forehead like maybe I can reach into my brain and scoop out whatever microchip Mikhail must have planted there while I slept. There's no other explanation, right? I mean, I *hugged* him. He made me cry... *and then I hugged him!* If that's not a sign of some high-level brainwashing, I don't know what is.

As if my life wasn't already on some janky, nightmarish carnival—the kind that doesn't just leave you hurling up your funnel cake, but also severs your legs off at the knees—things just went even more sideways.

The worst part is, I can still feel the gnaw of disappointment in my stomach. The ache that was ready to be filled by Mikhail's lips and hands and whatever other body parts he wanted to offer up.

I know what almost happened between us in that kitchen was a mistake—but I also can't stop thinking about it.

Sure, I've had mind-melting sex with Mikhail and carried his baby, but we never exactly cuddled. I kind of assumed he would feel cold and sterile like a gynecologist's exam table. But when I leaned against his chest, I wanted to curl up there. I *did* curl up there! A crime for which I'll never forgive myself. Because now, I know what it feels like to snuggle with Mikhail and I'll never be the same.

Especially because he all but rejected me.

I never want to see you without this on.

I twirl the hideous ring I chose for myself around my ring finger where Mikhail placed it. I should have thought about the consequences of my little prank long-term. It was fun to see Mikhail's reaction to the rings for a split second, but now, I have to actually wear the damn thing.

I have to wear this ring and live in this house and be married to Mikhail.

After everything I did to get free…

I sold my soul to the devil to escape this world, but here I am. It was all for nothing.

When I look down at my hand again, all I see is imaginary blood. Crusted to my knuckles, dripping between my fingers. I close my fist and swear I feel the cold handle of a knife against my palm.

My heart races, thundering against my rib cage until I'm shaking.

I close my eyes and take a deep breath.

I'm in Mikhail's mansion. I'm alone. I'm okay.

I never thought being in Mikhail's house would be a comfort, but I repeat the mantra to myself until the clamp around my chest loosens slightly.

When I open my eyes and look down, my hand is clean. The blood is gone. Before I can dwell on my Lady Macbeth moment too long, I hear whimpering coming from the hallway.

Dante.

I wrench open my bedroom door and am halfway across the hall before I smack directly into a wall of muscle. A bare-chested wall of muscle, actually.

As if my cheek has a very specific form of muscle memory, I know it's Mikhail even before he grabs my shoulders to steady me.

We stand there for a second. Just long enough to prove that his abs are every bit as fitness-magazine perfect as I thought they would be.

Then the whimpering coming from Dante's room rises to a full-on cry.

Mikhail lets me go and slips into Dante's room before I have full use of my legs again. Once I follow him inside, his muscular back blocks my view of what's happening until he kneels down next to Dante's bed.

"What's going on, *mal'chik?*" he asks, voice surprisingly tender.

Dante is sitting up, his blue eyes wide and shimmering in the soft glow of his nightlight, his lower lip pouted out. "I had a bad dream."

We have a routine for this. I lie down in bed with him and stroke his hair until he falls asleep. It's the only thing that has ever worked to calm him down.

I'm about to shove Mikhail aside and crawl next to Dante when, instead, Mikhail reaches for Dante's hand.

"Bad dreams are the worst."

"You get bad dreams, too?" Dante asks.

Mikhail nods. Somehow, that simple movement sends muscles in his back flexing and shifting. "Everyone gets bad dreams."

"What are your bad dreams about?"

Mikhail hesitates for only a second before he answers. "About not being able to save the people I love."

Who does Mikhail love? Anatoly and Raoul probably. Maybe Dante. It's only been a few days, but he's an easy kid to love.

I twist my wedding ring around my finger and smother the naive little voice that thinks I might be somewhere on that list.

Dante sighs. "Mine was about being chased by a dinosaur."

"Was it a big one?"

"The biggest." Dante shudders. He looks tiny tucked into the full-sized bed. "His foot was as big as your house."

Mikhail winces. "That doesn't sound good. Did he squish anybody?"

Dante chews on his lower lip and looks up at me. His chin dimples. "Mama."

I kneel next to Mikhail and grab Dante's other hand. I curl his fingers against my cheek. "I'm okay, baby. I'm right here."

"The dinosaur chased you and I didn't run after you. I was too scared. I—" He devolves into another round of tears.

"You couldn't save the person you love, either," Mikhail finishes. He pats his leg. "But that was just in a dream. In real life, you're brave."

"No, I'm scared," Dante argues.

"Of course you are. You have to be scared to be brave."

Dante looks at me, eyebrows raised like, *This guy is crazy, right?* But I stay quiet. I want to hear where Mikhail is going with this.

"If you aren't scared, then fighting a dinosaur isn't brave. It's just something you're doing. Just another normal day in your life. But overcoming your fear," Mikhail says, his large thumb rubbing over Dante's knuckles, "*that* makes you brave."

Dante frowns. "I guess so."

"*'I guess so'* isn't good enough. I need you to *know it*. I'm going to test you. Are you ready?"

Dante sits tall, nodding. "I'm ready."

"If you want to be brave, you have to be…"

"Scared!" Dante answers.

Mikhail smiles. "And when you're scared, you have to be…"

"Brave!"

He holds up his hand for a high-five, but Dante pushes right past it and wraps his arms around Mikhail's neck.

I'm pretty sure my heart stops.

I ran from Mikhail for years, terrified of what would happen if he ever caught up to us. But occasionally, when I let myself imagine the best-case scenario… I imagined *this*.

Dante having a real relationship with his dad. His dad wanting a relationship with him.

Kneeling there next to this mish-mashed little family of mine, I realize that agreeing to marry Mikhail is about more than keeping Dante safe. It's about making him happy.

It's about giving him everything he needs… even when what he needs is Mikhail.

"Mama," Dante mumbles, reaching towards me with grasping little fingers.

I lean in and let him hug my neck. "Do you want me to stay?"

He bites his lip, considering it. Then he puffs out his little chest. "I'm going to be brave."

Mikhail and I are almost through his door when he sits up again. "Mikhail? What happens if I can't be brave?"

"That's why you have me." Mikhail winks. "I'll take care of you."

God, I hope he means that.

"And Mama?" Dante asks.

My stomach drops, but Mikhail just nods. "And your mama."

Damn that naive little voice inside my head, but I hope he means that, too.

Back in the hallway with Dante's door firmly closed, I suddenly can't look away from Mikhail's bare chest.

The chest I cuddled less than an hour ago.

Or his biceps.

The biceps that just hugged our son after he had a nightmare.

Or his abs.

The abs I would scale like the world's sexiest climbing wall.

Mikhail says something and I have to rip my eyes up to his face.

The face so perfect the universe pulled a copy/paste and gave it to my son, too.

"What?" I ask, blinking at him like a confused newborn.

"Does that happen a lot?" he repeats. "The nightmares?"

"A few times a month, probably. Some months are worse than others. You handled it well, though."

Mikhail arches a brow. "But…?"

"You're good with him," I admit with no small amount of reluctance. "He likes you."

"The boy has good taste."

"Don't make me regret this," I groan.

Mikhail steps closer. He smells like cool mint and cedar. It just wafts off of his skin like he's a walking bottle of pheromones. "Regret what?"

I shrug weakly. "Being nice to you. Trying to… *coparent.*"

"What happened to *'You get him for Bratva stuff; I get him for everything else'*?"

"I'm trying to put it behind us and start over if you'll stop being pompous for five seconds." I huff out a breath. "The only reason I'm here is for Dante. I want what's best for him. And as much as I hate to admit it—"

"I'm going to love this," Mikhail says, crossing his huggable biceps over his cuddlable chest.

I do my best to ignore his words and his body.

"—you're good for him. That whole speech in there was inspired. You connected with him and I don't want to get in the way of your relationship."

Mikhail is thoughtful, his jaw flexing as he thinks. "He really loves you, Viviana."

"'The boy has good taste.'"

He rolls his eyes. "He really loves you, and I don't want to get in the way of that relationship, either."

The silence between us settles into something comfortable. Even with his chiseled-from-marble pecs on display, I don't have a hard time looking in his eyes.

"Then we're in agreement," I finally say. "We try to be civil. For Dante."

"You think you can handle that?"

"I can handle anything, thank you very much."

"Good." He starts to say something else and stops. His brow furrows before he finally forces the words out. "Because we have plans tomorrow. We can practice being civil."

"Plans for all of us?" I imagine another shopping spree and barely resist groaning.

"No. Just the two of us. You and me."

My stupid heart leaps, but I quickly lasso and hogtie it down. "Do I have a choice?"

"Of course you have a choice. But we're trying to get along, aren't we?" He dips his head. His breath whispers over my skin. "It would be civil of you to cooperate… so I'm not forced to carry you, kicking and screaming, over my shoulder again."

I'm tempted to ask about the spanking. *Is that on the table, too?*

But before I can find the words, Mikhail is back in his room with the door closed.

22

MIKHAIL

"Anatoly will hate us for coming here without him."

A blonde waitress bends over to bus the table next to ours. She's busy clearing away a few hundred dollars' worth of half-finished cocktails, but her barely-there skirt would have the entirety of my brother's attention if he were here. Which, admittedly, is part of the reason he's not.

Raoul nods, fingers drumming on the glass in his hands. He looks around the lounge but doesn't say anything. I know he isn't paying any mind to the waitress. He's looking for Fabio.

We've been all over the city today. Every so often, we have to make the rounds, pop in to visit the businesses we employ and the ones we protect. It hasn't been long since our last visit, but with Trofim's unsolved murder hanging over my head, I figure it's worth making sure no one has seen or heard anything strange. I don't want to take any chances.

Not least of all because I have Dante and Viviana to think about now.

Being on assignment means Raoul is focused, but I figured he'd relax once we got to the lounge. It's been under Novikov ownership for decades. Everyone knows not to fuck with us when we're here and the waitresses know how to be discreet.

Still, Raoul is tense.

It's strange enough that I'm close to checking in to make sure he's okay. Then the blacked-out door to the lounge opens and Fabio strolls in.

"He has got to be kidding," Raoul mutters.

No. Fabio is definitely not kidding.

He's in a blindingly white suit with a popped black collar underneath. He whips his sunglasses off to wink at the redhead working the bar and then strolls to the back corner where Raoul and I are waiting for him.

The man is barely five feet tall, but I'm not sure he knows that. He struts in like he owns the place.

Odd choice, since *I* own it.

Fabio pulls out his chair and drops into it, already waving down our waitress. "Where's Anatoly?"

"Busy."

"Shame. I like him. He's a good time."

"You two have a lot in common," Raoul drawls.

Anatoly would slug Raoul for that, but Fabio takes it as a compliment. I'm not positive it *isn't* one, but Raoul likes to play his cards close to the vest.

Once Fabio has thoroughly complimented the waitress on every inch of her exposed skin and has a drink in his hand, he shifts into the commercial real estate mogul I agreed to go into business with.

"To think I was trying to get these warehouses off my hands this time last year." Fabio snorts. "Now, they're about to make me more money than any of my other properties. One of which is the new Brooklyn development I invested in. You heard of that?"

"Unless it's a warehouse I can use, I don't care."

"It's going to be big," he says, plowing on ahead. "Sixteen buildings and over six thousand apartment units. My first foray into residential. But it still won't make me as much money as this deal is going to."

"Then let's focus on where the money is and stop wasting our time chatting about bullshit."

Fabio smiles, but it's dimmed compared to the previous wattage. "We're just here to sign on the dotted line, aren't we? The details have been figured out."

"We were talking in hypotheticals before," Raoul reminds him. "Now, Mikhail owns Cerberus Industries and we can set things in stone."

Fabio circles a hand in the air like he's bored. "The guns come in, I store them, you sell them, we all get filthy rich. Tell me where to sign."

Fabio is annoying; there's no getting around that. Unfortunately, he's also in possession of a shit ton of warehouses in Brooklyn, Queens, and the Bronx and—this is key—eager to climb the already overflowing ladder that is real estate in New York City. Fabio is the perfect blend of rich and desperate. I knew he'd dip into crime without a second thought if it meant he'd make a name for himself.

I grit my teeth and lay out the plan. "To keep our names from popping up too many places together, the money I owe you will all come directly from Cerberus and go to your trust."

He pulls the toothpick out of his olive and runs it through his front two teeth. "You think that's less suspicious?"

"Less suspicious than paying you hundreds of thousands of dollars per month from his personal account?" Raoul asks dryly. "Yeah, making it a business expense is less suspicious."

"Great. Sure. Whatever. We'll set it up." Fabio rocks his chair back onto two legs. "I've worked with Cerberus in the past. They rented out some space for a few months last year. I still have the assistant's number. I'll call her and arrange the payments to be—"

"No," I snap. Raoul and Fabio both freeze. I clear my throat. "You'll make those arrangements with me. Leave my assistant out of it."

Fabio looks surprised, but he doesn't argue. I'm sure he doesn't come across many *pakhans* who want to handle their own bookkeeping.

Then again, he's probably never come across the wife of a *pakhan* who wanted to continue working as a personal assistant. Where Viviana is concerned, he never will.

The last thing I want is people like Fabio having a direct line to Viviana. Both for plausible deniability on her part and for safety. The less the public knows about her and Dante, the better.

We shake hands, promising to be in touch soon. Fabio leaves his business card for the blonde waitress, slides his obnoxiously large sunglasses into place, and then makes his way out of the lounge.

"It's her job," Raoul says the moment we're alone.

"*Now*, you have something to say? You've been quieter than usual, which is really saying something."

"It's her job," he repeats. "Viviana's. As your personal assistant, she's supposed to—"

"Assist me. Personally."

"And yet you don't want her working with Fabio?"

I shake my head. "Leave it, Raoul. Fabio is someone I'd rather keep an eye on. This has nothing to do with—"

"Your feelings for her."

"I said to fucking leave it."

"And I will." Raoul pushes his empty glass to the center of the table and crosses his arms. "Once I do my job."

"Since when is your job to poke around in my personal life?"

"Since your personal life might interfere with what we've been working towards for the last six years."

"Viviana isn't going to interfere with anything."

"I know. Because you won't even let her take a phone call with Fabio to set up accounts. Why not?" he presses. "Is it that you don't trust her? Do you think she's a spy? Because if so, I'm not sure marrying her was the right call."

"Which is why I make the decisions and you do whatever the fuck I ask you to do," I snarl.

Raoul's eyes flare for a second, but he sits back.

I've always viewed Raoul as a friend. As a partner. But it's an uncomfortable truth that he was gifted to me by his family. That they intended for him to be a slave.

Occasionally, in moments like this one, it's impossible to forget.

"I wouldn't do anything to put our plans at risk," I add, a touch more softly. "We've all worked too hard at this to throw it away now. Viviana won't be a problem."

He doesn't look convinced. "She hates you. If she could get you sent to prison, she would."

"We're... planning on being civil now. For Dante's sake."

Civil. It feels like the wrong word for what happened last night. The way she and I sat with Dante... like a family.

I crumple the word and toss it away. I don't know what we are, but it isn't that. Not in any way that matters.

"According to Anatoly, you're taking her out tonight," he muses. "Sounds like a lot more than being 'civil' to me."

"Then that means it's working."

He frowns. "What's working?"

"My plan. We found out Trofim was murdered and Viviana showed up in my life on the same day. That doesn't strike you as strange?"

"We have no reason to think they're connected."

We don't. And they probably aren't. And yet...

"Just like we poked around for information today, I figured it would be smart to get Viviana alone and do a little digging. I'll soften her up and make sure she isn't hiding anything."

"That's why you asked her out?" He dips his chin, skeptical.

That was the last thing on my mind when I told Viviana we had plans last night. I wasn't even sure where I was taking her; I just wanted to be with her.

But this makes sense. This is a good plan.

"We should look into every possibility. Trofim was Viviana's ex-fiancé. If someone was out for him, they could be out for her, too. Or Dante."

"Viviana was in Chicago at the time. We found a woman's hair clip tangled in his sheets. It was probably an escort he hired and refused to pay."

"Probably," I agree. "But I'll find out more tonight. Whatever I find out, it won't change any of my plans."

That bears repeating: Viviana *won't* change any of my plans.

I'm going to make sure of it.

23

VIVIANA

I follow the sound of Dante playing down the hallway and into the sitting room. He's standing on the leather ottoman, a pillow held over his head. Anatoly is curled up on the ground in the fetal position.

"Have mercy on me!" Anatoly screams playfully.

Dante cackles hysterically as he dives off the ottoman. Anatoly catches him in mid-air and takes a pillow directly to the face for his efforts. He turns away and grins when he sees me, his hair mussed in every direction. To be fair, so is mine.

"Morning, Sleeping Beauty. Finally ready to join the living?"

"It's only—" I check the clock above the fireplace. "Wow. Is that clock right?"

Anatoly nods just before Dante assaults him with another pillow to the face.

I can't remember the last time I slept in. Definitely before Dante was born. Probably before I was engaged to Trofim, even. Years and years ago. A lifetime ago.

That's why my brain feels so jumbled. It has nothing to do with hugging Mikhail last night. And his bare chest? What could be mind-scrambling about that? Not a darn thing.

I'm not distracted because I'm waiting to hear his voice or wondering what surprise he has planned for the two of us tonight. No, it's all of the extra sleep that has me out of sorts. That makes the most sense.

"I didn't realize it was so late." Before Dante can swing his pillow a third time, I grab the end of it. "Have you had breakfast yet, little gremlin?"

"Stella made me pancakes!"

"Stella made pancakes?" Anatoly groans. "I can't believe I missed them."

"Wait. You didn't wake him up this morning?" I ask Anatoly.

He shakes his head. "When I came downstairs, Mikhail was already with him in the kitchen."

Dante is well taken care of in this house. Mikhail would never do anything to hurt him. I know this, but it doesn't stop that rotten bitch Mom Guilt from rearing her ugly head. She has been my constant companion since Dante was born.

"You could have come into my room after you woke up this morning. I would have eaten with you."

The same way I've eaten with you every single morning for the last five years.

Two days in this house and my son doesn't need me anymore. It's not true, but it *feels* true right now.

"I got Mikhail instead. I wanted to tell him I was brave last night."

I can't stop sheer shock from spreading across my face. "You went into Mikhail's room? While he was sleeping? And woke him up?"

I do manage to stop myself from asking my small child if Mikhail was shirtless. That would be inappropriate. Not to mention useless information. I don't need to know how Mikhail sleeps. It's of no consequence to me.

Dante makes a jumping swipe for the pillow, but I hold it out of his reach. He groans like this is the most boring conversation he's ever had, whereas I have never been more riveted.

"Talk to me and then you can beat up Anatoly," I tell him. "You woke Mikhail up this morning?"

"Yes," he sighs. "I ate pancakes and brushed my teeth, too. I did all the things I was s'posed to."

It takes nothing short of a full half-hour of pleading and screaming to get Dante to finish his cereal and use the restroom every morning. To get out the door on time, I'd have to sacrifice baby lambs on an altar somewhere.

But in Mikhail's house, Dante can take care of himself with no prodding whatsoever.

That isn't sending me into a shame spiral at all. Nope. I'm doing awesome.

"Why did you go into Mikhail's room?"

"I dunno," Dante shrugs.

"If you need something, you should come to me."

"I can go to Mikhail, too," he argues. "He's my dad."

The words drop with the force of an atomic bomb. It's all I can do to stay standing. I lose my grip on the pillow and Dante takes the opportunity to snatch it away while I'm reeling from those three little words.

He's my dad.

"Who told you that?" I ask, but Dante can't hear me. He's too busy divebombing Anatoly.

Anatoly tickles Dante into submission and suggests a game of hide-and-seek while I manage to collapse down on the couch and stare straight ahead at the wall. As soon as Dante runs into the closest closet, positive neither of us saw him, Anatoly claps a hand on my shoulder.

"You okay?"

I look up at him, eyes narrowing. "Did *you* tell him?"

"Not a word," he claims, hands raised in surrender. "Stella didn't say anything, either. We were up late talking last night and she was still using codewords just in case."

If it was any other day, I'd ask Anatoly what he was doing staying up late to talk to Stella, but I'm too deep in my own existential panic to focus on that now.

"Would Mikhail tell him?"

"No." Anatoly shakes his head with finality. "He wouldn't. I think... Kids have a way of just knowing this stuff. It's instinctual."

"I've stopped that kid from shoving a fork in a light socket and trying to eat marbles. Children have no instincts."

"They do about this," he insists. "I mean, my father never told me he was my dad, but I knew. I also knew he liked me less than my brothers. Kids read between the lines."

"There haven't been lines to read between," I mumble.

But of course there have.

Dante and I moved into Mikhail's house the day that we met him.

Mikhail sat by his bed with me last night and calmed him after a nightmare.

Mikhail swore to Dante that he would take care of both of us.

In a lot of ways, there hasn't been much need to read between the lines. The lines themselves have been pretty damn clear.

I drop my face in my hands. "What a mess."

"It's only a mess for *you*, Viv," Anatoly says unhelpfully, heading for the closet. "The rest of us are doing just fine."

Anatoly pretends to look for Dante behind a plant and under the sofa before he rips open the closet door and chases Dante around the room, wailing like a ghoul.

My son is fed, safe, and happy because of Mikhail. I should be thrilled. My horoscope this morning did say that I'm finding a new balance in my life and I should embrace it. Maybe Mikhail is that balance.

But is this what balance feels like? Like a boulder sitting on your chest, slowly crushing the life out of you?

Dante ropes Anatoly into one more round of hide-and-seek. "He's not very good at this game," Dante whispers to me after he opens his eyes and immediately sees Anatoly trying and failing to cover his massive shoulders with one of the curtain panels.

"I call for a rematch!" Anatoly cries just as Stella sweeps into the room.

"The tutor is here." Stella waves for Dante to follow her, but her eyes keep flicking to Anatoly untangling himself from the curtains.

"What's a tooter?" Dante asks, making a fart noise with his mouth.

"Get it out now because you are *not* going to do that when we meet her," I warn him. He continues making fart noises as I explain. "She's going to be like a teacher, but here in the house."

He frowns. "I already have a teacher. Mrs. Campbell is my teacher."

This. This is why I'm not thrilled.

As great as things may seem, Mikhail still pulled my son out of his school and away from the life we built. At the end of the day, Mikhail is a Bratva *pakhan.* He's used to everything in life going his way. If Dante or I try to push back, he won't be open to compromising.

I ruffle Dante's hair. "I know, but now, you have two teachers! How lucky are you?"

Dante grumbles something I can't hear, but it doesn't matter because we turn the corner and there she is. Dante's tutor.

The woman has pitch black hair pulled back in a severe bun on the top of her head. She's wearing wire-framed glasses perched on her thin nose and a green sweater vest over her button-down shirt.

I want to ask what came first: the job or the wardrobe. She looks like she stepped out of an encyclopedia page for tutors.

Instead, I hold out my hand and smile. "It's so nice to meet you. I'm Dante's mom."

"I'm Mrs. Steinman." The woman shakes my hand, but her attention quickly shifts to Dante. She kneels down in front of him and, in an instant, she comes alive.

A smile spreads across her face and everything that looked severe a second ago suddenly looks approachable. The bun flops back and forth when she talks, her eyes crinkle with the grin, and her glasses are in little half-circle shapes. She looks like a real-life cartoon character.

"I'm so happy to meet you, Dante!" she beams. "Do you want to help me get set up for today? I have so many activities planned for us that I'm going to need your help."

Dante twines his hands together behind his back and shuffles his feet across the carpet, but his nerves evaporate as soon as he pulls the giant, rainbow-colored dice out of Mrs. Steinman's bag.

I watch from the doorway as Dante and Mrs. Steinman take turns rolling the dice. Each number is associated with a different activity—a dance move, making a shape out of fuzzy pipe cleaners, finding alphabet sounds around the room. Dante is grinning from ear to ear as he rolls a four and then races over to make a butterfly out of red and orange pipe cleaners.

"She isn't going to disappear with him," Anatoly whispers from behind me.

I roll my eyes but slip out of the doorway and into the hall. "I know."

"Really? 'Cause you lurking over his entire lesson gives off nervous energy."

"I just met this woman fifteen minutes ago. Am I supposed to just walk away and leave her alone with my kid?"

"She's been vetted," he says like that is reason enough. "Mikhail actually paid to swipe her from her position with some senator's kids. She's the best of the best."

"According to Mikhail."

Anatoly sighs. "I understand the chip on your shoulder, Viv. I really do."

"I wish you'd stop calling me that."

He smirks. "And I wish you'd stop pretending you hate it—and us—so much. Maybe if you let yourself relax for a second, you'd realize that life here isn't so bad."

Anatoly is saying out loud what's been silently floating around in my head for the last twenty-four hours. So I tell him exactly what I've been telling myself.

"It's not so bad now, but it won't always be this way. Mikhail's life is dangerous. This world is dangerous."

"*Life* is dangerous," Anatoly retorts. "The only difference between being out there and in here is that, in here, Mikhail is going to do whatever it takes to make you and Dante safe and comfortable."

I snort. "I'll believe it when I see it."

"Then keep looking around, Viv. You're family now. Mikhail is going to treat you right." Anatoly tries to pinch my cheek, but I dodge him. "Maybe he'll even treat you *extra right* on your date tonight."

It's his turn to dodge when I take a swing at him.

"It's not a date!" I call as he jogs away down the hallway, still laughing.

24

VIVIANA

It's not a date.

It's just dinner… Dinner on the rooftop of a restaurant I'd feel too underdressed to walk past, let alone eat at.

I freeze as soon as the door to the rooftop opens. Blush and fuchsia pink flowers trail up brick columns and span the gaps between the exposed wooden beams running overhead. Candles flicker in the center of the table and in lanterns scattered around the roof. The space is large enough to fit twenty other tables, at least, but tonight, there is only one.

It's gorgeous.

And definitely not a date.

Mikhail's hand lands firm and warm on my exposed lower back. Stella chose a low-back, champagne-colored satin dress for me to wear. At the time, I thought it was overkill. Now, it's obvious I'd fit right in here… if there was anyone else around to "fit in" with.

Mikhail directs me out of the doorway and to our table.

"Is this for us?" I ask dumbly.

"No, actually," he says, pulling out my chair. "But don't worry—I killed the couple it was for on our way in. Their bodies are in the back alley. They won't be making their reservation, I'm afraid."

I blink at him, stunned for a full three seconds before I realize he's joking.

"Relax. Everything tonight is for us, Viviana." Mikhail gently pushes me back into the table.

He's in a blue suit that does dangerous things to his eyes. They are like melting glaciers. When I look into them, I swear I can see forever.

The thought jolts me back to reality. I lunge for my napkin and accidentally send the silverware inside clattering across the table.

I'm sure Mikhail notices my nerves, but he doesn't say anything. He orders wine and thanks the waitress as she pours our glasses. When Mikhail lifts his glass for a toast, all I hear is Anatoly's voice in my head.

Maybe he'll treat you extra right *on your date tonight.*

"Why did you bring me here?" I blurt.

Mikhail sighs and lowers his glass. He takes a sip before he answers. "I thought I should get to know the mother of my child."

A breeze blows across the rooftop and a pink flower petal flutters down from above, landing perfectly in the center of my plate. I arch a brow. "We can get to know each other back at the mansion."

Where there are other people. And fewer flowers. And I don't have to imagine what it would be like if this was a date and there was some chance that the night would end with Mikhail's lips on mine and this dress on the floor.

"I didn't want any distractions."

"Then you shouldn't have worn that suit," I mumble.

Mikhail leans closer and I can smell his minty freshness from here. "What was that?"

"I want to get to know you, too," I say quickly. "I have it on good authority that Stella and Anatoly are helping Dante make homemade slime. He definitely would have roped us into that experience if we were at the mansion."

"What is homemade slime?" he asks.

"It is what it sounds like: slime. It's just goo made from glue and food coloring and a bunch of other stuff from around the house."

Mikhail, a man I've seen beat his own brother into a pulp, looks horrified. "What do you do with it?"

"Nothing. Everything." I chuckle. "It's like Silly Putty from when we were kids. Did you ever play with that stuff?"

"I didn't play with anything," he admits. "There wasn't time."

"Here we go. The appetizers haven't even come out yet and I'm already learning shocking things about you." I grab my drink and take a sip. I'm no wine connoisseur, but even I know it's expensive. I plan to drink half a bottle, at least, if only to quiet down the nagging thoughts in my head. "What were you so busy doing that you didn't have time to play when you were a kid?"

"You grew up in the mafia. It's not so different from my world. You know what it's like."

"I grew up the only daughter of a don," I remind him. "I have no idea what it's like to grow up the second son of a *pakhan*. So, what was it like?"

Mikhail considers it for a second and then meets my eyes. "Bloody."

It doesn't have the same ring of amusement as the joke about killing the couple in the alley did. Probably because it's not a joke.

"Huh," I murmur. "Maybe our experiences weren't so different, after all."

I raise my glass for the toast I missed earlier. Mikhail dips his chin and clinks his glass against mine.

The waitress pops in and out every so often to deliver different courses, but otherwise, we are left alone. Large gas heating lamps burn in a circle around the rooftop, insulating us from the chilly evening. Still, goosebumps bloom up and down my arms when the wind blows.

"Cold?" Mikhail asks.

I start to refuse, but he is already standing up and slipping out of his jacket. He drops it over my shoulders and I almost moan at the residual warmth of his body. The scent of cedar and mint swirls around me. If I stole this jacket and sold it to some perfumer somewhere, I'd make a fortune.

"Thanks." I pull the sleeves more tightly around me. "It's a nice night, but I always run cold. My dad always said I get that from my mom. He said she shook like a scared little chihuahua the entire time he knew her."

Of course, she could have been shaking out of fear. Being married to a man who screamed at her every time another man even looked her direction, like it was her fault, couldn't have been good for her health.

It's probably why her heart stopped when she was only forty-five.

Or maybe he killed her.

I've never worked out which one, but after what my father did to Matteo, I wouldn't put anything past him.

"She died when you were little, didn't she?"

I only smile because I'm so surprised he knows anything at all about my life. "How do you know that?"

"You were engaged to my brother for six months. I got bored at all those godawful parties and fundraisers."

"So you asked around about me?" That shouldn't send a swirl of excitement through me, but it does.

"I overheard other people talking about you," he counters. "It was better than listening to people kiss Trofim's ass, so I tuned in."

"Glad my trauma caught your interest. That's what dead moms are for, after all: party chatter."

"Unless you're my father," Mikhail retorts, "and then dead moms are only around so you can blame them for all the bad behavior of your sons."

I knew Trofim's mom wasn't in the picture when we were engaged. All of the conversations about our union happened between his father and mine. It was a room full of men hashing out my romantic future without a female voice in sight. But Trofim never talked about her, and I didn't care enough about him to ask.

"What happened to your mom?" I ask softly.

"She married my father."

It's the only answer Mikhail offers and I can tell it's all I'm going to get.

"Well, if we succeed in being civil, it'll be the first halfway decent marriage I've ever seen up close," I admit.

Something I don't understand flickers across Mikhail's face before he schools his features. "Up close, every marriage is miserable."

"You really think so?"

"Best case scenario is 'til death do us part.' It's pretty fucking bleak," he mutters as he takes a drink.

"For a man who doesn't believe in marriage, you sure rushed into our wedding. Any chance this cynicism is an act?"

I'm teasing him, but deep down, I want to know. Why did he ask me to marry him? Why are we here on this rooftop, surrounded by flowers?

"The cynicism is from experience. The marriage is because of Dante."

Right. Dante.

He's here because I got knocked up during a one-night stand. A one-night stand that happened on the heels of Mikhail breaking up my very unhappy engagement to his brother. An engagement that only happened because my father murdered my previous fiancé right in front of me.

God... my life is a graveyard of bad marriages. Based on the ghosts swirling in Mikhail's eyes, I'm sure his past looks similar.

I sigh. "Is it too depressing to raise our glasses to shitty parents and their even shittier marriages?"

"Probably." Mikhail raises his glass anyway.

"I'd toast to not repeating their mistakes, but I'm not sure anyone would say our marriage is built to last. We've probably already made their mistakes."

"Our marriage is built on mutual benefits and personal responsibility," he says coolly. "I think that's a hell of a lot stronger foundation than love."

I snort. "I know centuries' worth of poets who would disagree with you."

"They can disagree all they want. While they were busy writing sad little poems about lost loves, I was learning from the real world. I know for a fact that when love is taken away from you, nothing can bring it back. It may make a man strong at first, but when it's gone... there's nothing weaker than that."

Mikhail is staring down into his glass. The words feel like an accident. Like they slipped through a crack in his usual armor and weaseled their way through another crack in mine.

I find myself leaning closer to him. "Has love been taken away from you, Mikhail?"

He blinks and instantly, the moment is gone. He shakes his head gruffly. "What about you?"

I don't owe him an explanation. Especially since he definitely isn't going to tell me anything. But I decide to be honest anyway.

"Once." I fold my hands around my empty glass. My fingers are cold. "It was a long time ago. I was young... stupid. It ended badly."

Suddenly, more wine is splashing into my cup.

Mikhail lowers the bottle and raises his glass yet again. "One last toast—to not repeating our own mistakes."

Easier said than done.

By the time our dessert plates are cleared away from the table, I'm full and warm in Mikhail's jacket. He offers me his hand to escort me down the stairs, but I'm not ready to leave.

I turn to the railing, taking in the glowing city streets below. The chatter and honking feels distant from this high up. I can romanticize it in a way I can't when a taxi is blaring its horn at me as I cross the street, Dante's hand locked in mine like a vice.

This top-of-the-world view makes everything down below look small... insignificant.

"Can we stay for a few more minutes?" I ask suddenly.

His face is unreadable as he lets the stairwell door close and follows me to the railing. "I thought you'd be ready to get back to Dante."

"He's definitely asleep by now. Besides, this is the first time I've been out in five years."

"You haven't been out since Dante was born?"

"Sad but true." I chuckle. "I hired a babysitter when I had to work late or when there was a work function in the evenings, but those only came up once or twice a year."

"What about dates?"

"Hazy, elusive things. If I focus really hard, I can almost remember what it felt like to have a social life. But it's been a long time. Actually, this is—" I grip the railing.

"This is what?" Mikhail's elbow brushes against my arm. Several layers of clothing separate us, but I swear I feel his heat radiate through my bones.

"This is the closest thing I've had to a date in as long as I can remember." As soon as the words are out of my mouth, I wince. "That sounded even more pathetic out loud than it did in my head. Which is saying something, because it sounded *really* pathetic in my head."

To my surprise, Mikhail laughs, and the sound sends warmth pooling low in my belly. The same way it did last night before our almost-kiss in the kitchen. Mikhail is stingy with his smiles and it only makes me want to gather them up and hoard them.

"It's not like you're hideous," Mikhail says. "Men must have asked you out."

"Wow. 'Not hideous.' If I was still on the market, that would be my profile on every dating app. What a rave review," I bite out sarcastically.

His hand whispers over my lower back again, drawing closer than we've been all night. "You know I like what I see. I've never denied that."

The night he bent me over the side of the bed and spanked me flashes in my mind. I saw his erection and accused him of liking it.

Am I supposed to deny it?

My face flames and words tumble out just to distract myself. "Actually, the morning I went to work and found you there instead of my boss, my neighbor had asked me out for dinner." I frown. "He's probably wondering what happened to us."

"Did you accept his offer?" Mikhail slides his hand possessively to my hip and I've never been more aware of my body.

"Yes, but…"

But I haven't thought about him even once since I walked away from him.

Not the way I've thought about you.

"But what?" Mikhail presses.

I flail for something to say. "But Tommy was a Capricorn. It probably wouldn't have worked out."

"Please don't tell me you put your faith in the stars."

I shrug. "The stars told me Trofim and I wouldn't be a good match. They were definitely right about that."

"The stars didn't need to tell you that," Mikhail snorts. "I was born at the end of September. What does that tell you about me?"

"You're a Libra. Libras are all about—" I inhale sharply. Mikhail's hand feels like a brand on my hip. "Balance," I choke out. "Libras are represented by the scales."

Mikhail turns to me, eyebrow arched. "Why does me being a Libra make you look like you want to jump over the ledge? I don't know a thing about astrology. Are Libras serial killers or something?"

In the case of this particular Libra: *probably*.

But bizarrely, that isn't what has my heart racing.

I paste on a smile. "It's stupid, but my horoscope this morning… It said I'm on the brink of finding new *balance* in my life."

Mikhail turns to me. I'm not sure how it happened, but instead of looking down at the view, I'm looking up at him. His skin is gold in the candlelight. The breeze brushes his dark hair away from his face.

"Is that all it said?" His voice is a tempting rumble that I feel in my toes. I'm surprised it doesn't shake the building. It should register on some Richter scale somewhere.

I lick my lips. "No."

His hand tightens around my lower back, pulling me closer. "What else did it say, Viviana?"

"It said I'm on the brink of finding new balance in my life… and I should embrace it."

Mikhail is good for Dante. He comes with some threats and baggage, but he wants to protect us from that.

Maybe I should stop fighting this pull I feel towards him. The pull I've felt since I first saw him leaning against the wall at my engagement party. The one that hasn't lessened for even a second since he threw me back on the bed in that bridal suite.

Mikhail leans closer. I tip my head back, part my lips.

I want him.

The thought rings through me like a gong and he must be able to hear it.

Because all at once, Mikhail pulls away and leaves me leaning on the cold metal railing.

"Sounds like your horoscope knows about your breakdown in the kitchen last night. You definitely 'embraced' me then." He shoves his hands in his pockets and walks to the stairwell door. He wrenches it open and points for me to follow.

I silently follow him down the stairs and through the restaurant. Pyotr is standing by the curb downstairs, but when he helps me into the backseat, Mikhail doesn't follow.

"Take her home," Mikhail orders. "I have work to do."

Without another look at me, Mikhail turns and leaves.

I spend the ride home staring out the window, playing and replaying the conversation on the roof. I can still feel where Mikhail's hand singed my lower back.

What happened? What did I do wrong?

As if he can hear my thoughts, Pyotr catches my eye in the rearview mirror. "Don't judge him too harshly."

"Who?" I snap.

Pyotr gives me a sympathetic smile. "Mr. Novikov has been through a lot. When he is responsible for someone, he takes it seriously. He doesn't allow anything to get in the way of him doing what needs to be done—not even himself. If he's keeping you at arm's length, there's a good reason."

Like he's uninterested. He doesn't want me. This marriage is a sham through and through.

If I'm transparent enough that Pyotr can see my disappointment, I'm sure Mikhail could, too.

Pyotr is trying to make me feel better, but as I mumble my thanks and walk into the mansion I now call home, I've never felt more alone.

25

VIVIANA

Push the board meeting from 10 to 2.

When I saw Mikhail's name light up my screen two minutes before six this morning, my stupid heart leapt. A more imaginative person might've said it frolicked, even, hopeful that whatever the hell happened at the end of our "definitely not a date" the other night was an emotional glitch Mikhail was going to apologize for.

Apparently not.

I mentally add a third tally under my *Days Since Mikhail Has Apologized for Being An Asshole* column. Then I text back. **Can do.** I even put a period at the end instead of an exclamation point. Like the no-nonsense hardass I am.

Mikhail isn't texting me as Viviana, the mother of his child and woman he nearly kissed before unceremoniously dumping her in a car and sending her away—he's texting me as Viviana, the assistant he inherited after a hostile takeover of Cerberus Industries.

It's getting hard to keep track of what and who we are to each other.

I'm his wife, but not really.

We're attracted to each other, but not together.

I'm the mother of his child, but we aren't a family.

So me being Mikhail's personal assistant is just another level of confusion on top of this seven-layer shit dip.

Today is my second day back at work since moving in with Mikhail, so my internal clock is still adjusting back to my work schedule. I have to drag myself out of bed and into the shower. Afterward, I twist my hair into a clip and toss my makeup bag in my purse.

Yesterday, I curled my hair and put on a full face assuming I'd be riding to work with Mikhail. But when I got downstairs, it was just Pyotr waiting for me in the driveway.

Today, I'll do my makeup on the drive.

My shopping spree with Stella and Anatoly included new work clothes, so I slip into a gray pencil skirt and cashmere sweater. This outfit alone is more expensive than the entirety of my combined work- and non-work wardrobe before meeting Mikhail. The cashmere feels like being cuddled by a flock of adorable baby sheep. It's so comfortable that it takes a concerted effort to not feel any gratitude towards Mikhail as I walk across the hall to wake up Dante.

But thoughts of Mikhail and baby sheep fly out of my head when I open Dante's door…

And find his bed empty.

"Dante?" I call, pulling back the blankets even though I know he isn't there.

I check the closet, but it's empty.

Shoving down gnawing panic, I check the sitting room and the kitchen, but they're empty, too. I don't see Stella or Anatoly. Dante's tutor, Mrs. Steinman, won't be here for another hour, at least. Out of desperation, I ask a maid I don't recognize if she's seen Dante, but she says something in Russian that lets me know neither of us are going to understand each other.

I sprint down the hallway back towards his room. "Dante! Where are you?"

Did Mikhail take him? Are they gone? Am I ever going to see him again?

I'm blinking back tears—seconds away from calling Mikhail for help or to scream at him, depending on if he's kidnapped my child or not—when I hear a muffled shout from the end of the hall.

From Mikhail's room.

I throw open the door and step inside.

The shades are drawn and the room is dim, but I can still see the rumpled, king-sized bed where Mikhail slept last night. Fully against my will, I breathe in the mint and cedar scent of him. It's stronger here than anywhere else in the house.

"Dante…?" I whisper as if Mikhail is going to lunge at me from behind a door.

"I'm in here," a little voice says tearily.

I turn towards the closet. The door is cracked open and I see a small, socked foot poking out of the shadows beyond.

Getting to my knees in my pencil skirt is an ordeal-and-a-half, but I manage it and crawl into the closet with him. Thankfully, Mikhail's closet could fit our previous apartment two times over. Claustrophobia won't be an issue.

"What are you doing in here, bud?" I ask softly. "Are you okay?"

Dante swipes a pajama sleeve across his nose. "I was looking for Mikhail."

"I think he's already at work." If his text at the buttcrack of dawn was any indication, he starts work in the middle of the night. "Did you need something?"

You could have come to me. You can always come to me.

The jealousy taking root in my chest is ripped up the moment Dante lifts his face and I see his chin wobbling. His blue eyes are glassy with tears.

"What's the matter, honey?" I wipe away his tears with the baby-sheep-soft sleeve. "Did something happen?"

"Is he leaving again?" he wails, throwing his arms around my middle. His face is buried in my stomach. "He came back, but he's leaving us again."

"No. He isn't going anywhere. He didn't—When did he leave us before?"

"When I was a baby," he cries. "That's why he wasn't there. It was me and you, but I… I want it to be Mikhail, too. But he's gone. He wasn't here before bedtime or when I woke up. He's nowhere."

When I stroke his cheek, I can't help but see his father in every inch of him.

"He's been away." I stroke his cheek and can't help but see his father in every inch of him. "But he'll be back soon. I'll make sure of it."

∼

Pyotr walks around to help me out once we pull up to Cerberus Industries, but I'm already out of the car and wrenching open the glass double doors by my damn self.

Jackie waves and says something nice about my sweater, but I'm too angry to engage in small talk today. My heels click down the tile hallway towards Mikhail's office like a war drum. When I reach his office, the only warning of my arrival is when the door bangs off the interior office wall.

"We need to talk," I bark.

Of course, Mikhail doesn't flinch.

He doesn't even look up, actually. He's signing some contract —probably his NDA with Satan. *I swear not to tell anyone you inhabit my body for your evil bidding eighty percent of the time in exchange for dangerously good looks and more money than any human has a right to.*

Whatever it is for, I swipe it off his desk with a violent sweep of my arm.

"I said we need to talk," I repeat icily. "It's important."

Mikhail clicks his pen, lays it perfectly parallel to the edge of his desk, and finally looks up at me. "What do you need, Viviana?"

"From you? Nothing. Absolutely nothing. *I* never needed anything from you."

"Is that why you came in here today? To tell me you don't need anything?" His eyes slide down and back up my body slowly. "Or is there something else?"

His old words ring in an obnoxiously horny part of my brain. *You know I like what I see. I've never denied that.*

The need twisting low in my gut despite everything this man has done to me and my son only fuels my anger. It's gasoline to my righteous rage.

"*I* don't need a damn thing from you. Your son, however, was crying on your closet floor this morning because he's scared you're leaving him again."

Mikhail's eyes darken. "I never left him. *You* took him away. I'm sure you cleared that up with him."

"You've been in his life for less than a week and you're already disappointing him. If you want to make me feel bad about keeping him from you, being a halfway decent father would do the trick. Right now, you're proving me right."

Anger bubbles just under his surface. I feel it like an electric charge in the air. But Mikhail's face stays calm. Impassive. Like it's carved out of a goddamn glacier with an avoidant attachment style and repressive emotional tendencies. "The kid was crying because he missed me. Sounds like he thinks I'm a little more than 'halfway decent.'"

I gasp. "You cannot be serious. Are you trying to spin him crying into a *good* thing?"

"I never cried when my father wasn't around and that definitely wasn't a good thing. You know what I think?"

"That the world revolves around you?" I guess. "Yeah, you've made that painfully obvious."

He continues on like I didn't say anything. "I don't think you're here because Dante misses me. I think you're here because *you* miss me."

"That is not true!"

It's not *entirely* true, anyway.

If this was just about what happened between us the other night, I'd carry on in silence. I would fight back by responding to his work texts with increasingly aggressive punctuation until he was forced to clear the air.

"*Dante* is the reason I'm standing here. *Dante* is the reason I agreed to marry you in the first place. *Dante* is the only reason you and I are in the same room right now."

"What about when you spread your legs for me and begged me to come inside you?"

In the silence that follows, I could hear a pin drop from a mile away.

Mikhail's face is unreadable. Anyone walking by probably thinks we're discussing schedules and upcoming meetings. But, oh boy, if they could hear... HR would have a field day with this conversation—with our entire relationship, actually.

Though the thought of Judith with the beehive hairdo from the nineteenth floor telling Mikhail what he can and can't do almost makes me laugh.

I hitch in a breath to try to respond, but Mikhail charges on ahead.

"Dante didn't exist yet, so I know that wasn't about him. Is it possible, Viviana, that you did want something from me that night?" His voice lowers, smoothing over my skin like velvet. "Do you still want it?"

Yes. Yes. *Which is the entire fucking problem.*

My cheeks burn. I throw his words from the night on the roof back at him. "You know I like what I see, Mikhail. I've never denied that."

He wags a finger in the air. "Except you are, Viviana. You're denying it right now. You're standing here because I'm following *your* rules. We got married and you said no sex. This is a business arrangement, remember? But the first time I don't walk you to the front door and kiss you under the porch light, you storm into my office and start making demands."

"For Dante!" I scream. "I'm making demands for Dante!"

"Using your son to get closer to me." He clicks his tongue in disapproval. "It's a dirty trick, even by my standards."

"I'm not—I would never—" Angry tears burn behind my eyes, but I refuse to let them fall.

This is what Mikhail wants.

He wants me to hate him. To yell and scream and give him an excuse to keep me at arm's length.

If that's what he wants, why should I fight to bring him closer?

I let that tiny seed of hope sprout in my chest, convincing me that maybe there could be more between us, if only because I like the symmetry of his face and the way his body feels against mine. But a relationship is built on more than that.

It's built on things I can't give him.

Like the whole truth. Every seedy detail of how exactly I was able to disappear for so long.

And things he can't give me.

Like his heart.

I take a deep breath and square my shoulders. "I don't care if you and I never speak again from this moment forward. But you can't do that to Dante. He knows you are his father. He figured it out. And just because you don't deserve a son like him, that doesn't mean he doesn't deserve to have his father in his life. Business is all you seem to understand, so try treating our son like a job. You need to show up for him every day. If you can't, you let me know so I can pick up that slack. He deserves better than either of us—but you and I are all he has."

Before Mikhail can say anything, I turn and leave.

I make it to the bathroom at the end of the hall before the tears start to fall.

26

VIVIANA

"See you *mañana*, Margaret." Steve raps his knuckles on my desk as he passes by towards the elevators.

Mikhail sent out a memo two days ago about my official name change, but Steve never checks the memos. He barely knows how his email inbox functions. If it was up to him, we'd all use carrier pigeons and smoke signals to communicate.

Everyone else who *did* read the memo has taken to my real name with smiles and visible, but unspoken, confusion.

I fight an eye roll and wave. "Later, Steve."

Mikhail's office is already empty. He left half an hour ago without a word to me. Walked right past my desk like I wasn't even there. Like I was a piece of furniture in the corner instead of his wife and the mother of his child.

On one hand, I'm glad he isn't spouting off about our marriage. It's not real and I don't want people to think I was some spy working on the inside to help my husband take over the company. That wouldn't be good for office morale.

On the other hand, being called into Mikhail's office fifteen minutes after my explosion to explain the quirks of Mr. Fredrickson's office phone was difficult with the enormous elephant in the room.

If you want the phone to connect, you have to pick up the receiver and then—Oh dear, would you look at that? The elephant shit on the desk again. *Anyway, about that phone*—

I leave right at five, turning off the light in Mikhail's office as I go.

Jackie is still down at the front desk. She's swapping her heels for a pair of walking shoes. She looks up as my own heels click past.

"Hey, Marg—er, Viviana." She chuckles awkwardly. "That's going to take some getting used to. Are you about to brave the subway in heels?"

I point to the black car idling outside the double doors. "Mr. Novikov assigned me a driver."

It's the sanitized version. Telling her my new boss is also my new husband and the father of my child seems like the textbook definition of an "overshare."

She whistles. "That's nice. New guy is sparing no expense. Is he treating you better than Mr. Fredrickson?"

Well, it depends. Mr. Fredrickson never put me up in a bonafide mansion or gave me a personal driver or more g-spot orgasms than I knew what to do with.

Then again, Mr. Fredrickson also never kidnapped me and my son from our home and then gave me emotional whiplash until I couldn't decide whether I hated him for being cruel or for making me want him anyway.

"In some ways," I conclude with a smile. "If you ever want a ride, just let me know. Your place is on the way to—"

My old apartment.

The apartment I do not live in anymore and may never return to.

Before I need to finish the sentence, Jackie waves me away. "It's okay; I'm actually headed to my first tap class today. It's in the opposite direction."

"Wow! Tap dancing. That sounds fun."

"Probably not." She lugs her duffel bag over her shoulder. "My therapist suggested I 'try new things.' Embarrassing myself in front of other adults isn't new for me, but doing it while wearing tap shoes is."

Jackie and I walk out together. I wave as she heads in the direction of the train station and then climb into the back seat of the waiting car.

"Home?" Pyotr asks.

Home is wherever Dante is. But I also feel a tug towards the apartment where we spent the last few years.

"Actually, I want to make a stop," I tell him. "There's something I need at my old apartment. You know where it is?"

Pyotr stiffens. "I know where it is, but we don't have a guard with us. Anatoly should be here if you're getting out of the car."

"I was out of the car all day and Anatoly wasn't with me," I point out. "For the last half-hour, Mikhail wasn't in the building, either. I think I can handle walking up to my own apartment for a few minutes. I'll be quick."

Pyotr seems torn, his hands drumming on the wheel while he thinks.

"I thought transportation was your job," I remind him. "Wherever I want to go, it's your job to take me there, right?"

I feel bad for putting Pyotr in a weird spot, but luckily, any hint that he might not be fulfilling his duties to the highest caliber is all it takes to kick him into gear. He shifts the car into drive and gets me to my apartment faster than I thought was possible.

"I'll be in and out," I promise as I slam the door closed and cross the cracked sidewalk.

Really, I'm not even sure why I'm going in at all. I guess, after the day I had, being somewhere familiar sounds nice.

My mailbox is overflowing. It's mostly coupons and weekly deals for the grocery store around the corner, but there are a few overdue bills in there. I need to remember to forward my mail to the mansion. I don't think I'll be moving out anytime soon.

I tuck the stack under my arm and climb the three flights of stairs up to my floor.

There are four different door hangers for the takeout place across the street on the doorknob. Also a note taped to the frame.

Give me a knock when you're back. —T

I rip the note down and duck inside. I don't have the bandwidth to explain this hot garbage heap of a situation to Tommy today. Maybe ever.

The apartment smells musty, the same way it smelled when Dante and I first moved in. We lived here for years, but it only took a few days to revert to its former state. I try not to take the betrayal personally and dump the mail on the counter.

I crack open the fridge and see a bag of shredded lettuce that has liquified on the top shelf. And one look at the milk is enough to tell me it's hours away from growing legs and claiming squatter's rights.

I could clean it all out… but why? I won't be back here again.

The conversation with Dante this morning sealed that fate. He likes Mikhail. He's on his way to loving Mikhail. Even if I'd rather live in my small apartment with my rotting lettuce, I have to do what's right for Dante.

I close the door and face the apartment. The little shoes tossed under our two-person dining room table. The one-armed Spiderman action figure that is doing a face-down plank on the shelf next to the television. All the little bits and bobs that made up our everyday lives.

It's just like it always was, except… I can see the cracks now, too.

The way the sole of Dante's shoes are tearing away at the toe. He outgrew them a month ago, but I was trying to make them stretch as far as they could.

And the shelf next to the television is bowing under the weight of the single action figure. I saved the water-damaged cabinet from the curb a year ago and meant to fill it with picture books for Dante, but there never seemed to be time. After I got off, the evenings were a mad dash of dinner, bath, and bedtime.

The hard truth is, I've spent more quality time with my son over the last few days than I have in months. Years, maybe. Because instead of every second being filled with rush and panic and *hurry up*, we can breathe.

We can *be*.

This apartment represents a lot for me. It's the first place that was ever truly mine.

But that doesn't make it perfect. I walk the rooms one more time, stashing a few things in my purse as I go—Dante's favorite moon nightlight, a few more pictures from the walls.

"You were good to us," I whisper as I make my way to the door. It feels ridiculous to talk to an apartment, but it also feels right.

I step onto the landing and pull the door closed behind me just as the door across the hall opens.

"Margaret?"

I'm tempted to sprint down the stairs and save both Tommy and myself this awkward encounter. But I take a deep breath and turn to face him. "Hi, Tommy."

He blinks like he didn't expect to ever see me again. "Where have you been? You disappeared. Your mail backed up downstairs. I even left a message with the landlord about you. He never got back to me."

"No surprise there. He has an unread message in his inbox about my leaky bathroom sink from three years ago."

"Where have you been?" Tommy asks again, ignoring my attempt to lighten the conversation. "Is everything okay?"

Yes.

And no.

But also yes.

I settle on a shrug. "I'm okay."

He runs a hand through his hair, a deep crease between his brows. "Is this about the other day? I know I kind of jumped you in the hallway when I asked about the date. I didn't mean it to be so aggressive. I hope you didn't feel cornered. Because if I scared you, I think I'd jump off the roof—*Oh my God*, that wasn't a threat. I won't really jump. It's just—"

I grab Tommy's arm and try hard to smile. "This isn't about you. Or the date. You did a nice job asking me out. I didn't feel threatened."

I didn't feel anything, actually.

Being around Tommy is the exact opposite of being with Mikhail.

Around Mikhail, I feel everything whether I want to or not. It's like I'm in an emotional amplifier. Everything feels heightened. Tommy is a damper.

"Thank God." He sighs in obvious relief. "But if this wasn't about me, then what was it about? You've never even gone on vacation before. Not that I keep tabs on you, but you know what I mean."

"I've had some… family matters come up." Talk about boiling down and sanitizing the big, dirty truth. "The last few days have been hectic."

"Do you need to talk about it? People have told me I'm a good listener. I know because I heard them tell me… since I'm such a good listener." He shakes his head. "I swear I won't tell any more terrible jokes on the date. Er—not a date. Just coffee?"

I just said goodbye to my old apartment; I should say goodbye to Tommy, too. He deserves that much.

He also deserves the truth.

"I could grab coffee." I raise my left hand slowly and tuck my hair behind my ear. I watch Tommy's eyes widen as he clocks my truly heinous wedding ring. "As friends."

"Wow. It really has been a hectic couple days for you," he breathes.

"You have no idea."

He sticks out his elbow and gestures to the stairs. "I'd love to hear all about it."

I slip my arm through his and let him lead me down the stairs.

I meet Pyotr's eyes through the windshield of the car for only a second before Tommy and I turn and walk in the other direction.

I'm going out with Tommy because it sounds fun and because he deserves some kind of explanation after three years of being neighbors. But some small, petty part of me hopes Pyotr will tell Mikhail about this.

An even smaller, pettier part of me hopes it will tear him up inside.

27

MIKHAIL

The moment my fist connects with the man's face, it's like the frustration that has been building inside of me for the last three days has finally found a conduit.

"I'm sorry, Mr. Novikov," he moans. "I didn't mean—"

I pound the words out of his mouth, hitting him again and again.

Fuck, it feels good.

For the first time since I stood on that rooftop with Viviana, her body warm against mine, her lips soft and opening for me, I can think clearly.

Maybe I should keep an asshole who steals from me within arm's reach whenever I'm with Viviana. In case the tension gets to be too much and I need to release a little pent-up energy.

Blood and spittle fly. My knuckles start to ache, but I don't let up. I drive the man down to the floor and then follow him. I kneel over his cowering body until his eye is swollen shut and his mouth is a mangled puddle of blood.

Raoul never tries to curb me when I'm doing business, but today, he clears his throat. Only once, but it's enough.

It's a subtle reminder. Of where I am. Who I'm dealing with.

Reluctantly, I climb off of the man and he rolls over, spitting blood and half of a shattered tooth onto the concrete. I turn to his two adult sons. They aren't restrained, but they didn't make a move to help their father.

Cowards.

"Your father can't explain himself right now, so maybe you boys can help me out here." I pace closer, noting the way they flinch back. "You pay me to protect your family business, correct?"

The long-faced blonde on the left nods. "Correct."

"You sell car parts upstairs and run a gambling ring out of the basement, and I make sure no one comes in and shuts you down. Do you know how I do that?" I ask, not waiting for an answer. "Cameras. A metric fuck-ton of cameras. No one comes in or out of here without me knowing about it. So, explain to me, gentlemen, how a cache of weapons I stored here ended up missing."

The blonde looks like he's going to be sick, so I turn to his brother. "Someone stole them. That's all we know. We came in this morning and they were gone."

"Except the only people coming and going have been the two of you and your father here." I kick the father in the stomach just to make sure he doesn't think he's going to slip my notice. "Maybe I'm stupid, but that would tell me that one of you three knows a hell of a lot more than you're saying. So, tell me: am I stupid?"

The blonde shakes his head so hard I think his teeth might rattle loose. "No, sir. You aren't stupid. But we don't know what happened."

I sigh. "Next, you're going to tell me you don't know who has been skimming the top of my cut of the gambling money for the last... How long, Raoul?"

"Thirteen months," he fills in coldly.

I whistle. "My, my. That's a long time for all three of you to be in the dark."

The way the color drains from their faces tells me they know exactly what I'm talking about.

I kick the father in the stomach again. He groans and curls into a ball, but neither of his sons argues on his behalf. It's like they don't even care about him.

Is this what it looks like when your relationship with your kids is built on the family business? When the only thing you have in common is the title you were born to?

Viviana's voice hasn't stopped echoing in the back of my head since she walked out of my office this morning, but the volume kicks up a few notches right now.

Business is all you seem to understand, so try treating our son like a job.

If this is what treating my son like a job looks like, I don't fucking want it.

I hope I'm never quaking on the floor like the man at my feet now. If I'm unlucky enough to find myself in that position, I hope someone will have the decency to put me out of my misery.

Although the alternative to treating Dante like a business is treating Dante and Viviana like a family… and I don't want that, either.

I stomp on the father's knee to clear my head. "You can't all be as oblivious as you look. One of you knows something about who has been stealing from me."

Just as the trembling blonde brother starts to open his mouth, my phone rings.

I grimace and take the call. "I'm in the middle of something, Anatoly. What the fuck do you want?"

"Viviana is gone."

I feel my hackles rise. Just like that, I no longer give a shit about the three men in front of me. Viviana is all that matters.

"Where is she?" I bark. "You were supposed to have eyes on her. Pyotr was her driver."

Raoul hears the tone of my voice and pulls out his phone. He starts tapping away, clueing himself into what's happening without me needing to say a word.

I left the office today without a word. I didn't even look at her, which was harder than I made it seem. Her skirt hugged tight to every angle of her curves. It was painful to see her walk past my door without asking her to come in. Without bending her over my desk and tasting her—

I growl, refocusing my thoughts. "What do you know, Anatoly?"

"So, I misspoke." I can hear the wince in his voice. "Viviana isn't gone so much as she is… out. Away."

I frown. "What the fuck does that mean?"

"Well, she wanted to stop by her old apartment after work and Pyotr took her."

"Pyotr wasn't authorized to make that fucking call."

"He's very sorry," Anatoly says. "He is also the one who told me where Viviana went."

"And where in the fuck did she go?" I didn't have patience to begin with. Even if I did, it would be long gone now.

Behind me, Raoul curses.

I spin around and he's looking down at his phone. When he sees me watching him, he curses again.

"What?" I bark. "Someone better start talking. Now."

I snatch the phone out of Raoul's hand. He has a security camera feed pulled up. I recognize Viviana immediately. The man next to her, however, I've never seen before.

"Who is he?" I growl.

"You've seen the footage, then?" Anatoly asks.

"Who the *fuck* is he?"

"Her neighbor. Just a random guy across the hall. Harmless as it gets."

On the screen, the "random guy across the hall" offers his elbow and Viviana takes it. They walk down the stairs arm in arm and just like that, I want to rip his shoulder right out of its socket.

"I have eyes on the two of them," Anatoly offers, as if that could ease the knot in my chest. "They went for coffee down the street. They're just talking."

I hang up and turn back to the three cowering men in front of me. "When I come back, I want to know which one of you is responsible for stealing from me. Take this time to come to a consensus. If you can't decide, I'll just kill you all."

I look at Raoul and he waves me to the door. "I'll lock things down here. You have other things to handle."

Things like my wife.

If Viviana thinks I'm going to sit back while she throws a tantrum and fucks some other man, she has no idea who she is dealing with.

I think it's time I teach her.

28

MIKHAIL

I double park in front of the coffee shop to a chorus of honking car horns. I climb out, eyes locked on the large front window. Drivers curse as they navigate around me, but I'm too busy scanning for a head of honey blonde hair. Listening for the smooth velvet sound of her laugh.

My fists tighten at my sides.

I'll fucking kill him.

"Easy there, chief." Anatoly lays a hand on my shoulder. I didn't even see him standing on the sidewalk. "Let's inhale some peace and breathe out some homicidal ideations, yeah?"

"Tell me where they are, Nat," I growl.

He sighs. "Pyotr and I have been here the whole time. I wouldn't have let anything happen."

There shouldn't even be the possibility of something happening. She should have been with me.

"My wife is out with another man. Something has already 'happened.'" I shove his hand off my shoulder. "Where the fuck were you? Why was she alone in the first place?"

"I was at the mansion with Dante," he snaps. "*You* were supposed to be with Viviana. You two work in the same goddamn building. I didn't think I needed to cover them both."

Viviana's voice echoes in my head again. *He deserves better than either of us, but we're all he has.*

I let them both slip through the cracks on the same day. *I failed them.*

I shove the thought away and march towards the coffee shop.

"What do you want me to do?" Anatoly calls.

"Leave. Take my car and get back to Dante."

Pyotr is standing by the car, doing his best to blend in with the passenger door. "Go with Anatoly," I spit at him. "I'll drive my wife home myself."

I don't wait around to make sure they follow my orders. My sights are already set on a woman sitting just inside, her back to the window. Her hair is twisted into a clip, the honey blonde ends spilling over and brushing against her neck.

I distantly register the shape across from her. The vague outline of a man who might be dead within the next five minutes if he doesn't play this right. Still, I can't pull my eyes from Viviana.

My wife.

I approach her from behind and bend low, my lips against the shell of her ear. "Pick a body part."

She goes rigid. Robotically, she places her coffee mug on the table in front of her. "Mikhail, what are you—"

"Pick a body part," I repeat coolly. "Something to remember your date by."

Acoustic folk music pumps through the speakers. The sound of coffee grinders and chatting customers carries on. But it all feels worlds away.

This close to Viviana, I can smell sweet vanilla floating off of her skin. I want to take a bite.

"Margaret?" The man across from her doesn't even know her real fucking name. *Pathetic*. "Do you know this—"

"If you don't pick, I will," I whisper, cutting him off. "I'll choose his tongue if he doesn't shut up."

Viviana turns to me slowly. "We're just friends."

"You're about to have a preserved reminder of your friend you can keep on your shelf. I'll start a collection for you." I trail my finger down her neck, watching as goosebumps bloom across her skin. "Any hand that touches you, I'll sever it. Any lips, teeth… Anything else…"

"We're just friends!" she insists, swiping my hand away from her neck.

The man across the tables leans forward. "It doesn't look like Margaret wants you here, man. Maybe you should—"

"Sit down, Tommy," Viviana orders. Her eyes never stray from mine. "This is my husband."

The poor sap across from her sinks down in his chair. "You're actually married? I thought…"

I want to kill him for the disappointment in his voice alone. Whatever he told her, he isn't here because he's her friend. He wants more.

Of course he does.

"You didn't tell him?" I arch a brow. "Interesting. Seems like something a *friend* would know, *Margaret*."

"I told him I was married, but I failed to mention that you were a domineering psychopath." She juts her chin out, challenging me.

I grab it and slide closer to her. The room around us fades as I smell the hazelnut on her breath. I could lean forward and taste it right now. Taste her.

Claim her.

"Your mistake," I growl instead. "If you want your *friend* to live, you'll get up and come home with me. Now."

Viviana rolls her eyes, but I can feel her trembling. Her pupils are blown wide. Her cheeks are flushed. She pulls her chin out of my hand and turns to her date. "I have to go, Tommy. I'm glad we got to catch up."

"Oh. Yeah, I—Me, too," he fumbles.

Then he lets me wrap an arm around Viviana's waist and lead her out of the shop without a word.

"Your date didn't even fight for you," I tell her once we're on the sidewalk. "He let you leave with me."

She jerks away from me and storms towards the car. "He didn't 'let me' do anything. I make my own choices."

She tries to wrench open the car door, but it's locked. I reach around her body and open it for her. I trace my eyes down the long line of her leg as she climbs into the passenger seat in her skirt.

"For his sake, I'm glad you chose correctly."

I close the door on her scowl and walk around the car. My cock is aching against my zipper. It's a miracle I don't turn around and sever her coward of a neighbor's head from his shoulders. Viviana may think they're just friends, but that's because she has no fucking clue the effect she has on men. The effect she has on *me*.

He wanted her.

And I want to kill him for even the thought.

Instead, I start the car and slam on the gas.

"If you were worried about my safety, you wouldn't be speeding through traffic right now," she bites out.

"If you were worried about your little friend, you'd let me put as much distance between us and that coffee shop as possible."

She snorts. "You're not actually jealous of Tommy."

Of course I'm not. Ridiculous.

"I'm going to do something stupid if I hear his name come out of your mouth one more time," I snarl. My knuckles are white around the steering wheel.

"Who is this little show for?" She twists towards me, her leg curled onto the leather seat so I can see the creamy white skin of her inner thigh. "You haven't spoken to me in days. You've been pushing me away ever since our not-a-date date night—which was *your* idea, by the way. You want to get to know me, but you don't want to be in the same room with me. Make that make sense."

None of this makes sense.

Nothing about Viviana and the hold she has on my thoughts or my emotions or my dick makes any fucking sense.

"You don't want me, but no one else can have me, either? Is that it?" she continues. "I don't understand who this little show is for. Are you trying to convince Tommy you care about me? Because he's gone. There's no one to act for. You can go back to ignoring me."

"You said his name," I growl.

The road is blurring in front of me. Blood pounds in my temples and in my balls. My body is too big for my skin and I'm going to explode.

I rip off the main road into an alley between buildings. I swerve around a rusted-out dumpster and turn into a waterlogged loading bay. It's dark and cool and the noise from the street has faded to a blur.

But Viviana is in full clarity.

"Why are we stopping here?" she asks, a hint of fear in her voice.

She's all I can hear. All I can smell. All I can see. Touch and taste are begging to join the party.

When I close my eyes, I see her at the table with another man. Smiling at him. Laughing with him. Would she have gone home with him if I hadn't shown up? Fucked him?

"You were partially right," I breathe. "No one else can have you."

But I still want her.

Her brows pinch together and her full lips are parted in an angry pout. "What are you doing, Mikhail?"

Before she can say something else infuriating, I grab Viviana around the waist and drag her over the console onto my lap.

"Something stupid."

29

MIKHAIL

Viviana's thighs sink around me like we were made to fit together this way.

I drag my hands up her legs, shoving her skirt up around her waist until I can see the pale pink triangle of her panties.

"I've dreamed about this," I murmur. "About what I'd do if I ever got between your legs again."

"What are you going to do?"

"Give you what you want." I slide my thumb under the delicate material of her panties, dipping into the wetness between her folds. "Fuck. I can feel how much you want it. You must like it when I take you from another man. First, Trofim and now—"

She shakes her head. "Tommy wasn't—"

I band my hand around her throat. "Don't say his name. The only name I want to hear on your lips is mine. I want you to scream it."

I unzip my pants and free my erection, stroking myself as I touch her.

She looks down and swallows hard. "I don't want to fuck you in an alley, crammed in the front seat like teenagers."

"No, you wanted to fuck me on a rooftop. That's what you wanted the other night." I gently scrape my thumb over her clit and her entire body jerks. "You wanted me to fuck you on top of the world. You wanted the entire city to hear us. You wanted them to know you are mine."

Her wide eyes are locked on mine. I feel her pulse thundering against my fingers.

"That's why you went out with your neighbor. To make me jealous."

"Were you jealous?" she asks, licking her full lower lip.

I tease my finger inside of her, dipping in and out of her heat until her thighs are trembling. "Should I be?"

She's panting, grinding against my touch. "He's just a friend. I don't want him."

"What about me, Viviana?" I lift her over my cock, sliding my swollen head over the soaked fabric of her panties. "Do you want me?"

She stares down at our bodies like she wants to memorize the image. Then, wordlessly, Viviana pulls her panties to the side.

Our eyes hold for a single second before I bury myself inside of her.

"Mikhail," she whimpers, somehow sinking deeper onto me. "You're—*Oh God.*"

I grab the clip in her hair and pull it free. Gold waves tumble over her shoulders. The warm vanilla scent of her shampoo fills the car. "Your buttoned-up, terrified little neighbor didn't deserve this. I would have killed him if he touched you."

She arches her back and curls her fingers in my hair. "He didn't touch me. It's only you. In six years, it's only been you."

Some dark part of me latches onto that.

"Say it again," I growl, driving into her.

She looks away, but I grip her jaw and force her eyes to mine. "Look me in the eyes and tell me every man who has been inside of you since it was me. Tell me now."

"Only you," she gasps, her body fluttering around my cock. "It's only been you, Mikhail."

Viviana hasn't been with anyone since that night six years ago. I was the last man to see her orgasm. The last man to spill into her.

I don't want there to be anyone else. I'll make sure there isn't.

Ever.

I curl my hand around her neck and bring her forehead to mine. I look into her hazel eyes as I pump into her again and again. "You're *my* wife," I snarl. "You belong to *me*."

"Mikhail..." She gasps, her back arching. I hit a new angle inside of her and she cries out. "You feel so good."

She feels perfect. Her body is tight around me. Each stroke is a test of my patience. My body aches to spill into her.

I fist my hand in her hair and pull, arching her neck. I press my mouth to her fluttering pulse.

"I'm the only man who gets to see you like this, Viviana. I'm the only man who gets to feel you tighten around their cock." She clenches, dragging a groan out of me. "If you want to feel this good, you have to come to me."

She nods weakly, her eyes drifting closed. "There's no one else."

There's no one else.

I wrap an arm around her lower back and pin her against me as I piston in and out of her until she's screaming.

"Please. It's been so long. I need—" She moans, working her body against mine until the car is rocking. Viviana fists her hands in my shirt and looks into my eyes. "I want you, Mikhail. Please."

I grab her neck and drag her mouth against mine. I part her lips with my tongue and taste the warm, sweet flavor I'll never be able to separate from her.

We're too close. I want her too much. My plans and self-control are balancing on a razor's edge. I should pull out and shove her in the passenger seat. Leave her to finish herself off. Show her what happens when she tests me.

But instead of taking my own advice, the thought gives me an idea.

"Touch yourself," I growl against her mouth. "Come for me."

Viviana slides her hand between her legs, working her clit at the speed of my thrusts. Her breasts strain against the buttons of her shirt.

This isn't enough. Fucking her in a cramped car in some random alley is never going to be enough.

"I'm c-close," she whimpers.

I need her spread out on the bed beneath me. I need her weight on top of me. I need to fill her from behind and I need to devour her from below and I need to feel her come quivering on my mouth and, and, and...

"Mikhail."

I need to take this woman in every way imaginable.

"Fuck me," she begs. "Please."

I need to see her pregnant with my child.

The thought sets off alarm bells in my head, but I can't hear them over the cries tearing from Viviana's throat.

My hand slides to her flat stomach as she contracts, pulsing her release around me. The image of her tight body carrying my baby fills my head as I pull her hips flush against my body and come deep inside of her.

Viviana drops her head to my shoulder, breathing heavily. "Holy shit."

I'm still twitching as I lift her off of me and drop her into the passenger seat. She sags into the leather, limp and sated.

It's been a long time since I've lost control like that. Of my body or my mind.

"It's been so long since..." Viviana's voice fades into a soft chuckle. She starts to grab for the spare napkins Pyotr keeps in the center console, but I swat her hand away.

"Don't clean yourself up. Leave it."

"You want me to walk around with your cum between my

legs? Why am I not surprised?" She bites her lower lip and tugs her skirt down into place. "You're a real brute."

"Only when my wife goes out with another man."

She groans. "It was coffee with a friend; not a date."

"Would it have turned into a date if I hadn't shown up?"

Viviana leans closer. Her makeup is smudged from my mouth and my hands, but her eyes are bright when they meet mine. "No other man has touched me in six years. You think I'd give it up for Tommy?"

It's only been you.

I strap that thought down so I can interrogate it later. Figure out why the fuck this woman gets under my skin.

"Besides, I wouldn't do that to you." She reaches for her hair clip in the center console and expertly twists her hair up. "I made you promise there wouldn't be any other women. That means there won't be any other men for me."

Helen hangs like a ghoul over my shoulder. I should really end that engagement before things get messy.

But I'd rather lay the seat back and take Viviana again, right fucking now. Show her that no other man could ever make her feel the way I do.

Instead, I shift the car into reverse. The last thing I need is to cloud my head even more.

"It's funny, though," she sighs, mostly to herself.

I grit my teeth. "What is funny?"

"You sat behind your desk this morning and accused *me* of being needy."

And now, I'm the one laying claim to her, demanding she never even thinks about another man, let alone touches one. Ironic.

Twelve hours ago, I was trying to pull away from Viviana and get some distance to clear my head. Now, she's in the seat next to me and it isn't close enough. She'll never be close enough.

"And?" I snap.

Viviana smirks. "Nothing. I just find it funny, that's all."

There's nothing funny about the chaos churning in my head or that, despite it all, I want her on top of me.

No, this isn't funny. It's a fucking mess is what it is. A mess I need to get out of now.

I'll dump Viviana at home and go clear my head with a run. Just a light, easy half-marathon. If my feet aren't numb and bleeding by the time I'm done, I didn't go far enough or fast enough.

Next to me, Viviana's stomach rumbles, cutting through the noise in my head.

"Are you hungry?" I ask.

Probably because that asshole neighbor took her for coffee when he should have taken her for dinner.

She shrugs. "A bit."

Instantly, I take the next right and head in the opposite direction of home. "I know a good place."

30

VIVIANA

Up until the moment we walk through the front door and into the small Colombian café on the corner, I'm positive Mikhail is going to fake me out at the last second and whisk me away to some secret, fancy restaurant.

It would be more believable that a restaurant with three Michelin stars exists in some Mary-Poppins-like fold between buildings than to think that he is taking me to dinner at a place where you order at the counter.

"They call numbers here," I whisper in awe as we wait in line. "They're going to give us a number on a little piece of paper."

"I'm aware," he drawls.

More people come in behind us. A couple of teenagers laugh and shove each other. Half the tables in the cramped dining room are already taken by families or friends sitting around pitchers of beer.

Mikhail didn't rent the building out for us. He isn't trying to pay off the rest of the patrons to hurry up and leave.

And when the woman behind the counter hands him his receipt and tells him to step to the side to wait, he just nods and shifts over to wait for our food.

Huh?

"You've been here before?"

"It's Raoul's favorite spot in the city. He makes us eat here every time we're in the neighborhood. They have great empanadas."

Mikhail doesn't want another man to touch me for the rest of my life.

Mikhail likes empanadas.

I gather up the random scraps of information and tuck them away like a squirrel hoarding acorns for winter. I don't know when Mikhail is going to shut down again and pull away, so I have to get as much out of him as I can while I'm able.

A man calls our number and Mikhail grabs a plastic tray with our plates on it. He places a hand low on my back and directs me to a table. I sit down on a pea-green vinyl chair and pray the mess between my legs isn't leaking onto my skirt.

I forget all about it, though, when I take a bite.

"Holy shit," I moan. "This is incredible."

"I told you."

I wave my empanada in the air between us. "Is this how you apologize for three days of silent treatment? If so, feel free to ignore me more often."

"I could never ignore you," he rasps around a bite. Then Mikhail lowers his empanada and looks me in the eyes until my knees feel a little shaky. "This is how I apologize: I'm sorry."

I push through the shock and give him a silent golf clap. "That was very evolved of you. Night and day from the brute I was just in the car with."

He rolls his eyes. "I'm not sorry about what happened with your neighbor; I'm sorry about Dante. I shouldn't have disappeared on him. It was wrong. I can own that."

"Oh." I breathe quietly. "Why did you?"

"You two come as one. It's hard to ignore you and still see Dante."

"So you *were* ignoring me! I knew it."

"Trying," he admits, eyes narrowed. "Next time it happens, I'd suggest getting my attention in a way that doesn't endanger the lives of innocent civilians. I was about to burn that coffee shop to the ground."

Why? Is this about his pride? Maybe Mikhail only cares if I'm out with Tommy because of how it would make him look if his wife was openly dating other men.

Or maybe… Mikhail can't handle the idea of me being with another man because he is desperately in love with me.

Might as well go look for that universe tucked inside Mary Poppins' bag because, once again, that is more likely.

As much as I don't want to confront this particular ache in my chest, I can't stop myself from toeing close to the line. "You accused me of liking this possessive side of you, but I think you might get off on being possessive." I take a bite of empanada. With Mikhail's eyes on me, it tastes like sawdust.

"I wasn't even your fiancée the night you burst into my bridal suite to save me."

"I wasn't there to save you," Mikhail corrects sternly.

"Right, right. I forgot. You just so happened to show up the night before my wedding to overthrow your brother, even though you could have beat him down and stripped the signet ring off of his hand at any point in the prior six months. He spent more than enough nights drunk off his ass and defenseless, believe me. You had plenty of opportunities."

He sighs like an exasperated parent. I should know—I'm fluent. "At the risk of you throwing yourself at me in gratitude for saving you—"

"No risk of that," I lie.

"—I will admit that one of the many reasons I chose to eliminate Trofim on that night in particular was because I didn't want to damn you to a life tethered to him."

Okay, I might be more grateful for that than I'll ever be able to fully express. So I don't bother.

"I'm just glad you can be honest. You *were* there to save me that night."

"I wanted to stop my brother from making an alliance with a powerful mafia family before I could take control from him," Mikhail explains haltingly. "And... I also thought it might be nice of me to do it before the wedding so you wouldn't feel obligated to follow him into his likely exile."

I wince. "I didn't even think of that... My father definitely would have tried to force me to go."

"Then you'd be dead, too." Mikhail says it under his breath, but I still hear him.

My heart jolts. *"Dead?"*

He studies me for a second, making a decision. Then he nods. "Trofim is dead. Has been for a while, apparently."

I can't even pretend to enjoy my food now. I drop the other half of my empanada on my plate and wipe my mouth with shaking hands. "Do—do you know what happened to him? Who—How it happened?"

"Nothing definitive yet. Raoul and Anatoly are working on it, but he was cremated before there was even an autopsy."

"So there's no way to figure out what happened?"

"A retired detective who worked the scene mentioned some hair tie or clip or something tangled up in Trofim's sheets. They think there was a woman there with him that night."

"A woman?" I feel nauseous. I suddenly wish I hadn't eaten a single bite.

"What's the matter, Viviana?" Mikhail leans forward, and I freeze. I can't move. Can't breathe. "Don't tell me you're jealous of the woman my brother was fucking."

A shaky laugh huffs out of my tight chest. "God, no. I just hope the woman got out of there okay."

"I'll let you know when I find her."

"You're looking for her? Why?"

"Because she may be the last person to have seen Trofim alive."

My heart is wedged firmly in my throat. "You think she killed him?"

"Or she knows who did." Mikhail shrugs. "It's worth looking into."

"Why, though?" I blurt. "I mean, you exiled him. Why look?"

"He's my brother."

"The brother you exiled. The brother who killed Anatoly's mother and treated everyone like shit. I don't want to be harsh, but… who cares if he's dead?"

Forget crossing lines—I'm burning them. I'm eradicating lines and dancing on the other side of decency.

Of course, Mikhail doesn't mind. "He is associated with the Bratva. If someone killed him, I want to know why and make sure it has nothing to do with me and mine." He sits back, a smile playing on his lips. "But I had no idea you were so ruthless. You really hated Trofim, didn't you?"

"I didn't hate him. I just—Okay, yes, I hated him," I admit. "But only because Trofim represented all of the worst parts of this world. He was heartless and brutal for no reason. He only cared about gaining power and he didn't care who he crushed on his way to the top. Men like him are why I didn't want Dante living in it."

"What about men like me?" Mikhail asks with surprising softness. "I got rid of Trofim. I protected you. But you still didn't want Dante in my world."

"It was more complicated than—"

"He was my son and you knew that," Mikhail interrupts. "Did you think I would hurt him?"

We haven't talked about why I kept Dante away from Mikhail. Not really. Not at length. If the other option wasn't talking about Trofim, maybe I would try to change the subject.

"I didn't know what you would do," I tell him honestly. "I barely knew you, Mikhail. I saw you around at a few parties. Then you burst into that bridal suite the night before my wedding and told me you were bad. You looked me in the eyes and said that you weren't going to be good for me. What was I supposed to think?"

"He is my son."

"Exactly. *Your* son. The son of the new Novikov *pakhan*. But I didn't want that for him. I still don't." I tug my lower lip into my mouth, trying to find the words. "It's not about you anymore. I know that you're going to take care of him now. But you can't stop what's coming for him. His future."

"I don't want to stop it," Mikhail declares proudly. "Everything I'm working towards right now, I'm going to pass on to him. He's going to carry on my family's name."

The thought weighs heavy in my chest, but I understand. I do. Mikhail is proud of what he's done and he wants to share it with his son—with *our* son.

"But not yet." My voice breaks in a plea. "Right now, he's a little boy. I want him to be a little boy."

Mikhail's blue eyes make a slow study of me. "That's why you're the perfect mother for my child, Viviana."

My heart stutters, and I have to remind myself. He didn't say *perfect woman* or *perfect wife*.

"We balance each other out," he explains.

"Does that mean you agree to give him more time to be a normal kid before all of the Bratva training?"

"It's not like I'm shipping him off to boot camp." The corner of his mouth twists upward wryly. "Marriage is about compromise, isn't it?"

Just a few months ago—and for the last six years—I had some image of Mikhail in my head. Some idea of the man he was. But nothing I imagined could have come close to doing him justice.

"You're different than I thought you'd be," I find myself murmuring. "Nicer."

"What did I tell you about falling in love with me, Viviana?"

I laugh, but the idea isn't as ridiculous as it was the day we got married. "Would that be so bad?" My face feels warm, but I say it casually. It's just a thought. Not something I'm going to turn over and over in my head while I toss and turn in bed tonight. "I mean, if we're going to be married, we might as well try to be happy."

"Which is why you can't fall in love with me." There's a hard edge to his voice now. He gathers up our plates and piles them on the plastic tray.

"You really think love makes people *un*happy?"

"I think letting your emotions dictate your life is the quickest way to losing control. And I have no interest in losing control."

He walks the tray to the trash can, dumping the food and stacking the dirty tray on top of the others. On the way towards the door, he casually slips a hundred-dollar bill into the tip jar.

I'm not sure Mikhail will ever let me close enough to understand exactly how he operates.

Maybe that's for the best.

Sometime in the last half-hour, it started raining. Pouring, actually. Rain pounds on the red awning above the door and flows down the pavement in sheets.

Without a word, Mikhail slips out of his jacket and slides it over my shoulders. It smells like mint and citrus. I pull it tighter around my shoulders even as I ask, "What about you?"

"It would take far more to hurt me." His eyes dip to the neckline of my white shirt for a beat before he turns back to the deserted sidewalk. Then he grabs my hand and pulls me after him. "Come on."

We run out into the rain and instantly, I'm soaked. Rain drips down my back and over my eyes. If my makeup wasn't already ruined from what we did in the car earlier, it would be destroyed now. Mikhail's jacket is heavy and waterlogged. It hangs down into my eyes until I can't see.

Maybe that's why I don't notice Mikhail stop on the curb.

I'm staring down at the ground as I jump over the overflowing gutter and into the street. Then headlights blind me. A horn blares. A car hurtles toward us.

I don't have time to react or panic before Mikhail yanks me back. I smack against his hard chest, his arm banded around my back like iron.

His jacket has slipped down around my shoulders. Rain pelts my face, plastering my hair to my face.

But I barely feel it.

Mikhail is breathing heavily. His eyes are wide. He strokes a warm hand over my cheek, brushing wet strands of hair from my face.

"You almost died."

He says it so softly I'm not sure how I can even hear it over the pounding rain—over my pounding heart.

"But you saved me."

It's becoming a trend: Mikhail saving me. I could almost get used to it.

His thumb presses gently to the corner of my mouth and I turn towards it. I exhale against the calloused pad of his thumb, pressing the barest of kisses there.

His arm tightens around me, pinning me to his body.

"What are we doing?" I breathe.

The question shatters the moment. Mikhail jerks back, putting a safe distance between our bodies. But as he looks both ways to make sure no more cars are coming to splatter me against the asphalt, I hear him whisper a confused response.

"I have no fucking idea."

31

VIVIANA

He didn't use a condom.

The realization should have hit me sooner. Preferably in the moment before I pulled my panties to the side and practically begged Mikhail to fuck me in a cramped car parked in some random, dirty alley.

But no. I never even considered the consequences.

This is what happens when you spend six years getting orgasms from various battery-operated devices. Toys don't have sperm. Toys can't get you pregnant. Toys can't seduce you with their gravelly voices and calloused hands until your brain is mush and your body is on fire.

But Mikhail can.

Case in point: the five-year-old boy sleeping across the hall.

The last thing I need in my life right now is another Bratva baby. No siree. I scrub my loofah between my legs a little harder, like that might undo what we've done.

When I get out of the shower, I'm sore both inside and out. I debate leaving this one to chance. Surely I won't get pregnant after one time, right? Then I once again remember the five-year-old boy sleeping across the hall, pull on my big girl panties, and text Stella. I have a feeling she'll be more discreet about it than Anatoly or Raoul would be.

This is no big deal at all, but if you could pick me up some Plan B if you're out, that would be great. No pressure. Thanks!

No problem, she texts back a minute later.

No follow-up questions. No nosing into my personal life.

I knew I liked her.

Thirty minutes later, there's a soft knock at my door. I answer it, expecting to find Stella on the other side with a nondescript paper bag. We'll exchange it without a word like we're making an illicit drug deal and then never speak of this again.

Instead, I find an entirely-too-amused Anatoly leaning against the door frame.

"Someone had some fun after I left today, huh?" He waves the box under my nose. I snatch it out of his hand and try to close the door, but he wedges it open with his foot. "Sorry, but the delivery boy needs a tip."

"Here's a tip: remove your foot from my door before I chop it off."

He snorts and pushes his way into the room. I'm still standing by the door as he flops onto his side on my bed, his head propped up on his beefy arm like a gossiping girl at a sleepover. "Tell me everything."

"Or I tell you nothing and you leave."

He pouts out his lower lip. "If you keep treating me like this, I'll start thinking you don't want me around."

"I'm glad you're finally picking up all my subliminal messaging."

It's not true. Anatoly is the closest thing to a friend that I have in this house.

Unfortunately, he's also Mikhail's brother. Which is wild to think about. Anatoly's mother must have been a real fun-loving gal, because he certainly didn't get his temperament from his father.

"You and Mikhail are perfect for each other," he complains, rolling onto his back. "Neither of you want to tell me anything."

Curiosity gets the best of me and I softly close the door. "You talked to Mikhail?"

"I tried when you guys got back. He wasn't in a chatty mood."

The drive home was silent. Mikhail didn't say a word. Just like the last time we kissed, he shut down and pulled away.

The difference was, I didn't have anything to say, either.

"Has Mikhail ever been chatty?"

"No," he grumbles. "Especially not after he's been with you."

Even after my very abrasive shower, I can feel Mikhail's body against me. The way he stroked my face after he pulled me out of the road. I can hear the torment in his voice as he led me to the car.

What are we doing, Mikhail?

I have no fucking idea.

I blink and realize Anatoly is staring at me. His smirk is gone, replaced with something more pensive.

I twist away from him, opening and then closing a drawer I don't need anything out of. "I doubt his mood has anything to do with me."

"Bullshit! You two are so wrapped up in each other, it's ridiculous. Take that, for instance." He gestures to the box of emergency contraception in my hand. "You literally can't keep your hands—and other body parts—off of each other. But when I come asking, no one knows a thing. *Nope, nothing to see here. Just incontrovertible evidence of spontaneous, unprotected sex.*"

"Or maybe it's just none of your business," I snap. "How did you get this anyway? I texted Stella."

"And Stella texted me," he says casually. "She knew I was out, so she asked me to pick it up on my way home. I got some suspicious looks from the pharmacist, let me tell you."

"Stella could have at least pretended it was hers," I mumble.

"Except I know she isn't seeing anyone."

"People can have sex without being in a relationship," I argue. "You should know—you've done it hundreds of times."

"Yeah, but that's me. Stella is… different." Anatoly frowns like something is only just occurring to him. Then he shakes his head, clearing it away. "Before she even explained, I knew that little delivery was for you two lovebirds. How was it? Explosive? Magical? Like a fairytale?"

"This *little delivery* should be all the sign you need that whatever happened between Mikhail and I wasn't a fairytale moment. It wasn't a happily ever after; it was a stupid mistake. One I plan to rectify."

I tear open the box and rip through the silver pill pack.

"Would it be so bad?" Anatoly asks softly.

I said the same thing to Mikhail at the restaurant. *Would it be so bad if I loved him? If he loved me?*

Mikhail's response is still fresh in my mind. It's easy to parrot it back to Anatoly. "Letting your emotions dictate your life is the quickest way to losing control. And I have no interest in losing control."

Swallowing the pill feels like trying to swallow a rock. But I chase it with a long drink of water from the bathroom sink.

When I walk back into the bedroom, Anatoly is shaking his head. "I think it would be nice. Dante would love to have a sibling."

"Dante doesn't know what he wants," I spit. "He's a little kid. It's why I never wanted him in this world in the first place. I want him to have a choice. To be able to decide his future. Here, it's all laid out for him."

"It wasn't for Mikhail."

I frown. "What does that mean?"

"Mikhail was the second son. The spare. But he rose up and took what he wanted. Dante could do the same thing. Fuck knows you and my little brother are both stubborn enough. I'm sure that will rub off on Dante. Nothing is predetermined."

I lean against my dresser, suddenly exhausted. "If you think reminding me that the father of my child overthrew his own brother so he could become the *pakhan* is going to make me feel better, then I'd suggest never trying to make me feel better ever again."

"What I'm telling you—" Anatoly sits up, hands folded in his lap. "—is that Mikhail isn't like Trofim or my father or your father. He makes his own path. He always has. I mean, he married you, even though he—"

"Even though he what?" I press.

"Even though he could have just taken Dante away," he continues smoothly. "He chose to take care of both of you. You're safe with him."

I'm safe with him... as long as I stay under his thumb and do what he says. I'm safe with Mikhail... as long as he can control me. As long as he doesn't find out how far I was willing to go to stay away from him.

That's not safety.

That's a ticking time bomb.

"Even if that was true, it's not a good enough reason to have another baby."

The last thing I need is one more person who is counting on me to take care of them. I can try to play this game as long as I can—toe the line, do what is expected of me. But if Mikhail ever finds out what I've done, I'll be just like Trofim: a memory and a pile of ash.

32

VIVIANA

Faces float out of the darkness like steam. Clouds that form and fade away before I can reach them.

Mikhail.

Trofim.

My father.

Matteo.

I sprint away from them, running until my lungs feel like they're going to burst. Every turn I take, another face blocks my path. No matter which way I run, I can't escape.

"Viviana." A chorus of voices calls from the darkness. "Viviana."

I clap my hands over my ears, but the sound isn't coming from the room around me. It's in my head.

Then I hear Dante's voice.

"Mama?"

I open my eyes and he's standing in front of me in his favorite superhero cape. I smile and wave, but he looks right through me.

"Dante?" I kneel down and open my arms to him. "I'm right here."

He spins in a circle, eyes searching the darkness. "Mama?"

"I'm right here. Dante! I'm right—"

Strong hands grip my shoulders, dragging me back into even deeper shadow. I try to stay where I am, but there's nothing to hold onto.

"Dante!" I scream as the voices call my name. As countless hands grab onto my clothes and my skin, tearing and ripping at me.

But Dante fades into the darkness.

I spin around and ghostly pale faces float above me. Trofim sneers. Matteo is weeping blood, red and thick down his cheeks. My father scowls at me.

Then they launch themselves at me.

I scream, thrashing back and forth to get free.

Then I hear my name again. This time, the voice is a deep, soothing rumble.

"I've got you, Viviana."

Strong hands slide under my shoulder blades and lift me out of bed.

"Put me down," I mumble, still fighting weakly.

I'm so tired that I don't realize what is happening until I'm curled against a warm chest, the smell of mint and cedar wrapped around me.

I blink my eyes open. "Mikhail?"

I'm cradled in his arms, but his jaw is set and firm. He looks angry.

"Put me down," I repeat.

He gives a quick shake of his head. His arms tighten around my body.

Mikhail carries me down the hall and into his room.

His comforter is thrown back like he got up in a hurry. When he lays me down, the mattress is still warm.

I'm on Mikhail's side of the bed.

In Mikhail's room.

I'm painfully aware that the large t-shirt I'm wearing barely reaches my thighs. But that doesn't matter once I watch Mikhail walk across the room to close the door. He's wearing nothing but a pair of black briefs. His body is broad and strong. Muscles ripple with every step. The poetry that could be written about his arms alone could fill several erotic collections.

Heat burns down my body. Both because of Mikhail and his body, but also because he scooped me out of bed and brought me to his room like I was a child. Desire and embarrassment twine together until I couldn't pull them apart even if I wanted to.

Mikhail slides into bed next to me and I sit up. "I can go back to my room."

"Stay." It isn't a question or a command. It's some strange in-between space. The in-between space where Mikhail and I seem to always exist.

"Why?"

"I heard you crying in your sleep." He cushions his head on his arm and looks over at me. "I couldn't let you suffer alone."

I want to tell him that I'm fine. *I have bad dreams all the time. I don't need anyone to save me. I can save myself.*

Instead, tears burn hot and heavy down my cheeks. I have no idea where it's all coming from, but the tap is on and I can't turn it off.

Without a word, Mikhail grabs me by the waist and curls me against his body. He takes deep breaths and, slowly, my body responds. I inhale and exhale with him until my tears dry and my chest doesn't ache.

Until it's hard to tell where my body stops and his begins.

"Go to sleep, Viviana," he whispers against my neck. "I'll take care of you."

I know it's not true. Anatoly tried to convince me of the same thing and I built an argument against him.

But there is no argument in the world that could convince me not to sink into the warmth of Mikhail's body.

It's been so long since anyone took care of me. So long since there was someone I could count on. I want to count on Mikhail… even if it's only for tonight.

His arms tighten around me, and I snuggle against him.

For the first time in as long as I can remember, I feel safe. I close my eyes and drift to sleep.

33

MIKHAIL

"Is bacon made from chicken?" Dante asks as he slips his third strip from the plate at the center of the table.

Viviana plucks it out of his hand just as he tries to take a bite. "No, it comes from pigs. And you've had two strips already. Eat your fruit and then you can have some more."

He grumbles, but stabs a strawberry with his fork. "Do pigs come from chickens?"

Viviana sighs and launches into an explanation on why interspecies births aren't possible, and it's all so... normal.

I can't remember the last time I sat down at a table and had a meal. Since Viviana and Dante moved in, I've taken most meals in my office. Or I get home too late and eat leftovers at the island in the dark.

This is... different.

Especially as Dante ducks his head and tries to slyly grab another piece of bacon without Viviana noticing. She lets him get all the way to the plate and lift a strip of bacon before she rears back and swats it out of his hand.

"Stuffed!" She picks up the bacon and takes a bite. "Get that outta my house, Dante. You aren't sneaky."

He sags in disappointment, but he can't quite stop a smile from spreading across his face. Viviana ruffles his hair and pours him some more milk.

It's normal, but also bizarre. Watching them feels like watching some nature documentary. Because this is *nothing* like breakfasts in my family.

My parents weren't playing with me or gently reminding me to eat my fruits and vegetables. We weren't smiling and laughing together. I can't remember a single time my entire family sat down to share a meal.

The only reason I woke up early this morning and ordered a big breakfast is because I couldn't stay in bed with Viviana for another minute.

She was asleep next to me, her lips parted, her lashes fluttering as she dreamed. I could have stayed there next to her for hours. But I knew when she woke up and rolled over that I'd be done for. She would blink up at me, a sleepy smile on her face, and I'd want her too fucking much. More than is good for either of us.

What are we doing, Mikhail?

I have no fucking idea.

So I got up and took a cold shower, but here I am anyway.

Wanting her.

Even worse, I want whatever Viviana and Dante have. This ease that lets them love each other and coexist.

They've had five years of practice, so it makes sense that they're good at it. But it still makes me wonder if this is what things would be like if I'd known Viviana was pregnant with Dante.

Would breakfast together be the norm? Would I be the one blocking his attempts to wolf down an entire package of bacon in the morning and ignore his fruit bowl?

No.

Everything would have been different.

I never would have been that parent. We never would have been that kind of family. We can't be. I stood over Alyona and Anzhelina's graves and promised I'd never replace them. Anzhelina was so young that I barely even know what being a father was like, anyway.

Viviana's hand lands on my wrist. "Mikhail?"

I jerk away from her touch and don't miss the hurt that flashes there.

She would leave if she could. I can see it in her eyes when I look at her. If I gave her the opportunity, she'd take Dante and run. I can't forget that.

She tips her head towards our son. "Dante said your name."

Dante is looking up at me out of the corner of his eyes. He's chewing nervously on his lower lip. Viviana does the same thing when she's nervous.

"What's up?" I ask as cheerfully as I can.

He shifts in his seat. "I like Mrs. Steinman and the games she has. She taught me checkers and sometimes, I get to color with markers. But I want to go back to my school."

Viviana stiffens, but doesn't say anything.

"Mrs. Steinman is your school," I tell him. "She's your teacher now."

Dante looks from his mom to me, trying to make sense of this. "Am I ever going back to kindergarten?"

"You're in kindergarten right now."

He shakes his head, huffing in frustration. "Am I ever going back to my friends? To my normal school?"

They would both leave if they could.

I carry my plate to the sink and rinse it off. "No."

"I'm not going to see Emerson anymore? Or Gianna?" He grabs Viviana's hand and tugs on it, his voice watery. "We were supposed to have a pajama party because we learned all of our sight words. I have a book from the library and Mrs. Witt says we get in trouble if we don't take them back."

"You're not going back." It comes out more harshly than I mean it to. I take a breath. "This is your normal school now, Dante. You aren't going to see them again."

I can see him shaking his head out of the corner of my eye. "But—"

"You need to get dressed. Mrs. Steinman will be here soon. Your mom can help you."

Viviana is staring down at her plate, but her knuckles are white around her fork. It takes a significant effort to lay it down on the table and stand up. But when she does, a paper-thin smile is smeared across her face.

"Come on, bud. Let's go find some clothes to wear."

Dante starts to argue, but Viviana swipes the last strip of bacon off the plate and dangles it in front of him.

He snatches it out of her hand and trots down the hallway, happily snacking.

I'm alone for a blissful fifteen seconds before Anatoly whistles. "You're going to get it from Viv later."

"Go away, Nat."

"She looked *piiissed*." He plucks a raspberry out of the fruit bowl and plops it in his mouth. "What do you think, Raoul?"

Raoul slinks out of the back hallway, his head down. At least he has the decency to look ashamed for eavesdropping. "It wasn't great."

"He asked me a question and I told him the truth."

"When he asks if Santa Claus is real, make sure you really let him have it," Anatoly suggests. "Kids these days are too soft, anyway, with all of their childhood magic and hope."

"Fuck off. It's not the same." I shove away from the counter and head for my office.

Anatoly and Raoul fall right into step behind me. "If you want my advice," Anatoly starts, "you should—"

"I don't."

"You should take it easy on both of them."

I slam to a stop and spin around. "I'm giving them a roof over their heads and making sure Dante has the best education money can buy. I'd say that's 'taking it pretty easy.'"

"That's all nice, but it's not the same as freedom." Raoul slides his hands into his pockets, his shoulders hunched. "Living with you was better than being with my parents, but it still wasn't quite... At first, it wasn't the same. It took some getting used to."

I understand why Raoul sees similarities here. The only reason Viviana has any connection to the Novikov Bratva at all is because her father handed her to Trofim on a silver platter. But it's different. *Viviana* is different.

She isn't some consolation prize of war. She isn't a slave.

She's my wife. The mother of my child.

She's... different.

But I can't explain that now without Anatoly making kissy faces at me and I'm not in the mood.

So I nod. "Yeah. I'll keep my cool. I'll give them both time to adjust."

And I mean it.

∽

Or... I *want* to mean it.

Then, ten minutes later, Viviana throws open the door of my office. I swear I see heat rippling off of her.

"You had no right," she growls, arms crossed over her chest. She's changed into her work clothes and the buttons on her top are straining with every ragged inhale. "No. Fucking.

Right. Dante misses his friends and his life and you told him he was never going to see them again. He's heartbroken."

"He looked heartbroken," I snark. "It took twenty whole seconds and a strip of cold bacon to take his mind off of it."

"That shows how well you know him. Dante needs time to process. He's okay now, but I'll be the one holding him—*again*—while he cries—*again*—because of you—*again*."

Even Anatoly thought I was harsh with the kid, so I can own that. But the rest of it?

"Whose fault do you think it is that I don't know my own son, Viviana?" I stand up, rounding my desk slowly. "*You* kept him from me. *You're* the reason he's not prepared for the life he's going to lead."

She flicks her hair over her shoulder, one leg cocked to the side. "A life where he hides away in this mansion all day and doesn't have friends? Doesn't sound like much of a life to me!"

"Better than hiding from who he really is. It's better than running forever."

Fire burns in her eyes and I still want to pull her close.

What in the fuck is wrong with me?

"We were only running because of *you*!" She squeezes her eyes closed and rubs her fingers into her temples. "I can't do this. I can't—I want to take Dante home."

"He *is* home."

"To *my* home. *Our* home," she says, squaring her shoulders. "You can still be in his life, but there's no reason we need to live together."

"We're married."

"Legally," she points out. "In every other way, it wouldn't make any difference whether I'm here or not. It's not like you care."

Of course I don't care. Why the fuck would I care?

Why the fuck do *I care?*

"I care whether my son lives or not. You can't protect him in that shitty apartment. The doors are paper-thin and the security is nonexistent."

"I did just fine for the last five years."

"Because no one knew who you were, *Margaret!*" I stop in front of her, looking down. "Is this about Tommy?"

It takes her a second to switch gears, to understand what I'm talking about. *Who* I'm talking about.

"My neighbor? You think this is about—Jesus, Mikhail, this isn't about him. This is about me and Dante. This is about what's best for us!"

"This is about what you think is best for *you*," I sneer. "You want to hide out in that apartment and pretend to be Margaret. You want to date a boring man like Tommy and hide from what you really want."

Her eyes narrow to slits as she glares up at me. "And what do I really want, Mikhail?"

I lean towards her. Instantly, her face softens. Her full lips part. She's so responsive to me. She can't help herself.

I want to pin her against the wall and show her what she wants. I want to give it to her. Now. Later. Every day until I'm fucking dust in the ground.

Instead, I step away. "This isn't about you and me, Viviana. It's about Dante. What he needs is to learn what it takes to become *pakhan*."

"He's five!"

"Which is five more years of freedom and innocence than most heirs get."

"You said—" Her voice breaks and she swallows past a lump in her throat. "You said he could have more time."

"And you said you wouldn't try to come between me and Dante anymore," I remind her. "Moving him out of my house wouldn't exactly bring us all together, would it?"

"So you're not going to let me leave?" The words are little more than a whisper. Viviana can't even look at me. She's staring at the wall over my shoulder, her gaze far away.

I knew Viviana would leave if she could, but hearing her admit it out loud does something strange to me.

I shove the feelings aside. They don't matter.

"We're a family," I tell her, the words ringing every bit as cruel and hollow as I intended them to sound. "Families stay together."

34

MIKHAIL

Raoul and Anatoly are huddled together in the entryway. When I walk into the room, they split apart, looking guilty.

"Viviana just left," Anatoly explains. "If you wanted to catch a ride to work, you missed it."

"I'm working from home today."

And maybe every day this week. This month. However long it takes until I don't feel every inch of distance between myself and Viviana. When I stop thinking about closing that distance, maybe then I'll head back into the office.

"Does that mean we're going back to deal with the father and sons?" Raoul asks.

Anatoly perks up. "The idiots who stole from us? I wanna come!"

"You need to stay here with Dante."

"It's been so long since I killed someone. Weeks," he

complains. "Our reputation is becoming a problem. People are too afraid to cross us now."

"That's a good thing," Raoul points out.

"Not for me." Anatoly kicks his shoe petulantly against the seam between marble slabs.

"You can come next time," I tell him. "Right now, you need to stay with Dante. Viviana is a flight risk, but she won't leave without her son. I want you to keep him close."

"This is all because I'm better with kids than Raoul. Charisma is my curse," Anatoly sighs dramatically.

Raoul ignores him, focusing on me. "You think Viviana is going to make a run for it?"

I shrug like I don't care. Like it doesn't matter to me either way. "She wants to. She asked me if she and Dante could move back into her shitty apartment."

"And you said…?" Anatoly prods.

"No, obviously. She can't take my son away from me."

Anatoly rolls his eyes, looking towards Raoul. "Glad he decided to take our advice and go easy on her."

Raoul is deep in thought, which usually means he's about to say something I don't want to hear. Thankfully, my phone rings before he can. I pick it up without checking to see who is calling, grateful for the distraction.

"Hello?"

"Why am I hearing that you've been waltzing around town with some blonde bitch?" my father barks.

So much for a distraction.

"Nice to hear from you, too, Otets. How have you been?"

"I'd be better if you weren't throwing away your future for some no-name bimbo."

My hackles rise at the way he's talking about Viviana. If he knew who she was, he wouldn't be complaining. He's the one who set her up with Trofim in the first place. The Giordanos would be a "good match" for our status, in his eyes.

Even still, the way he's talking about my wife makes me want to cut out his tongue.

"It's no longer any of your business who I'm seen with."

"The only reason you have any *business* is because I built it and handed it to you."

"I took it," I remind him.

"So that means I should sit idly by and let you run it into the ground?" He pulls away from the phone to cough violently. When he comes back, his voice is hoarse. "You are thirty-five, Mikhail. It's time to think about what comes next. You need to sire a legitimate heir, which isn't going to happen if you're out sticking your dick in everything with two legs. Believe me, that's how things get complicated fast."

Anatoly can't hear what our father is saying, but I can tell by the strain in his face that he knows who I'm talking to.

"This isn't complicated," I tell him. "The woman is no one."

If my father looks into Viviana, he'll figure out who she is in an instant. He'll realize I already have an heir with the daughter of Agostino Giordano and all hell will rain down. Helen Drakos and her father won't take kindly to the insult, that's for sure.

"If she's no one, then keep her in your fucking bed," he snarls. "There are eyes everywhere, Mikhail. If this gets back to Helen, our plans could go under fast."

"*My* plans," I correct. "Unifying with the Greeks was my idea."

He sighs. "Then you should care more than anyone about seeing it through."

The line beeps in my ear as it disconnects. I curse under my breath and pocket my phone.

"I assume our dear father knows about your house guests?" asks Nat.

"Just one of them," I say. "But he doesn't know about Dante or that it's Viviana. I want it to stay that way."

Raoul frowns. "For how long? You can't keep them a secret forever."

"Until I know who killed Trofim and can make sure they aren't coming for Viviana or Dante next. That's how long."

Until I can get this ache in my chest under control.

Until looking at Viviana and not *touching her doesn't make me feel like I'm crawling out of my own skin.*

"If you want her to *want* to stay," Raoul advises, "maybe you shouldn't use her kid to blackmail her into it."

Anatoly winces in agreement. "It's not a great way to get close to her."

"Then it's a good thing I'm not trying to get close to her."

They both go unusually quiet. I feel them staring at me

without even needing to check. They don't believe a word out of my mouth.

"Viviana is here because of Dante," I explain in an unconvincing monotone. "The only reason we're married is so she doesn't end up dead. I figured you, out of all people, would understand that, Anatoly."

He flinches at the cruel, casual mention of what happened to his mother. I shouldn't have thrown it in his face, but then again, they shouldn't have backed me into a corner.

Before I can say anything else, Raoul steps between us, almost like he's shielding Anatoly from me. "You've been through hell, Mikhail. We both know that and we understand it. But treating Viviana like shit isn't going to undo the past."

"I don't know what you're talking about," I lie.

Raoul lowers his voice. "It won't bring them back. Nothing can undo the past. Believe me, I've tried."

My molars grind together. "If you're still here paying penance, you're free, Raoul. I never forced you to stay."

"Which is exactly why I have," he fires back. "My family sent me here like I might be able to make up for the ones you lost. I knew I could never take their places, but I vowed to be loyal to you and try to undo the pain my family caused yours. I'll be loyal to you until the day I die, Mikhail—but it still won't bring them back."

"Playing house with Viviana won't bring them back, either!" I roar. My words echo off the marble floor and the high ceilings. I drag a hand through my hair, instantly regretting the outburst. "Fuck."

"I'll say so," Anatoly mumbles. "This shit is heavy, brother. You don't have to carry all of it alone."

Raoul claps a hand on my shoulder. "We won't let you. I can't change the past, but I can push you towards the future you deserve."

"A quick death and a Viking's funeral?"

Nat laughs, but Raoul just shakes his head. "I can push you to open up that black heart of yours, Mikhail. No matter how much it pisses you off."

35

VIVIANA

"Mama, you hide and I'll count to sixty-seven!" Dante slaps his hands over his eyes and turns to the nearest tree.

I laugh and groan simultaneously. "I thought we were on a walk."

Hands still over his eyes, he turns to face me. "Walks are boring. I want to play hide-and-seek!"

Considering this is the first walk Dante and I have taken on a weekday while the sun is still up, I don't find it boring at all.

Mikhail didn't come into the office at all today, but he texted me at quarter to four. ***No more business today. Head home.***

Calling the mansion "home" felt like a slap in the face at first —a reminder of our shouting match this morning. Then Pyotr pulled down the drive towards the mansion and I realized… I *like* it here.

And I mean, yeah, of course I do. What kind of person is upset when they come home to a personal chef making five-star dinners and enough clean toilets for a whole football team? Mikhail lives in a kind of luxury that I didn't even have growing up. My father was don of the Giordano mafia family, but he wasn't God. Which is almost who you have to be to live the way Mikhail does.

But it's more than the luxury. It's also the ancient oaks and the sprawling lawn. The stone trail that winds through meticulously landscaped gardens. It's the vines that twine around the bars of the wrought-iron fence and the birds that flit from post to post.

It's the fact that my son greeted me at the door the moment I walked in, his arms around my legs and a smile on his face.

"Let's go for a walk!" he declared.

Five minutes later, here we are.

The guards trailing a respectable distance behind us at all times are a bit of a dark cloud on the otherwise beautiful day, but hey, nothing can be completely perfect, right?

"Mama!" Dante has pulled his hands away from his eyes and is blinking at the brightness. "You're supposed to go hide!"

"Fine, but sixty-seven is kind of a big number. What if we do fifteen?"

He shakes his head, his hair flopping over his forehead. "I can count high now. Today, I counted to sixty-seven. Mrs. Steinman said it was a big im-poo-ver-ment." He sounds the word out slowly and shakes his head. "What's that word?"

"Improvement."

He beams. "Yeah, it's a big improvement. So I'll count and you hide, okay?"

Two weeks ago, he couldn't count past fifteen. His teacher kept sending me passive-aggressive emails to work with him at home since *"he should be able to count to twenty-five by now."*

"Okay," I agree. "I'll hide."

Dante turns back to the tree and starts counting like it's a race to sixty-seven. I stand and listen as he flies right past fifteen like it's nothing. It's incredible. I want to cheer him on, but there isn't time. I jog down the path and duck down behind a bush that is way too small.

I keep expecting him to bring up our conversation at breakfast this morning. The way Mikhail snapped at him. About wanting to go back to his old school and see his old friends. But Dante seems... fine.

He's learning a lot, we have more time together, and he's safe. These are all good things... So why does it still feel wrong?

Dante pops his head over the bush. "Found you!"

"Wow. That was fast." My knees go snap, crackle, and pop as I stand up. *Getting older is no joke.*

"Because you didn't do a good job hiding. I could see your leg sticking out."

"Look around, kiddo. There aren't very many hiding options out here for me." I ruffle his hair. "I'm bigger than you are."

His forehead squishes for a second while he thinks. Then he grabs my hand and drags me towards the house. "Let's play inside!"

Dante drags me back up the hill, through the back door of the mansion, and down the hall towards the guest suites. "I'll count again, but find somewhere good to hide," he orders, eyes narrowed. "*Really* good. Not a baby spot. Actually try hard."

I hold up my hands in surrender. "Fine. I'll give it my best shot."

He starts counting and I hurry down the hallway.

The only time I've been in this wing of the house is the day Dante and I moved in. I saw it briefly during the tour, but otherwise, there hasn't been much reason for me to venture over here.

I test a few doorknobs and find them locked. Then, as Dante's counting enters the forties, I find a door that opens. I duck inside and softly pull the door closed behind me.

It's a sitting room with connected bedrooms on either side. Leave it to Mikhail to have a guest suite in his house that is nicer than any hotel I've ever stayed in.

But what really catches my attention are the *three* bouquets of red roses gathered on the coffee table. There have to be six dozen roses here, at least. But why are they sitting in some unused room in the back of the house?

There's a ribbon wrapped around one of the vases, a small card attached to it with a little heart scrawled in the corner.

Just like the one I saw in Mikhail's office the first day after his takeover of Cerberus Industries.

The day I accused him of having a wife—only for me to become his wife the very next day.

Does he have some girlfriend on the side?

Do I care?

I made it part of our arrangement out of spite, mostly. I didn't think Mikhail would agree to marry me if I told him he had to be celibate.

Maybe that's why he agreed... because he *isn't* celibate.

All of these thoughts run through my head in a matter of seconds as I turn the card over and see the loopy writing on the other side.

One rose for every hour I thought of you today.

I drop the card like it's poisoned and count the roses in the vase. Twenty-four. One for every hour.

Aside from being nauseatingly corny, my stomach twists for a very different reason. Someone out there with neat penmanship and enough money for hundreds of dollars' worth of roses is thinking about Mikhail. She's leaving him cheesy notes and he's hoarding them away in a back room.

Does he like this?

Is he sweet with her?

Does he think of her, too?

Voices in the hallway just outside the door stop my spiral in its tracks.

"I'm looking for my mama," Dante says. "We're playing hide-and-seek."

"Don't let me get in your way," Stella tells him cheerfully. "I'm just dropping something off."

If the flowers are all the way back here, Mikhail clearly doesn't want me to see them. I'm not sure what he'll do if he finds out I know about his secret admirer. So I'd love for

Stella not to see me looming over them like the jealous snoop I am.

Just as the door is opening, I dive into a tall, narrow wardrobe in the corner and close the door.

Stella walks in and I can hear Dante plodding along behind her.

"Mama is hiding really hard," he explains. "She used to hide in easy places when I was a baby, but I'm big enough to find her now."

Things shuffle around on the other side of the door. Blankets moving, Dante's footsteps heavy on the wood floor.

After no more than fifteen seconds of searching, Dante declares, "I don't see her."

Stella chuckles and the door clicks closed.

One bullet dodged.

Now, I just need to get out of this room before I discover Mikhail's secret stash of love letters from this woman wrapped up in her lingerie—*oh my God, does that really exist? I don't want to know*—and find a new place to hide.

First step: get the fuck out of this wardrobe.

The worry that I'd get caught by Stella overrode my claustrophobia for approximately thirty seconds, but now, my lungs are tight and panic is creeping in.

I reach for where the handle should be, but it's too dark to see anything. My fingers scrape against flat wood again and again.

"There has to be a handle," I whisper out loud, mostly to keep myself calm. "There has to be."

But given the fact that I've clawed my way across every inch of the inside of the wardrobe door without finding one, I'm starting to think there doesn't actually *have* to be a handle, after all.

I'm also starting to think I'm going to suffocate and die in here.

Whatever reason I had for hiding in here in the first place—I genuinely can't remember through the fog of panic—it isn't a good enough reason to die for. So I pound my fists on the door.

"Help!" It's hard to scream when my lungs are so tight, but I push through the crushing fear and yell as loud as I can. "Help me! Please!"

Dante is right outside. He'll be here to save me in just a second.

Except this house is a literal mansion. He could be ten rooms away by this point—way too far to hear me.

Maybe no one can hear me. No one is coming to save me and I'll be stuck in here. I'll die here, trapped and alone.

Tears pour down my face now. I pound on the door, screaming inconsolably. I have no idea how long it has been. Minutes? Hours?

I'm fighting for my life right now. If I don't get out of here, I'll die.

I've had this nightmare too many times to count over the years. Nightmares of being locked in a trunk, a few meager holes drilled in the lid to provide oxygen.

When I close my eyes, I can still see the men who peered

down at me through the holes, laughing as I cried for my father—for *anyone*.

Suddenly, the wardrobe door opens.

Light blinds me, but I throw myself out of the door, fists swinging.

These assholes kidnapped the wrong girl.

"What the hell—"

A large hand grabs my fist out of the air and deftly twists me around. Arms curl under my armpits and around my shoulders, pinning my arms back so I can't move.

"Let me go!" I shriek, thrashing and kicking back at the person holding me. "Let me go!"

"Holy fuck, Viv. What is happening?"

Anatoly?

I blink and, all at once, I realize… I'm in Mikhail's mansion.

I'm in a guest room.

I'm not in a warehouse trapped in a trunk. I'm not twelve years old. I'm not dying.

"Calm down." Anatoly loosens his hold on me as I go limp with relief. "It's me. You're okay."

The panicked tears shift to something else. Something soul-deep I've kept buried for a long, long time. I drop to the floor, sobbing while also trying to suck in deep lungfuls of air. I sound like a broken vacuum cleaner, heaving and coughing and weeping.

Anatoly kneels next to me, his hand firm on my back. He

doesn't say anything or do anything. He just sits with me until I can breathe again.

When I finally look over at him, his face is white. "What in the fuck was that, Viv?"

"Claustrophobia," I croak.

"No." He shakes his head. "That wasn't a normal fear. That was—I don't know what that was."

And if I have it my way, he never will.

"Where's Dante?"

There's a long pause. I know Anatoly wants to push for answers. I can see in his face that he doesn't believe me, that he's worried about me. Finally, he pushes himself to standing.

"I think he forgot about hide-and-seek when Mikhail got home." He offers me his hand and helps me to my feet. "I was supposed to come find you. Dinner is ready."

I swipe at my sticky cheeks. I am *not* ready for a formal dinner right now. I need a shower and Xanax and twelve hours of dreamless sleep.

Unfortunately, I'm at the beck and call of Mikhail Novikov.

I hold my arms out to the side. "Do I look okay?"

"No," he drawls, studying me. "You don't."

That's because I'm definitely not.

I grimace. "Gee, thanks, Anatoly. Is that how you catch all the ladies? Insulting them?"

Without waiting for a response, I shove past him for the

door, suddenly desperate to get out of this frying pan and into the fire.

36

VIVIANA

Mikhail knows.

One look at him as I entered the dining room and I could tell he knew what just happened with Anatoly. He knew I was locked in a closet. He knew I freaked out.

Now, we're thirty minutes into dinner and I'm positive.

What I'm not sure of is *how* exactly he knows. I haven't seen him touch his phone since Dante and I sat down to dinner. I also haven't seen Anatoly—or anyone else, for that matter.

And yet, Mikhail knows.

He slides my water glass towards me for the third time in half an hour. "Take a drink."

"I'm fine."

"Your voice is almost gone. Drink."

My voice is raspy and tomorrow, it will definitely be gone. But for now, I just sound like I smoke a casual four or five packs per day. Perfectly normal.

I take a sip to appease him, offering a thin-lipped smile once I'm done. "How's that?"

His eyes answer for him, trailing over my face with practiced patience. He's taking inventory. I'm sure he can see my red, puffy eyes.

Mikhail Novikov doesn't miss a thing.

Next to me, Dante grabs another breadstick and tears off a bite. "This is the best day ever."

Only a five-year-old could have an existential crisis about never seeing his friends again and then, twelve hours later, claim it's the best day ever because he gets to eat spaghetti and meatballs.

"You like it?" Mikhail asks.

"Uh-huh," Dante confirms, his mouth shoved full of garlic breadsticks. "Mama bought me this for my birthday last year. It's my favorite."

"Is it really?" Mikhail looks smug and not at all surprised. There's no way on earth he didn't realize he was ordering from mine and Dante's favorite Italian restaurant. Mostly because there's no other reason he would be eating an overly-salted, previously-frozen breadstick.

"I don't even want to know how you found out about this place," I tell him. "Though I think you should do the world a favor and set your spies on more important missions."

"I'd rather make sure you and Dante have everything you could ever want here."

Mikhail doesn't even look at me as he drops this bomb. That's what this calm affection feels like—a nuclear bomb meant to lay waste to the anger and resentment I've been harboring since the moment I opened my apartment door and found Mikhail standing on the landing.

I'm supposed to forget what happened this morning because he came home with three different types of carbs? The life I imagined for my son is worth a lot more than the two-for-one meal deal at Antonio's.

Mikhail will have to try a lot harder than that.

"A boy cannot live on cheap Italian food alone," I mutter.

As yet another sign that Mikhail is trying to make peace, he doesn't say anything. Instead, he drops another breadstick on my plate.

We circle around Dante for the rest of the night without ever talking to each other. It's surprisingly easy because Dante is proactive about filling silences. Before I can even worry that he's too absorbed in coloring to make conversation and I'll finally have to figure out something to say to Mikhail, Dante snaps his head up and asks if I'd rather swim in a pool full of ice cream or Skittles.

"Can you both put me to bed?" Dante pleads, hands folded behind the back of his skateboarding dinosaur pajamas.

Mikhail is already halfway out the door, but he backtracks and kneels down by Dante's bed without any hesitation. "Sure, kid. What book do you want to read?"

Is this everything I dreamed of for Dante? Sure.

Am I going to let it melt my heart and buckle my knees? Hopefully not.

The problem is that Mikhail is a good reader. His voice is deep, so his grumbly impression of a bear makes Dante giggle. Then, as we're leaving the room, he holds out his fist for a fist bump.

"If you want to be brave, you have to be…"

"Scared!" Dante pounds his fist with a grin.

"And when you're scared, you have to be…"

"Brave!"

They fist bump again and Mikhail ruffles his hair. "Goodnight, *malysh*."

Mikhail steps into the hall, but I linger by Dante's bedside, hoping Mikhail will be gone by the time I come out.

"I love you, bud." I kiss Dante's forehead. "If you need anything, I'm right across the hall, okay? I'm always there for you."

"And Mikhail, too? He's here for me?"

My heart tries to thaw, but I resist. "Yep. Mikhail, too."

Dante snuggles up under his blanket and I blow him a kiss before I pull the door closed.

"He was in a good mood tonight." Mikhail is leaning against the wall a few feet away, but he might as well be whispering in my ear. A shiver works down my spine and I fight hard to repress it.

"Probably because you loaded him up with spaghetti and breadsticks. It's hard to be sad when you're jacked up on garlic butter." I spin away from him, heading for my door. This conversation is over, as far as I'm concerned.

"That makes your bad mood even more impressive."

I have every intention of walking into my bedroom and locking the door, but I find myself turning to face him.

Mikhail is right behind me now, closer than I thought. I have to take a step back to avoid running into his chest.

"Where there's a controlling, lying asshole, there's a way."

"This is about this morning." It isn't a question; he already knows the answer.

"This morning. Yesterday. Last week," I list off. "This is about every single second I've spent with you since the moment we met six years ago."

"I distinctly remember you being in a *very* good mood during some of those seconds." He leans closer, the mint and cedar scent of him drawing me in even though I should be flinging myself in the other direction. His blue eyes scrape over my face. "Why were you crying?"

I blink.

Oh, yeah. This way madness lies, for sure.

I back against my door, fumbling for the doorknob. "Do you get some kind of pleasure out of emotionally confusing the people around you? Because you're losing me with the subject changes."

I finally get the door open and try to slip inside, but Mikhail wedges himself in the doorway. "Talk to me."

"I don't want to."

"I didn't ask if you wanted to," he growls, his patience slipping away.

I snort. "Which is exactly why I don't want to! You saved me from Trofim so I could get away from this world, but you didn't give me a choice when you dragged me back. Now, you're not giving me a choice in how I raise my son. So, no, I don't want to talk to you."

"I saved you from Trofim because it was a convenient pitstop on the way to taking over the Bratva."

"Right," I groan. "You never cared about me. You would have let me rot with Trofim if it hadn't been convenient for you to do otherwise. God forbid I think you cared about me for even a second. You've made all that perfectly fucking clear, Mikhail. What *isn't* clear is why you suddenly think you know what is best for my son despite having only met him two weeks ago."

"The only reason I don't know him is because—"

"Because of me," I finish. "I know! God, Mikhail, I fucking—I know, okay? I know I kept him from you and that was wrong, but it doesn't change the fact that I have five more years of experience than you in raising a kid. I know what is good for Dante."

Mikhail closes my bedroom door and looms over me, his square jaw clenched. "If you knew what was good for him, you never would have kept him from me in the first place."

"Which is why I'm not going anywhere!" I throw my arms wide, gesturing to my new bedroom. I blow out a breath, suddenly exhausted. "I can see that you're good for Dante, whether I like it or not. It's why I'm not grabbing him and fleeing into the night."

"You asked to leave."

"Exactly," I point out. "I *asked*. I could have tried to escape, but I asked you instead."

Mikhail doesn't give anything away. He's watching me, assessing every word out of my mouth. Somehow, this moment feels more exposing than any we've ever had.

"I want you in his life, Mikhail. I just… I want other people in his life, too. Friends, teachers, teammates. Dante is an extrovert. He makes friends everywhere he goes and likes playing with other kids. If we keep him locked up here, he'll grow to hate it."

Mikhail takes a deep breath. "I want him to have the best education money can buy. He wasn't getting that at his other school."

"I know. He can count to sixty-seven now." Just like that, the bubble of tension pops and I can't find the energy to stand anymore. Panic attacks always leave me exhausted. I walk backwards to the bed and sink down on the edge of the mattress.

"I want us to make choices together. When it comes to Dante, I want us to be equals." It's a longshot, I know, but I can't help but ask.

Mikhail sits next to me on the bed. The mattress sinks under his weight and I shift towards him without meaning to. Our thighs brush and electricity sizzles under my skin.

Down, girl. That is not why we're here.

Mikhail seems perfectly in control of himself, which just fucking figures. "I don't do 'equals.' I don't think I've ever seen it done before. Not in the Bratva."

"Me either. My parents weren't equals. At *all*," I admit. "Every decision my mom ever made was wrong, according to my father. He yelled at her for every little thing. Even things she couldn't control."

"Like?"

Mikhail doesn't deserve any explanations from me, but I can't stop myself. There's so much I can't tell him. But I can share this.

"Attention from other men. She was beautiful and men paid attention to her. She couldn't help it."

"You must look like her," Mikhail murmurs, almost softly enough I don't hear it.

I pretend I don't and keep going. "My father hated it and he'd scream until she was crying on the floor. I think he was worried she'd see how many options she had and leave him. I still think she would have if she hadn't died."

"How did it happen?"

"Heart attack." The rest of the story sits on the tip of my tongue. I almost swallow it down, the way I have most of my life. But this time, I let it fly. "Supposedly. If you ask me, my father poisoned her."

"And you still let him marry you off to Trofim."

I turn to him. "You know I didn't have a choice."

Our eyes meet and hold. Something passes between us that makes my heart race and my stomach flip. "I know enough about you to know you can be very persuasive. You have a way of getting what you want—a way of changing people's minds."

He has no idea exactly how far I've gone to get what I want. If I'm lucky, he never will.

"Have I changed yours?"

He turns away and drags a hand through his golden brown hair. It sticks up and he looks so much like Dante it hurts. "We can try."

"Equals?" I gasp.

He shrugs, a loose agreement. "The reason I went into your bridal suite that night is because I was tired of things being done the way they have always been done. I wanted to make changes, make this world better. Why not give this change a try?"

Because you're supposed to be a cold, heartless bastard. You're supposed to push me away and make me hate you.

My head spins and I physically need to lie down. I curl onto my side, tucking my pillow under my cheek. "Today has been too much for me. I need to sleep."

I close my eyes and when I feel Mikhail stand up, I assume he's leaving.

Then his weight shifts onto the mattress behind me.

"What are you doing?" I snap, rolling over. Exhaustion has left the building. Now, my heart is hammering against my chest.

Mikhail lies down next to me, his strong arms wrapped around a pillow. "You said you wanted to sleep."

"That doesn't explain what you're doing here."

In a blink, his arm is around my waist. He tugs me towards him, smothering me in the delicious warmth of his body. "I've heard you having nightmares every single night since you moved in," he says quietly in my hair. "It's distracting. And it can't be good for you. When's the last time you woke up rested?"

The night he carried me to his bed. The night I fell asleep with his body wrapped around mine.

My throat is sore and my muscles ache. I need a good night's sleep. That's the only reason I sigh and sag against his chest. "The way you smell should count as chemical warfare. No one could resist this."

He chuckles, a soft rumble deep in his chest. I lean in closer until I feel him in my bones. Until I'm breathing at the same pace as Mikhail, my body matching his rhythms like it's done that forever.

I settle down quickly. Within just a few minutes, my limbs are heavy and my thoughts are fluid.

When Mikhail whispers in my ear, I'm not even sure it's real. "If this is war," he breathes, his lips against my forehead, "you might be winning."

Actually, I'm positive: it's not real.

It can't be.

37

MIKHAIL

"She came out of that closet like she was fighting for her life." Anatoly shakes his head. "I've never seen anything like it. I almost checked to make sure she wasn't in there with someone."

Anatoly texted me that something happened to Viviana before we sat down to dinner last night. Then she walked into the room with puffy, bloodshot eyes. She looked like hell.

"She told you she was claustrophobic?"

"Yeah, but it was more than that. She looked legitimately freaked. She didn't even know it was me when I opened the closet door. When I looked in her eyes, she was a million miles away."

I moved Viviana into my house. I'm taking care of her and her son. She works ten feet away from my office door every single day.

And yet… I still can't protect her.

I fist my hand against my thigh. "I tried to ask her about it, but she dodged the question."

"Was that before you two fell asleep cuddling or this morning when you woke up spooned together?" Anatoly's tone is neutral, but his face is straining so hard against a smile I think it's going to crack.

I punch in the code for the conference room harder than I need to. The poor pin pad isn't the reason for the frustration clawing under my skin, but it gets the brunt of it.

"She's my wife," I remind him, as if that explains a goddamn thing.

"She sure is. And yet I don't think anyone would accuse you and Viviana of having a normal relationship."

It's definitely not normal for me. Any other time I've been in bed with a woman, it has been to fuck before I make a hasty exit. But I've slept next to Viviana twice now, no fucking involved.

It's bizarre.

And the reason why my showers have veered into icy territory the last few mornings.

Anatoly drops down into a chair and crosses his feet on the table. "In all seriousness, between all of the snuggling—"

"I thought you were being serious," I growl.

Anatoly smiles and continues. "—maybe you could figure out who fucked up your girl so bad. She was terrified. I've seen PTSD up close enough to know what it looks like. She was having a flashback."

It was bad enough listening to Trofim push Viviana around the night before their wedding. But the idea that someone actually terrorized her to the point of lasting trauma... It makes me murderous.

"I could look into it."

Anatoly and I look up at the same time to find Raoul in the doorway.

"Sneaky bastard," Anatoly murmurs.

"No, that's you." Raoul flicks him in the back of the head before turning his attention back to me. "I can look into Viviana's history—her father's, too. There's a lot we don't know about them."

"It's not a bad idea."

Especially because the more I know about Viviana's potentially traumatic past, the easier it will be to murder every single person responsible for it.

"You're right: it's not a bad idea; it's a *terrible* idea," Anatoly snaps. "Things with Viv are fragile."

I frown. "'Viv'? Since when do you call my wife by a nickname?"

"Since I got to know her the old-fashioned way," he says smugly. "By talking to her. I'd try that before you let Raoul go poking around in her history."

"I asked her what was up last night and she wouldn't answer."

"I can only imagine how hard you tried," Anatoly spits sourly. "Demanding answers from someone isn't the same as talking to them. You have to give a little to get a little."

I wrinkle my nose. "Are you telling me to fuck it out of her?"

My cock twitches at the idea. It wouldn't take much to get the rest of me on board, too.

"You two don't need any encouragement where that's concerned." Anatoly shudders. "But no, I'm suggesting you tell your wife a little bit about yourself and hope that she reciprocates. It's how normal people build lasting relationships."

"You don't know shit about a lasting relationship."

"You know a lot less than you realize," he mutters.

For a split second, I wonder if Anatoly is interested in Viviana. It would explain the nickname and why he seems to know how to connect with her.

But… no, he wouldn't. He wouldn't dare.

"Besides," I continue, "Viviana and I don't have a relationship; we have a business deal. A mutually-beneficial arrangement."

"So does that mean you want me to—" Raoul starts, but he's interrupted by a knock on the door.

The woman from the first floor front desk—J… Janie? Jackie? —opens the door, an extravagant bouquet of twenty-four roses in her arms.

"These arrived for you, Mr. Novikov," she explains. "The delivery driver was tired of coming all the way up here every day, so he left them with me."

I wave for her to place them on the table. "Thank you."

"They're beautiful." She breathes them in one last time before she leaves.

"Viv will love those," Anatoly grumbles.

The first day I brought her into my office, Viviana thought the flowers on my desk meant I was married. But Anatoly wasn't there for that.

"How do you know?"

"The closet I pulled her out of," he explains, "was in the guest room where Stella has been storing all of your many, many bouquets from Helen. Viviana looked like she wanted to kick over the coffee table on her way out of the room yesterday."

Helen's existence is an ongoing problem. Her insistence is even worse. I never wanted to marry her in the first place. The engagement was a practical matter—the easiest way to get access to the ports I wanted and make sure the Greeks were happy.

Now, she sends me two dozen roses per day as a sign of her devotion to me. Meanwhile, I'm thinking about another woman around the clock and running out of dumpster space to throw away the fucking flowers.

"What are you going to do about Helen?" Raoul asks.

I have no idea.

I do, however, have a plan for the flowers.

"Deliver those flowers to my assistant once our meeting is over, Anatoly." I can hear the board members gathering in the hallway outside. The meeting hasn't even started and I'm already anxious for it to end. "And make sure the note is visible."

Anatoly glances down at the card and sighs. "Of course. Ignore my advice and goad her into another fight. That'll help."

Probably not.

But it will almost certainly get me what I want, what I need: a reason to stay far the fuck away from Viviana Giordano.

38

VIVIANA

I stare at the flowers on the corner of my desk for ten minutes before I can't stand the sight of them anymore. Especially the card.

I can't see you soon enough. All my love.

I search every inch of the vase and bouquet without finding a name. Apparently, Mikhail's secret admirer wants to remain a secret.

Fine.

But she can remain a secret on *his* fucking desk.

The bouquet is heavy, so I have to carry it with two hands, but I still hold it away from my body. If I touch as little of the vase as possible, maybe the hollow ache in my gut will disappear. Maybe jealousy won't seep into my pores and destroy me from the inside out.

My hands are full, making knocking an impossibility, so I kick Mikhail's office door open.

"Delivery," I grumble. I plop the vase on the corner of his desk. It wobbles for a second before settling. "These came for you."

Mikhail doesn't even look up. He's typing away on his computer, far too busy with work to worry about trivial things like extraordinarily large bouquets of red roses. "Who are they from?"

That is the million-dollar question.

"You would know better than I would."

"Read the card," he demands.

"I've seen you read books to Dante. Contrary to popular belief, I know you're capable."

That earns me an arched brow. "I can do a lot of things that I pay you to do for me, Viviana." He circles a hand lazily in the air. "Go on. Read it."

I don't even reach for the card. I don't need to. I have the message memorized.

"'I can't see you soon enough. All my love.'"

"Was there a name?" he inquires innocently.

Some woman just sent him all of her love and he doesn't even blink. How often does this happen to him? How many women out there would kill to be in my position?

"No name," I grit out. "Is that all?"

Mikhail finally looks away from his computer. He leans back in his chair and folds his hands over his stomach. His jacket is draped across the back of his chair and the cuffs of his shirt are rolled around his forearms—an HR-worthy offense on its own, if you ask me. Indecent exposure.

His eyes stroke over my face—and lower. There's heat in his gaze. I saw it this morning, too, when I woke up with his erection pressed between my thighs. I tried not to touch him as I slid out of bed to take a shower, but when I looked back, Mikhail was looking at me exactly like he is now.

"Do you like it?"

I blink, momentarily stunned at the way he's reading my mind. Then his eyes flick to the bouquet.

"Flowers are flowers," I drawl. "They'll be dead in a few days."

"We'll all be dead eventually." Mikhail stands up, pacing slowly around his desk. He circles around me, his breath hot on my neck. "That doesn't mean we can't find some enjoyment in the time we have."

"Do you need anything else?" I blurt. "I have a lot of work to do."

"Your job is to do what I ask you to do. Right now, I'm asking you to tell me what you think of these flowers." He leans back against the front of his desk, his legs stretched long so I'm caged between them.

"And I told you," I snap. "They're flowers. Roses are cliché and desperate."

"I like them."

My heart drops into my stomach and any hope that I could keep my jealousy at bay evaporates.

"Of course you do! Because the woman who sent them wants to fuck you. I'm sure you *love* that." I try to turn towards the door, but Mikhail grabs my wrist and pulls me closer. I yank my hand back. "You also love the flowers because they're driving me absolutely insane and you know that, too."

His legs are warm around my hips. "I do know that."

"Is that why you won't tell me who they're from? Because you think it's fun to see me jealous?"

He grips my hip, his fingers spread around the curve of my ass. "You're sexy as hell when you're jealous."

The wind in my sails dies without even one last pitiful gust. I blink at him. "What?"

Mikhail stands up and turns me around, pinning me against the desk where he was just sitting. I can feel the residual warmth of his body in the wood. More importantly, I feel the warmth of his fingers as they slide under my skirt.

"I'm not telling you who they're from because it doesn't matter." He drops to his knees and presses a kiss to the inside of my knee. "I'm not telling you because the only name I want in your head—the only name I want on your lips—is mine."

This morning, I wondered if a knee-length skirt with a full zip down the right side was too risqué for the office. As Mikhail slides the zipper from top to bottom and lets the material puddle on the floor at my feet, I have my answer.

The skirt is positively filthy.

Mikhail spreads my thighs and drags his thumb over the soaked lace of my panties.

"Mikhail," I gasp, my head lolling back without my permission. "Someone will see. The door."

He pulls away for half a second to slam the door closed. Then his stubbled face slips between my legs, parting them so he can drag his tongue over my slit.

"Fuck." I fist my hand in his hair. "Mikhail."

"Just like that," he growls, his breath hot on my skin. "Let them know you're mine."

I don't know who the *them* he's referring to is.

The proverbial *them*?

Our poor coworkers who are within earshot of his office?

The woman who sent the flowers?

Giving Mikhail exactly what he wants doesn't give me any pleasure, but the flick of his tongue over my clit? That does the trick.

"Mikhail!" I moan a little louder. As if the woman who sent the flowers can hear me.

Mikhail grips my hips and slides me to the very edge of the desk. The only thing keeping me from slipping to the floor is his very competent mouth, sucking and tasting every inch of me.

Papers flutter to the floor and a cup of pens tips over, but I don't care. I actually think it's physically impossible to care about anything at all when Mikhail's tongue is inside of me.

"Oh my God." I tug on his hair, unsure if I'm trying to pull him away or drag him closer.

It feels so good it hurts and I lose the ability to speak. Instead, I moan. I grind myself against his mouth and squeeze my thighs around his ears. I seek and seek and seek until, with one last flick of his tongue, I *find*.

The orgasm rips through me like a bolt of lightning. My muscles contract and hold as pleasure I didn't know was possible in under sixty seconds erupts inside of me.

When I can finally move again, I grab Mikhail by the shirt and bring him to my mouth. His lips are shiny from me, and I lick him clean.

He growls as I do, a sound so animalistic I break out in goosebumps. Then he spins me around, bends me over his desk, and drives into me in one thrust.

I arch my back, taking every inch of him.

Mikhail drags his hand down my spine before he slaps my ass. "Good girl."

"Fuck you," I hiss. But the words devolve into a moan as he slides out of me slowly, making sure I feel every inch. When he slams back into me, I can't even remember why I was upset.

"This pussy is mine," he grunts, driving me further and further across the desk. I'm practically lying on my stomach, legs wrapped around his waist. "Now, everyone will know."

I reach for the edge of the desk but I hit something cold, instead. The vase is there, condensation gathering on the glass.

He wants me to be his? Fine.

But that means he is mine.

I don't even think before I push it off the desk. It shatters on the floor, water splashing onto the wall.

"Viviana." My name tears out of his throat. I feel him twitch and pour deep inside of me.

The fact that some other woman is sending him flowers, but I'm the one he's buried inside of now is enough to send me over the edge with him.

Once I can stand without falling over, I clean up as best I can, but it's not looking good.

"I walked in here looking nice. Now, my shirt is wrinkled and my hair is a mess."

"I'll fix it." Mikhail reaches over and plucks the clip out of my hair so it falls in loose waves around my shoulders. "Your hair looks better down."

My face flushes. You'd think I'd be beyond blushing by this point, but apparently not. "That's nice, but the trouble is that my hair was *up* all day. But after fifteen minutes in your office, it's suddenly down? That's going to raise some eyebrows."

Mikhail leans against his desk, legs crossed at the angles. "If you don't get out of here, you're going to raise a lot more than eyebrows."

He looks down at the front of his pants and, what do you know? Another blush.

"I have work to do," I remind him.

"Tonight, then," he says, a sultry promise in his voice. "After dinner."

"Dinner with who? Just you and me?" I ask.

"Everyone. Anatoly and Raoul, too." He swallows, and I could be mistaken, but Mikhail Novikov looks nervous. "It'll be a true family dinner."

My heart leaps as if he just invited me on the world's most romantic date night.

He might as well have.

Mikhail follows me out of his office and then leaves for the rest of the afternoon. He and Anatoly have Bratva business to attend to. It's for the best—I wouldn't trust myself not to repeat what we just did several more times today.

A few of my coworkers eye my loose hair and rumpled shirt with suspicion, but no one mentions hearing any wild moans or cries of passion coming from the area of Mikhail's office, so I take that as a good sign that we got away with it.

Hopefully.

Either way, I ride my orgasmic high all the way home.

Everyone is already in the kitchen when I get there.

"You're working your wife too hard," Anatoly proclaims, throwing his arm around my shoulder as I walk into the kitchen. "Viv is the last one home."

"Mama!" Dante throws his arms around my legs, squeezing tight. "We're having pie for dinner!"

"Chicken pot pie," Mikhail corrects, coming out of the pantry.

He has a bottle of wine tucked under his arm and a juice box in his free hand. His shirt is unbuttoned, displaying a sliver of his muscled chest.

My throat closes and there is only one thing I'm hungry for.

"Ah. That explains the new hairdo," Anatoly mumbles. He's looking from me to Mikhail and back again like all the details of our sordid morning at work are written in the air between us.

I wipe the lust off my face and take Dante's hand, letting him lead me to the set table.

"You sit here, Mama." He directs me to a chair next to the one he has claimed. Then he pulls out the chair on the other side of him. "Mikhail can sit here."

Anatoly pulls out a chair for Raoul. "Looks like no one assigned us seats."

"You can sit next to me next time, Uncle Nat," Dante assures him.

Anatoly winks at him. "Thanks, big man."

Anatoly told me things could be nice here if I would relax and try to enjoy it. Is this what he meant? Mikhail pouring wine while Raoul dishes out pot pies. Anatoly humming songs to see if Dante can guess them.

I catch Mikhail's gaze over the top of Dante's head and, for a second, I can see it: our future. A life.

Maybe this can work after all.

Then the doorbell rings.

I hear Stella walk to get it and then voices in the entryway.

Mikhail, Anatoly, and Raoul are on their feet several seconds before I recognize anything is wrong.

"Fuck," Anatoly mutters.

Mikhail turns to me. "Take Dante upstairs and don't—"

But it's too late.

Iakov Novikov steps into the dining room. He's as tall and broad as I remember, though significantly grayer. He takes in our scene. His lip curls in a sneer when his eyes land on mine.

"Am I interrupting?" he rumbles.

"It's a family dinner," Anatoly says coldly. "So… yes."

"A family dinner? How sweet. If that's the case, then you're missing someone." I assume he means himself, which would be bad enough, but then Iakov gestures to someone just out of view of the door.

A tall, thin woman with jet black hair and impossibly sharp cheekbones steps into the doorway.

The woman's eyes land on me and narrow. "I'm Helen."

She says it like I—or anyone else—should know who she is, but I don't have a clue. I'm about to look to Mikhail for guidance.

Is this woman insane? Is Dante in danger?

Before I can, Iakov fills me in with a sickening grin. "Helen is Mikhail's fiancée."

39

MIKHAIL

The room is deadly silent. Helen is wearing a tight smile over my father's shoulder, but even she can't find the words for this situation.

There's a first time for everything.

When I bothered to spend any time with her over the last five years, she usually couldn't shut up. I considered it practice for the lifetime I would spend tuning her out.

Now, I don't have a choice but to pay attention.

Dante's fork clatters against his plate before I get the chance. "What's a fee-nan-say?"

I suppress a snort. Leave it to a five-year-old to break the ice.

"Stella," I call as I slide Dante out of his chair. Stella pokes her head out from behind Helen like a meerkat popping out of her hole. She was definitely lurking there to eavesdrop. I don't even blame her. "Take Dante upstairs and put him to bed."

"But I didn't get cake!" Dante complains. "Mama promised I could have—"

"We'll take a slice upstairs with us," Stella assures him. She smooths her hand down his little back, leading him away from the fallout area. "You can eat it in bed while we read."

That gets him moving. Dante forgets about everything else, too focused on getting a corner slice to notice that his mother is currently homicidal.

But *I* notice.

Viviana is stone-faced, but there's a fire burning in her eyes. She's looking at Helen the same way she glared at the bouquet of roses on my desk today. Except now, it's Helen she wants to rip apart petal by petal.

Watching her do just that would satisfy whatever dark fantasy has my cock hardening, but I'd hate to make Stella clean up all that blood.

"Now that we're all here, let's eat." My father herds Helen towards the table.

I block their path. "First, let's talk."

Helen presses her hand to my chest. "What do you want to talk about, darling?"

"I want to talk to my father." I pluck her hand off of my chest and let it fall to her side. Helen's already angular face sharpens. She looks like she could cut glass. I step around her and look at my father as I add, "*Alone.*"

Anatoly's chair scrapes away from the table. "Helen, you can wait for Iakov in the entryway. When they're done chatting, you can both happily fuck off to—"

"Sit down," Viviana blurts. She pulls out Dante's empty chair. "Join us, Helen. I'd love to get to know Mikhail's fiancée."

She doesn't look at me. Won't. I can tell it takes physical effort on her part to keep her eyes locked on Helen instead of sliding over to me.

"Great," I announce. "While you two get to know each other, I'll speak with my father. Otets, I'll show you to my office."

My father brushes past me gruffly. "I know where the fucking office is."

Helen sits down next to Viviana, her face icy. Next to her, Anatoly is firing off silent pleas for me not to leave him alone with the two women. I've seen my brother take down half a dozen trained fighters at once, but this is the first time I've ever seen him scared.

If this shit wasn't such a nightmare, it would almost be funny.

I turn my back on my brother and follow my father to my office. The moment the door is closed, he turns on me, face red. "What kind of game are you playing, Mikhail? Do you have any idea what you're doing?"

"Before you showed up, I was having dinner."

His top lip curls in barely contained rage. "Don't be fucking cute. This marriage has been in the works for six years, but you wait until the home stretch to throw it all away. Why?"

"Circumstances changed."

That's putting it mildly.

He barks out a humorless laugh. "You're going to throw away our plan for that bitch out there and her little brat?"

"That 'brat' is my son," I growl. "Watch how you talk about him."

"Your—" He drags a hand down his face. "After growing up with Anatoly and seeing what happened to him—"

"What *you* let happen to him," I correct. "You could have stopped it."

He ignores me. "After all of that, you still fathered an illegitimate child."

"He is hardly illegitimate if we're married."

The information sits between us for a few silent seconds. My father stares at me like the disappointment I've always been to him.

The second child who talked back. The spare who never quite knew his place. The son who favored his bastard brother and overthrew the eldest.

I've never made him proud.

It's never felt quite so good.

"Helen and her father will wage war over this," he warns. "Are you ready to fight for your whore?"

I rise to my full height, looming over my father's hunched form. "I'll kill anyone who threatens my family. Anyone who insults them. Including you."

There's a lot more he wants to say, but he's wise enough to keep his mouth shut. He knows without me saying it that he has no power here. Not anymore.

I was prepared to kill him six years ago. He knows I'd do it now in a heartbeat.

Finally, he sighs. "When are you going to announce Dante as your heir? If you're ending your engagement to Helen, people will want to know why. An heir is a good excuse. If you don't do it soon, people will question his legitimacy."

If I don't announce him soon enough, they'll question his birthright. If I announce him *too* soon, they'll kill him before he can inherit.

There is no winning.

I understand more and more why Viviana wanted to avoid all of this. Life would be easier without all of the politics.

"I would never let anyone question the legitimacy of my child," I growl. "I would never let them disrespect my own flesh and blood the way you let people disrespect Anatoly. That was a choice you made, and I don't intend to make the same one."

Before my father can say anything, someone clears their throat in the doorway.

When I turn, I see Anatoly is staring at me, ignoring our father entirely. I know he heard what I said. But there is more important shit going on than his tender feelings right now.

"You should probably come back to the dining room," he mumbles. "Things are, um… heating up."

I can only imagine. "How long after we left before Viviana told Helen the news?" I ask.

Anatoly bites back a laugh. "Thirty seconds. She flashed her wedding ring and Helen spit wine across the table."

This isn't how I imagined breaking the news to either of them, but it is more efficient. Two birds, one stone.

"Handle it, Anatoly! We're busy," our father snaps. "They're two women, for fuck's sake. I'd hope you can keep them in line."

"Shows how much you know about Viviana." Anatoly smirks.

My father spins towards me, eyes wide in his patented mix of shock, disgust, and disbelief. "Viviana *Giordano*? I fucking knew I recognized her. First, you took Trofim's job—now, his wife?"

"She was never his wife," I snarl. "She never belonged to him, even when they were engaged. *She's mine.*"

He scrapes a hand down his softening jaw, laughing even though none of this is funny. "Fine. She's yours. But so is this shitstorm. I'm not responsible for the chaos headed our way —*you are.*"

My father storms out and I make no attempt to stop him. He has never done a thing for me. Why start now?

Anatoly leans in. "I wasn't kidding about getting to the dining room. The two of them might have already killed each other while I was gone."

I sigh. *No rest for the wicked.*

We emerge from the office. I hear raised voices the moment I step into the hallway.

"I don't know who you think you are," Helen hisses, "but *I* am his fiancée."

"And I'm his wife!" Viviana snaps back.

I didn't realize how nice it would be to hear her say that. To claim me.

"Just because you have that hideous ring on your finger, you think that gives you some power?" Helen snorts. "This marriage has been in the works for five years."

"And I carried his child six years ago," Viviana spits right back. "I had him well before you were in the picture."

Fucking hell. I should have introduced these two sooner.

I'm trying to decide the likelihood of getting Viviana to reenact this conversation later in the bedroom when Anatoly claps a hand on my back. "Good luck, brother."

"You're not coming in?"

He's already ducking down the hallway like he's expecting shrapnel any second. "I think you can handle this on your own."

"Coward!" I call after him.

He gives me a two-finger salute and disappears around the corner.

"I'm sure you've had a lot of men," Helen says to Viviana. "Whores usually do."

I blow out a breath and step into the mayhem.

40

VIVIANA

I'm going to kill her.

Actually, I might start with Mikhail. He's the one who decided to marry me after he'd already proposed to another woman.

I guess that explains why he never dropped to one knee and gave me a ring. He'd already been through that song and dance with Ms. Sour Puss here.

Helen Drakos has the kind of face meant for bland editorials —the sullenness of high fashion. As soon as she wears an emotion, her face twists and creases like it can't wait to be rid of it. She looks like overdried leather drenched in mismatched foundation.

"If you keep sneering like that, your face will get frozen that way," I warn her. "It's not a good look."

Her forehead crease deepens, but before she can say anything, Mikhail is standing between us.

I hate that, even now, he looks good. Rumpled and more strung-out than he was ten minutes ago, but good.

"You're two brides away from a reboot of *Sister Wives*, Mikhail. When were you going to tell me?"

"When the cameras showed up," he retorts without a beat of hesitation.

I slam my palm into his chest before I can stop myself. Of course, Iron Man doesn't even budge, so I'm forced to spin away from him and Helen, who is gawking at me over his shoulder. Seeing them side-by-side like this, I can understand why they got engaged. They look good together.

Which makes everything about this so much worse.

"I won't be here when that happens. I have no interest in whatever the hell this is. If you two want to be together, go ahead. I won't stand in your way."

I storm towards the hallway, waiting for Mikhail to hurry after me.

Wait, Viviana. Don't go.

I choose you. I love you.

But nothing happens.

His warm hand doesn't wrap around my wrist to draw me back. The rumble of his deep voice doesn't shatter the deafeningly-loud silence.

I should disappear without another word—*if he doesn't come after me, he isn't worth my time, anyway*—but I don't have quite enough self-respect for that. Instead, I stop in the doorway and face him.

Mikhail hasn't moved, but Helen has. She's standing just behind him now, her manicured claw clamped on his shoulder.

I want to snap her fingers off at the knuckle and jam them into her eyes.

"Go upstairs, Viviana," Mikhail says coolly. "I'll be up in a few minutes."

"Are you—Are you *dismissing me?*" I growl. "So you can be with *her?*"

Helen smirks and... yep, I'm going to kill her. Mikhail, too.

With the fury boiling up inside of me, I wouldn't be surprised if I could breathe fire. I'd turn them both to ash right now.

But when I open my mouth, nothing comes out. Not even when Mikhail says, "I'll come talk to you next."

"Don't fucking bother," I hiss.

Finally, I turn around and storm out.

Embarrassment and rage fuel me as I take the stairs two at a time and slam my bedroom door closed. But by the time I'm pacing the floor of my bedroom for the tenth time, it's jealousy creeping through my veins.

I'm jealous that Mikhail is downstairs with Helen right now, giving her even a second of his attention when he should be upstairs with me.

It's not fair to think a one-night stand would keep him from ever looking at another woman again, but I'm not in the mood for "fair" right now. I want Mikhail to tell me he never even thought about another woman after that night in the bridal suite. *Helen? Never heard of her.*

I want all of his thoughts to be consumed by me. I want to open up his closet and find a shrine to me plastered on his walls.

I'm tearing myself apart imagining some version of Mikhail sitting on his floor crafting a collage of my face when the man himself walks into my room, shoulders back, hands in his pockets.

I promptly lunge for the lamp next to my bed and hurl it at him.

It shatters against the wall, a good three feet away from his face.

"You missed," he says flatly.

I stomp around the bed, prepared to grab the second bedside lamp and make sure I absolutely don't miss this time. But Mikhail finally decides it's time to stop me.

He grabs my arm and jerks me back. "No more throwing lamps."

"Of course you'd say that. You're the one who deserves to have a lamp thrown at his face." I try to twist out of his hold, but his fingers are like iron around my wrist. "Let me go!"

He pulls me closer, pinning me between his body and one of the posts of my four-poster bed. "Talk to me."

He smells delicious. It's infuriating.

"I hate you."

"No, you don't."

No, I don't. But I wish I did.

"Don't tell me what I feel." I fidget, but Mikhail is like a brick wall. A warm, fragrant, well-muscled wall. "You don't get to send me up to my room like a child while you talk to your fiancée and then—"

"Ex-fiancée."

"Oh, no," I drone. "Down from two wives to zero. How sad for you."

He drags his calloused finger over my pulse point. "Your heart is racing."

I slap his hand away. "Don't touch me."

"But you like it so much," he says with a smirk.

After everything that just happened, he has the audacity to smile? To *tease* me? Even worse, my heart has the audacity to speed up. I feel like a sexually charged hummingbird. I hate him for it.

I slam my fist into his chest. I'm more likely to break my hand than hurt Mikhail, but I can't just stand here. I have to *do* something.

"You lied to me." I hit him again. "I asked you if you had a wife. The first day we met, I saw those fucking roses on your desk and I asked you if you had a wife—"

"I didn't have a wife," he explains, grunting as I continue to hit him. "I also didn't answer the question."

He dodged it. The same way he dodges everything he doesn't want to discuss.

The same way he dodges the fist I aim at his square jaw.

It's enraging to hit nothing but empty space, but I should've known he's too fast, too calm for me to land so much as a single blow on that smug face of his. Fuming, I step back and brush my hair out of my eyes. "You really think you're above reproach here? You were *engaged*. That's information you should have shared."

He arches a brow. "If you want to get into a fight about which of us has kept more important information from the other, I'll win."

He's talking about Dante, but there's more I haven't told him…

More secrets hanging over us like anvils on fraying strings.

Right now, I wouldn't mind so much if a few of them dropped. It would put me out of this misery.

"Engagement isn't legally binding. But what you and I did?" He spins my rainbow-colored ring around my finger. "It's official."

"Screw the law. What matters to me is that that woman down there was planning to marry you!"

He curls my hand up in his and pins it against his chest. I can feel his heart beating against my wrist. "Too bad for her, I'm already married."

"Under duress," I remind him, putting as much space between us as possible. Which, right now, is about six inches. "I married you under false pretenses and coercion."

"What about when you came on top of my desk today—twice? That wasn't under duress."

"Being a good fuck doesn't make you a good person."

If it did, Mikhail would be the best person in the world. Saint-like levels of goodness.

Blood thrums through me, pooling in places I wish it wouldn't. I can hear my heartbeat in my ears. Can feel it between my legs.

"I never claimed to be a good person, Viviana." His fingers slip around my hand, tracing the lines of my palm. I hate that he's being gentle with me now like he didn't just rip my heart out of my chest.

But goosebumps bloom across my skin. My mind and body are clearly not on the same wavelength.

"I remember. You said you'd be the worst possible thing for me." I stretch onto my toes, upper lip curled back in a snarl. "I think you undersold yourself."

Mikhail holds my gaze for a second. His icy blue eyes are penetrating. I'm positive he can read every confused, lust-drenched thought in my head.

Whatever he sees there, he decides to slam my wrist against the post above my head and press our bodies flush together. "Then let me amend a few things."

His lips crash against mine before I can even gasp.

41

VIVIANA

His mouth slams against mine, forcing my jaw open wider so he can taste me. But his lips are soft, tender, teasing.

Like everything with Mikhail, it's a dichotomy I don't understand.

I press closer, sliding my tongue into his mouth to try to figure it out... before I remember I hate him.

Then I clamp my teeth down on his lower lip until the metallic tang of blood fills my mouth.

He growls and rears back. When he swipes his hand over his mouth, it leaves a trail of bright red blood on his skin. I want him to curse and rage and vent, but instead, he just sighs and asks, "Do you feel better?"

"Hand me the other lamp and we'll see."

He grins, but it's devilish. Dark. His blue eyes are almost black. There's a dangerous sheen in them I've never seen before.

"There are better ways to take out your anger, Viviana." He thrusts his hips against me. His erection is hard and hot against my stomach. "Want me to show you?"

"I want you to choke while I watch."

He bands his hand around my throat. "We can take turns."

Making death sound delightful—add it to the growing list of things about Mikhail that don't make sense.

Along with why seeing him with another woman only makes me want him more.

From the moment I saw Mikhail, I was drawn to him. Sucked into his orbit. Years later, I'm still out here spinning around him like horned-up space junk. It's not fair.

"Fine. You first." I lunge for his neck, but he shifts out of the way. I catch his cheek instead, leaving four red slashes across his face.

He snatches my arm out of the air and gathers it with the other one in his grip. He arches me back, the wood of the bed frame groaning under the pressure.

"Hurting me isn't going to make you feel better, Viviana." He presses his teeth into my neck and my collarbone. Then he chases the hurt with his lips.

I hold my breath and try my best to look unaffected even while every nerve ending in my body is buzzing.

"If you want to feel better, I can help."

"Fuck you," I growl.

It's unoriginal, but it's the only thing I can think of while his breath is hot on my skin and his knee is forcing my thighs apart.

He chuckles softly. "That was the idea."

He bites the collar of my shirt and pulls. The thin material shreds off of me. There's no hiding from his watchful eyes now.

My chest is heaving, my nipples pointed and aching against the lace of my bra. Mikhail circles his tongue there, scraping his teeth against my pebbled skin.

"You're fucking gorgeous," he breathes. "And all mine."

The words send a zing of pleasure through me, but it's vestigial. Some leftover remnant of whatever I felt for him this morning.

But now? After he lied to me and sent me upstairs to my room so he could talk things out with his fiancée?

I feel nothing for him.

This means nothing.

He means nothing.

Which is why it's perfectly okay for me to take what I want. He told me not to fall in love with him when we got married.

Well, there's no chance of that happening anymore. So what's a little hate fuck in the meantime?

I tug against his hold on my wrists and find his mouth. It's a war of teeth and lips and tongues. The taste of iron blooms in my mouth. He's still bleeding.

Good.

Mikhail unzips my skirt for the second time today and palms me. Then his fist closes and he rips the lace of my panties off of my body. The fabric cuts into my hips and I cry out, but the sound is lost as he drives two fingers into my aching pussy.

"You're dripping." Mikhail bites my earlobe and I have no idea how to make sense of the pleasure and the pain of it all.

"Then get your fingers out of me and give me what I really want."

Mikhail curls his fingers inside of me until I whimper just to prove a point. Then he pulls his hand away, unzips his pants, and slams every inch of himself into me.

"Is that what you want?" he growls against my skin. His teeth drag over my neck with every word. "You want me to make you feel good?"

It feels *so* good. Which complicates everything.

"Even if it's good now," I pant, "it'll be hell later. This is the only thing you and I have ever been good at."

He drags in and out of me in slow, steady strokes. The friction makes my toes curl. My head lolls back against the wooden post.

Mikhail releases my wrists so he can grab onto me for better leverage. I claw my nails down his back and at his shoulder blades as I pull him closer.

"You know what would make me feel good? If you *sucked* at this." I moan as he fills me completely, my body spasming around him. "Maybe if this didn't feel good, I could forget about…"

He swirls his tongue over my nipple and palms my breasts. "Forget about what?"

I could forget about the future I've begun to imagine. The life we could all have—you, Dante, and me. Maybe if the sex was horrible, I'd be able to see clearly that despite whatever fantasy I have built up in my head of what a marriage to you could look like, it's just that: a fantasy. I need to let it go. You aren't right for me. You can't be. You'll never be.

Instead of saying any of that, I tear Mikhail's hand away from my chest and wrap his fingers around my throat. I stare into his icy blue eyes, challenging him.

He strokes in and out of me, his jaw flexing as he hits deeper and deeper places. "You want me to hurt you, Viviana?"

"You already have," I whisper, trying to hide the tremor in my voice. "You've ruined my life and fucked up my head. Might as well add my body to the list. How much worse could a few bruises be?"

He leaves his hand around my throat, but he doesn't tighten his fingers. He doesn't make any move to do anything except fill me again and again.

I'm stretched around him, aching and pulsing. I'll come like this if he keeps going, looking into his eyes as he pumps into me.

And that terrifying thought is enough for me to slap him across the face.

The sound echoes between us, but before I can even pull my hand away, Mikhail jerks out of me, flips me over, bends me on the end of the bed, and cracks his hand across my ass.

I yelp, but the sound is lost to another spank in the same exact place. I can feel each individual finger.

My skin is already tender and hot, but Mikhail hits me again.

It should hurt. *I want it to hurt.* And it does—but not in the way I want it to. It's a pain that demands more of the same. I find myself arching my back, seeking out his hand.

"You want me to leave bruises?" he growls, spanking me so fast that my body is rocking against the bed. The headboard is slapping against the wall, matching his steady rhythm. "I'll mark up your pretty skin, Viviana—but when you see the bruises later, you won't want to stay away from me. *You'll want more.*"

I know he's right. It's not even over yet and I want more.

More of him. More of this.

As if he can read my mind, Mikhail grips my hips and slams home in me.

"Fuck!" I fist the sheets and try to crawl away from him.

This was obviously a mistake. The more of Mikhail I get, the more I want. Falling apart around his cock isn't going to fix anything; it's going to make everything worse.

"Don't run. You asked for this," he growls, tightening an arm around my body. He hauls me against him, sliding deeper. "Now, you can't take it?"

His hand crawls up my stomach to my neck, bending me so my back is flush against his chest. Every stroke of his cock lights me up and I can't fight back another moan.

"I hate you," I pant, even as I slam my hips back to take more of him. "You're a fucking monster."

His other hand slips between my thighs, circling my soaked clit. He digs his teeth into my neck and I cry out.

"I'm *your* monster," he snarls in my ear. "And you love it."

Mikhail drives himself deep inside of me again and he's everywhere. His warmth and touch and smell are all around me and I can't resist him. My resolve splinters and then shatters.

I cry out again and again, waves of release I've never experienced before crashing over me until I can't breathe.

Mikhail groans as I clamp down around him. He throws me on the bed and digs his fingers into my hips. He thrusts into me harder and harder and harder before he finally just stays there, buried in me and roaring through his own release.

I feel his heat explode inside of me.

He stays there for a long time. When he slides out at last, I assume he's going to leave. I wait for the door to slam and for the room to go quiet.

What we just did terrifies me. Sex has never been like that with anyone—so rough… so good. Every time Mikhail and I venture into a vulnerable place like this, he pulls away.

He's going to leave me here, bruised and spent and used.

And I'm right. His footsteps recede. A door opens, then closes. The room goes quiet.

And then… the door opens again?

More footsteps, growing closer. I can barely summon the energy to look over my shoulder, but when I do, I see Mikhail come out of the bathroom with a damp washcloth. He pulls me closer to the edge of the bed and sets to work cleaning me up. He trails his gentle touch over the tender skin he spanked not even ten minutes ago. He wipes the soaked inside of my thighs, the mess he made of my pussy, dabbing away all the evidence he left behind with one careful stroke after the next.

Then he settles me under the blankets and slides in beside me, his hand finding the curve of my waist under the sheet.

"Do you feel better?" he rasps quietly, the first words either of us have spoken in several long minutes.

I see the options floating in front of me—*yes; no; maybe; better than I've ever felt in my life*—but I can't circle just one. I'm feeling everything at once. Way too much to sort through.

So I settle on the truth instead. "I hate that you're engaged to that woman. That you've been with her and—"

"I've never touched her. Marrying Helen was only ever going to be a business deal."

I frown. "That's what this is, though, isn't it? A business deal?"

What we just did doesn't feel like business. The way I want to curl against Mikhail's chest and let him hold me until the sun comes up definitely doesn't feel like business.

Mikhail must not know what to call it, either, because he doesn't say anything. He just folds his arm behind his head and stares up at the ceiling. "There are no more secrets, Viviana. I've told you everything."

There's so much I haven't told him—what happened to Matteo, how I wanted Mikhail the first time I saw him, how I *still* want him. There's even more I can't ever tell him.

Mikhail is coming clean with me and I can't promise him the same.

Maybe that's why I settle on something I *can* tell him.

"When I was twelve, I got kidnapped."

Mikhail turns to me, his brow pinched together. "What are you—"

"It was only for twelve hours. Maybe less." I chuckle humorlessly. "Barely a kidnapping in a lot of ways. But for those twelve hours... they kept me in a trunk."

Each time I blink, I'm back there. I can feel the dark pressing in, my lungs growing tight.

Mikhail's hand slides down my arm to my wrist. He draws circles there with his thumb, reminding me he's next to me. Grounding me.

After everything that just happened, that shouldn't be a comfort. But it is.

"That's why you were crying the other day," he infers. "That's what your nightmares are about."

I nod. "It was a long time ago. I should be grateful that all they did was lock me in a trunk. It could have been so much worse." I wrap my arms around myself and tug the blanket up to my chin. "Maybe if it was worse, my father would have killed them. Maybe that would have helped me find some closure—*get over it*, as my father liked to say."

"They're still alive?"

Mikhail is shocked. Of course he is. He would never let someone hurt his family and live to tell the tale. It's one of the many ways that he is a better man than my father will ever be.

"I think. Or I mean, I assume. I have no idea who they were. I should have asked, but... I wasn't in my right mind at the time. I was just grateful to be alive," I admit. "Whoever they were, my father paid them off and they let me go. It's clean as far as ransom situations go, but I still can't be in a tight space. When it's dark and the walls are closing in around me, I'm back in that trunk."

"You were only a child," Mikhail growls. "If those men had a problem with your father, they should have taken it up with your father, not you." His hand shakes with rage.

"I think you're more upset about this than my father was." I'm trying to lighten the mood, but Mikhail still looks murderous. I curl my hand over the bleeding scratches I left on his cheek. "I don't like to feel trapped—in a space or... a relationship."

He goes rigid. "You've said a lot of things tonight, Viviana. But comparing me to the men who kidnapped you is the worst of it."

"I'm not—That's not what I mean." I release a shuddery breath. "I just want you to understand how it feels for me. It's why I fought so hard to get away from this whole world. I wanted to be able to choose what happened to me and I never wanted anyone to hurt me or Dante the way I was hurt as a little girl."

Mikhail studies my face, tracing every inch of me for so long that I don't think he's going to say anything. "The only time you'll be hurt, Viviana," he says in a soft rumble, "is when you beg me for it."

For the first time since he came crashing back into my life...

I believe every word he's saying.

42

MIKHAIL

"I'm surprised you're here, brother." Anatoly is sitting behind my desk, his hands steepled in front of him in mock seriousness. "I didn't expect you to come up for air for several more hours."

"I have no idea what you're talking about." I wave him away from my desk. He hops up and I reclaim my chair.

I'd still be in Viviana's room if she hadn't fallen asleep. I can't blame her. After this morning and then tonight, she deserves the rest.

"I'm talking about what the rest of the household staff can't seem to stop talking about." Anatoly wags his brows. "The hallways in this house really carry sound. Did you know that?"

I usually try to show a bit more restraint, but it was impossible tonight. Viviana was feral. I wasn't much better.

What we did felt primal in more ways than one. After Helen's surprise appearance, it was like neither of us could settle until we'd staked our claims.

"You spend your time gossiping with the staff now?"

"Just Stella." He says her name a bit too casually. If I was Anatoly, I'd jump on that. But at least one of us has to have a little decorum. "She's thrilled for the two of you, by the way. She thinks you guys are living out a real life love story."

"It isn't love," I snap.

Stella only needs to look at the bruises already blooming on Viviana's throat and ass to know this isn't some fairytale. What kind of Prince Charming spanks the princess until she comes?

Anatoly narrows his eyes. He doesn't buy it, but I don't care. He doesn't need to buy it.

I just need it to be true.

For once in his life, Anatoly decides to keep whatever he's thinking to himself. Instead, he smirks. "What's so important it dragged you away from your woman?"

Pulling away from Viviana's naked, sleep-warm body should be counted as torture. Few things could have gotten me out of that bed.

This is one of them.

"Someone kidnapped her."

Anatoly frowns. "I'm going to assume you'd be a lot more upset right now if Viviana was missing, so kindly explain what the hell you're talking about."

"When she was little," I grit out. Even thinking about it has my blood rushing in my ears. "They locked her in a trunk. It's why she is claustrophobic."

"It's why she tried to rip my head off when I opened the closet door," Anatoly infers, the pieces coming together. "A-ha. I knew there was more there."

Raoul opens the office door and slips inside. "Sorry I'm late."

"It's okay. You just missed learning about Viviana's kidnapping."

I can tell Anatoly just wants to confuse Raoul the way I just confused him, but Raoul only nods. "When she was twelve?"

"How the fuck do you know that?" I snap.

"After we talked the other day, I looked into her past like you asked." Raoul looks from my blank face to Anatoly's, his frown deepening with every passing second. "That's what you wanted, isn't it?"

Anatoly throws up his hands. "No, man! We talked about this. Mikhail needs to get to know Viviana the old-fashioned way. No private investigators and no background checks."

Raoul shrugs. "Guess I missed that memo. I dug up some stuff."

"Like what?" I ask.

At the same time, Anatoly barks, "Don't say a word, Raoul."

"I'll remind you both that *you* work for *me*." I wave Anatoly off and turn to Raoul. "Do you know who kidnapped her?"

"No. It was a small blip in the information I found out, but I could dig deeper. I could get names if you want them."

"Oh, I fucking want them," I growl. "And I'm not going to stop until every single person responsible for hurting Viviana is dead."

"And he says it isn't love." Anatoly is mumbling and snorting under his breath.

"What was that?" I curve my hand around my ear and lean towards him. "I couldn't hear you. Speak up."

He's wise enough not to say it a second time.

"I'm wondering if you want us to keep monitoring Helen and the Greeks," he says instead. "They might try to retaliate against Viviana."

I wish they would. I'll kill them, too.

"Do both," I announce. "Any threat towards Viviana or Dante needs to be monitored."

"And the men who kidnapped her eighteen years ago qualify as a 'threat'?" Anatoly drawls, unconvinced.

"Anything causing my wife distress is a threat. The fact that those men survived to live another day bothers her. I intend to fix it."

Whatever Anatoly thinks about my motivations, his eyes glimmer with the promise of bloodshed. "What do you have in mind?"

"Their scalps could make a nice wedding gift," I muse.

"You want them dead and you want it to hurt," Raoul summarizes. "Done and done."

"When can you bring them to me?" I ask.

Raoul and Anatoly look at each other, silently communicating something. They've been working side by side for years and it shows.

Anatoly runs a nervous hand through his hair. "This kind of mission could have some blowback, brother. Especially towards Viviana. If these men found out she is involved, they could come looking for her."

"I'd like to see them fucking try."

"You might like to see it, but Viviana wouldn't." Anatoly waits for understanding to dawn.

I sigh. "You want me to get her out of here."

"Her and Dante," Raoul adds. "For their own safety."

They're right. Viviana could become a target if the men involved in her kidnapping all those years ago find out we're going after them for revenge. Since the bastards love kidnapping children so much, Dante isn't off the table, either.

"So I'll send them away while I stay here and kill those men with my bare hands."

"You'd leave Viviana and Dante in a strange new place without you, me, or Raoul with them?" Anatoly shakes his head, answering his own question.

Well, when he puts it like that...

"Fuck." I flop back in my chair. "Fine. You two handle it. But take pictures. I want there to be plenty of evidence to show Viviana. To prove that they're dead."

"Don't you worry 'bout a thing," Anatoly reassures me,

practically rubbing his hands together in glee. "You enjoy your honeymoon; Raoul and I will handle everything else."

"It's not a honeymoon; it's a distraction."

"I bet it will be very *distracting*." He hops out of his chair and heads for the door. "Oh, by the way… Nice scratch marks."

Unfortunately, he dodges just in time to miss the stapler I hurl at his head.

43

VIVIANA

No nightmares.

It's the first thought that pops in my head as I start to wake up.

The next is, *Holy fucking shit, that feels good.*

I reach between my legs and run my fingers through Mikhail's hair. His hands are hot on my thighs, spreading me wide open so he can feast on every inch of me.

"Good morning to you," I manage as he slips his tongue inside of me. "What a way to wake up."

Mikhail lifts his face to smile at me, but his thumb slides in to replace his mouth. He circles my clit and my hips jerk off the mattress.

"You were already so wet." To prove it, he plunges two fingers into me. I barely have to stretch to accommodate him. "Were you dreaming about me?"

My face flames. "Wouldn't you like to know?"

The dream wasn't concrete—no clear series of events or faces. But I felt… happy. Safe. And I knew Mikhail was there with me.

"I don't care about dreams." He kisses my stomach, my hip. "I prefer reality."

When this is my reality, I tend to agree.

Mikhail fucks me with his fingers and his tongue until I'm gripping the headboard and screaming out my release. When he crawls up my body, I reach for the erection tenting his gray pajama pants. But Mikhail pins my hand to the mattress.

"Later," he says, a dark promise in his eyes.

"Why not now *and* later? We can do both."

"Unfortunately, we're in a bit of a rush." He presses his forehead to mine, blowing out a harsh breath. "It'll have to wait until we're on the plane."

I jolt upright. "Plane? What plane?"

"My plane."

"Of course you have a plane." I roll my eyes. "I mean, why are we getting on a plane? Where are we going?"

Mikhail smiles cryptically, which might be the single most attractive thing I've ever seen. "Get dressed. You'll find out when we get there."

I have a million more questions, but I know Mikhail won't answer any of them. Strangely… I don't need him to.

Is that trust? Is this what trusting someone feels like? God knows I'm not very familiar with the concept. But this is nice.

"Okay." I slide out of bed on wobbly legs. "Do you want to get Dante ready while I shower?"

"I'll get Dante ready, but—" Mikhail snags me on the way to the bathroom, pulling my naked body against his. He palms my still-throbbing center. "Don't shower. I want you to smell like me."

His eyes are hooded. Mikhail is usually tough to read, but there's no hiding the fact that he wants me. And there's no denying that I like it.

"Okay." I stretch onto my toes and kiss him, tugging on his lower lip with my teeth. Then I turn and walk into the bathroom.

Do I swing my hips a little more than normal? It's impossible to say.

But as the bathroom door closes, I hear Mikhail curse under his breath.

I can't bite back a grin.

∽

"I want to drive the plane!" Dante runs down the center aisle towards the cockpit. "Can I steer?"

I laugh. "Probably not, bud. I think the pilot should do that."

"George would probably let you look around the cockpit once we're up in the air," Mikhail whispers in his ear. "Until then…"

Mikhail opens a secret compartment in the wooden paneling to reveal a mini fridge stuffed with juice boxes and pudding cups.

Dante forgets all about getting into the cockpit and begins stockpiling snacks and drinks in his seat like it's the end of days. To be fair, I also thought the world would end before I'd ever be on a private plane again. This time is a little different than the last, though.

"He's going to be in a sugar coma by the time we get there. Which reminds me…" I rest my chin on Mikhail's shoulder. "Where are we going?"

He wraps his arms loosely around my back. "If you're trying to catch me off-guard, you'll have to do a better job of distracting me than that."

I lean against his solid body, my stomach fluttering with a whole lot more than pre-flight jitters. "I have a few ideas."

Any "ideas" I have are forgotten as Dante throws his arms around both of our legs. "I'm so excited!" he screeches.

"He's already vibrating and he hasn't even cracked open a juice box," I mutter to Mikhail. "This is going to be a long flight."

"How long?" Dante asks. "Where are we going?"

Mikhail pats his head. "We're going on vacation. That's all you need to know."

He frowns. "What's 'vacation?'"

I cringe. Survival has been the name of the game for the last six years. There wasn't time, money, or energy for random trips. Still, it feels like a bona fide Mom Fail that my son has never heard the word "vacation" before.

"A vacation is an adventure," I explain. "A fun thing you do just because you want to."

Dante gapes at me like I just told him we're going to live in a magical treehouse and eat nothing but candy for the rest of our lives.

Then he frowns. "But we don't have any money."

If it was possible to die from humiliation, those six words would kill me stone dead.

Mikhail already knows my situation with Dante wasn't exactly lucrative before he came along. That was obvious enough, given my job as a personal assistant to a man with chronic Funyun breath and the apartment held together with tape and hope.

Still, the fact I've said that we don't have money out loud enough times for my five-year-old to repeat it now verbatim is a punch to the gut.

I'm still reeling, trying to figure out what to say, when Mikhail kneels down in front of Dante. "Do you know who owns this jet?" he asks. When Dante shakes his head, he points to himself. "I do. And the house where we live?"

"You? You own the castle?" Dante guesses.

Mikhail nods. "What about the swimming pool and the pantry full of snacks and the cars in the garage?"

"You," Dante answers a bit more confidently.

"Exactly. I own all of that and I'm sharing it with you and your mom," Mikhail explains. "All of this stuff is *ours* now."

Dante gasps. "The jet is mine?"

"That's right. Yours and mine and your mom's. We all three own it. And we all three have enough money and time to go wherever we want in the world, whenever we want."

"Disney World?" Dante blurts. "Can we go there?"

Mikhail shrugs. "Sure. It's not where we're going today, but we'll go one day."

"Where are we going today?" he asks.

I expect Mikhail not to answer. I'm actually about to warn him that if he doesn't answer, we'll be in for many hours of Dante repeating the same question ad nauseam.

But Mikhail surprises me with an actual, factual response.

"Costa Rica."

"What?" Dante and I blurt at the same time for very different reasons.

"I have a house there," Mikhail continues, as casually as if he's telling us he owns two pairs of shoes. Like it's no big deal.

"What's Costa Rica?" Dante asks.

I try to explain it to him, but I give up and hand him my phone so he can watch a travel video for Costa Rica on YouTube. That quickly transitions to him watching a movie, which ends with him slumped in his seat with drool on his shirt and a half-finished juice box clutched in his fist.

"I can't believe you're taking us to Costa Rica," I mumble for what has to be the hundredth time in an hour.

Mikhail and I moved to the back of the plane so we wouldn't wake Dante up. According to Mikhail, we have a lot of plans once we arrive, so it'll be good that he's rested.

"You didn't need to do this," I tell him.

"I don't do anything I don't want to do."

I suppress my snort. *I don't doubt that for a second.*

"So why did you *want* to do this?"

"Because I can," he says nonchalantly. "We never had a honeymoon."

"We skipped a lot of wedding traditions. No proposal, no engagement party, no rehearsal dinner, no reception—"

"No wedding night." Mikhail looks me over, the heat in his gaze setting my insides on fire.

I reach for the blanket folded under his seat with shaking hands. "Do you mind?"

He waves me on. "What's mine is yours, remember?"

I drape the blanket over both of us, snuggling in close. Then I slide my hand under the blanket and scrape my nails along the seam of his pants. "Does that make this mine, too?"

The low growl in Mikhail's throat is hard to interpret, but by the time I have his hard length in my palm and he's snarling a long string of curses under his breath, I'm pretty sure I understand perfectly.

44

VIVIANA

Vacation Mikhail is officially my favorite Mikhail.

Which is really saying something. Normal Mikhail is tough to beat. The man knows how to wear a suit. And the gruff Bratva *pakhan* who is always in control and never shows weakness revs my engine just fine.

But shirtless on a beach with his tan muscles rippling in the sunlight and saltwater curling the ends of his hair?

That's even better.

Curse the person or persons responsible for such trivial things as "public decency" and "indecent exposure" and the phrase "get a room." Because I can't look at Mikhail without wanting to lay him out, taste every inch of him, and then go back for seconds.

Mikhail is standing down by the water, his feet in the surf. He stretches one arm over his head, arching into the movement to stretch his back. Every inch of the man is perfect. Tan skin stretched over muscles I didn't think existed anywhere except medical textbooks.

I'm tucked away under an umbrella with a sunhat on, but I'm feeling suddenly flushed.

Holy hell, this is torture.

"Come play with us, Mama!" Dante waves a plastic shovel frantically in the air.

"Yeah, Mama," Mikhail echoes, amusement dancing in his eyes. "Come play."

The two of them have been working on a "sand mansion" for the last half-hour while I've been pretending to read my book. Really, the book was just a ruse. I've been peering over the top of the pages to watch Mikhail father our child… like the debauched pervert I am.

That's what most perverts are into, right? Good parenting. Wholesome values. Strong paternal role models. Sick, twisted stuff like that.

I heave myself out of my lounge chair and across the sand. Some manual labor will be a good distraction from the dirty thoughts swirling around my head.

An hour later, we put the finishing touches on the sand mansion's in-ground swimming pool just as the tide comes in.

Dante's lower lip is getting wobbly with fear, so I try to lighten the mood. "I hope they have flood insurance."

He doesn't know much about insurance and it's not a great joke anyway, so I can see the tears welling in his eyes.

Then Mikhail roars, throws Dante over his shoulder, and sprints away from the shoreline, screaming about a tsunami. Dante erupts in giggles. When Mikhail plops him in the sand, he hops up and chases Mikhail back towards the water, the ruined sandcastle already a distant memory.

Oh, yeah—Vacation Mikhail is the best.

We walk back to Mikhail's beach house—one of half a dozen different beach houses dotted around the globe, I've learned—and dinner is already on the table. It's fried pork and red beans with coconut rice on the side. Apparently, Mikhail keeps a local chef on retainer, so we've been eating nothing but the best since we arrived two days ago.

Even Dante digs right in. "This is my favorite food," he announces around a mouthful.

"You've said that about every meal since we got here," Mikhail points out with a laugh.

"Because they've all been my favorite."

"I want to move here for that alone," I whisper, jabbing a finger at Dante's almost-clean plate. "He has never eaten so well."

Neither have I. Clearly, keeping my hands off of Vacation Mikhail requires a lot of energy. I've been doing nothing but eating and relaxing since we got here, but I still end every day absolutely exhausted.

After dinner, Mikhail offers to read books to Dante. I climb into our bed wearing a skimpy baby blue nightie to wait for him. I even light a sea breeze candle next to the bed for ambience.

The next thing I know, I'm waking up to bird calls and sunlight streaming through the windows.

"Nooo!" I roll over and groan into my mountain of pillows.

My nightie is twisted around my body and I can feel some drool crusted on my lip. Not exactly the mood I was hoping to set.

"Not what I expected to hear from a woman who went to sleep early and slept in an extra hour this morning."

I peek over at Mikhail. He's sitting on the attached balcony with the doors wide open, a cup of steaming coffee in his hand, wearing a button-down shirt with the top four buttons undone. The view of his hard-as-rock torso is not doing anything to ease my annoyance with myself.

"I wasn't supposed to go to sleep early," I complain. I try and fail to smooth down my bedhead as I sit up. "I had... *plans*."

Last night, I would have dropped to my knees in front of Mikhail and let him touch the back of my throat. I was prepared to be a seductive vixen. We were going to defile every inch of this bedroom.

In the early light of morning, saying any of that feels embarrassing.

"Well, now, we have plans this morning." Mikhail throws a white robe on the end of the bed. "My masseuse is here."

"Your masseuse?"

"I make an appointment with her every time I stay here." He unbuttons his shirt and lets it fall to the floor. Then, with no warning whatsoever, he drops his shorts as well. "Since Stella will be out with Dante all morning touring my animal sanctuary, I asked for a couple's massage."

I would gawk at the fact that he has his own animal sanctuary, but I've swallowed my tongue.

Mikhail doesn't seem to notice as he pads naked to the closet, his firm ass flexing with every step. But when he pulls on his robe and turns back to me, he looks too smug to be completely innocent. "I'll meet you downstairs."

When I get downstairs, I'm wound tight. I'm sure Mikhail's masseuse is amazing, but this isn't the kind of tension a couple's massage is going to fix.

A woman I assume is the masseuse, given her clean, neutral uniform and soothing smile, is in the hallway outside of the downstairs guest room. She has a towel draped over one arm and a glass container of oil in the other.

"Good morning, Mrs. Novikov."

It's the first time I've heard my new name. I like it.

"Your husband is getting situated on the table," she tells me. "You can go on in and join him. Once you're both ready, I'll come in and—"

"Actually," I interrupt, unsure of what's going to come out of my mouth even as I'm speaking. "How much would I have to pay you to just… leave?"

She frowns. "I'm sorry?"

No, I'm *sorry. I'm so horny I've lost my mind.*

"I want to cancel the massage and I'll pay you to quietly leave. Right now."

She stares at me for a few more seconds, her expression blank. Then it hits her. I watch it happen. A blush spreads across her face and she swallows nervously, trying to hide her smile. "Would you like me to leave the oil?"

"That would be great." I sheepishly take the bottle from her.

I wait until she is out of the house and well beyond earshot before I slip into the room.

Two massage tables are set up in the center of the room. The lights are dimmed and a few candles flicker in the corners. There's a diffuser pumping some kind of essential oil into the air, but all I can smell is Mikhail. Mint and cedar.

Maybe it has something to do with how much of him is exposed. He's face-down on the table and naked except for a small towel laying over his ass. He doesn't move a muscle as I close the door.

My heart is thundering in my chest. I've been with Mikhail enough times that this shouldn't be nerve-wracking, but it absolutely is.

Every time we've had sex before, it's been almost by accident. One thing leads to another and suddenly, we're fucking.

It's a no harm, no foul situation. Completely out of my hands, more often than not.

But this is a choice I'm making. A risk I'm taking.

I try not to think too much about the deeper meaning as I drop my robe on the floor and stand next to the massage table. I pour oil into the deep ridges along his spine and spread it over his skin with trembling fingers.

Mikhail readjusts slightly, taking a deep breath. His ribs expand, his shoulders flexing. Then he settles… and I get to work.

I knead the tension out of his shoulders and his lower back with smooth circles, digging my fingers into his golden skin and bands of muscle. I have no idea if this is good for him, but it's beyond great for me.

Eventually, I shift down to his legs and work the heel of my hand up the backs of his thighs and over his calves. I've never found a man's calves attractive before, but I think I've discovered a new fetish.

Once I've finished with all the exposed parts of him, I shift to the final frontier.

Slowly, I slip the towel off of his ass.

Mikhail tenses. I know because I can see it. The muscles of his lower back pull taut and a single dimple forms in each cheek. I can't resist pressing my thumb there.

"Where is my wife?" he asks, still lying face-down.

Some possessive part of my brain lights up at that. He thinks another woman is touching his ass and he asks about *me*. One gold star for Mikhail.

I don't answer. My throat is closed tight with nerves.

So I slip my hand over his hip and curl it around to the front of him.

Before I even have a chance of touching anything, Mikhail snatches my hand away by the wrist and sits up. He's been receiving a relaxing massage for the last fifteen minutes, but there's nothing relaxed about his face now. His jaw is clenched and his eyes are narrowed. He looks like a bull ready to charge.

Then he sees me and it clears.

"Viviana." He sits up and pulls me between his legs. His eyes slip over my naked body. "You're not Paulina."

"I hope that's okay."

My breasts are heavy and aching. I can feel my heartbeat between my legs.

He pinches my pointed nipple between two fingers and presses a kiss to my jawbone. "It's more than okay."

"Good."

My hands are slick with oil and I wrap one around his quickly-hardening cock. I stroke him as I drop to my knees and then take him in my mouth. The oil tastes like mint, which makes me wonder what all Paulina uses it for. How often is this kind of thing happening for her?

"Fuck." Mikhail leans back on his hands, his legs spread to make room for me. "This is the best massage I've ever had."

I run my tongue along the underside of him, licking and stroking until his hips are bucking for more.

So I give it to him.

I slide down his shaft until my nose is pressed to his stomach. Until I can feel him twitch in my throat. Mikhail curls his fingers in the back of my hair, holding me there. "Goddamn, this mouth. Viv… this mouth."

I come up for air and take him again, soaking up every moan and muscle twitch and curse word.

I didn't realize until this very second how much I want to show Mikhail that I appreciate him. I could write a letter or buy him an edible arrangement, but we've never been good with words.

This is what we're good at.

This is how we communicate.

As I swallow him down again and again, I hope he understands what I'm saying.

Mikhail fucks my mouth, his hands firm on either side of my face. I'm fine finishing him like this. I want to give him whatever he wants. But he pulls me off of him, panting.

I stand up. "How do you want me?"

He roughly palms my breast. His eyes are black. "Careful asking a question like that, Viviana."

I bite my lower lip and repeat, "How do you want me?"

He grips my chin and pulls my lips to his for a quick kiss. "You're the masseuse. You tell me."

Butterflies flutter in my stomach, but I fight to look more confident than I feel.

I lay him on his back and crawl onto the table, stroking my fingers over his oiled-up skin. I massage his pecs and his abs, trickling my fingers over every single ridge and valley. When I follow the trail of golden hair beneath his stomach, his cock twitches.

I wrap my hand around him, making long, even strokes. "You hold a lot of tension here. I can help with that."

I straddle him backwards and slowly lower down onto him.

"You're perfect." He grabs my ass and thrusts into me, sinking in the rest of the way. "Fucking perfect."

The words pierce straight through my already-flimsy armor.

I thought I wanted to show Mikhail I appreciate everything he's done for me. I *thought* I was in lust with Vacation Mikhail and fucking him would clear my head. But I think this goes deeper than that.

Mikhail presses on my lower back and leans me forward, groaning as we find a new angle.

"I'm so fucking deep in you," he growls.

You have no idea.

I fall onto all fours and Mikhail quickly resituates and enters me from behind. He forces me down onto the massage table until my cheek is squished against the cushion. He drives into me harder and harder and I'm grateful.

When he's fucking me like this, I can't think about anything except taking him.

Then, suddenly, Mikhail slides out of me and flips me onto my back. I feel exposed in every way imaginable. Like all he has to do is look down and see the thoughts running through my head.

This isn't a business deal.

I want everything you can give.

I'm weak and pathetic and I fell for you, even though I swore I never would.

He hooks my legs over his shoulders and enters me slowly, watching my face to see how I react to every stroke.

Tears well in the backs of my eyes, but I blink them back.

I am not going to cry during sex. I am not *going to cry during sex.*

He circles his thumb around my clit. There's no rush to his movements. He is content to take his time, but I feel like I'm cooking over an open flame. If I don't get out of here, I'm going to say something stupid. I'm going to tell him I love him.

I clench every muscle I have, squeezing him. He groans, an eyebrow arching. Then he smirks. "Do it again."

I tighten around him and his mouth falls open. He tips his head back and I can see his pulse pounding in his throat.

"You're so tight." His thumb picks up pace and now the spasms are beyond my control. My pussy flutters around him.

I paw at his chest. "I'm close."

His jaw is clenched with the effort not to finish first. "Come around me, Viviana. I want to feel you. I want—"

His words are lost to a roar as my orgasm tears me wide open, taking Mikhail down with me.

But as I cry out, tears pricking the corners of my eyes, I can't help but wonder what Mikhail wants.

I can't help but wonder if it's me.

45

MIKHAIL

I can see Viviana and Dante from the balcony of my bedroom when Raoul calls. "How's the honeymoon?" he asks through the phone.

Phenomenal. Confusing. A mistake.

"Careful, my friend—you're spending too much time with Anatoly. You're starting to sound like him."

"I just wanted to sound casual in case Viviana was around." He waits. "So… is she around?"

"No. She's on a walk with Dante."

Viviana and I spent most of the night twisted in the sheets, but when I opened my eyes this morning, she was already gone. And she's stayed gone.

She and Dante went with Stella to the store to pick up some snacks, they went for a mid-morning swim, and now, they're walking hand in hand down the beach. I'd ask if she's trying to avoid me, but I'd have to be in the same room with her to do that.

And when I'm in the same room with her, I can't think straight.

I turn away from the view and walk into the bedroom. "Are you calling with an update? I can't stay on vacation for-fucking-ever."

"I'm actually surprised you've lasted this long."

"Then don't test my patience," I growl. "Have you dealt with it or not?"

Anatoly and Raoul have kept me updated with a few texts here or there, but otherwise, it's been quiet. For the first time in years, I put my phone down and took a step back from work and the Bratva. It's been nice.

That doesn't mean I'm not ready to get home and give Viviana the peace of mind she deserves.

"It's been dealt with," Raoul tells me. "You can come home."

"Perfect."

When Viviana and Dante get back from their walk, I'm waiting in the living room. Vivian's golden hair is wild from the wind and her cheeks are pink. She's shaking sand out of Dante's hair and laughing. "That's what you get for trying to tunnel across the beach like a little mole. Now, you have to take a bath."

Dante starts to groan, but then he sees me. And his face lights up.

I'm so fucked.

It's all I can think as my son throws himself at me and wraps his arms around my neck.

"Me and Mama saw a crab! It was red and walked on the sand on tiptoes like this." He balances on his toes and walks in a clumsy circle. "Mama wouldn't let me touch it."

"Because your mama is smart. That thing would have pinched your little nose off." I snap two fingers towards his nose and he claps his hands over it and shrieks.

"Bath, mister," Viviana reminds him, swatting him towards the hallway. "Then we'll have dinner."

Dante rolls his eyes, but listens to his mom. A few seconds later, the bathroom door clicks closed.

"Dinner might be in the air," I tell her.

She was heading towards the end of the couch to sit, but she stops and stares at me. "On the plane?"

I nod. "I think it's about time we headed home."

"You don't want to wait until morning?"

"Dante can sleep on the flight," I point out. "And I have some things to take care of."

She tugs her lower lip into her mouth and nods absently. I can see in her eyes that she's a million miles away.

The five feet between us right now is almost too much to handle, so I can't handle the far-off gaze on top of that. I wrap an arm around her waist and haul her against me.

Instantly, some deep, dark beast in my chest relaxes. With her sun-warmed skin against mine, I feel like I can breathe for the first time all day.

"You don't want to go?"

"No, it's not—Well, yeah," she chuckles. "Of course I don't want to go. It's gorgeous here."

"If you like the house, I'll build you one in the city."

She smirks. "Why do I think you're serious?"

Because I am.

Because I'd do almost anything you asked of me without a second thought.

God, I am so fucked.

She sighs. "It's not the house. It's… everything. It's how I feel when I'm here and all the free time we have. Plus, you're different here."

I twist a strand of her hair between my fingers. "I'm not different."

She gestures both hands to me—to *us*. To the way we're curled together on the couch, my hand in her hair, her head on my chest.

"You just seem more relaxed here." She nuzzles her cheek against my chest. I can feel her warm breath on my skin. "I like seeing this side of you."

I want to deny it, but there's no point. Things have shifted between us over the last few days. Whatever walls were up between us have been heavily damaged, if not destroyed entirely. I mean, she's stroking her thumb over my knee while I hug her to my chest. This feels more intimate than the sex.

It's probably just that we're in a little bubble here. There's no one around except for us and Stella, but she has been making herself very scarce. Here, I'm not wrapped up in the politics of the Bratva. I haven't thought about Trofim's murder in days.

Once we're back to normal life, things will go back to normal.

Maybe that's why I announce, "We'll have to take more vacations. Just the three of us."

Viviana looks up at me with a smile. "Really? You'd want to do that?"

No. Fuck no. This is a business arrangement. I'm not going to get attached. I don't have time for Viviana to be in love with me and I won't be the husband and father she wants.

There's no point getting any closer. It will just fuck everything up.

"Sure." I press my thumb under her chin and tilt her head back for a kiss. She sighs into my mouth and I feel it in my bones. In my balls.

If I don't get up now, we won't be getting up for a while.

I gently push her off and stand up. "We need to pack. I'll call the pilot and we'll leave after Dante's bath."

Viviana looks a little taken aback, but she agrees. Vacation is over.

∼

Within two hours, we're on the plane.

Dante is on one side of me. He's wearing a flannel blanket like a superhero cape around his neck, but his head is resting on my arm. He fell asleep on the car ride to the airport and didn't wake up as I carried him onto the plane.

Viviana tucks her feet up underneath and leans against my other arm. Her breath is warm and even against my shoulder. She smells like vanilla.

Would it be so bad to let them both in? I could be the father Dante needs and the husband Viviana wants. This long weekend proved that. I can be there for them.

But each time I get close to crossing the line, I imagine a life without them.

I imagine standing over yet another set of graves.

I imagine walking through my house and seeing signs of them everywhere; being reminded day in and day out that I once had everything I could ever want… and it was taken from me.

I can't do it again.

I won't.

Once the plane lands, the vacation will be over for good. This person I became, whoever the fuck he is, will be dead and gone.

Viviana readjusts, shifting closer to me and tucking her hand around my elbow. Her fingers dig in, squeezing tight.

Just a few more hours.

Then it's back to business.

46

VIVIANA

The plane touches down after midnight and everyone is exhausted.

That's what I tell myself, at least, as Mikhail wordlessly gets out of his seat and grabs our luggage. The words run on a loop in my brain as he carries a still-snoozing Dante to the car and buckles him in.

We're all exhausted beyond words, I think as the ride back to the mansion is perfectly silent.

Mikhail is sitting in the front seat next to Pyotr while I'm in the back with Dante. He's an arm's length away, but it feels so much farther. Especially after days of downright casual affection. Hands twined together under the dinner table, brushing my hair away from my face, stroking my hand down his arm.

Touching him like that felt natural.

Not anymore.

Goodbye, Vacation Mikhail and your cuddles. You shall be missed.

When we get to the mansion, Pyotr takes our luggage inside and Mikhail comes around to my side of the car. He opens my door and I think he's going to offer me his hand to help me out.

Instead, he says, "I'll take Dante up to bed. Wait for me in the living room. We need to talk."

Does anyone else hear a funeral march playing or is it just me?

"What do we need to talk about?"

"Later," is all he says. His mouth is pressed into a flat line and he won't look at me.

He won't look at me, but he wants to talk? Raging alarm bells layer in over the funeral march to create the world's worst symphony in my head.

Mikhail carries Dante into the house and I slump along slowly behind them. The first day we arrived, walking into the mansion felt like walking into my own prison cell and locking the door behind me.

Now, it feels like stepping into my own coffin.

Mikhail and I just had four of the best days I've ever had. In my entire life. I'd naively hoped we were past the hot and cold part of our relationship. That every high didn't need to come with an equal but opposite low. Apparently not.

Worst-case scenarios rip through my head on fast forward.

He isn't just going to avoid me for the next few days; he's going to kick me out of the house. Mikhail is going to annul our marriage, take custody of Dante, and boot me to the curb. He's going to sic bloodthirsty hounds on me and feed my body to vultures and make sure all my favorite TV shows get canceled—not necessarily in that order.

The house is quiet. I assume it's because everyone is asleep, but when I walk past the kitchen, I hear hushed voices.

"… didn't think you'd be back until tomorrow," Anatoly whispers.

"Me, either," Stella says. "Mr. Novikov changed our departure time. He wanted to leave as soon as possible."

Mikhail said he has business to take care of. Is it me? Am *I* the business?

"You know how he gets," Anatoly muses. "He likes to nip things in the bud as soon as possible."

"But tonight?" Stella lets out a long sigh, her voice dropping even lower. I lean towards the doorway to hear better. "Viviana is tired. He should let her sleep before he—"

"Did you forget something in the car, Miss?" Pyotr asks.

I practically jump out of my skin, yelping and stumbling into the doorway in full view of Stella and Anatoly.

The two of them are huddled over the island. When they see me, they spring away from each other.

Pyotr is standing in the entryway, smiling and completely oblivious.

"No, I didn't forget anything," I mumble before rushing down the hall to the living room.

I try to sit on the sofa, but my body is buzzing. I can't relax. What was Stella going to say? Mikhail should let me sleep before he…?

Murders me?

Breaks up with me?

Ties me up in the dungeon and tortures me?

The plausible options aren't great. What's even worse is that I'm not sure which of them is the most terrifying.

The possibility that this could have something to do with Trofim's murder isn't off the table, but I don't know how I'd ask about that without putting the idea into Mikhail's head that *I* have something to do with Trofim's murder.

When Mikhail walks into the living room, I'm a bundle of exposed nerves. My hands are shaking and my stomach twists. I feel sick.

"Thanks for waiting," he says. "It's been a long weekend and I know you're tired, but—"

"I should go to bed," I blurt. "We both should. I'm not in the right headspace to talk. We should do this in the morning."

Yes, my life crumbling around me will feel better in the morning.

He shakes his head. "No. We're doing it tonight. It's important."

My throat closes up. I seriously consider stuffing my fingers in my ears and singing *la la la* until he goes away. Would that work? I guess you never know until you try.

My fingers twitch towards my ears just as Mikhail continues. "I have a gift for you."

I freeze. "A gift?"

"It's why we went away for a few days," he explains. "I needed to get things in order here."

"I'm sorry..." I shake my head. "You're giving me a gift? Like, a present?"

"Is there another kind?"

I almost bring up the Trojan Horse and ask him if this is anything like that, but I decide not to test my luck. I thought Mikhail was going to break up with me and now, he's giving me a gift. This is a net positive, for sure. Though my anxiety hasn't seemed to have gotten that message.

"Where is it?"

He waves for me to follow him. "In the basement."

The basement? I've never been in the basement. I'm not even sure I know where the basement door is. Up until fifteen seconds ago, I would have said the mansion didn't have a basement at all.

So I have a hard time believing going into the basement is a good thing.

Still, I follow Mikhail on leaden feet. As it turns out, the reason I've never seen the basement door is because it's tucked into an alcove behind the pantry. I haven't cooked a single meal since we've lived here, so beyond grabbing Dante some fruit from the bowl on the island or sneaking a bag of Cheez-Its for myself, I've never been back here.

Mikhail pulls out a long key and unlocks the door.

The stairwell disappears into darkness, but I can see every single one of the metaphorical red flags lining every inch of the path forward.

Three days ago, my horoscope told me the path ahead was "murky." I applied it to my relationship with Mikhail and thought, *Obviously. I mean, duh. When isn't it?* But maybe I should have taken it more literally. Maybe it was trying to warn me about this exact moment.

I freeze at the top of the stairs and Mikhail reaches back for me.

"The stairwell is narrow, but it opens into a large room," he explains. "You won't be claustrophobic down here."

"I'm actually not worried about tight spaces right this second. I'm more worried about being chained up down here and left to die." I say it as a joke, but every joke has a kernel of truth. Or, in this case, a giant heaping pile of truth with a kernel of a joke.

My heart is thundering in my throat and my breaths are coming to me in shallow gulps.

"You'd have to do something pretty bad to deserve that." It's annoyingly vague and potentially suggestive.

Trofim's face flashes in my mind. Mikhail hated his brother, but if he thinks I had anything to do with Trofim's murder, would he consider that bad enough to deserve imprisonment? Would he leave me down here?

When we reach the bottom of the stairs, Mikhail releases my hand and presses his palm to my lower back. He guides me down a narrow hall and stops in front of a metal door.

"You told me the other day that things could have been easier for you if your father had killed the men who kidnapped you."

My eyes flick from Mikhail to the door and back again, trying to understand what's happening. Unless there is a surprise party behind this door—which I highly doubt is happening at one in the morning—I don't see how this is a gift for me.

"Y-yeah," I stammer. "Yeah, I said that."

"You needed closure. Someone hurt you and your family didn't do anything about it. That was wrong of them." Mikhail's eyes glow in the darkness. He looks more serious than I've ever seen him. "Family should look out for family."

He knows. Oh, God, he knows. Mikhail thinks I had something to do with Trofim's murder and now, he is going to look out for his brother, even in death. He's going to throw me in this room and... I can't even think about what he'll do.

Maybe things will be better if I confess. If I tell him right now what my father made me do... If I explain that I was pregnant and desperate and out of options, maybe he'll take mercy on me.

"Mikhail, I don't know what you—"

My admission goes stagnant on my tongue as the door swings open.

The room is bare and damp. The light is muddy and I have to blink into the darkness before I see the three men leaning against the far wall. Their hands are suspended above their heads by stainless-steel chains. And I smell blood.

The metallic tang burns my nose and I stumble back into Mikhail's chest. "What is happening? Who are they?"

Other people who have crossed Mikhail? Am I going to hang on chains next to them?

"These were the men who kidnapped you," Mikhail explains calmly. As if he's describing a painting in an art gallery instead of the contents of an active torture chamber. "They worked for a small-time drug lord and made their money targeting the children of wealthy families. They built their fortunes ransoming little kids like you back to their families. And now, they are all dead."

Adrenaline is pumping through my veins, but I can't move. Can't breathe.

"Raoul and Anatoly found them while we were gone," he explains. "I didn't want you or Dante to be in danger if they were part of a larger organization and decided to come back to finish what they started. But they were nobodies. Monsters who preyed on little kids to pay their bills. They deserved what they got."

"This is the gift," I breathe. "You... You tracked down the men who kidnapped me."

I should be horrified. I should be disgusted and repulsed. Mikhail tortured people and called it a gift. He had men killed and then presented them to me like a present.

"You and I are married, Viviana. We are family now." Mikhail turns my stiff body towards himself, his warm hand stroking down my arm. "Which is why I'm going to look out for you."

Mikhail found out something bothered me and he took care of it. I had a problem; he fixed it.

It's bizarre and bloody and horrifying... but it's him.

It's us.

I throw my arms around his neck and kiss him.

After a beat of hesitation, Mikhail hauls me against his body. He crushes his mouth to mine and carries me up the stairs to his bedroom.

47

VIVIANA

Mikhail's room is dark, but silvery moonlight streams through the open window. Shafts of it slice across the bed as he lays me back and kisses my neck.

He nibbles down my jaw and my collarbone. When clothes get in the way, we toss them off and find each other again.

It's been days of this. Days of kissing and touching and fucking until we were exhausted. But this time feels different. This isn't Vacation Mikhail. We aren't in some borrowed room with the sound of tropical bird calls and the ocean just outside the window.

This is real life—which makes it so much better.

"I can't believe you did that for me," I pant, kissing his neck and shoulders while I try to catch my breath.

Mikhail slips down my body, his stubbled face scraping over my chest and my ribs. He kisses every inch of me, swirling his tongue across my stomach and toying at my hips with his teeth. I throw my arms over my head, crying out when he jerks my panties down and drags his tongue across my slit.

Ten minutes ago, I thought the best-case scenario involved a divorce and a custody agreement. Now, I'm gripping my husband's hair and riding his face to the world's fastest orgasm.

"This can't be real," I moan, exploding on his mouth.

I'm still pulsing, desperate for something to contract around, when Mikhail presses himself to my pussy and slides in to the hilt.

"Fuck," he growls. "You're still coming."

He pumps into me, drawing out the pleasure until I think I'm going to scream. I scrape my nails through his hair and hold him to me. "I never want this to stop."

I'm talking about him being inside of me, but it's layered. I don't want the sex to end, because, well, like, *obviously*—but I also want to stay married to him. I want to live in this house with Mikhail and Dante. I want to eat meals together and talk about our days.

I want Mikhail to be the person I fall asleep next to. The first face I see when I wake up.

"I always want to touch you." He sucks my nipple into his mouth, flicking the pebbled point with his tongue. "I think about it all the fucking time."

I grab his face and pull his mouth to mine.

Our lips crash together with bruising force, but that's okay, because I need this to hurt. I need to keep our lips sealed together. If I don't, I'll tell him the truth. I'll utter the three scariest words I've ever thought, let alone said. And I can't do that.

Not when I have no idea how he'll feel about me in the morning. Not when he doesn't know the whole truth of how I escaped from my father and kept Dante hidden.

If he was willing to slaughter the men who kidnapped me eighteen years ago, there's no telling what he'd do to the person who killed his brother.

Mikhail spreads my thighs wider and splits me open. He buries himself deep inside of me and I've never been so full.

"Come for me again," he grits out through clenched teeth. He strokes his thumb over my clit. "Milk mine out of me, Viviana. Come."

My release is instantaneous. It's like my body exists to obey Mikhail. He tells me to come, I ask how hard… Well, I'm beyond the power of speech. *But I come.*

"Mikhail." I wrap my arms around him, holding myself as close as possible to him as I explode. "I'm coming. Oh, God, I'm—"

He falls on top of me, his forehead pressed to mine. His blue eyes are wide open and looking into mine as he twitches inside of me.

I curl my palm around his cheek. "I feel you."

His eyes close and the words I actually want to say sit in my throat like a rock.

I love you.

I squeeze my eyes closed to bite them back and ride the release instead, contracting around Mikhail until I'm limp and sated. Until he slides away and lies down on the bed next to me.

We stay like that for a while, quiet and spent.

Then I reach over and press my palm to the warm skin above his heart. "I can't believe you did that for me."

He huffs out a laugh. "That wasn't just for you. It was for me, too, Viviana."

"Not the sex," I chuckle softly. "What you did. The gift. I can't believe you did that."

He wipes his face clean and scowls. "It's what your father should have done two decades ago. I was just cleaning up someone else's mess."

I've never known Mikhail to be humble before. Especially not after he went to so much effort.

"You're right. My father should have done something about those men. But *you* didn't have to." I can feel his heart thudding out a steady rhythm against my hand. It's grounding. "My entire life, I existed to be used by someone else. It was always what my dad wanted. And then what Trofim wanted. For six years, I was on my own, but even then, my life revolved around staying anonymous and protecting Dante. I think… being here and not having as much to worry about made me realize how much the kidnapping still affects me."

"So I brought up old traumas?" he snorts. "You shouldn't be thanking me for that."

I blow out a breath. "No. It's just… Being here with you has been healing. I feel safe. Protected. I'd feel that way even if you hadn't killed those men."

"I guess it was a waste of time then," he mutters.

I lift myself up on my elbow and look down at him. "It wasn't. Because even though I feel safe here, I know now how far you'll go to protect me. I'm grateful for that, Mikhail. No one has ever cared about me enough to bother."

He's been staring up at the ceiling while I talk, taking my gratitude reluctantly. But suddenly Mikhail jerks off the bed.

"I killed a few assholes," he snaps. "Don't read so much into it."

The whiplash is jarring. I watch him retreat into the bathroom—retreat from me—and I can't do anything to stop it. The confession I've been holding tight for days feels pathetic now. I can't love him. *I don't.* Whatever I'm feeling is just a residual vacation high. It's exhaustion and relief that I'm not trapped in a dungeon somewhere.

I roll over and face the wall. Hot tears slip down my nose and drip onto my pillow. My shoulders shake, but I fight to keep them still.

This is why I told Mikhail the night we got married that we couldn't have sex: it complicates things. Sex makes me think I feel something for Mikhail when all I really want is meaningless orgasms.

The bathroom door opens and I catch my breath. I listen to his footsteps, some naive part of me expecting him to grab my shoulder and apologize. To roll me over, kiss me stupid, and tell me he loves me, too.

When he settles silently into bed behind me, the tears come even faster.

48

MIKHAIL

The mattress shakes as Viviana sobs silently next to me.

I want to drag her against my chest and hold her. I want to lick away her tears and fuck her slowly until she melts all over me.

Which is exactly why I wait until she is asleep before I scoop her into my arms and carry her back to her own bedroom.

When I set her down, Viviana rolls onto her side and curls her arm around her pillow. Her hair is a mess of golden curls around her shoulders. Her lips are swollen from kissing me. And her eyes are puffy from crying over me.

I can't look at that anymore without wanting to claw my heart right out of my chest, so I turn around and march out of her room. It's late, but there's no chance I'm going to sleep now. So I go down to the kitchen for a drink.

"Ah, the prodigal son. I figured you'd be down eventually." Anatoly is sitting at the island with a beer. Raoul is across from him.

I drop down into a booth and hold out my hand. A second later, one of them, I don't know which, slides a beer towards me. I take a long drink and set it down empty.

"Busy night?" Anatoly asks.

"Whatever crack you're going to make about us fucking, stuff it. I'm not in the mood."

Anatoly holds up his hands. "No cracks. Got it. We'll all be moody and solemn."

"And silent," I add.

Raoul nods. "We'll be quiet. But you don't have to be."

"Is this who I am now?" I snort. "I sit up with the two of you 'til sunrise and chat about my feelings? This isn't fucking therapy."

"Thank God for that," Anatoly retorts primly. "Some of the shit you've done would go way beyond doctor-patient privilege. They'd send your ass straight to prison."

I smirk despite myself and blow out a deep breath. "Whatever version of me Viviana thinks she knows, it's not real."

No one has ever cared about me enough to bother.

I should have shut her up the moment she opened her mouth. No good has ever come from a post-fuck conversation. It's why I usually get out of there as soon as possible. There are too many hormones and emotions swirling.

That's the only explanation for why Viviana thinks I *care* about her.

"I don't care about anyone," I spit, my inner thoughts bleeding out. "People are either useful to me or they're not. The only reason she's here is because of Dante. If it wasn't for that kid, Viviana would still be in her shitty apartment. She probably wouldn't even be my personal assistant anymore," I add. "She would have pissed me off too much and I would have fired her."

Or brought her into my office daily to bend her over my desk and teach her a hard lesson.

I take another pull of the dregs of my beer to wash the thought away before I go upstairs and do something stupid. Something worse than hearing one sob story from her childhood, tracking down the men responsible, and torturing them to death for ever hurting her.

"I didn't have those men killed because I care about her," I blurt. "I did it because there is a certain way things in this world should be done. When people mess with your family, you kill them."

"Amen," Anatoly agrees.

"It's why I'm looking into who murdered Trofim. Because he may have been a heartless bastard—"

Anatoly raises a finger. "I take offense to that usage of the term."

"—but he was blood. Family."

"Yeah," Raoul drawls, face screwed up in thought. "But you also want to make sure whoever killed him isn't going to come for Viviana and Dante, too."

"You were supposed to stay quiet." I jab a finger at him in warning. "And sure, fine, that's another reason. I told Viviana

I'd look out for her and Dante, and I will. It's what is expected of me as her husband. But I can't promise anything else. I don't want anything else."

"Well…" Anatoly starts with a wince.

But before he can finish his ill-advised sentence, little feet pad into the kitchen behind me. Dante shuffles into the kitchen, rubbing an eye with his pajama sleeve.

In a second, I'm out of my chair and kneeling in front of him. "What is it, bud? What do you need?"

"How did we get here?" He blinks around at the kitchen and Anatoly and Raoul. "We were at the beach."

"You fell asleep on the plane. You didn't wake up when I carried you to your room," I explain.

He frowns. "So the adventure is over?"

Yes. If I know what's good for me.

"We'll go on plenty of other adventures, but yeah, this one is over." I scoop him up with one arm. "Say goodnight to Uncle Nat and Uncle Raoul."

Dante gives them a sleepy grin and blows a kiss over my shoulder.

"Goodnight, little man!" Anatoly calls after him.

We're only halfway up the stairs when he lays his head on my shoulder. I sigh and pause as we reach the landing. My bedroom door is wide open and Viviana's is cracked. Dante must have gone both places looking for me.

"Why did you come all the way downstairs to find me?" I ask him. "Your mom is in her room."

"I know."

I think that's the only explanation I'm going to get until I lay him down in his bed and pull his covers over him. Then he chews on his lower lip and I see so much of Viviana in him. "Mama looked sad."

My heart squeezes. "What?"

"I went in her room and she was red and puffy. It's the way she looks when she cries."

"Does she cry a lot?"

Only when men she trusts rip her heart out and stomp on it.

He wrinkles his nose while he thinks. "Not so much as she used to. At our old house, she cried a lot. She said she didn't, but I could tell."

"Why did she cry?"

Getting information about Viviana from Dante is low, but my snooping is balanced out by the fact that Dante is five and knows nothing.

He shrugs. "I don't know. When I cry, it's because I'm hurt or because someone does something mean. But I never saw Mama get hurt. And I was never mean to her. Well... *almost* never."

"That's good. You should be nice to your mom."

One of us should be, at least.

"I am. And you are, too, right? That's why Mama likes living here so much?"

"Did she tell you that?"

"No. I can just tell."

That was before tonight. Before I muddied the waters and fucked everything up.

This thing with Viviana could've been civil and clean. We could've taken care of Dante and lived together peacefully. Instead, I listened to my dick and now, everything is a mess.

Before I can figure out what to say, there's a knock on the door. Anatoly pops his head in.

"I'm busy."

"I know." He gives Dante a tight smile before he focuses on me. "It's important. It's about the Greeks."

The grim look in his eyes tells me all I need to know.

Retaliation.

I expected it, but it still would have been nice if they'd chosen any other night aside from tonight.

"I have to get going, bud." I readjust the comforter around his shoulders. "Are you okay now?"

His brows pinch together. "Will you be safe? Will you come back?"

Nothing in the world has prepared me for this moment. For my son looking at me with worry in his eyes, afraid on my behalf.

I smooth his hair back and press a kiss to his forehead. "I'm always safe. I'll always come back."

"Good." He throws his arms around my neck. "I love you."

My chest aches. It's a physical pain, the way those three little words penetrate my heart.

"I love you, too."

It's easy to say. There's no denying it. Not the way I can with Viviana. The way I *have to.*

I kiss Dante's forehead again and slip out of the room.

Anatoly is waiting there, a gun on his hip. "They launched an attack on the lounge. The guards are dead and I'm waiting on a count of the waitresses, but it doesn't look good."

"Fuck the body count." I march past him down the hall. "It changes nothing. They attacked us. I'll kill them all."

49

VIVIANA

It takes me a few seconds to realize where I am.

Within the last twenty-four hours, I've slept in three different rooms. First, the beach house in Costa Rica. Then Mikhail's room. Now, I'm waking up in my bed.

Alone.

My head hurts from crying. My cheeks are still sticky from tears. I sit up and reach for a tissue on the nightstand, but I freeze when I see a shadow in the corner shift.

I slam back against the headboard before I realize it's Mikhail.

"You scared me."

He's sitting in an armchair in the corner, his elbows resting on his knees. He's not looking at me; his eyes are fixed on the floor.

"You can't leave," he says without glancing up.

"It's the middle of the night," I point out. "Where would I—"

"You can't leave." He looks up at me and my throat closes.

There's blood crusted over a slash on his forehead. More blood dried in the grooves around his knuckles. His hair is disheveled and there is pure hell in his eyes.

I shove the blankets away and stand next to the edge of the bed, as if whatever bloodied him up is in the room. As if I can do something about it that Mikhail hasn't already.

"What happened to you?" I breathe. "Are you—"

"No walks," he interrupts. "No work. Nothing. You cannot leave. Do you understand me?"

He sounds haunted, raspy, mournful. Wherever he's been, he still isn't out of fight mode.

"Viviana," he says, rising to his feet. His shirt is ripped and there's a dark stain on the hem of his pants. "Do you understand me? This is an *order*."

"I thought I wasn't a prisoner here," I say softly.

"If you were a prisoner, I'd be keeping you away from the world. But I'm trying to keep the world away from you." His voice cracks and he scrapes a hand over his jaw. "I can't—I can't let anything happen to you. I can't—"

"Can't *what*? What happened? Where have you been?" I reach for his hand. My fingers barely brush his wrist before he spins away from me and paces across the floor.

"I can't focus on keeping my men alive if I'm worried about one woman doing something stupid and getting herself killed."

The words are ice-cold. *Don't read so much into it.* He isn't protecting me because he cares; he's protecting me because my death would be a distraction.

"I've managed just fine without you," I snap. "If I'm such a distraction, why don't you just forget about me and focus on your job?"

"I can't!" he roars.

Between one blink and the next, Mikhail is looming over me. His chest is heaving and his jaw is set. There's something wild in his eyes I've never seen before.

"If I could forget about you, I would have done it by now," he hisses. "I would have done it before I broke into your bridal suite that night. I would have forgotten about you the moment I saw you at your engagement party to my fucking brother."

I can't breathe. Can't move. If I do, I'll break this moment. This glimpse into Mikhail's head will shutter closed forever.

"I never should have looked at you." He says it softly like he's talking to himself and I'm not here. "I hadn't looked at anyone for three years. Why should you have been any different?"

If he wants me to answer, he's out of luck. My throat is closed tight. I couldn't find the words right now even if I wanted to.

He drags a blood-crusted knuckle across my cheek. "You smiled at me. You were the first person in fucking years to do that. Everyone else was too afraid—afraid of me, afraid they'd say the wrong thing and set me off. But you just smiled and introduced yourself."

I remember. *I'm your new sister.*

I had no idea what I was doing when I walked up to the handsome loner in the corner. Truth be told, I still have no idea what I'm doing.

Mikhail brushes his finger over my bottom lip. I can taste blood.

"Whose blood is this?" I ask softly. "Are you okay?"

Maybe he's talking like this because he's hurt and confused.

Even if that's the case, though, he ignores my question.

"When I looked at you, you smiled, and… I wanted you." Mikhail drops his hand. "That's why I couldn't let you marry my brother. Not because I wanted to fuck you, but because he didn't deserve you. If you married him, you wouldn't have survived it. You would have ended up like Alyona, and I didn't want to watch it happen again."

Alyona.

The name sparks in some deep, forgotten part of my brain. I heard it in passing a few times. Trofim and his father talking to each other, complaining about "Alyona and the baby" and how they "fucked him up."

I didn't know what or who they were talking about. Asking Trofim questions never got me anywhere I wanted to be, so I stayed quiet.

But with Mikhail…

"Who was she?" I whisper.

"My first wife."

Out of all the things Mikhail could have said, that answer didn't even register as an option.

My chest hitches, but I try not to make a noise. Mikhail was *married* before. To someone else. I don't have any right to be jealous, but I am.

Did she leave him and break his heart? Is that why he's so closed off with me? Because his true love is running around out there without him?

Mikhail sighs and I can see the exhaustion written all over his blood-stained face. Maybe it's the only reason he's saying any of this. He's too tired to realize all of his walls are down. I don't want to make a noise and remind him.

"We got married young. I thought I loved her, but I don't know anymore. I loved her as much as I could at the time," he amends. "I was young and stupid. I thought I could take care of them."

"'Them'?" I ask before I can stop myself.

Alyona and the baby. I close my eyes, half-wishing Mikhail would refuse to answer. I don't think I want to hear this.

"My daughter. Anzhelina."

He has another kid. Mikhail has another wife and another child. I'm just one in a long line.

Alyona. Helen. Me.

"She was only three months old." His voice catches and every thought in my head disappears.

"'Was'?" I rasp, echoing yet another word like some dumb parrot. "What happened to her?"

"They killed her," he croaks, eyes closed. A single tear carves through the smear of blood on his cheek. "Alyona wanted me to stay with her and Anzhelina. The fight with the Colombians amounted to no more than a turf war and she didn't like how often my father sent me to the front lines. She thought I deserved some level of protection as the *pakhan*'s son. Like Trofim. But I wasn't Trofim; I was just another soldier in my father's eyes. So when one of our warehouses was attacked, he sent me to lead a group of men and take it back. But it was a distraction. The real target was the inner circle. The family. And since they couldn't get to my father or Trofim… they went after *my* family."

He's hurling the information at me so fast I can't process all of it, but I understand what's important.

Mikhail had a family… and he lost them.

The room spins, but I fight to stay standing. If Mikhail is still standing after everything he lost, it's the least I can do. Be here to support him.

"Mikhail, I—"

"All the men had been pulled to the main house—this house —and there was only one security guard at the gate to my house. He didn't stand a chance. Alyona took Anzhelina into the safe room, but they pried it open. They dragged them out and—" He swallows hard. "I had the house torn down and I kept the caskets closed at their funerals."

Silent tears pour down my cheeks, but I force back a sob and reach for his hand. "Mikhail, I'm so sorry. I had no idea. I would have…"

What would I have done? Would I have let Mikhail raise Dante to make up for the child he'd already lost? If I'd known his daughter had been stolen from him, would I have still kept Dante a secret?

I don't know. So I don't finish the sentence.

Turns out, I don't need to.

Mikhail rips his hand away from me. When he looks at me now, I know he's seeing me. Wherever he went to dig up that story, he's back now. So are his walls.

"I stood over their graves and I swore I'd never let myself be that weak again. That I would never let anyone bring me that low. It's why I proposed to Helen. I was going to marry her to solidify my alliance with the Greeks. Then…" He looks at me pointedly.

He found me.

We got married.

We fell in—

"I found out about Dante," he finishes sharply, slashing through my naiveté. "I have the power and position to keep you and Dante safe, but I won't let myself be distracted with a family or childish notions of love. You two will be safe here. That's all I can promise."

Hot and cold. Up and down. I've cycled through every possible human emotion since being startled awake five minutes ago and I can't stop the tears from pouring down my face.

"It doesn't have to be like this," I whisper. I hate that I'm begging. I don't know why I even bother. I know it won't do any good. "We could be happy, Mikhail. You and me and Dante… we could—"

"Stay inside and stay out of my way. I have enough to worry about."

He turns and leaves without even a glance back.

My knees wobble. Everything in me wants to collapse into a heap on the floor and sob, but I can't. Not when I have Dante to think about.

I need to figure out what is going on.

The hallway is empty. I don't know where Mikhail went, but I take the stairs down to the first floor. All I can think about is getting to the front door.

I'm crossing the entryway when I hear footsteps behind me.

"Everything is okay, Viv," Anatoly says in a way that makes it sound like everything is absolutely not okay and he knows it as well as I do.

I ignore him and reach for the handle. It holds fast and the wooden door thuds against the frame. I instinctively reach to turn the bolt, but it isn't there. Instead, there's a keyhole.

"He just wants to keep the two of you safe," Anatoly continues. "He's doing this to—"

"He changed the locks." I run my fingers over the smooth metal. Then I spin around, facing my brother-in-law. "He changed the fucking locks, Nat."

Anatoly winces. "It's not safe for you or Dante right now."

My chest feels tight. I focus on filling my lungs with air and blowing it out as I walk to the window.

Part of me expects to find bars installed over the glass.

Somehow, the reality is worse.

Armed guards stand on the porch. I can see two men just outside the front door and two more stationed at the corner of the house. I don't need to run to the sliding doors out to the patio to know there are more guards there.

We're surrounded.

My breathing picks up. I inhale and exhale so fast that I can't tell the difference between them anymore. My lungs burn from the effort of working so hard.

"Viv, it's okay." Anatoly lays a hand on my back. "This is temporary. Mikhail wants to take every precaution. He wants to keep you safe."

"This isn't about me," I rasp before a sob steals my ability to speak.

He doesn't want to worry about two more funerals.

He just doesn't want to be distracted.

Tears soak the collar of my pajama shirt and I don't bother wiping them away. Finally, I drop to my knees the way I wanted to in my bedroom. Why not? It's not like there's anywhere else to go but down.

I look around at the huge entryway and the high ceilings, but I might as well be back in that trunk. I can feel the walls closing in. Early morning sunlight streams through the windows, but my vision is going dark.

"Viviana!"

Anatoly's voice is far away. I can barely hear him over my wracking sobs. I press my forehead to the cool tile floor. My heart is racing and my lungs are closed in a tight fist.

"I'm right here, Viv." Anatoly pats my back and tries to lift me up. "It's okay. I'm right here."

I know he is, but it doesn't matter.

The problem is that *he* isn't.

The only person I want to be here with me is the same person who trapped me here.

So I squeeze my eyes closed and let the darkness wash over me.

50

MIKHAIL

Raoul is standing on the opposite side of the lobby. He's wearing a tuxedo, but anyone paying close enough attention would know he doesn't belong here. He's too rigid, his dark eyes scanning the theater-goers constantly for possible threats, for any sign that our plan has been found out and we should retreat.

But there's no chance of a retreat tonight. I'd rather go down in a hail of enemy gunfire than spend another minute in the mansion.

I haven't seen Viviana since early this morning, but I spent every single moment all day aware of exactly how far away from me she was. I could practically count how many steps it would take to go to her. How many seconds it would take for me to strip her down and do what we do best.

But I know as soon as I empty my frustration inside of her, we'll be at the same fucking impasse.

She'll still be a distraction I can't afford.

And I'll hate myself for wanting her anyway.

Two chimes ring through the theater's sound system, signaling the end of intermission. Everyone shuffles to the two sets of double doors that lead to the main theater.

I look at Raoul and he nods. We follow the crowd towards the doors, but break away at the last second for a hallway that leads to the private boxes.

"There's still time to change the plan," Raoul mutters under his breath. "One call and someone else can pull the trigger."

He's been watching me closely all day. Raoul has a way of knowing when I'm at a tipping point. He's worried I'm about to go off the edge.

He should be. Hell, maybe I already have.

I shrug. "Me, someone else, it's all the same. What does it matter?"

If Anatoly were here, he'd say it matters a hell of a fucking lot. He is pissed Raoul and I are doing this without him—but Viviana likes Anatoly. They have a bond. I want him there with her right now.

"It matters because you have more… responsibilities than you used to."

He's talking about the Bratva, sure. But I know what Raoul is actually thinking of. *Who* he is thinking of.

Dante.

Viviana.

What happens to them if I die tonight?

I shake my head. "This is my mess. I'm going to be the one to clean it up."

He sighs. "Could you see if Helen was there?"

I sat through the first act of the show, but I don't have a clue what it's about. My attention was on the private box closest to the stage.

The box we're walking to now.

"No. But I identified our target."

Even from the back of the theater, I recognized the man in the security footage from the attack on the lounge last night. Yanis Drakos is Helen's uncle and the head of security for his brother. But last night, he led the charge on a business that has been in Novikov control for decades. He murdered my guards and innocent waitresses.

He started a war.

So if Helen is stupid enough to be sitting next to him after what he has done on her behalf, she deserves whatever is coming.

If Raoul disagrees with my call, he doesn't mention it. Instead, he checks his weapon as we mount the stairs and then sends a text to one of the men waiting in the audience below.

"The security working the exits were disposed of just before intermission. Our guys have replaced them now. We have fifteen minutes before the drugs wear off and the guards wake up. They're tied up, but the noise—"

"So we kill him before fifteen minutes is up."

If things go my way, this won't take more than one or two.

Raoul nods wearily. "You make the kill and we move out before they lock the theater down. The police are on our side tonight. They've agreed to give us a small window to flee. We could shoot our way out in a pinch, but neither of us want to do that."

As nice as a full-out fight would be for the tension crawling under my skin, I have no interest in taking out innocent bystanders.

"It's an execution. We get in, kill him, and get out. It's simple."

It should be simple, anyway. But just as we're about to round the final corner to Yanis Drakos' box, I know something has gone wrong.

There are voices in the hallway.

I peek around the corner and see two men standing guard outside the door. There's the bulge of a weapon on one man's hip.

Raoul freezes next to me. He's as surprised as I am.

Yanis has never had guards outside of his box before. They definitely weren't here during the first act, either.

He knows. Somehow, Yanis knows something is going on tonight and he's prepared to fight.

Raoul is going to pull us out. He doesn't like the looks of this and neither do I. If Yanis is expecting an attack, it means things just got ten times more dangerous for everyone involved.

But retreating now would be a sign to the Greeks that I'm intimidated. It would be like throwing open the gates of my house and telling them to take whatever they'd like. Letting them get away with an outright attack on the Novikov

Bratva would be handing them Viviana and Dante on a silver platter. Because they won't stop with the lounge they destroyed. They'll keep coming until Viviana is out of the picture and Helen is stationed at my side.

But that isn't going to happen. *Ever.*

Raoul reaches for my arm just as I whip around the corner. Before either of the guards can react, I grab the closest one and press my gun below his ear.

"Don't make a sound or I'll paint this wall with your brains."

Raoul curses behind me before he pulls his gun on the second guard. "Don't move, *cabrón*."

I quickly think through logistics, but there's no way we leave these guards alive. They're a risk. I just don't yet know how we kill them quietly.

Then the emergency exit behind me opens and killing them quietly becomes the last thought in my mind.

I pull the trigger half a second before Raoul does the same. The two guards drop dead, but two more charge into the hallway to replace them.

If I had any doubt that the Greeks saw this attack coming, it's gone now.

There isn't even time to wonder how they figured it out. There's only time to kill the newest threat in front of us.

The guards seem shocked to have walked into the middle of an active fight, which gives us a one second head start. It's enough for Raoul to shoot the first man to walk through the door between the eyes. His friend ducks and fumbles for his gun, but I kick him in the stomach. He sprawls on his back and I kneel down next to him.

I press my gun to his neck. "How many more of you are there?"

Before he can answer, I hear raised voices coming from the theater. *So much for being discreet.*

Raoul's phone is buzzing nonstop, messages pouring in from the men stationed inside the theater. "We have to go."

I kill the man on the floor and stand up. "Go if you want to, but I'm finishing this."

He wants to argue. I can see it in his face. Then his expression clears and he nods. "I'm with you."

I kick open the door to the private box. Beneath us, the theater is in chaos. One performer is still singing, either trying to keep people calm or completely unaware of what is happening. But my focus is on the small space in front of me.

Two guards form a human wall between me and what I know is Yanis Drakos.

"Don't die for him," I advise them. "Don't throw your lives away for this asshole."

But a woman hiding in the corner of the box shrieks, drowning out my words, and the entire theater erupts in panic.

One of the guards lunges forward, his shoulder catching me in the stomach. I slam back against the door, breathless for a second. Then I bring the grip of my gun down on the man's head as Raoul fires at the other guard.

The man's arms loosen around my middle. I manage to kick him off and then land a second blow to the center of his chest. He collapses onto the other guard, who is clutching a gaping wound in his throat.

At the same time, Raoul and I finish them.

With his disposable guards wiped out, Yanis presses his palms together and drops to his knees. "Please. Please! I ask for mercy, Mikhail." His mustache quivers with fear and sweat.

"We have to go," Raoul whispers.

I haven't been keeping track of time, but we must be at least halfway through our fifteen-minute window by now and the entire theater knows something is wrong.

That window is closing fast.

It's fine.

This won't take but a second.

I press my gun to Yanis's sweaty forehead. "Even if I had any mercy, I wouldn't waste it on you."

I pull the trigger. Yanis collapses in a limp pile of limbs as the woman in the corner screams again and again and again. She is sobbing and shaking, her heels scrabbling against the thin carpet in an effort to get even further away from me. The only way out for her is over the balcony.

It's an idea.

Then again, it's not always a bad thing to leave a witness.

"I don't have anything to do with Yanis's business," she weeps. "He tells me nothing. Please. Please don't—"

I wave for her to be silent. "Tell Yanis's niece that *she* started this war. Her uncle's blood is on Helen's hand."

Then I dip my chin in farewell and leave the woman to deal with the cooling corpse of her lover.

51

VIVIANA

Someone knocks on my door, but I don't respond. I don't even move.

Whoever it is, they'll come in if they want to. Actually, they'll come in if Mikhail wants them to. That's what everyone around here does: whatever Mikhail asks.

It's probably Anatoly or Stella. I swear they've drafted a rotating schedule. They've been in and out of my room all day, taking turns, trying to wear me down.

"Mikhail is a good guy," Anatoly said the first time I let him in. "I know he has imprisoned you in this house and isn't letting you or your son leave despite the fact you have well-documented claustrophobia, but it's for your own good."

Fine, maybe that isn't *exactly* what he said, but it's close enough.

Stella focuses her emotional appeals on Dante. "Dante looks to you to see how he should respond. If you seem happy, he'll be happy," she explained. "You have the power to make this a fun adventure for him."

It's genius, really. If I wasn't half a second from a mental breakdown, maybe I'd pull myself together and be there for my son.

But Dante is the exact reason why I haven't left this room since my panic attack this morning.

I've spent years of my life pretending things were fine when they weren't. But that well has run dry. I'm too exhausted to pretend. The best thing I can do for Dante right now is stay far, far away.

There's another round of knocking and I curl the blankets under my chin and stare at the door. As expected, after I don't answer a second time, the door slowly opens.

I grab a pillow, ready to hurl it at the ginormous target that is Anatoly's head. But it isn't Anatoly *or* Stella in the doorway; it's Pyotr.

"Hi, Viviana."

Mikhail's driver practically lives in his black suit and white button-down. Mikhail told me he doesn't enforce a dress code for the staff; Pyotr just likes wearing a suit. I've never seen him out of it.

I stare blankly at him, making it very clear how much I want him in my room right now. He gives me a tight smile of acknowledgment and holds out a tray of food. "I brought your dinner."

"I'm not hungry."

I've been nauseous all day. Panic attacks always leave me

feeling like I'm hungover. Usually, a little fresh air helps, but, well… that's not an option.

"You should eat," he insists. "It will make you feel better."

I don't bother asking why Pyotr thinks he knows what is best for me. Everyone in this house acts like they know what is best for me. I'm tired of arguing with them about it.

"I can't believe they have you on servant duties," I snap. "With the house on lockdown, I guess there isn't much else for you to do. It's hard to transport people where they want to go when they are imprisoned."

His mouth tightens into a thin line. "Stella was worried you weren't eating. I volunteered to bring this up. She said you haven't been especially… welcoming."

"Because they haven't been especially empathetic," I bite back. "Everyone is so far up Mikhail's ass that they can't see how absurd this all is. I'm trapped here, Pyotr."

"I know."

"You say that, but—" I groan. "If I'd known this is how things were going to go, I would have tried harder to run after Mikhail brought us here. Actually, I would have stayed hidden. I would have kept moving again and again."

Dante would have been miserable starting over at a new school over and over again. It wouldn't have been sustainable.

Plus, even just the thought that these last few weeks with Mikhail never would have happened makes my stomach twist until I think I'll be sick. No matter how bad things are now, I can't bring myself to regret everything that has happened—just the way they've ended up.

"What I can tell you, Miss, is that no one is enjoying themselves right now."

It's the closest anyone on Mikhail's staff has come to criticizing him and it takes me by surprise.

"Careful," I warn. "I'm sure even the walls have ears around here."

He smirks. "If they did, I'd probably be fired by now."

I raise my brows. "Are you telling me you aren't on the straight and narrow like you appear?"

"I wouldn't go that far." He sits on the very corner of the bed, as far from me as possible. "But I have some... *feelings*... about what is happening to you right now. I've spoken my mind to a few people, but no one seems to feel quite as strongly about your situation as I do."

Since I moved in, Anatoly and Stella have been there for me. More than anyone in this mansion, I considered them my friends.

Was I wrong to trust them if they won't help me now?

"It makes sense," Pyotr continues. "They don't have the same background I do."

"What background is that?"

"One much like yours." He smiles, but there's so much sadness in his eyes that I reach over and take his hand. He squeezes my fingers gently. "My mother was forced into the mafia against her will. Her father was wealthy and married her off to the son of a don. When I was five, she took me and ran."

I frown. "Then why are you here working for Mikhail now? If she wanted you to get away from this lifestyle, why did you come back?"

"Because she died."

I gasp. "Did they find her? Did they…"

I can't even finish the thought. I've spent enough nights dreading what could happen to me—first, if Mikhail found me and Dante. Now, if I take Dante and run. I don't want to hear all of my worst fears confirmed.

"It was a car accident."

I sag. "Oh."

He lets out a humorless chuckle. "A little boring, right? She ran from danger, but it found her anyway. It was an ordinary accident. The sun was bright and she ran a red light. A truck T-boned our car on her side. She died and I survived. So I went back to live with my dad."

The story is heartbreaking, but one detail still sticks out.

"I'm sorry, but… *why are you here?*" I repeat. "I mean, your father was the son of a don. How did you end up as Mikhail's driver?"

"How did I fall so far from grace, you mean?"

My face flushes. "I'm sorry, I just—"

"It's okay." He waves me away. "It's a fair question. The answer there is a bit mundane, too, I'm afraid. My mother didn't just run from my father because of his connections to the crime world. He was also a mean drunk. The drinking only got worse after she left and even worse after she died.

By the time I was old enough to head out on my own, my grandfather had disowned my dad. We were living in a hovel on the edge of town without two pennies to rub together."

"So you applied to work for Mikhail?"

He shrugs. "My life taught me how to keep secrets. And even though I seem like I'm on the straight and narrow now, I have a decent-sized rap sheet. Mikhail knew I would never say a word against him because I have no interest in being noticed by the police. It was mutually assured destruction that sealed our working relationship."

"How romantic," I drawl.

"I respect Mikhail and I like working for him, but..." Pyotr lowers his voice like maybe the walls have ears, after all. "— that doesn't mean I agree with what he's doing to you, Viviana."

I give him a sad smile. "Thanks. If only sympathy could get me out of here."

He pauses. "Is that what you want? To get out?"

I blink at him. *Is this a test?*

"It's not exactly a secret that I'm not happy about being trapped here. The panic attack this morning probably clued a few people in."

"Being upset and wanting to leave are two different things." He's staring at me with an intensity that forces me to stare back. "Think about it, Viviana. Think through all of the possible benefits and consequences, and... if you do that and still want to leave, I'll help you."

"Why?" I blurt. "Why would you do that for me?"

He pats my hand with his. "I wouldn't be doing it for you. It would be for *her*."

52

MIKHAIL

The kitchen is busier than I've seen it in years. Dante is sitting on the counter, kicking his feet against the cabinet door below him as he helps Stella arrange cookies on a baking sheet. Anatoly is leaning across the island, tickling Dante's side every few seconds and sending him into a fit of giggles. Raoul is lounging at the table, disconnected from everyone, but watching closely.

I take account of each and every one of them in an instant.

I also take account of the one person missing.

"Where is she?"

Everyone stiffens at the sound of my voice except for Dante. He's still giggling from the latest round of tickling. He turns back to me with a smile. "Mama is sick."

For a split second, I believe him. *Viviana is sick and no one told me? Why the fuck am I just hearing about this now?*

Then I see Anatoly's face.

I storm out of the kitchen and am halfway up the stairs when Anatoly catches my arm. "I think you should let it go, Mikhail. She isn't doing well."

"It's been two days," I growl. "She can't stay in her room forever."

Though, now that I say it out loud, maybe it's not such a bad idea. Out of sight, out of mind. It didn't work the last six years, but might as well give it another go, right?

"It won't be forever. She just needs some time."

I hate that Anatoly thinks he knows Viviana better than I do.

I hate even more that he might be right.

It's easy for him to get close to her and Dante. He doesn't have as much to lose if something happens to them. He won't spend the rest of his life feeling like he failed them. Not like I will, at least.

"We don't have time," I spit. "The Greeks are on our asses. There was another attack last night only hours after we took out Yanis. If they attack here, I need her to be ready."

"Viviana is always ready to fight," Anatoly says with a sad smirk. "But she… she had a panic attack."

I frown. "When?"

"After you left her room yesterday morning. She was…" He drags a hand over his face. "It was fucked, man. I've never seen her like that."

My immediate thought: *It should have been me.* I should have been the one to find her, to comfort her. Not Anatoly. *Me.*

"I don't care if she's mad about the safety measures. They're for her own good."

"She wasn't mad," he corrects. "She was terrified. When she realized you'd changed the locks, she felt trapped."

"She's trapped in a mansion. Poor girl."

"With locked doors and guards watching every window. Even a mansion can feel like a cell when you can't escape. The walls started closing in on her and she was hyperventilating. I mean, she crumbled right in front of me. She collapsed and I thought I was going to have to call the doctor. Thankfully, she passed out and started breathing normally again."

Guilt burns through me hot and fast, but I shove it down. "I did what I had to do to keep her and Dante safe. Just like I always will."

Anatoly nods. "I know. Deep down, I think she does, too."

Very, very deep down, maybe.

"But she needs time," he says again. "Give it another day and I'll talk to her. I'll see if I can—"

"I don't need you to talk to my wife, brother."

Anatoly looks down at the floor. "I didn't mean—"

"She's coming to dinner tonight whether she likes it or not." I walk back down the stairs, brushing past Anatoly on my way. "Since you two are so close, I'll let you make sure she shows up."

He sighs behind me, but wisely doesn't respond.

Fifteen minutes later, he walks into the dining room with Viviana trailing behind him.

I don't have time to be pissed that she listened to Anatoly and came downstairs, because it's the first time I've seen her face in days—and she looks worse than I imagined.

Her skin is pale and her lips are cracked and dry. Her eyes are red-rimmed. If I didn't know any better, I'd think she really was sick.

"Mama!" Dante jumps out of his chair and hurls himself at Viviana's legs. The force of it sends her stumbling back half a step. "Are you all better?"

Viviana's eyes flick to mine for just a second before she quickly looks away and hugs Dante to her. "I'm better, baby." Her voice says the exact opposite. It's a husk of itself, hoarse and ragged and broken.

He drags her to the table by her hand. "Sit with me, Mama."

Anatoly moves to the other side of the table to make room for Viviana and Stella brings out a plate for her. Dante wedges himself between me and his mom with a bright smile. He's the only person in the room who can manage one tonight.

"Did you know 'hat' and 'cat' are rhyming words?" Dante asks the table. "Also, 'gat' and 'dat.'"

"Those last two aren't words," Anatoly points out.

Dante hits him with narrowed eyes. "But they rhyme."

Anatoly holds up his hands in surrender. "Too true, little man."

The entire meal is stiff and awkward except when Dante quizzes us with everything Mrs. Steinman has been teaching him during his tutoring sessions. He asks Raoul if he knows

The Muffin Man and almost falls out of his seat in delighted shock when Raoul sings the song along with him.

Seeing my usually-somber second-in-command sing children's nursery rhymes should be enough to break me out of any funk, but it doesn't so much as touch the dark cloud over my head tonight. Mostly because Viviana hasn't so much as touched her dinner.

I interrupt the third round of singing by pushing Viviana's plate closer to her. "You need to eat."

She juts her chin out but doesn't look at me. "I'm not hungry."

"Considering you haven't eaten all day, I don't think that's possible."

"She had *some* lunch," Anatoly offers in her defense. But he closes his mouth when I glare at him.

"Eat," I demand.

Slowly, she turns to me. Her cheeks look sunken-in. I didn't think that was possible after only a few days, but Viviana looks gaunt, skeletal.

I did that. This is my fault.

Without breaking eye contact, Viviana lifts her fork to her mouth and takes a bite. She chews slowly and I swear I can see her turning green. It takes visible effort for her to swallow.

"How's that?" she asks coolly.

"A good start. You need to keep your strength up. We don't know what is coming for us."

"Something is coming?" Dante looks up at me, a purple juice mustache on his upper lip.

Viviana smooths down his hair. Her nails are bitten down to the skin. "Nothing is coming, bud. Mikhail is just talking silly. You have nothing to worry about."

"He does," I counter. I bend down to Dante's level. "We all do. There are people out there who want to hurt us and we have to be ready."

"Mikhail!" Viviana hisses at the same time Anatoly knocks my knee under the table.

"He deserves to know what is going on," I tell them both. "He needs to understand why I have to send him away."

All at once, the air sucks out of the room. I can hear my own heart beating in my ears.

"I'm going away?" Dante's voice wavers.

It's better for him to be upset now than to be unprepared. I'm doing him a favor. "You wanted to go back to school, didn't you? That's where I'm sending you. To school."

Viviana gasps. "But I thought you didn't want to—"

"In Russia."

Viviana moves so fast I almost don't see her. In a second, she's out of her chair with a protective arm wrapped around Dante's chest.

"Like hell you are!" she hisses. "Stay away from him. You aren't sending him anywhere."

Raoul shoves away from the table, poised to take action wherever it might be necessary. Anatoly just looks exhausted.

"He isn't safe here," I tell her as calmly as I can. "He needs to get out of the city. No one knows about him yet. If I send him away, we can keep him anonymous until I've cleared up—"

"This will never be 'cleared up'! There will always be danger!" she cries out. "It's why I didn't want to come back here in the first place. Now, you expect me to stay trapped in this house while you send him halfway around the world? Absolutely not. No!"

"We can talk about this like adults," Anatoly suggests, rising out of his chair. "We should all sit down and think this through—*after* Dante goes to bed."

"There's nothing to talk about," Viviana growls at him. "You can't take my son away from me."

Suddenly, Dante darts out of Viviana's arms and runs down the hall. I hear his little feet scampering on the steps.

I start to follow him, but Viviana steps into my path. "Let him be. He wants to be alone."

A door slams somewhere upstairs.

"You don't know that."

"I do," she insists. "He is hiding in a closet right now because he knows I won't follow him in there. *He* knows I don't like feeling trapped."

The casual mention of her claustrophobia is a reminder as much as it is a challenge. She's driving the knife of guilt in a bit deeper.

All of this is my fault and she wants me to know that.

As if I don't already.

"I'm not doing this to hurt him."

"That doesn't mean you aren't hurting him anyway," she spits. "You're hurting all of us."

The knife in my gut twists and saws.

"We're in the middle of a war. Do you think I should let the two of you wander around in the yard and pick flowers when, any minute, a fucking army could tear down the gates?"

"I think you should give us a choice!" she fires back. "I think you should talk to me. We are both his parents. You told me that we would work together."

I also told her I wouldn't send him away. But that was before we landed in the middle of a war. Things have changed since then.

"How about, for right now, we work together to get my son out of a fucking closet?" I snarl. "Let's focus on that."

None of this is resolved, but this is an issue we can both agree on.

Viviana grudgingly follows me upstairs.

53

VIVIANA

It takes twenty minutes and a king-sized chocolate bar to lure Dante out of Mikhail's closet. I couldn't even blame him—I wanted to crawl in there right along with him, to be honest, claustrophobia be damned.

Now, he's in bed, nibbling on the top of his chocolate bar and looking reproachfully at the two of us like we might snatch him up by the collar and haul him out of the house at any second.

I would never do that.

Unfortunately, I can't say the same for Mikhail.

"You're safe here for tonight," Mikhail tells him. "Nothing will happen to you while I'm with you."

"Then why do I have to leave? Why can't I stay here?"

"Because I can't always be here with you. Sometimes, I have to leave."

Dante flings a hand at me. "Mama is here. She's always here."

Against my will, but the kid does have a point.

Mikhail sighs. "Listen, Dante… I should have found a better way to tell you about your new school. If it helps, I think you'll really like it."

Fat fucking chance.

"It doesn't help," I mutter softly enough that only Mikhail can hear me.

His shoulders stiffen, but he keeps talking. "Let's put a pin in this for today."

Dante wrinkles his nose. "What?"

"It means Mikhail wants to talk about this another day," I explain. "He and I are going to think this over and talk more about it. Nothing is decided, okay?"

It's not a lie. Not really. Mikhail's mind might be made up, but that doesn't mean for a single second that I'm going to let him take my son away from me. Not when I've worked so hard to keep us together.

Dante's lower lip wobbles, but he nods. "Okay, Mama."

Mikhail reads him a book about dragons throwing a taco party and Dante laughs when Mikhail pretends to breathe fire all around his room. But as soon as the book is over, I see the worry crease between my baby boy's brows.

I hate that he is wrapped up in this.

I hate that Mikhail dropped this stress on his shoulders.

I hate that there's nothing I can do to make it better.

By the time I kiss his forehead and step into the hall,

whatever malaise settled over me the last two days is gone. I don't want to lie in bed and cry—I want to breathe fire.

Mikhail closes Dante's door and I'm there in an instant, jabbing a finger into his chest. "You're a liar."

He sets his jaw. "Let's do this somewhere else. I don't want Dante to hear."

"Oh, *now,* you think about Dante? You weren't thinking about him when you announced at dinner that you were planning to ship him off to the middle of nowhere!"

"Russia is hardly the 'middle of nowhere.'"

"It's not here with me!" I snap. "That's all that matters. Do you understand that he is only five years old? You can't rip him away from his mother!"

Mikhail snatches my finger out of the air and hauls me against his chest. My heart gallops. The smell of him wraps around me and I have to fight the instinct to lean into the warmth of his body.

Despite everything, pressing myself to him like this is the only thing I've thought about the last two days. I want to lay my cheek over his heart and breathe in time with him. I want him to comfort me the way he's always been able to.

Except the man I want to comfort me isn't the man standing in front of me right now. Hell, maybe that man never existed. For all I know, this has all been a trick to get to this moment: Mikhail stealing my son.

Mikhail peers down his nose at me. "If I don't rip him away from you now, someone else will, and in a way that's much more permanent."

I rise onto my toes, ready to fight him tooth and nail. But as our bodies slide together, Mikhail's facade cracks.

His throat bobs. His eyes flicker across my face. For the first time, every thought in his head is plain to see.

He wants me the same way I want him. Probably against his will.

More than that, he doesn't want to send Dante away. I remember what Pyotr said the other night: *No one is enjoying themselves right now.*

Instead of arguing with him, I go for a gentler approach. I press my palm to his stubbled cheek. "You aren't the same man you were back then, Mikhail."

He stares down at me, unreadable and unrelenting.

"You're different," I continue. "You understand the risks and you've done everything to account for them."

When he understands what I'm saying, he jerks away. "Don't."

He spins around and pushes through my bedroom door. I follow him across the hall. "Don't what? Don't tell you the truth?" I ask. "Don't tell you that I trust you to keep us safe?"

"Don't act like you understand anything."

"I'm not Alyona, Mikhail. And Dante isn't—"

"Don't!" he roars, rounding on me.

I gasp and fall back against the closed door. Mikhail freezes, regret flickering across his face before he can hide it. He drags a hand through his hair and spins away from me.

"If there is something I don't understand, then tell me," I beg. "Fill me in. I'd love to be right there with you making decisions. That's what a marriage is."

He snorts derisively. "This has never been a real marriage."

If I hadn't already spent the last two days sobbing, I'd probably cry. As it is, I'm all dried up.

"No, I guess not," I breathe. "But it could be. If we let ourselves feel what I know we're both feeling, then this could be the realest thing I've ever—" I clear my throat, choking down a sob.

Mikhail is a statue in the middle of the room. His shoulders rise and fall with his breathing, but he doesn't move. Doesn't speak.

I take a step closer and reach for him. My fingers whisper across his shoulder blade. "We'll never be a family if you send him away."

Mikhail jerks to life. He spins to face me, blue eyes wild. "We won't be a family if Dante is dead. He'll be safer in Russia. That's all I want."

"Trofim wasn't safe there," I point out, swallowing down my nerves. "Someone found him."

"This is different."

"I don't see how," I lie.

It's very different. For one, I'd never hurt Dante.

But I lift my chin and meet Mikhail's eyes. I don't let him see the anxiety brewing under the surface.

"We'll talk about this later," he says, stepping around me. "When you're being rational."

"I *am* being rational! You're the one not being—"

But the door closes and Mikhail is gone.

Again.

I'm alone in my room.

Again.

I stand there for a few minutes, waiting to make sure Mikhail won't change his mind, turn around, and come back to apologize. The fact that part of me still expects him to is more pathetic than I know what to do with.

So when the hallway stays quiet and the door stays closed, I slide the lock home, pull a duffel bag down from my closet, and start stuffing things inside.

I don't want to leave. I can admit that much to myself. Despite everything that has happened between us, despite the fighting and the lies and the kidnapping—*I still want him.*

But what I want has never been a factor where Dante is concerned. I have to do what is best for my son, always.

When I finish packing the bag, I tuck it deep under the bed and shove some extra, rolled-up blankets around it for camouflage. I hope I don't need it.

God, I really don't want to need it.

But I've already lost my heart to a man who will never love me back.

I won't lose my son to him, too.

54

MIKHAIL

I toss my third—or shit, I don't know, it could be my fourth, fifth, or tenth—drink back, but I don't even taste it.

There's no familiar tingle in my extremities. No warmth low in my gut. Despite the alcohol, I feel ice-cold inside and out. Numb.

Maybe that's why I don't flinch when my office door flies open and my father is standing in front of me, practically frothing at the mouth.

"What in the fuck are you doing?" he snarls.

I hold up my glass. "Having a drink. Or, I was having a drink. I just finished it."

"You're drunk." He swipes out to bat the glass out of my hand, but I pull it back with plenty of time to spare. I'm wasted, but even still, I'm faster than the old bastard.

"Not drunk," I correct, placing the glass safely on the corner of the desk that used to belong to my father. "Just drinking. Now, what the fuck do you want?"

A deep, angry growl squeezes out of his throat. "I want to know why you're sitting here kicking your heels up while we are being attacked."

"If you're talking about the assault at the lounge, I've responded to that."

He snorts. "Yeah, by killing Yanis Drakos in front of an entire theater full of witnesses."

"No one who matters saw me. Even if they did, they won't breathe a word."

"It doesn't matter either way. If you don't end up in prison, you'll be in the grave. The Greeks aren't going to stop until you pay for humiliating Helen."

"Helen humiliated herself," I drawl. "She fell in love with me without any encouragement. She let her feelings get in the way of what should have been nothing more than a solid business deal."

Which is exactly why I won't do the same thing with Viviana.

I don't care that I can still feel the way her breasts pressed against my ribs. It doesn't matter that I've been half-cocked since she pressed her hand to my cheek. It sure as fuck doesn't make a difference that she all but admitted she loves me. I won't make this shit any messier than it already is.

"Helen isn't the one who let her feelings get in the way of things, son," he snaps. "That was you. You let this *woman* turn your head and make enemies of the Greeks."

"This isn't about her. It's about my son."

He rolls his eyes. "The bitch probably got pregnant on purpose. You destroyed her wedding to Trofim right when she was banking on a connection to the Novikov Bratva. She needed to tie one of you down and beggars can't be choosers, eh?"

I remember everything about that night in vivid detail. Neither of us were thinking with enough clarity to manipulate anyone. The draw between us was magnetic. I couldn't have pulled out of her even if I'd wanted to.

And Viviana still doesn't want anything to do with this world.

"That's my wife you're talking about."

"Yeah, she's your wife," he agrees. "She's also your brother's murderer."

Even if I was drunk, that sentence would have sobered me right up. My blood runs cold and I sit tall. "Explain yourself."

My father tosses an envelope onto my desk. "It's all in there."

I pull a flash drive out of the envelope. "What is this?"

"Play it and you'll—"

"I don't want to play it," I bark. "I want you to tell me why the fuck you are accusing my wife of murder before I kill you for insulting her."

My father has the audacity to smirk. "I wouldn't have thought I'd know more about this than you. I don't have an army of men at my command and doing my bidding anymore. It seems you've gotten distracted from your investigation. Does Viviana have anything to do with why you haven't found who killed Trofim?"

Viviana has *everything* to do with why I haven't really cared that Trofim was killed at all.

He hurt her. He was going to make her miserable for the rest of her life. So, fuck him.

The only reason I cared in the first place is because I thought the same person might come after Viviana or Dante next. There's a good reason why he died six years ago and I'm just finding out now.

"I've been looking into it. Raoul says there's reason to believe Trofim hired a prostitute. Or he brought some random woman home and she killed him. Either he owed her money or he pissed her off. Maybe both."

His smirk spreads. "The prostitute theory might not be so far off."

"Careful," I warn. "That's twice you've gone too far. I won't allow you a third."

"Or maybe my theory holds some water," he retorts. "My thought is that Viviana knew she was pregnant and wanted to make sure that her child's father was guaranteed to be *pakhan*. The easiest way to do that would be to kill Trofim."

"I was going to be *pakhan* whether Trofim lived or not. I won it from him. It was over." I wave him off. "Get out of here with your bullshit theories against my wife."

"Maybe I'm right, maybe I'm not, but that doesn't mean I don't have evidence against her all the same." He points to the flash drive. "If you do watch that, you'll see your wife walking into the house where Trofim was staying and then walking out half an hour later covered in blood. The next time anyone sees him, he's dead."

"There were no cameras. Raoul checked."

"Trofim didn't even know they existed. I had them installed without his knowledge." He lifts his chin. "You may have tossed your brother to the wolves, but I wanted to keep an eye on him."

"Then where were you six fucking years ago? If you had these tapes, then you knew Trofim was dead. Why didn't you say anything?"

"I didn't know he was dead," he argues. "I thought he fell off the map, which was understandable after you embarrassed him so publicly. I didn't remember the cameras and dig up the tapes until I heard he was gone."

"Who told you?" I ask.

"Not *you*," he says through gritted teeth. "I may not be *pakhan*, but I'm still your father. I'm Trofim's father. I deserved to know he died, and you kept it from me."

I roll my eyes. I don't have time for his sob story. Especially when I'm still trying to process the fact that Viviana might have something to do with all of this.

"Why didn't you tell me you thought Viviana was his killer when you saw her at dinner the other night? You recognized her."

"I don't *think* anything; I *know* she killed him," he corrects acidly. "And when I was last here, I didn't know Trofim was dead. It wasn't until I recognized Trofim's ex-fiancée sitting next to you that I decided to call him. When he didn't answer, I did a little digging. It was easy enough to piece it all together."

I run a hand through my hair, trying desperately to clear my head and think.

What does this mean?

Why would she do it?

Why wouldn't she tell me?

"You're sure it's her on the tapes?" I ask.

"Positive. She's very... *identifiable.*" There's a suggestion in his tone that I should kill him for. Maybe I would have five minutes ago.

But now...

My wife killed my brother.

The woman has been a distraction since the moment I first saw her. She's thrown my life into chaos and consumed way too many of my thoughts. I made excuses for her before. I told myself it wasn't a problem.

But now? This is different... isn't it?

"Well?" my father charges. "What are you going to do?"

"I know what *you're* going to do." I stand up and wave him away. "*Leave.* Now. If you tell anyone what we talked about here, I'll kill you."

"You'd kill your father over the woman who murdered your brother?" he spits.

I don't answer because, the truth is, I have no fucking idea.

But I'm going to find out.

55

VIVIANA

My bedroom door flies open like the lock doesn't exist.

The wooden frame shatters, spraying splinters across the floor. I have enough time to wonder if this is the attack Mikhail was warning me about.

He was right. Someone is coming for us. I need to get to Dante.

Then the thoughts disappear like smoke because it's Mikhail himself stalking across the scattered shards.

"What the hell are you—"

He rips the comforter away where I had it clutched to my chest and presses me back into the headboard. His hand is an iron choker cinched low on my throat. His thumb drives painfully into my collarbone. I whimper and stretch away from him, but he doesn't give me an inch.

I want to say something, but the look on his face makes it impossible. I've never seen him like this. Rage is rippling off of him like a physical force. The heat of him soaks through my thin nightgown.

Does he know about the duffel bag I packed?

Does he know about—

Before I can even cement why I should be afraid, Mikhail crushes his lips to mine. He closes the distance between us in a second and then he's everywhere.

I can tell myself that I don't want Mikhail until I'm blue in the face, but all it takes is one touch for me to melt. Need throbs between my legs.

I moan against his mouth and Mikhail hauls me against him and lifts me off the bed like I'm no more substantial than a ragdoll. His arm tightens around my lower back until I'm struggling to breathe. His hold and his mouth are relentless. I have no choice but to give what he wants.

As stars begin to speckle my vision, Mikhail drops me onto the mattress. I fall sideways with a gasp. I'm still a mess of limbs, trying to make sense of what he's even doing here, when Mikhail grabs the hem of my nightgown and shreds it straight up the seam.

That's not difficult to interpret.

"Why?" I rasp.

With the way we left things, I didn't expect him to come back tonight. I certainly didn't expect this.

"Because you're mine."

It's the only answer I get before he opens the ruined shreds of my nightgown and crawls over me.

He slides up my body slowly. I feel his erection, hard and insistent, over my ribs and between my breasts.

I'm dazed from the surprise of him being in my room—*doing this*—and from the intensity of how much I want every second of it.

He unzips his pants and his cock rests against my skin, hot and velvety soft. I press my breasts together, creating more friction as he slides between them.

Then he swats my hands away, grabs a handful of my hair, and drives himself into my mouth.

My throat bobs as I take him. He tips his head back and groans when I swirl my tongue around him and suck him deeper.

The last few days have been hell for both of us. I'm pissed at him, but that doesn't mean I don't understand that he's under stress, too. If this is how we both choose to burn off some frustration, I'll take it. I dig my fingers into his muscled ass and pull him deeper.

"Fuck, Viviana." He thrusts and holds.

Then in a blink, he's gone.

He rips my hands away from his body, slides off the bed, and, with one jerk, flips me onto my stomach. I barely have time to register what is happening before he drags my hips to the edge of the bed and sinks his cock into me.

"Oh my God." I arch off the bed, gasping as my body quickly adjusts to him. It's like pressing on a muscle you've overworked. It hurts in a way that makes me want to press harder. I lift my hips, taking him deeper.

Mikhail moves like we're in a hurry. Are we? Is there a clock counting down somewhere I can't see?

He wraps his huge hands around my waist and slams into me. I cry out, falling face first into the mattress. The bed rattles on the frame and the sound of our bodies slapping together echoes around the room.

My body flutters around him, desperate to grab onto something. But he's coming and going so fast.

"Mikhail," I gasp, struggling for purchase on the bed. Heat is building low in my belly, but it's happening too quickly. I didn't spend days thinking about this for it to be over in a minute. I want to feel every inch of him inside of me. "Mikhail, we aren't in a rush. We can—"

Suddenly, his hand wraps around to muzzle my mouth.

I'm so shocked that, for a second, I'm frozen.

Then I open my mouth and clamp down hard on his finger.

He spits a curse in Russian, his hold loosens, and it's enough space for me to crawl away from him. He slides out of me, his cock twitching in the air between us. "You're treating me like a fucking sex toy. If you want to pound a Fleshlight, check your bedside drawer."

He grabs my ankles and yanks me to the end of the bed. His thumb strokes over my slit, dipping inside of my wetness. "Why would I, when you're here and ready?"

I bite my lower lip, swallowing down a moan. "I'm not your prostitute; I'm your wife."

Mikhail rotates his wrist and slides a finger inside of me. He curls against my walls, stroking the words out of my head and every bit of resistance out of my body.

I part my legs for him, my knees wilting on either side of his hips. He slips a second finger inside of me and I fall against his chest.

"I know you're not a prostitute," he whispers against my temple. "You open your legs for *free*."

"Hey!" I shove off his chest, but his thumb circles over my clit and my breath hitches. The argument stutters out of me. "You c-can't talk to me like—"

"I can do whatever the fuck I want with you."

My face burns. I try to shove him away, but he holds me steady with one arm while he slides a third finger inside of me.

"Are you going to tell me to stop?" he growls. His blue eyes are practically black. Whatever version of Mikhail is in front of me now, he isn't here to apologize or find some relief. He's here to fight.

I have no idea what this is about, but I'm more than happy to oblige.

I claw my nails down his abs, drawing a groan from deep in his chest. Then I wrap my hand around his cock. He's still wet from being inside of me, and I stroke him from root to tip.

His breath catches. I know he's just as helpless here as I am.

Whatever it is that draws us together, it's got a tight hold on us now.

"I don't want you to stop," I purr, twisting my hand around him. "I want you to fuck me—*hard*. If you *actually* want to punish me, you'll have to walk away."

He swallows, debating it. Debating leaving me on the bed, throbbing and desperate. It really would be a cruel and unusual torture.

The problem is, it would torment him, too.

There are no winners in this little game. Mikhail seems to realize that at the same moment I do.

We surge towards each other, lips crashing together so hard it hurts. I scrape my nails through his hair and tug at the strands, angling his head to give me better access.

He rips his hair out of my grip and pins my arm to my side. With his other hand, he presses his cock to my pussy. He drives into me in one stroke, but I'm more than ready for him this time. I take all of him, gasping against his mouth.

He moves slower this time, letting me feel him. But I don't have any illusions that he's doing it for my sake. Mikhail wants to feel me, too.

I tighten around him and he growls. He moves like he's going to lay me down on the bed, but I hook my leg behind his knee. He stumbles back, barely managing to catch us from tumbling across the carpet.

"What the fuck, Viviana?" he snaps.

In answer, I plant my feet on the floor and grind down against him. I ride him into submission, pressing him onto his back.

He could have us both on the bed in an instant if he wanted, but he stays down. I plant my hands on his chest and let the frustration and anger and confusion that has been building in me for days funnel into this one act. Maybe, finally, I'll be able to let him go. If I can fuck him into the floor and take what I want, maybe I can prove to myself that Mikhail isn't special. I'll ride him out of my system and be done with this toxic rollercoaster we've been on.

It's hate fucking. Toxic, violent, turbulent hate sex, pure and simple.

"I'm close," I murmur, my nails biting into his skin. I move faster, riding him until I'm panting.

I clench around him, wanting nothing more than to take him down with me. Mikhail must have the same idea. He grits his teeth and growls, "Come for me like my pretty little whore, Viviana."

He grips my thighs and pulls me against him again and again. When I'm close enough, he sucks my nipple into his mouth and his teeth clamp down over sensitive skin, and I can't fight it for another second. I need this.

"I'm coming," I cry, leaning back to let him find a new angle in me. "Mikhail, I'm—"

Falling.

I yelp as my back hits the floor. My body is convulsing around nothing, achingly hollow as Mikhail looms between my legs.

He's stroking himself fast, his top lip curled back like he's disgusted with himself.

"I'm doing what I should have done that night in the bridal suite," he growls, pumping his cock with his own hand faster and faster.

I lie there in shock and he comes with a muted groan, coating my stomach with the hot, sticky splatter of his release.

Even dumped on the cold floor, I'm still riding my orgasm. My pussy pulses weakly around what should be Mikhail while my head is spinning.

What is he talking about?

Once Mikhail empties himself on me, he stands up like it's a race to see who can get dressed first. He's zipping his pants when I manage to get to my feet.

I grab his arm. "What the fuck was that?"

He jerks away from my touch. The force of it sends me back onto the bed. I bounce on the mattress. "What is this? What are you—"

"I know what you did."

I start to ask what he means, but when I look in his eyes, I realize I already know.

56

VIVIANA

He knows.

He knows I killed Trofim.

I have no idea how he knows, but he knows.

I knew this moment would come. I just didn't think it would happen while I was still flushed from an orgasm and sticky with Mikhail's cum on my abdomen.

"How did you find out?" I whisper.

He doesn't answer. Maybe he can't even hear me. Based on the scarlet flush creeping up his neck, he might not be hearing anything but the thundering of his own heart.

I can't even blame him.

"Were you planning to kill me, too?" he growls, leaning forward to spit each word in my face. "Maybe you can take out both Novikov heirs and wind up with Anatoly. Has that been your plan all along? If so, you've picked the most pleasant of the bunch, I have to admit."

Mikhail being jealous of my friendship with Anatoly would stand out as important on any other day. Today, it isn't even a footnote.

"No!" I cry. "No, I don't have a plan. There was never a plan."

"You flying to Russia and tracking down Trofim was an accident? That's what I'm supposed to believe?"

Some desperate part of me still hoped this was a misunderstanding, but that confirms it.

He knows everything.

I can't hide it anymore.

"It wasn't an accident, but I didn't want to do it. Please, Mikhail." Tears are rolling down my cheeks now, dripping onto my bare chest. I've never been more vulnerable than I am right now. "Please."

"Is this how it went? Did Trofim beg for his life as you murdered him?"

I squeeze my eyes closed. I can still feel his brother's blood on my hands as I walked out of his house. The way the blade glanced off of bone.

"I didn't want to do it," I repeat, gasping for breath as tears I've buried for six years come pouring out. "My father didn't give me a choice. *I didn't have a choice.*"

Mikhail doesn't move, but I feel the shift in the air. He's listening now, alert. "What did your father do?"

I know what he's asking, but I have to start at the beginning. If there's any hope of Mikhail understanding, I have to start at the very beginning.

"I was going to marry another man. Years before Trofim," I explain as quickly as I can. "He was poor, but he loved me, and I loved him."

"I don't want to hear about—"

"My father murdered him," I blurt. "He found out that I was going to marry Matteo and it would have made me useless. He couldn't use me as some political pawn if I was married to another man. So he kidnapped Matteo, tied him up, and made me watch as he murdered him."

Some nights, when I'm running through the empty darkness of my nightmares, I can hear Matteo's screams. I hear him begging for mercy.

He never gets any.

Neither do I.

"My father would do anything to make sure he didn't lose control over me, including killing Dante." I look into Mikhail's dark eyes, begging him to believe me. "If he thought being pregnant with your child would be a risk to our family, he would have never let me keep him."

He stares down at me, his expression unreadable. That's okay, because as long as he's standing here, there's hope. As long as he's listening to me, there's a chance I can fix this.

"So I did what I needed to do to make sure that Dante would survive," I plow ahead. "I did what I needed to do to make sure Dante would be the son of a *pakhan*, because that's what my dad wanted."

"My father's theory wasn't so far off, then," Mikhail mumbles. I have no idea what he's talking about. Before I can ask, he commands, "Tell me what happened. All of it. Now."

"Okay. Okay." I nod and try to speak through hiccupping sobs. "After you told me to get out of the hotel and away from this life while I still could, I went on the run. My father tracked me down after a few weeks—the same day I took a test and found out I was pregnant. He was going to take me to get an abortion and put me straight back on the marriage market. Trofim didn't work out, but he had the next rich asshole lined up for me to marry. I felt like a pig at market. I felt—"

"Trapped," Mikhail finishes.

I swipe the tears from my cheeks. "Yeah. So I told him the baby belonged to you. I knew that would mean something to him. But things were still so up in the air with your family. No one knew if Trofim would come back and fight for the crown or if your father would stand up to you. Being pregnant with your baby only meant something if you could hold onto your position as next in line to be *pakhan*. So my father told me he would let me go… if I killed Trofim."

Mikhail opens his mouth to respond, but I need to get this out. All of it. Right now.

"He probably didn't think I'd agree, but there was no other way out. Not that he was actually giving me a way out, either. I knew it was bullshit. I knew as soon as Trofim was dead and my plane landed, my father would be there to drag me back home and sell me to the highest bidder. But getting on that flight to Russia was my best chance at making a run for it. I had a new identity lined up; I just needed to get far enough away from my father to put my plan into action."

"You didn't have to kill Trofim." Mikhail narrows his eyes. "If all you wanted to do was escape, you could have taken the flight and ran."

I shake my head. "I know what happens when lineages get messy in our world. If Trofim took back power, he could have come looking for me. If he found me, he never would have let Dante live. Even if Trofim *didn't* get power back, he could have killed Dante out of spite." I drop my face into my hands and blow out a deep breath. "I struggled over what to do for days. I weighed the options back and forth, and I decided… The best way to keep Dante safe was to kill Trofim. So I went to Russia. I showed up at his house, and I—"

"Manipulated him." Mikhail paces away from the bed. His body is tight. His hands ball into fists at his side. "The same way you're manipulating me."

"What?" I breathe. "No! I didn't—"

"Raoul said they found a woman's hair clip in his bed." He snatches my golden claw clip off the nightstand and flings it at me. "I bet it looked a lot like this."

My eyes close to hold back the hot tears. "I didn't touch him, Mikhail. As soon as I got there, he was on top of me. He thought you'd sent me there to live in exile with him. He thought—"

"He thought you were trustworthy," Mikhail hisses.

This isn't about Trofim. I know that. Mikhail knows who his older brother was. After what he did to Anatoly's mother—after what he would have done to me—there's no way he actually feels sympathetic for how his brother's life ended.

"Trofim practically herded me to his bedroom. He was drunk and muttering about finishing what we'd started. If I hadn't had the knife strapped to my thigh, I wouldn't have been able to fight him off. He would have—"

"Enough!" Mikhail roars. "At least when I kill a man, I'm honest with myself about it. I have a good reason."

"Dante is a good reason!" I yell. "He's my *only* reason. And if you could forget about your wounded pride for half a fucking second, you'd see that!"

Mikhail's hand is around my neck in a heartbeat. He angles over me, pushing me back into the mattress. "If you think I'm going to let you manipulate me the way you do everyone else, you're very fucking wrong."

I can't breathe. Can't move. Mikhail is clenching my throat too tight. For the first time, I'm not sure he's going to let go.

Finally, just as black begins to creep into my vision, he throws me back on the bed. "You're my wife in name only. This arrangement between us exists only to protect Dante and ensure no one questions his parentage."

"Mikhail," I plead, "let me explain everything. Please, just—"

"Give me a reason," he barks. "Why should I give you another second of my time?"

"Because you..." A few minutes ago, I thought I knew the truth. I thought Mikhail and I were both fighting back the same feelings. But looking into his cold face now, I'm not convinced Mikhail has any feelings. Still, I say it anyway, praying saying it out loud will make it true. "Because you love me."

He laughs—actually *laughs*. His face is twisted into a cruel mockery of a smile. "I don't love you, Viviana. I don't even fucking know you."

"You do know me! I've told you everything now. There are

no more secrets. Please." I can't see him through a haze of fresh tears. "Mikhail, please let me explain. I didn't even—"

"Dante is my responsibility now and I'm going to send him away. I'm going to keep him safe, from my enemies… and from you."

He turns towards the door. The tears run unchecked down my cheeks.

"Are you going to kill me?" I ask weakly.

I know how these things go. He might keep me around for a little while, but eventually, he'll get tired of me. If Mikhail really hates me as much as it seems like he does, I don't stand a chance.

His back stiffens. "I don't know yet."

Then Mikhail pulls my ruined door closed behind him as I drop to the floor and sob.

57

VIVIANA

I open my eyes and see a figure standing next to my bed.

I jolt awake, my heart slamming against my ribcage as my spine slams against the headboard. *This is it. He's here to kill me.*

"Mama?"

The little voice scatters the cloud of panic. I blink and see Dante staring up at me, wide-eyed.

"I'm sorry," he blurts. His eyes are shiny like he's been crying, too. "Mama, I didn't mean to—"

"Shhh. Don't be sorry." I slip my hands under his arms and scoop him up the way I used to when he was a toddler.

He learned to stand on a toy box to open his door. Then he would pat my mattress and call for me, too small to see over the side of my bed. That was back when I could carry him anywhere I wanted without a second thought. Before he grew too big to fit comfortably in my lap.

I curl my arms around his sleep-warm body and hold him to my chest. "I'm glad you're here, baby. I missed you."

He nuzzles his face into my neck. "I don't want to go away, Mama."

"You're not going anywhere," I whisper. "You're safe here with me."

I still have the duffel bag under my bed. I can get him out of here. Not now, though. With all the guards around the premises and eyes on me, I'll need help.

I hope Pyotr's offer is still good.

Dante sits up. He's frowning and he looks so much like Mikhail. It still hurts, but not the way it used to. Now, it's the ache of a missing limb. The pain of losing something vital you can never get back.

I squeeze Dante's hand. *I won't lose him, too.*

"What is it, bud? What's wrong?"

"Call Mikhail," he whimpers. "Tell him I don't want to go."

"We can talk to him later. Maybe in the morning."

I tried talking. It didn't do any good.

"He isn't in his room," he says. "I went there first. I was going to ask him to promise to let me stay, but he's gone."

I don't want to think about what it means that Mikhail isn't in bed in the middle of the night. Is he too worked up to sleep? Or is he too busy planning my punishment?

"He'll be back," I assure him. "And when he comes back, we'll talk to him. I'm sure we can convince him to let you stay."

Mikhail's voice is still echoing off the walls of my skull. *Dante is my responsibility now and I'm going to send him away. I'm going to keep him safe, from my enemies... and from you.*

He didn't leave any room for doubt about what he wants to do. I don't think I'll be able to convince him to do anything, but maybe Dante can.

"Just call him," Dante begs, shaking my arm. "He has to listen to you."

"Why do you think that?"

"Because you make the rules," he says.

The innocence shining through his absolute certainty that I am the ultimate power in this house brings tears to my eyes. I hug him close.

"Please call him. Just try. Please."

I know it won't do any good, but I reach for my phone on the bedside table. "I'll call, but I don't think he'll answer."

Actually, I know he won't.

If I thought there was any chance Mikhail would answer, I wouldn't even try. Dante does not need to be present for whatever hellscape that conversation would turn into. My son looks at me, hopeful, as the phone rings and rings.

I give him a tight smile, doing my best to look upbeat. Hopeful, just like him. Part of me *is* still hopeful. There's still Pyotr and his offer. It's the only bright spot in this long tunnel of darkness. There's still a chance we get out of here.

After thirty seconds, the ringing stops and the call goes to voicemail.

"Sorry, D." I toss my phone onto the mattress next to me. "I'll talk to him tomorrow, okay?

He sags. "What if tomorrow is too late?"

It would be a lie to say the same question isn't burning in the back of my mind. I have no idea when this little world we've built could come tumbling down or when Mikhail will pull this rug out from under me.

The only thing I do know is that Dante is here right now. We both are.

"It won't be too late. We have time." I wrap my arm around him and smooth his hair out of his face. "We have nothing but time."

We fall asleep like that, Dante snoozing next to me. It reminds me of the years we spent in our tiny little apartment. There were so many nights when he had nightmares and I would crowd into his toddler bed with him. We'd wake up smashed together, his knees in my spine and his elbows in my ribs.

Those were good nights.

∼

But when I blink my eyes open, the bed is empty.

I can see the nest of blankets where Dante was curled up, but he isn't there anymore.

"Dante?"

Boom. Boom. Boom. The walls start to shake.

I duck down, my first thought going to gunshots.

When the sound stops, I turn to the door. It's closed. The frame is still splintered and cracked on the inside from when Mikhail tore through it last night, but somehow, the door is locked.

The banging starts up again, and I realize it's a hammer. Someone is pounding on the other side.

I leap out of bed and yank on the doorknob, but it doesn't budge. Somehow, it might be sturdier than before Mikhail broke it.

"Leave it be, Viv," Anatoly sighs. He sounds weary. "You aren't getting through this."

"What are you doing?" I jerk on the handle, but the door doesn't even rattle in the frame. Whatever Anatoly is doing, it's *solid*. "Are you locking me in here?"

"Please don't…" He sighs again. "You'll get out soon, okay? Mikhail just needs some time."

"Time to decide if he's going to kill me?" I spit.

"He won't do that."

Anatoly sounds sure, but I'm not. As I crawl to the wall and slide down it, I can't even find the energy to panic over being trapped in this room.

All I can think is, *It's too late.*

There's no way out of here. Even Pyotr can't help me now.

58

MIKHAIL

"I finished with her door." Anatoly leaves a hammer on the corner of my desk. "What did you do to it, anyway? It looked like the Kool-Aid Man had been in there."

I grimace up at him. I try to ignore Anatoly on a good day. And after everything that happened last night and less than an hour of sleep, today is not a good day. "What the hell are you talking about?"

He mimes crashing through a wall and rumbles in a fake-deep voice, "Oh, yeah!"

"You're talking about a damn commercial." I drag a hand over my face.

"No, I'm talking about you tearing through Viviana's door like it's a banner and you're the home team at a football game, only to have me bolting her inside six hours later."

"Is there a question somewhere in there? I'm not in the mood for a word puzzle."

"Why?" Anatoly kneels down so he can meet my eyes.

I stare back at him. "You know damn well why."

He groans and spins to standing, pacing across the room. "So she killed Trofim. Who the fuck cares?"

Raoul opens my office door, a steaming mug of coffee in his hands. I'm reaching for it before he even makes a move to hand it to me.

"She lied about it," Raoul says, picking up on what we're talking about as if he never left the room. "She should have told him."

"Why?" Anatoly snorts. "So Mikhail could have pulled this Annie Wilkes bullshit even earlier?"

"Enough with the fucking references," I growl.

"You're just mad because you don't read and aren't as cultured as I am," he fires back. "And I'm mad because no one in this room ever liked Trofim, so why do we care that Viviana killed him? I think we should throw her a parade. I mean, honestly, raise your hand if you cared for one single second what happened to Trofim?"

To no one's surprise, all of our hands stay down.

Anatoly throws up his own hands like he's made his point and then flops down into a chair.

"This isn't about Trofim," I snarl. "This is about Viviana. She killed our brother, didn't tell me I had a son, and is now my wife. If I don't stop and consider what the fuck all of that means, then I don't deserve to be *pakhan*."

"It doesn't mean anything. It means that fate brought you both together," Anatoly says, like either answer is completely acceptable. "Viviana isn't some mastermind working this all to her benefit. She would have kept hiding forever if you hadn't bought Cerberus."

I've almost forgotten about Cerberus... not that the board members are upset about that, I'm sure. They're probably hoping I'll never show up to another meeting so they can quietly reclaim their company. If the Greeks don't want peace and I lose shipping access along the Eastern seaboard, they might as well. Taking over Cerberus will have been for nothing.

"She told you her father made her kill Trofim," Raoul points out. "Do you believe her?"

I shrug. "We all know Agostino is a piece of shit. I wouldn't put it past him to threaten her."

I wouldn't put it past him to kill Dante, either. Viviana had good reason to be worried about what he'd do.

"Imagine asking your daughter to do your dirty work," Anatoly sneers. "What a coward."

"Agostino threatened her, but Viviana chose to follow through. She chose to kill Trofim rather than take that flight to Russia and disappear."

"Because she was worried that our psychopath of an older brother would come after her for revenge. *Which he absolutely would have!*" Anatoly argues. "Viviana was right. She didn't have another choice."

"*I* was the other choice!" I shout. I drum my fingers around the steaming coffee mug in my hands, watching the ripples move across the dark surface. "She could have come to me. I would have protected them both."

The room is quiet and I know instantly I've said too much.

Raoul and Anatoly know me better than almost anyone else in the world, but they still aren't used to getting this kind of peek into my head.

Anatoly slides to the edge of his chair, getting as close to me as he can without actually standing up. "She'd just watched you beat Trofim to a pulp the night before her wedding. The two of you had sex and then you told her to leave… She probably didn't know coming to you was an option."

Also, I told her it wasn't.

Viviana wanted to know if I was there in her bridal suite that night to replace Trofim as her groom. I assured her it would never happen.

"Why don't we sort out what is going on with the Greeks and then come back to handling this?" Raoul suggests. "We are fielding attacks all over the city. We can't deal with what's going on inside the family until we deal with the shit from the outside."

I shake my head. "If we don't deal with Viviana soon, there will be an uprising on the inside once the men find out."

"Then no one can find out," Anatoly offers.

"The same way we weren't going to let anyone find out about Trofim's murder?" I snap. "Our skeletons don't stay buried, brother. The men rallied behind me when I exiled Trofim, but if they find out my bride killed him, they'll think the same thing father does: that it was to ensure Dante had a clear line to power. I'll look weak, like she manipulated me. They'll doubt my leadership."

"No one gives a flying fuck about Trofim!" Anatoly shouts as he jumps out of his chair. "Literally no one."

"They may not care about Trofim, but they care about honor."

"Killing a man to protect your child is honorable! What Viviana did under that kind of stress—*while pregnant,* no less—is badass. If you weren't the one she lied to, you'd see it, too."

Anatoly even sounds like Viviana now, almost word for word. I hear her voice echoing in my head. *If you could forget about your wounded pride for half a fucking second, you'd see that!*

"The only thing I'd see is that you've taken a strong interest in *my* wife," I spit.

Anatoly glares back at me, refusing to take the bait. "Dante and Viviana are family. I'll always defend my family—even from themselves."

A slow clap from the doorway draws all of our attention.

My father is standing on the threshold, a smirk on his face as he applauds Anatoly. "That's very sweet. Unfortunately, while you're sitting in here 'defending your family,' the Novikov Bratva is being dragged through the mud out there." He turns to me. "I assume you know about the latest attack."

I don't. Raoul's subtle glance in my direction is enough for me to know that my second is handling it.

"We are more than capable of defending ourselves," I tell him icily.

"I know that," he says. "But if you take the deal I just secured, you won't have to."

I want to slam my office door closed and tell my father it's a closed meeting. He had decades to lead the Bratva the way he saw fit. All of that culminated in him poised to serve it up to Trofim on a silver spoon.

Unfortunately for him, I don't trust his judgment.

Unfortunately for me, I'm not in a position to turn down ideas right now.

I wave him in wearily. "Explain yourself."

He closes the door behind him and saunters towards my desk, stopping in front of Anatoly. My half-brother, to his credit, refrains from shoving our father out of the way. Instead, he stands up and shifts into the corner. Even a few feet away, he's a looming presence. He practically casts a shadow over Otets, who stretches his neck as long as it will go.

I know for a fact that Iakov Novikov hates that his bastard son stands a foot taller than he does.

"I was able to get a message to the Greeks. Helen's father is willing to stop this war in its tracks… if you marry Helen as promised."

"He's already married," Raoul interjects dourly.

The only thing my father hates more than Anatoly towering over him is Raoul being my second. He offered Raoul to me as a slave; I put him in a leadership position. If today wasn't already fucked beyond belief, his double helping of annoyance would bring me a lot of joy.

My father ignores Raoul and focuses on me. "You're married to Viviana now, but that could change. Especially if you do what honor demands. Everyone here seems to care a lot about 'honor,' after all."

"Not that you know anything about it," Anatoly mutters.

Our father snaps his attention to Anatoly. "I know that my son was murdered and I deserve retribution." He turns slowly back to me. "I deserve to kill her."

"Fuck no!" Anatoly growls.

"Trofim was already in exile. That lessens the severity of what she did," Raoul posits. It's rare for him to interfere in a conversation with my father. If he's doing it now, that means something.

"He wasn't just in exile," Anatoly argues. "Trofim was sent away for being a sadistic, worthless fuck. Mikhail sent him away and would have happily let him die in squalor. The only reason we're having this conversation now is because Viviana did the world a favor."

"That's my son you're talking about!" my father bellows.

"And you're talking about killing my *sister*," Anatoly fires back. "Viviana is more my family than Trofim ever was, so *fuck you.* You're not killing her."

I wave a hand at Nat. "Relax."

He spins towards me, eyes wide. "You can't be considering this. All so you can marry Helen and have access to a few ports? Take them some other way, Mikhail. You don't need to do this."

"This isn't for Helen. I don't care about Helen," I explain. "It's about Dante."

"Don't lie to yourself *and* me. Dante needs his mom and you know that!"

"He won't need anything once he's dead. Which will happen if we stay in this war with the Greeks." I shake my head. "I'm not having another funeral for my child. I won't do it."

"Mikhail…" Anatoly's face breaks.

On the day I buried Alyona and Anzhelina, Anatoly was the only person at the funeral with me. I told him not to come, but he showed up anyway. I never told him how much that meant to me.

I meet his eyes, holding my gaze steady. "There's no way to save Viv. She made her choice. Now, I have to think of Dante and what he needs. We need to end this war with the Greeks if anyone is going to be safe again."

Anatoly frowns, but my father steps in front of him, grinning. "I knew you'd see reason, Mikhail. Where is she? I'll take her off your hands and you—"

"She's still the mother of my child." When I stand up, he stumbles back a step. "I'll decide how and when she leaves my house. When that time comes, I'll let you know."

Anatoly drops his head in defeat, staring down at the floor. But his hand is clenched on the arm of his chair.

This fight isn't over. Not by a long shot.

59

VIVIANA

I'm half-awake when I hear the door open.

I don't think I've slept at all in hours, or maybe days. I have no sense of time anymore. Ever since Anatoly barred my door, I've been in a timeless purgatory. Waiting for Mikhail to decide if I should live or die.

For that reason, I should probably be on edge when a shadowy figure appears in my doorway… but I'm not. I blink through exhaustion, watching as the shape grows closer.

"Has he decided?" I rasp. My voice is hoarse. The last person I spoke to was Anatoly when he barred my door shut.

"Come on. Get up," a deep voice says.

Strong hands wrap around my elbow, tugging me out of bed.

I pull away from whoever it is. It's not Mikhail. That's all I know. It's the only thing that matters.

The smell is wrong and the voice is deep, but it doesn't send shivers down my spine. Or maybe I'm too far gone for spine shivers.

This is what hopelessness feels like, I think. *I'm too numb to feel anything at all. Even the things I thought I'd have to be dead to forget.*

"Viviana," the voice hisses in my ear, "get up right now if you want to live."

I blink again and it's like I'm coming out of a dream. It's like a filter has just been ripped away from my eyes, finally letting me see the world in front of me.

Anatoly is kneeling next to my bed, his square face etched with solemn lines. It's nothing like the wrinkled smiles and joy I'm used to from him.

"What are you talking about?"

He shakes his head and keeps tugging me out of bed. "There's no time to talk. We only have time to move. *Now.*"

My feet hit the floor, but I don't trust myself to stand. Meals have shown up every few hours while I've been here, but I haven't felt like eating much. The only time I've actually stood up has been to run to the bathroom and heave.

My teeth feel soft and my stomach churns at just the thought. "Are you taking me to Mikhail? Is he going to kill me?"

Anatoly starts tossing things from my closet into a trash bag. "Mikhail would regret killing you. Trofim wasn't the kind of man anyone should mourn. You killed him, but you don't deserve to be punished for it."

I'm frozen by the side of my bed, trying to sort through the muddy soup of information in front of me.

Mikhail doesn't want to kill me, so he sent Anatoly to take me away?

"Why can't I just stay here in the house?" I ask. "Mikhail said we would have a marriage in name only. If he isn't going to kill me, doesn't that mean I'll stay here?"

"If you stay here, you're dead."

The finality in his words splashes over me like a glass of ice water. For the first time in… I have no idea how many days, I feel wide awake.

"But you said Mikhail would regret if he—"

"Iakov wants you dead," Anatoly explains, shoving handfuls of random clothes into the trash bag. I see him scoop up a bikini and a winter hat in the same fist. "The only way to end the war with the Greeks and keep Dante safe is for Mikhail to marry Helen, but Iakov demanded that we give you to him as an honor killing."

Anatoly is telling me that Iakov wants me dead, but all I can focus on is, "Mikhail is going to marry Helen?"

Anatoly grabs my arm, peering into my eyes. "If we don't move now, you aren't going to get out of here alive. Be sad and jealous later. Right now, you need to live."

I am nowhere close to understanding what is happening here, but I trust Anatoly. So I bend down and yank my duffel bag from under the bed. "Leave the trash bag here. You packed a bunch of nonsense. I've had the essentials packed for days."

Despite it all, Anatoly smirks. "I knew you had some fight left in you, Viv. Now, let's go."

He looks both ways in the hallway and then heads for the stairs. I freeze in my doorway.

"Dante."

Anatoly hesitates, checking to make sure we're still alone. "He's already downstairs in the car. I carried him down asleep."

Dante is a heavy sleeper. Last December, he slept through the back half of a Christmas orchestra concert and for the entire train ride home. Hopefully, he stays asleep through whatever comes next.

The house is dark as Anatoly and I make our way down the stairs and across the first floor.

I keep expecting someone to pop out of the shadows to stop us, but the house is silent. Even Stella seems to be in bed for the night.

I look around, wondering when I'll see it all again. Somehow, this mansion became home. The people inside of it, even more so.

I don't want to leave.

But Anatoly holds the garage door open and ushers me inside. The garage is as dark as the rest of the house, but I don't dare turn on a light.

"Your car?" I assume, nodding to Anatoly's green jeep in the farthest parking space from the door.

Anatoly shakes his head and points to the black sedan in the center.

"We're taking Pyotr's car?"

"He comes and goes all the time," Anatoly explains. "No one asks questions."

Who would be asking questions? The guards? Mikhail?

I lug my duffel bag towards the car and notice a blanket-covered lump in the backseat. I toss my duffel bag into the passenger seat and move to open the back door.

"Where are you going?" Anatoly asks.

"I'm going to sit with Dante." I pull open the back door, but before I can slide inside, Anatoly is behind me. He grabs my shoulders and hauls me back.

"What?" I hiss. "I won't wake him up."

"That isn't Dante."

Anatoly holds out a hand to keep me back and peers into the backseat like he's waiting for the lump to explode.

"What do you mean, it isn't Dante?" My heart is like a jackhammer against my ribs. "He's supposed to be here."

Isn't he?

Or was it a lie?

Anatoly doesn't answer me. Instead he grabs the corner of the blanket and whips it back.

"No!" The cry that comes out of Anatoly is guttural. It's dripping with enough shock and horror that I don't need to see anything to know that something is horribly wrong.

The blanket settles at my feet, a bright red stain oozing across the fabric in the center.

No.

I squeeze my eyes closed, too afraid to look.

When Mikhail told me about the moment he found Alyona and Anzhelina dead, I couldn't imagine how it must have been for him. How the sight of your child, limp and lifeless, must haunt your every second for the rest of your life.

I thought, *I wouldn't survive it.*

That's what I'm positive is about to happen to me when Anatoly backs out of the car… and lays Stella's limp body over the stain.

I'm mortified by my own relief that it isn't my son. Then I take in her white skin. Her eyes rolled back in her head.

"Stella…" Anatoly smooths her hair away from her forehead and falls over her body. He presses his ear to her chest, listening for a heartbeat. I don't need to test it to know she doesn't have one.

"She's dead," I whisper in horror.

Anatoly shakes his head, pumping both of his hands into her chest. Her entire body spasms with the effort, but it's useless. She's been gone for a while.

I grab Anatoly's shoulder. "She's dead, Nat. She's gone. We have to—"

I don't know what we have to do. *Who did this? Why?*

"You can't be gone," Anatoly moans. He presses his forehead to her body. "Please, baby, come back."

My heart cracks and shatters for him, but another horror is dawning over me. I look in the car, but it's empty. Just a bloodstain where Stella was dumped.

"Where's Dante?" I try to jerk Anatoly away from Stella, but he's so much stronger than me and lost in his own grief. "Nat, where is he? Where's Dante?"

"Don't worry, Viviana. He's safe."

The third voice finally snaps Anatoly out of it. He lets Stella go and sits up—just in time to watch as Pyotr raises a gun and shoots him directly in the chest.

Smoke swirls from the gun in Pyotr's hand as Anatoly topples back over Stella's body.

I can't even scream; I'm so shocked, I just stand there. My hands are clapped over my mouth. My heart is a useless, clenching fist in my chest.

Then a shrill scream slices through the air.

Pyotr struggles to keep hold of the small body plastered against his leg, but he manages to grab my boy by the collar and hold him back.

Dante is weeping, lunging for Anatoly's motionless body on the cement floor. And my heart bleeds. Nothing else matters except getting to my son.

I reach for him, but Pyotr turns the gun on me.

"Don't move until I tell you to, Viv." His voice is a cruel sneer. Nothing like the kind, soft-spoken man who was in my room the other night, offering me tales of his own sorrow and promises of freedom.

None of this makes any sense. I have no clue what is happening.

"What are you doing? Why did you—" I look down at Anatoly's body on the ground and I can't even say the words.

Why did you kill him?

"Was Anatoly telling me the truth?" I ask, trying to make sense of this. "Was he saving me or are you—Is this your plan? I would never have agreed if I knew you were going to do this."

I want Mikhail. The thought pangs through me with bruising force.

"Mama!" Dante weeps. He's clinging to Pyotr's leg because he's five and he needs someone to hold. He shouldn't be seeing any of this. I should be the one comforting him. I want to protect him, but I can't. I don't know how.

"Let him go," I beg Pyotr.

Pyotr starts to open his mouth, but behind me, the garage door slides open and yet another figure joins the fray.

"I wondered if you'd try to escape your fate," Iakov says with a sigh. His hands are in his pockets, oddly relaxed given the scene in front of him. "This is why I like to handle matters like this in person. If you want someone killed right, you have to do it yourself."

The last person I expected to see here tonight is Mikhail's father. Then it hits me: he's Trofim's father, too.

"Whatever this is," I beg, "let Dante go. Take me instead."

A smile twists across his face. "Actually, I think I'll take you both."

60

MIKHAIL

Raoul and I left the mansion hours ago. I wanted plausible deniability on our side for anything that went on there while we were gone.

Plus, the Greeks have caused enough havoc to our businesses across the city that we had a few fires to put out.

Raoul is still out securing some of our more important holdings just in case this peace my father brokered with the Greeks doesn't pan out, but I couldn't focus on work. Not when the rest of my life is still raining down like volcanic ash around me.

When I pull into the garage, I'm surprised to see Pyotr's car in its usual space while Anatoly's car is gone. The plan was to take the black car and fly under the radar in a way Anatoly's radioactive-green Jeep isn't capable of. I wouldn't have assumed Nat would be back already, let alone have had time to be back and then leave again in his own car. Especially since he hasn't called me with an update yet.

I check my phone and, sure enough, nothing from Nat.

Given my life experience, I'm accustomed to anticipating the worst-case scenario. It's the first place my mind goes when something is out of the ordinary: someone has betrayed me or someone is dead. There's rarely another option.

Still, I try to shove that idea down and stay calm.

Anatoly and I reached an understanding about the Viviana situation, but that doesn't mean he's not still pissed at me for not jumping for joy when I found out my wife killed our brother. I wouldn't be surprised if I walked inside and the asshole was wearing a Team Viv t-shirt he'd made by hand.

He called her his sister. He considers her family.

I made a bigger mess of this whole situation than I ever could have imagined. I'm not the only one tangled up in it, either—I took everyone else down with me.

I climb out of the car, already texting Anatoly. **Get back here and meet in my office. I want an update.**

I send the message and instantly hear an electronic *ding* coming from the corner of the garage.

I stop short, listening.

The garage is quiet. But that doesn't mean it's empty.

I place my hand on the gun on my hip as I call Anatoly. His phone starts to ring. I hear it in my ear, but I also hear the chime echoing off the cement floors and metal walls, bouncing the sound all over the place. It's hard to track, but I follow it around Pyotr's car…

And stumble upon the worst-case scenario.

I drop to my knees. "Anatoly!" I grasp my brother's arm and

flip him over. Blood is bubbling slowly out of a hole in his chest and his eyes are closed.

His blood is flowing. *That's a good sign.*

But there's so much of it. *Not so good.*

I shake him, but he doesn't stir. Doesn't even seem to register that I'm here.

Then I see Stella beneath him. Her body is twisted at unnatural angles and her skin is mottled, pale, cold to the touch.

The only good news is that I don't see any other bodies in the garage. Viviana and Dante aren't here.

I grab my phone and dial Raoul as I feel for Anatoly's pulse. It's faint against my fingers, but it's there.

Raoul answers on the first ring, music playing in the background. He was headed to the lounge to check on the security situation there when I left him. "Hello?"

"Send the doctor to the mansion. *Now*," I hiss. "Anatoly is down."

"What the fuck happened?" Raoul balks, pure shock laced in every word.

"I have no clue. Viviana isn't here. Stella is down, too."

Stella is dead, but I can save that reveal for later on. There's nothing anyone can do for her now, anyway.

"Fuck. I should have come back with you. I should have—"

"Call the doctor and have an ambulance ready," I bark. "That's what you can do now."

Raoul blows out a shaky breath, but I hear him tapping away on the other end of the line. He's no doubt sending a message to the Bratva doctor. Anatoly needs more than what Dr. Sidorov can offer out of his little black bag of tricks, but at least Dr. Sidorov can get him to an emergency room without raising suspicions. The last thing anyone needs right now is a team of first responders crawling all over the mansion. Especially when I still have no idea who shot Anatoly to begin with.

The mansion is dark and quiet when I get inside. I search each room, moving slowly, anticipating a gun in my face at every turn. But there's nothing.

"Dr. Sidorov is on his way," Raoul tells me over the ongoing call. "I'm going to meet them at the hospital."

I don't answer. If anyone is nearby, I don't want to lose the element of surprise.

But there isn't anyone nearby.

I make it upstairs and Viviana's door is unlocked. The only person who had the key is Anatoly, so he must have gotten that far into the plan, at least, before he was shot. The room beyond is empty, clothes scattered haphazardly across the floor.

Dante's door is closed and I hesitate outside of it for a few extra seconds. I cling to the bliss that is not knowing what I'm going to find on the other side. For a few more seconds, I can pretend he's perfectly safe and asleep in his bed.

Then I push the door open and discover the ugly truth.

His bed is empty.

Dante was supposed to stay. No matter what happened with Anatoly and Viviana, Dante was supposed to be here.

If he's gone, I can only imagine what happened.

"I need every available set of eyes on the lookout for Viviana and Dante," I snarl into the phone. "I don't want them getting far."

"Dante is gone, too?" Raoul asks.

I grit my teeth and jog through the house back to Anatoly. "Viviana must have taken him. She must have—"

I get back to the garage to find Anatoly still lying on the floor, unconscious and bleeding.

Could she have done this?

I backed her into a corner. I made her feel like she didn't have another choice. She already killed one of my brothers; why not the other?

"Viviana must have shot Anatoly and escaped with Dante," I tell him. "I want her found and brought back to me. *Now*. She isn't getting away with this again."

61

VIVIANA

The world around me is darkness.

No light, no shadows. There's no variation in the absolute blackness around me.

I try to lift my hand in front of my face, but my arms are heavy. My limbs are sluggish and cold. I look down, but I can't see my own body.

"Help!" My voice is a dry rasp, paper-thin and weak.

Pain sparks in my joints with every movement. It radiates behind my eyeballs and I groan.

A sound echoes and builds. Builds. Builds.

Soon, the floor is vibrating. My teeth rattle as the hard floor at my back splinters and cracks open. A faint light creeps from inside the crack, just enough that I can see a hand reaching for me.

I twist away from the fingers inching towards me, but I can't move. My legs are lifeless and my arms flop across my chest like bags of wet sand.

"Mikhail!" I don't mean to cry for him, but I can't help it. It's instinctual. "Mikhail, help me!"

More hands protrude through the ground and claw at me. Shattered nails leave long gouges in my skin that weep blood.

This is it, *I think.* This is how I die.

One more hand, cold as the grave, erupts next to my head and clamps down over my mouth and nose.

I sit up, gasping.

The room around me spins and I have to work to blink it back into focus. Not that there's much to focus on. It's a bland room—concrete floors, white walls, a metal door.

I stare down at my body, relieved to see I'm not covered in claw marks. That nightmare, at least, isn't true. Though I'm pretty sure I've woken up from one nightmare just to find myself in an even worse one.

I drop my face into my ice-cold fingers and try to remember what happened.

It's a blur of blood and fear. Especially since I'm ninety-eight percent positive I was drugged. It would explain the small red pinprick on my right bicep. Someone injected me with something.

I have to forage through my scrambled head for every thought, but all at once, my head is clear. All of my energy funnels into the only thing that matters.

"Dante!"

I know he isn't here with me, but that doesn't stop me from spinning around and checking the floor around me. It's the same way I used to wake up in the middle of the night when he was only a baby, patting the blankets around me like maybe I lost him between the sheets. He was always in his bedroom safe and sound in his crib.

But this time, that thought isn't a comfort. We aren't in our little apartment in the city. Dante isn't safe and sound in his crib.

We're in a waking nightmare and I have no clue where my baby is.

I crawl to my feet and lunge for the metal door. I don't even make it a foot before my body is jerked painfully back.

My tailbone cracks against the cement, the wind whooshing out of me.

That's when I hear the rattling of chains. That's when I feel the frigid metal wrapped around my wrists and ankles. My skin is already so cold I didn't notice it before.

"Hello!" I scream, not even stopping to think if it's a good idea.

I have no idea who is on the other side of this room. But if there's even a tiny sliver of a chance that it's my son, I'm going to scream with everything I have.

"Hello!" My dry throat aches, but I yell as loud as I can. "Who's there? Help me!"

A key slides into the door. Metal tumblers click and turn painfully slowly, giving me too much time to imagine who might be on the other side.

Maybe Mikhail is here to save me. He's going to get me and Dante out of here and avenge Anatoly's murder.

Then the door opens and a man I've never seen before is lurking in the threshold. His face is half in shadow, but the yellow glint of his smile is hard to miss.

"'Help'!" he mocks, his voice shrill and cruel. "'Who's there'?"

"What do you want with me?" I spit.

There's a single yellow light above the door. It casts ghoulish shadows across his face as he steps further into the room.

"I want to find out what's so fucking special about you," he says in his normal voice. "The woman who started a war."

Is this guy one of the enemies Mikhail was trying to save me from? Is Iakov Novikov working for the other side?

"I didn't start anything. I have nothing to do with any of this."

"That's not what I've heard. First, you were engaged to Trofim. Now, you're married to Mikhail. The Novikov men are fascinated with you." He clicks his tongue, eyeing me appraisingly. "What I want is to figure out *why*."

Slowly, the man pushes the door closed behind him.

The room is small, but with him towering over the only exit —which I suspect is now locked—I feel like I'm being buried alive. With every inhale, there's another shovelful of graveyard dirt weighing on my chest. Less oxygen to take in. Less room to move.

Less hope of getting out alive.

"Please," I rasp, clinging desperately to reality. If I let myself fall apart in front of this man, I don't know what will happen. "My father—he has money. If that's what you want, I can get it to you."

I haven't spoken to my father in six years, so using him as a lifeline is a stretch, to say the least. Even if I called him right now and told him what was going on, he'd probably let this man do whatever is swirling around in his sick head as punishment for disobeying him.

No one is coming to save me.

His mouth curves into a smirk. "I don't want your money, darling."

A shiver moves down my spine. With every step he takes towards me, I feel myself slipping out of my body. With every passing second, I'm further and further away from this room.

When I close my eyes, I see the beach house in Costa Rica. I see Dante and Mikhail building sandcastles on the beach, the turquoise blue water stretching out forever behind them. I can feel the soft sheets of our bed and feel Mikhail's warm bulk against my side.

When we were there, I imagined a different future for all of us. I could see us becoming a family, growing together and carving out something like a normal life amidst the chaos.

So I go there now as the man wraps a clammy hand around my arm.

"I won't hurt you." His words grate against my eardrum, ripping me out of my fantasy world. "Just stay quiet."

A whimper forces its way up my throat as he forces me down to the floor and presses a knee between my legs. Just as he tries to pry my locked thighs apart, I hear another key in the door.

Lovely. That must be more of them. An audience to watch my torture.

Except the man on top of me freezes. He looks back at the door, confused. He clearly isn't expecting anyone else.

Then the door flies open so hard it bounces off the wall and the man springs away from me like I'm on fire.

The fear disappears in an instant, replaced by a stupid, stubborn, blinding hope.

I'm saved, I think. *Someone's here to save me after all.*

62

MIKHAIL

The hallway is dark, save for the lone light above me. The hospital hallway groans and clicks and twitches with noises from the rooms lining the corridor. I pace back and forth and the light overhead flickers with me, like the energy radiating from my body is fucking with it.

"Have you found anything?" I ask the second Raoul answers his phone.

"I'm looking. *Everyone* is looking," he says. "There's nothing yet."

"The security cameras—"

"Off," he growls, every bit as frustrated about yet another setback as I am. "Someone turned every single camera between Viviana's room and the garage to standby. The one at the gate showed Anatoly's car leaving, but it's too dark to see inside it."

Could that have been Viviana? I wouldn't have thought she knew where the security cameras were or how to work the system. Then again, I also wouldn't have thought she'd be capable of killing Trofim and lying about it, or shooting Stella and Anatoly in the chest.

That'll teach me to underestimate people.

My hand tightens around the phone until I'm sure I'll crush it like a can. "Keep looking. We need to find them."

"How's Anatoly?" Raoul asks.

"Unconscious, but stable."

When he wakes up, he'll be thrilled to know the surgeon credits his barrel chest for why he doesn't have an exit wound, which probably would have caused him to bleed out. The bullet will stay inside of him until the day he dies, but that day won't be today. It's a win.

"Call me with updates," Raoul says. "I'll do the same."

I want to be out there looking for my son, but someone has to be here with Anatoly. Maybe he heard where Viviana was going before she fled. He might be able to give us some insight about what happened and where to look for her.

I just need him to fucking *wake up.*

I drop down into an uncomfortable plastic chair and comb my fingers through my hair. Maybe I should have let my father kill Viviana the way he wanted. Would Dante be safe in bed if I had? Would Anatoly be uninjured? Would Stella be alive?

Would any of that change my mind?

The thought of a world without Viviana makes me wonder if I don't know what it's like to be shot in the chest, after all.

Even after everything she has done, letting her be killed would fucking hurt.

Why can't I just let her go? I let her get inside my head even after I swore I wouldn't. I took risks I shouldn't have, and for what?

This entire night proves why love is the worst kind of parasite. You let it in and think it's good for you. Somehow, you convince yourself that whatever shit comes your way because of it, it was worth it. Inevitably, though, at the end of it, you're used up, miserable, and alone.

But I won't make that same mistake again.

My head is still in my hands when I hear a crash from the hospital room behind me. "What in the—" Another crash echoes into the hall. "Where the fuck am I?"

I'm on my feet and in the room before any of the nurses can even get around the nurse's station. Anatoly is standing next to his hospital bed with his IV pole on the floor. The bags are leaking across the floor—not that it matters, because he's actively ripping the IV out of his arm.

"You better leave that in, brother. Unless you want to die."

He looks up at me. He's deathly pale, but his usual smile spreads across his face. "It'll take a hell of a lot more than a shot to the chest to kill me."

Not much *more*, I want to say.

The nurse in charge of Anatoly disagrees, too. "Lie down," she barks, shoving him back into bed while simultaneously calling for a maintenance team to come take care of the mess. "You've been unconscious for hours and the first thing you do when you open your eyes is jump out of bed and start tugging on tubes." She shakes her head, inserting another IV into his arm with a little more force than strictly necessary. "Stay in bed before you do something stupid and collapse your other lung."

Anatoly isn't scared of anything, but he looks cowed by this fierce, middle-aged nurse. He apologizes softly and dips his head in respect as she finishes her work and leaves.

Once she's gone, he peeks up at me. "I think I'm in trouble."

"You were almost dead. You've been unconscious for hours."

His eyes go glassy. I can tell he's deep in his head, reliving the moments before he was shot.

"Do you remember anything?" I ask.

His jaw flexes and his eyes narrow and when his voice emerges, it's a feral growl like nothing else I've ever heard from him before. "I remember everything."

I nod solemnly. "Good. The more detail you can give me, the sooner we can find them." I lay a hand on his shoulder. "I know you care about Viviana, but she isn't going to get away with this."

"She?" Anatoly frowns. "What are you talking about?"

"I'm talking about you getting shot in the chest, brother."

"Did you check the cameras? Did you watch any of the footage of what happened?"

"They were all offline. I don't know how she did it, but she must have—"

"*She* didn't do anything," he interrupts, explaining it to me the way he explained electricity to Dante last week. "Viviana had nothing to do with this."

I shake my head. "But if she didn't, who—"

"Pyotr." The heart rate monitor behind Anatoly's bed spikes. If he doesn't calm down, the nurse will be back in here with a stern warning for him, I'm sure. Though one look at the murderous grimace on Anatoly's face might be enough to scare even her off. "I don't know who he's working for or why he did it, but… it was Pyotr."

I drop down into the chair next to Anatoly's bed, physically unable to stand.

Viviana didn't do this.

Viviana didn't do this.

It's the only theory I've had for hours and this new information doesn't compute.

"Tell me everything," I rasp. "Every single detail. I need it all."

So Anatoly does.

"An hour after you and Raoul left, I went to Viviana's room like we planned. She asked about Dante, like we both knew she would, and I told her he was waiting for us in the garage. I knew once she saw Dante wasn't down there that she'd throw a fit, but I figured I'd rather explain it to her there than in the hallway outside of his bedroom. I was gonna give her the old, *'It's either leave without Dante or die at the hands of Iakov'* ultimatum. I figured that would knock some sense into her."

"Un-fucking-likely," I mutter.

"But we never got that far, because as soon as we got into the garage, Viviana saw something in the backseat. She thought it was Dante. Hell, for a second, so did I. I thought maybe he was hiding under a blanket or something. It was small enough that it could have been—" He squeezes his eyes closed, blowing out a tight breath. "It was Stella. She was already—I don't know when he did it, but Pyotr shot her, too."

A tear rolls down his cheek. I reach out and squeeze his shoulder.

Love is a parasite, but that doesn't mean I don't feel bad that my brother got bit by it, too.

He thought he was being covert, but I've known about him and Stella sneaking around for months. Now, she's gone. I know how deeply that pain hurts.

"I'm sorry," Anatoly croaks out. "I was so focused on Stella that I didn't even see Pyotr coming. I looked up and h-he shot me." He shakes his head like he still can't believe it. "I didn't even hear the door open. I was fucking lost. Then, suddenly, I was down and... I don't know what happened after that."

He took my family. That lying fucking *mudak* stole my wife and child, that's what happened.

"Pyotr took Viviana and Dante," I tell him icily.

"Dante is gone?" Anatoly slams his fist into the thin mattress. "Fuck. I'm sorry, Mikhail. I should have—"

"Should have what? Been faster than a bullet and taken Pyotr out before he could get away?" I finish for him. "Yeah, that would've been nice. But since we're all human here, let's just focus on what comes next."

Anatoly sighs. "Yeah. Okay."

"He didn't count on you surviving and was probably hoping

he'd have a few more hours before we figured it out. That's why he took your car instead of his."

Anatoly gasps. "He took my car?!"

"I'll get you another one," I snap. "Help me find Viviana and Dante and I'll get you whatever lime-green monstrosity you want."

"I'm not mad he took my car, you idiot. I'm—" Anatoly twists around, looking on either side of the bed. Whatever he's doing, I know his nurse wouldn't like it. "Where the fuck is my phone?"

I spot it, grab it off the desk behind me, and hand it to him.

"I'm not mad he took my car," Anatoly repeats. He turns his phone around to show me a little flashing dot in the center of the screen. "I'm *thrilled*. Because the asshole doesn't know about the tracker I keep in the glove compartment." Anatoly is tapping away. "I'll send the live location to you and Raoul now."

My phone buzzes a second later.

"And Mikhail?" Anatoly calls as I'm already halfway out the door. "Before you kill him, tell Pyotr I sent you."

I nod. "I'll make sure he hurts, Nat. I'll make sure he knows why."

63

VIVIANA

It only takes a second after the door opens for all of my naive hopes to die.

"Fuck off, Lukyan," Iakov Novikov barks. "Leave the woman alone. She's been through enough."

The guard—Lukyan, apparently; I won't forget that name—gives me one last look before he slouches out of the room like a puppy who just got a good swat on the nose.

Iakov saved me from whatever vile things Lukyan had planned. The trouble is, whatever Iakov has in store might be worse. Actually, I'm positive it is.

I scoot away from him until my back is against the farthest wall. He watches me with dark eyes, his face unreadable. "This cell is horrendous," he remarks after a long, pained silence.

I blink at him, waiting for the other shoe to drop. Waiting for him to grin and tell me he's thrilled I'm finally in hell where I belong.

Iakov Novikov leans through the door to my cell and looks in each corner like he's physically repulsed. "Honestly, this is deplorable. Inhumane."

I know better than to get my hopes up at this point, but it's hard to keep the human spirit down. I can't stop myself from asking, "Are you going to let me go?"

He laughs. "Of course not. You're a murderer. But that doesn't mean we should treat you like an animal." He angles around to talk to someone in the hallway. "Get her a mattress or something. She'll be here for a while; we might as well make her comfortable."

"How long will I be here?" I blurt. "What are you planning to do with me?"

"That is the question, isn't it?" he muses as he turns back, drumming his fingers together in thought. "If you'd stayed in the mansion, Mikhail probably would have overseen the whole thing. He wouldn't have let me have too much fun. He would've forced me to make it quick. But now..." He grins and I'm forced, for the first time, to see how much Iakov looks like Anatoly. They have the exact same smile. My heart breaks for my friend. "Now, I get to do with you as I please. I plan to take my time making sure your punishment is just right."

I force down a shiver. I don't want him to see one single shred of my fear. "Did you even care about Trofim? You don't seem to care about Mikhail. You don't seem broken up about the fact that Pyotr killed Anatoly while kidnapping me." I shrug. "I don't understand how you could look at your three children and decide Trofim is the one to fight for."

"Trofim was my true heir!" he roars, launching himself into my room.

I fly back against the wall so hard I see stars.

Iakov blows out a breath and seems to steady himself, stopping a few feet short of me. "Mikhail is a strong leader, but he has never been able to manage that soft heart of his. He isn't a monster the way his brother was."

"You *want* your son to be a monster?"

"I want my family to survive in this world," he corrects testily. "I want my children to build empires and rule them. If they have to be monsters to do that, then so be it. *Heroes* get themselves killed. *Heroes* bleed out on a garage floor because they tried to help their brother's killer escape. *Heroes* are useless to me."

"Anatoly was a better man than you'll ever be!"

"Perhaps." He shrugs. "That doesn't count for much now, does it? He's dead and I'm still here."

Without thinking, I lunge at him. I throw all of my energy into reaching for his neck so I can squeeze the life out of his fat throat the way he deserves.

But, once again, the chains jerk me back.

Iakov looks startled, at least, as he backs towards the door. "Careful, Viviana. You'd hate to scare the boy."

I don't know what he means…

Until Dante appears behind him.

His head is down, chin to chest, golden brown hair covering his eyes. His shoulders are shaking. My heart drops into my stomach as I plummet to my knees. "Dante?"

He glances up at me quickly and then looks away. I watch a tear roll down his nose.

"What did you do to him?" I growl.

If Iakov thought I wanted to kill him a second ago, he has no idea what I'm thinking now. If he so much as hurt a hair on Dante's head, I'll skin him alive. I'll shred the meat from his bones and feed it back to him.

My hands shake with rage.

"What did I do to him?" Iakov repeats like the idea is absurd. Like he didn't just abduct Dante from his bed and shoot his favorite uncle in front of him. "I didn't do anything to him. I would never hurt my grandson."

I snort in disgust. "Too late for that. He's traumatized."

Iakov looks down at him, assessing. "So it appears. But unfortunately, that is what it takes. If he wants to make it in this world, he has to be prepared to see things he doesn't like. To *do* things he doesn't like. Mikhail never would have trained him up properly."

"He'll kill you," I warn. "As soon as he realizes Dante is gone, he'll kill you."

There's no need to specify who I'm talking about. Iakov already knows. Mikhail may hate me, but he loves our son. That's the only thing I know anymore.

"He'd have to find us first." Iakov smirks. "Besides, I'm sure he's busy planning the funeral for his bastard brother."

Iakov starts to leave and I panic. Right now, I can see Dante. He's safe and alive in front of me. That's better than the unknown.

"Please!" I rasp. "Let Dante stay with me. I'll take care of him."

"I'm not sure you're in the best position for that right now," Iakov demurs. He pulls Dante close, forcing my son to hug his side. "I'll take the boy under my wing. Don't you worry."

That's exactly what I'm afraid of.

I ignore Iakov and focus on Dante. I give him a smile—my best approximation of one, anyway. "I'm okay, bud," I tell him. "I'm okay and I'll see you soon, alright?"

Dante nods, but he still won't look at me. It's probably hard for him to see me chained up like this.

I fold my hands behind my back to hide the shackles and blow him a kiss. "I love you, baby."

"I love you, too, Mama," he mumbles through another sob.

My heart splits wide open, spilling out on the floor in front of me.

Then Iakov shuts the door and he's gone.

The room feels even smaller than it did before. The silence is painful. I may never get out of this room—I've made my peace with that. But the only thing I can cling to as I curl into a ball in the corner of the cell is that Mikhail won't abandon our son.

No matter what has happened between us, I have to believe he'll do what's best for Dante.

It's the only hope I have left.

64

MIKHAIL

The entire time I'm flying across town, I'm sure I'll find Anatoly's abandoned car idling along some curb, the driver's door thrown open, with Pyotr nowhere in sight.

He has to know I'm coming for him. He has to know that, by crossing me, he's signed his death warrant.

He killed Stella, tried to kill Anatoly, and kidnapped my wife and child. Even if he has already fled, he could never get far enough away. When he dies—which he will—it will be by my hand.

And my God, it will fucking hurt.

When I reach the beacon location, I do find a neon green Jeep that can only have belonged to my brother idling along the curb—but it isn't empty. As I edge down the sidewalk, I hear Pyotr's voice coming from the rolled-down window.

Idiot. His death is going to come even sooner than I hoped.

"It's me. *Again*," Pyotr growls, a phone against his ear. "I held up my end of the bargain and I'm waiting for word from you.

You have what you want. Now, I need what you promised. I know you're good for it, Iakov. But you need to call me back."

I knew I'd come to regret not killing my father the same night I exiled Trofim. I should have suspected he was involved from the very beginning. But even as the rage deep in my gut burns and grows, I want to laugh.

Pyotr betrayed me, thinking my father was going to keep whatever bullshit promises he made?

I almost feel bad killing the fool.

Actually, I don't. He deserves whatever is coming to him.

"I'll wait here another ten minutes, but any longer than that isn't safe," Pyotr continues. "Please call me before—"

The words die in his throat when I press the muzzle of my gun to his temple.

"Hang up the phone," I growl.

Pyotr clings to the phone for another second. It's like he's waiting for my father to pick up. Like maybe some lifeline will appear on the other end of the phone and save him.

But there's no salvation coming for him.

"Now."

Finally, he hangs up and drops the phone in his lap. He raises his hands into the air. They tremble in front of him.

"Mikhail, I—" He swallows nervously.

"Get out of the car."

"Let's just talk about this," he pleads. "I want to explain myself to—"

I cock the gun so he can hear it. "How about *that* for an explanation? Do you understand my side of things now, Pyotr?"

He nods and reaches slowly for the door handle. He slides out of the car reluctantly, his eyes locked on mine.

The street is dark and deserted. The only streetlight working is at the far end of the block. We're shrouded in shadow, but I'd like to be somewhere a little more private for what I have planned.

I tip my head towards the alley behind us. "Start walking."

A cross between a growl and a whimper works out of his throat. "Mikhail, you have to understand—"

"The only thing I need to understand is that Anatoly will be pissed if I get your brains on his upholstery," I interrupt. "But I'm sure he'll understand I didn't have a choice if you don't start walking."

Pyotr marches slowly to the alley. He looks up and down the road, but there's no one in sight. Just the two of us.

The stupid suit jacket Pyotr insists on wearing blends into the darkness of the alley. All I can see is the white of his neck peeking over the collar. So that is where I aim.

I snatch Pyotr up by the back of his scrawny neck and slam him against the brick wall. The air in his lungs gushes out in a single huff.

"Where did you take Viviana and Pyotr?"

"It was your father!" he rasps. "Your father organized everything. I was only the transportation. It's my job to—"

"It's your job to do as *I* tell you. You stopped working for my father six years ago and you fucking know it." I spin him around and crack the gun across his face. A gash opens across his cheekbone, spewing blood. He scrambles to shield himself from another blow. "Tonight didn't happen because you were confused about your duties. Tonight was you starting a war with me. Now, I want to know why."

"You're going to kill me either way," he says, spitting blood onto the pavement. "Might as well get it over with."

I wedge the gun under his chin, leaning in close. "I'll kill you if I'm feeling merciful—if you earn it. Keeping you chained in the basement until Anatoly is well enough to get his own revenge is another option I'm toying with."

His eyes flare with panic. He's seen firsthand what Anatoly is capable of.

"Do I need to remind you that you killed his girlfriend?"

Something like regret flashes in Pyotr's eyes. "I didn't know they were—Anatoly must have told Stella his plan. She saw me messing with the car you'd loaded with supplies and tried to stop me. It was his fault that she was in my way."

"Go ahead and tell him that when he comes to find you in the dungeon. He'll love hearing how it was *his* fault that you murdered his woman and shot him in the chest."

"I don't know why I'm surprised," he mutters. "Anatoly fucks up and you still can't find fault with him."

I choke him with the barrel, crushing his windpipe against the wall. "He didn't 'fuck up.' He got shot by someone he trusted. Our only mistake was calling you a friend."

And letting myself get distracted. Maybe if I hadn't been so preoccupied with Viviana, I would have noticed that Pyotr was a spy.

Pyotr chokes out a laugh. "A *friend?* Do you treat all your friends like servants? I've worked for you for six years and I've never been invited to a family dinner. You were happy keeping me under your foot. I was never going to move up the ranks."

I blink at him. "This is about jealousy? You're mad that you and I aren't best fucking pals?"

He juts his chin out, looking every bit like an oversized child. "Considering you are the spare son who claimed the title you wanted, I'd expect you to resonate with my circumstances. I didn't plan to be a driver forever."

"So you ask for a fucking promotion!" I snap. "You don't kidnap my wife and child!"

"Iakov promised that he and I would reclaim the title. I was going to rule in Dante's stead until he was old enough, and then—"

I laugh in his face. "You thought my father was going to let *you* lead? God, it's even more pathetic than I thought. You're a fucking idiot."

"He was lonely," Pyotr spits. "He lost all of his sons for one reason or another. I became a substitute of sorts. On long drives, he confided in me. We became close. He and I both agreed that Trofim was the right choice and that Iakov should reclaim his position to save the Bratva; we just didn't see a way to unite the men behind an aging figurehead when you had already fucked everything up so much. Then Dante came along. I was actually the one to suggest the idea, and Iakov—"

"My father made you feel like a special little boy," I sneer. "He played you for the fool you are and made you believe that he would reward you for betraying me. You did his dirty work. Now, he has my wife and son and you are being hung out to dry. There's no world in which you were ever going to be even a temporary *pakhan*."

Pyotr sags against the wall as realization dawns.

"You might as well play him back and tell me where he took Viviana and Dante."

"He tricked me," Pyotr whispers to himself.

My phone vibrates in my pocket. I wouldn't usually check messages in the middle of an interrogation, but Pyotr looks like he's going to be sick. I'm not worried about him running away.

I found them. He's holding them at your old house. Finish up and meet me there.

I force down the rage, stowing it away for later, and lower my gun to Pyotr's stomach.

"Wait!" he gasps. "I'll tell you—"

"I don't need anything from you anymore." I pull the trigger and he hunches over, screaming as hot blood coats my hand. "That's for Anatoly."

I step back and shoot one kneecap, my ears still ringing from the first shot. "That's for Stella."

As he clutches one leg, I take aim at the other. "That's for Dante."

He sinks to the ground, weeping as his ruined legs splay wide. I aim directly between them and fire.

Once the screaming dies down, I say, "And *that* is for touching my wife."

Pyotr falls sideways onto the damp pavement, blood pooling around him. Usually, I'd stand here and enjoy the sight of him bleeding out in abject agony. But he's screaming so much that I'm worried about drawing too much attention.

"Ultimately, I don't care why you betrayed me," I tell him, even though I'm not sure he's in much of a listening mood. "The only thing that matters is that it's the last thing you'll ever do."

He lifts his bloody face just as I pull the trigger.

The light in his dark eyes fades and he crumples into the alley like the pile of wasted potential he is.

In a lot of ways, I'd count this as a mercy. Pyotr's pain lasted five minutes when it should have lasted years.

Lucky for him, I have somewhere to be.

65

MIKHAIL

As soon as Alyona and Anzhelina died, I had the house destroyed. I could have repaired the bullet holes and replaced the bloody carpets, but I never would have walked the halls of that house without seeing their bodies. Without smelling gunpowder in the air. The house had to be razed into nonexistence.

But while the building was reduced to rubble and carted away, the property itself remained in Novikov control. For the same reason I couldn't live in the house, I didn't keep up with what happened to the land. It's not like I wanted to go for picnics on the ground where my family had been slaughtered. My idea of a relaxing afternoon wasn't strolling alone around the lawn where I once imagined my daughter growing up.

While I was busy blocking that nightmare from my memory, my father decided to make good use of my tragedy.

And apparently, he has a sick sense of irony.

The wrought-iron gates are rusted, the hinges barely clinging to the rest of the fence. It doesn't look like anyone has touched them since I tore down the driveway and left this place in my rearview almost ten years ago. I'm sure that's what my father wanted people to think, anyway.

Raoul is already inside the gates. I can see him and a few other men pacing around a concrete dome rising out of the ground. As I get closer, I see the metal door set into the concrete.

It's a cellar.

"It was all Anatoly," Raoul tells me as soon as I get out of the car. "After you left the hospital, he looked at the history of the tracker from his car. He could see everywhere Pyotr had been. The idiot left the mansion and drove straight here. He didn't make any stops or try to evade detection at all."

"I'm not surprised. We're talking about a man who thought Iakov was going to let him lead the Bratva."

Raoul's eyebrows rise. "You're kidding."

"We'll laugh about it later." Actually, I doubt I'll be laughing about any of this any time soon. "Right now, I want to get inside."

"Since I'm guessing Viv and Dante weren't with Pyotr when you found him, they have to be down there. I just don't know who else is down there," Raoul admits. "I wanted to wait for you to—"

"I'll go in." I check my gun. There are only two shots left, but it's more than enough for what I have planned for my father. I don't want to waste my time on torture. I just want him dead.

Raoul looks nervous, but he doesn't try to stop me. He knows better.

My men lift the hatch and I step down into the darkness.

A steep, narrow stairway leads down into a maze of hallways lit only by yellow emergency lights lining the corners of the low ceilings. Clearly, whoever built the hatch utilized the preexisting basement. The space is sprawling, but it's broken down into a web of tiny rooms with metal doors.

Cells, I realize as I clear empty room after empty room. *They're prison cells.*

I shove aside thoughts of what my father had planned for this place. Was he going to trap everyone who wasn't loyal to him down here? Would I have found myself in one of these cells one day?

The hypothetical doesn't matter. What matters is that my wife and son are in these rooms, buried in the ground beneath where I already lost one family.

I won't lose another.

I shove aside the possibility that I'm too late. I have to assume there is time and that, this time, I'll save them.

But as I turn the last corner and find a dead-end, I don't have to work to clear my mind. Every thought in my head except for one disappears as I see a small, shivering figure curled up in the hallway.

"Dante?"

His head pops up and I know instantly it's my son.

"Dad?" he croaks, sniffling back tears. Then he's on his feet and sprinting towards me. He throws his arms around my neck and I'm too stunned to move—to speak.

Dad.

He called me *Dad.*

"I knew you'd come for us," he cries, squeezing me tight. "Pyotr is bad and hurt Anatoly, but I knew you were good."

He saw Anatoly get shot. He was there for all of it.

I suddenly regret not taking more time dispatching Pyotr. He deserved so much worse.

I scoop Dante up and carry him with me down the hall. "Where's your mom?"

He points a shaky finger towards the last door on the right. "The man left, but he didn't unlock her door. I can't get her out. She's crying, but I can't help her." He hiccups, trying to control his sobs while he's talking a mile a minute. "The man scared her, I could tell. He scared me, too. I told him to let her go, but he wouldn't. The chains are big. And now, he's gone and he chained her up and they're big. I can't break them. Even you can't break them. Is she going to be stuck here? Is she going to die?"

"Hush now, son. No one is going to die," I assure him. And I realize I mean it.

It's why I told Anatoly to get Viviana out of the mansion in the first place. I wasn't going to let my father kill her. She may have lied to me about killing Trofim, but she is still my son's mother.

That alone is a good reason to keep Viviana alive. Whatever else I might feel for her isn't important.

It turns out my father didn't leave a key behind because the door is already unlocked; it's just heavy enough that Dante can't open it on his own. As to why Viviana isn't trying to open it from the inside... I don't want to think about that yet.

I lower Dante to the floor and he instantly clings to me. His fingers dig into the collar of my shirt, holding tight.

"I'll be right back, but I have to go make sure your mom is alright."

His blue eyes are panicked. "Is she okay?"

Fuck, I hope so.

"I'm sure she is," I tell him. "But I need to go in there and check on her. I want you to stay right here, okay?"

He nods, his chin dimpling with the effort not to cry.

"Good boy." I kiss the top of his head and then turn to face the door.

I didn't feel a thing walking down into the bunker. But now, facing a door I know Viviana is behind, my heart jolts.

I don't want to parse out why.

I don't want to think about what she's been through.

I don't want to do anything except get her out of here and figure out what happens next.

As soon as I open the door, I hear the rattle of chains. Viviana is huddled in the corner, her arms coiled around herself to protect from the cold concrete and damp walls.

She looks up as the door opens and she is half-wild. Her face is pale and her green eyes are circled in purplish bruises. Her hair is a matted tangle over her shoulder. She looks hollow and sick.

But when she stands up with hands fisted at her sides and her mouth set in a firm line, all I can think is…

I want her.

After everything, I still fucking want her.

"Mikhail?" she rasps.

Her excitement isn't as genuine as Dante's. For good reason: she doesn't trust me the way she once did.

That goes both ways.

"My father is gone and Pyotr is dead," I inform her. "Dante is in the hallway."

She blinks, processing it all in a second. Less than.

"Anatoly?" she whispers like saying his name out loud might jinx it.

The only good decision my father ever made was choosing Viviana as a bride for his son, I think. She's tough enough for the title, that's for sure. She looks like she could collapse at any second, but she's staying on her feet and assessing the situation.

She's a warrior at heart.

"Alive. He's the reason I found—"

"Thank God," she sobs.

Then she hurls herself at me, but I'm just out of reach. The chains jerk at her wrists and ankles. She's frozen in front of me, arms extended. If the chains weren't there, I'm positive she'd be face-down on the floor right now. Her face is crumpled with exhaustion and relief and fear and a million other emotions I can't even begin to name.

Even though I know I shouldn't, I step forward and close the gap between us.

She falls against my body with a sigh. She smells like damp and dirt, but under it all is the sweetness I'm used to. The vanilla honey scent that I'd have to burn my mansion down to get rid of.

"Mikhail..." Viviana sobs my name like she's still trying to convince herself that I'm real. She holds me tighter, burying her face in my neck.

I let her hug me. I let her soak the sleeve of my shirt with tears as I pat her back. I can feel her heart thumping in her chest and I count each beat.

She's alive. Feeling the proof eases some clenched part of me.

"Mama?" Dante peeks his head into the cell and Viviana cries harder.

She reaches for Dante, but doesn't let me go. She pulls me into the hug until we're all huddled on the floor.

This is for Dante, I tell myself. *I'm doing all of this for Dante.*

When they're ready, I break apart the chains and lead them both out of the bunker and straight into the backseat of the car Raoul is driving.

Within minutes, Dante curls into his mom's side and falls asleep. Viviana's cold fingers have been folded in mine since we were still navigating the hallways of the bunker.

"This isn't how I thought today would end," she whispers,

looking up at me. When I frown, she squeezes my hand like that's explanation enough.

Nothing with Viviana has gone the way I thought it would. Since the moment I saw her at that engagement party, she has surprised me at every turn.

Which is exactly why she has to go.

"The day isn't over," I say coldly.

She stiffens next to me. "What does that mean? Aren't we going home?"

"Dante and I are going home," I explain. "But when we get back to the mansion, you're going to leave." She tries to pull her hand away, but I snatch her wrist. "Don't wake up Dante and cause a scene. This will be easier if he stays asleep."

Her eyes flick from our son to me and back again. She shakes her head. "You aren't going to make me leave. You just saved me. Twice."

"Anatoly wanted to save you." It's not a lie; it's just not the entire truth.

I told Anatoly to save her, but admitting that doesn't change what needs to happen.

"He wouldn't have helped me escape without your permission," she protests. "You don't want me to die, Mikhail."

"I may not want you to die, but that doesn't mean I want you," I lie through my teeth, every word ripping out of me in burning agony. "I thought being with you would keep Dante safe. Now, I'm in a war with the Greeks and the truth is… you're not worth it."

The blow lands exactly like I thought it would. She gasps and a tear slips down her cheek. "You expect me to leave and let you take my son from me?"

"I'm keeping Dante whether you make a scene or not. You aren't *letting* me do anything. Your only choice here is deciding what Dante's last memory of you should be. Do you want it to be cuddling in the backseat of this car, or screaming and crying as you're dragged off my property?"

Raoul would hate to drag Viviana away, but he'd do it if I asked.

She stares at me in disbelief as tears flow silently down her cheeks. I didn't know it was possible for someone to look so beautiful while they cry.

She looks broken. Shattered. The fire I've always seen in her eyes dims. "You aren't going to change your mind."

It's not a question, but I explain myself anyway. I say the one thing I know she can't disagree with.

"Ending this war with the Greeks is how I can keep Dante safe."

People in my own Bratva are pushing back against me. I won't fight on two fronts. Not when it could put Dante at risk. I'm going to do everything I can to keep him safe.

"So you're going to marry her?" she asks softly. "Helen?"

"That doesn't concern you."

"As long as I have this ring on my finger, it concerns me."

I hold out my open palm. "Then give the ring back. You hate that fucking monstrosity anyway."

She jerks her hand away. "I made a vow. Until death does us part, this ring is staying on my finger."

A couple days ago, I would have loved hearing that. I would've taken her home and showed her exactly how much I loved hearing it, several times over.

Now, it's too late.

I slide my matching ring off. Viviana's name is indented in my skin thanks to her smart ass addition on the inside of the band. I toss the ring into her lap. "Then take mine. I don't need it anymore."

Her chin dimples, but otherwise, she tries not to react. Slowly, she pockets the ring and then wraps her arms around Dante.

The rest of the drive is silent as she softly cries into his hair, kissing his temple as he sleeps. She holds him like it's the last time. Because it is.

I wait for her to change her mind and rail and scream against my decision, but when I carefully pluck Dante from the car and hand him to Raoul, Viviana doesn't say a word.

She doesn't speak again until Raoul and Dante disappear inside the mansion.

"You promised me that you'd let him be a little boy first and an heir second." She sniffles, her breath hitching with stifled sobs. "If there's any vow you keep, please make it that one."

"I don't owe you anything, Viviana."

"But you owe *him*," she spits. "You owe your son a real father since he won't have—since I won't be—"

Since he won't have a mother.

Since she won't be with him.

"I promise," I growl, cutting her off. She has cried more than enough tonight. I can't take any more. None of it changes what I need to do. "I'll remember."

Viviana holds my gaze. Seconds skew and twist until I'm not sure how long we've been standing here.

I'm still waiting for her to argue that she should stay. Part of me wants her to. Maybe she'll make a good point and change my mind.

She doesn't. And I can't waste any more of my time or energy on her. It's what got us into this mess in the first place.

"There's a car waiting for you." I gesture towards the garage. "Pyotr's car, actually. It's the one Anatoly was supposed to take you in tonight. The car is yours to keep."

"Am I supposed to thank you?"

I ignore her. "You can go wherever you want. But I suggest you go far."

"This isn't about what I want," she mutters. Then she clears her throat. "I don't have any money. I didn't have much savings before and I haven't been to work in weeks."

"There's money in the car. Enough for you to get started. Plus the rings."

She frowns. "What about the rings?"

"Pawn them. They're fucking hideous, but they're expensive."

"Yeah. I guess so." She nervously works the gaudy ring around her finger with her thumb. "You know, for a second there, I thought we were going to make it work."

"Make what work?"

Pain flickers across her face. She shrugs. "You. Me. *Us*. For a second, it seemed like we might be happy."

"This was never about being happy."

It still isn't.

Because if it was...

I shake my head. "This is a business deal. It's about what benefits me."

"And I don't benefit you anymore?" she asks softly.

The problem is that I don't benefit you, Viviana. Being close to me is a promise of death. I'm saving you by sending you away. You'll hate me for it, but it's the only thing I can do to keep you safe.

"No," I say simply. "You don't."

She swipes at her cheek, brushing away a tear I can't see. "Well, I guess I should leave while I still can."

It's what I told her the night we spent in that bridal suite. Only, back then, I actually wanted her to leave. I wanted her to get out before Trofim or her father dragged her back.

Now, she needs to leave while *I* have the strength to let her. Otherwise, I'll drag her back inside the mansion and bar the doors.

"Goodbye, Viviana," I say as I'm already turning towards the house. I need to walk away and end things here. Keep it short and sweet. But I can't stop myself from adding, "Take care of yourself."

She releases a shuddering breath. "Goodbye, Mikhail."

I don't watch her get in the car or pull down the drive. I can't. Even when I hear the security system chime, alerting me to the gates being opened, it takes all I have to sit in my office and not tear down the driveway after her.

I have to do what's right for the Bratva and what's right for Dante.

After six years and a lifetime of chaos, Viviana Giordano is finally gone for good.

66

VIVIANA

Iakov Novikov is chasing me.

It's what I tell myself again and again as I drive away from my son in Pyotr's car.

I'm being chased by a powerful man who is going to be even hungrier for revenge now than he was before Mikhail stopped his plan in its tracks. I don't know that I'll be able to protect *myself* from Iakov, let alone Dante, as well.

He's safer with Mikhail. As much as I wish it wasn't true, it is.

It's also the only reason I can drive away from Dante without falling apart.

Though, ten minutes away from the mansion, I do in fact fall apart.

I manage to pull the car along a curb through a haze of tears. Then I press my forehead to the steering wheel and cry and cry. I weep until there's nothing left. Until all I can do is sit back in the seat gasping for breath.

This car may have belonged to Pyotr, but the citrus and cedar smell of Mikhail is practically woven into the upholstery. Each breath is like burying my face in his neck. It's like being back in his house, back in his arms.

I need to get away from it. I throw the door open and stumble into the grass. By the time I drop to my knees, I'm already heaving.

There wasn't much in the way of food in Iakov's bunker, but my body tries desperately to empty itself anyway. I want to blame my nausea on the stress and the grief.

I *pray* it's because of the stress and the grief.

Deep inside, though, I know better.

When I'm finally done, I flop back on the grass and stare up at the black night. The sky is overcast and gray. The city lights paint everything a dingy orange. I lie there until the early morning dew soaks through my shirt and my body is grumbling at me to either eat something or throw up some more. Or both.

I climb back into the car and drive until I see the glow of a twenty-four-hour pharmacy. The girl behind the counter is young and she doesn't look up from her phone as I raid the shelves for supplies.

She checks me out without hesitating over anything I place on the belt. I'm sure she's seen it all. Especially at two in the morning.

Then I make my way to a motel.

Running is oddly familiar to me. Dante and I lived in the same apartment for years, but the mindset of being on the run never quite left my system. It's only in the last few weeks that I let myself consider the possibility that we would settle down somewhere. Naively, I thought Mikhail's mansion could become home.

I may not want you to die, but that doesn't mean I want you.

I block out the echo of Mikhail's words. I can't dwell on them now. Not when my survival depends on me staying sharp and being ready for anything. Curling into the fetal position and nursing a broken heart isn't an option right now.

I look around at the faded couch against the water-damaged wall, at the threadbare comforter tossed over a bed too many people have slept in.

Then, finally, I force my gaze down to the pregnancy test sitting on the rickety table.

I expected the two pink lines, but still, nothing could have prepared me for how quickly they appeared or how vibrant they are.

I'm not just pregnant. I'm *really* pregnant.

Forget Plan B. Forget Plans C, D, and E, also. I'm deep in the alphabet, scrambling for what in the actual fuck I'm going to do now.

I've been here in this exact position before, but this time is different. This time, Mikhail has Dante and Iakov is out for blood. The odds aren't just stacked against me; I'm being slowly crushed underneath them.

In a sign of just how desperate I am, I grab my phone out of my bag and dial a number I haven't used in years.

My father answers on the second ring. "It was only ever a matter of time before you came crawling back on your knees."

I close my eyes, fighting through a wave of nausea that might have nothing at all to do with being pregnant. "Aren't you going to ask where I've been?"

"You don't think I already know?" he snorts. "You've started a war, girl. Then again, if you're calling me, I'm guessing that means Mikhail has done the smart thing and ended it before it could begin."

Now. I'm in a war with the Greeks and the truth is... you're not worth it.

I hate that my father is right.

I hate even more that I can't afford to hang up on him.

"This isn't about Mikhail—it's about Iakov," I explain. "He's coming for me because of what you made me do."

"I didn't *make* you do anything. You had a choice. And if you'll remember, you didn't uphold your end of the bargain."

"My end of the bargain was to risk my life killing Trofim and then hand you my son. It was a shit deal and it was never really an option."

"Is the bastard boy with you now? Or am I right in assuming he's with his father while you're in some rat-infested motel?" I don't answer, but I don't have to. He laughs. "You stabbed me in the back and lost the boy anyway. Now, you're on the run and desperate. It's just like the last time I came and scooped you up off the pavement."

He has no idea how right he is. Down to the positive pregnancy test sitting in front of me.

"I won't survive this time."

Every cell in my body wants to lie and tell my father I'll make it on my own, but I know I won't. My choices over the last six years are catching up with me. I tried, but it just wasn't enough. I wasn't smart enough or brave enough to make it.

Dante's face flashes in my mind. I can still feel his head heavy on my shoulder, his soft breath against my neck.

I squeeze my eyes closed, willing myself not to dissolve into more tears. *Not in front of my father.*

"Please," I beg. The word is bitter, but appealing to my father for help is my only choice. "I'll do anything."

He hums as he considers and I can hear the amusement. He's loving this far more than he should.

Then his answer comes as swift as an executioner's ax.

"No."

I freeze. "What?"

"No," he repeats. "You have a current and a former Novikov *pakhan* after you. All because you turned your back on me and ran."

"Dad—"

"I was willing to help you before, even after you ran the night before your wedding. I was willing to pick up the pieces of your broken promises. But now... Now, you need to face real consequences, Viviana. You need to understand what it's like when I'm not playing the hero and cleaning up your messes."

If I wasn't so panicked, I'd laugh. My father has never been the hero. Not once.

But I can't even formulate coherent thoughts, let alone words.

"Good luck," he says into the stunned silence. "I'm sure I'll see you soon."

The line goes dead and I throw my phone against the wall. It leaves a dent, but it's just one of many in the trashed room.

"You won't see me once I'm dead!" I shriek.

I swipe my arm across the table in front of me, sending the pregnancy test and half of the supplies I bought from the drugstore flying across the room.

The anger fuels me for another ten seconds before I collapse on the floor and start gathering up the mess.

I have no idea where I'm going to live, how I'm going to get more money, or where my next meal is coming from. I can't afford to throw a fit.

I stack the non-perishables and water bottles on the table and then drop to my hands and knees to find the pregnancy test under the bed. I don't need it anymore. I already know what the result is. But I have to stare at it some more to convince myself this nightmare is real.

I'm pregnant with Mikhail Novikov's second child.

I'm on the run.

I'm all alone.

I press my hand to my stomach. *Maybe not* all *alone.*

I'm about to sink down onto the bed and let myself slip into a few blissful hours of unconsciousness… when there's a knock on the door.

I groan. I'm sure someone called about the shouting and banging, but given the grunts and groaning going on next door, I don't think my neighbors have any right to complain.

"I'm sorry about the noise," I call through the door. "I'll quiet down."

No answer. After a few seconds, there's another round of knocks.

I look through the peephole, but it's been painted over, because of course it has. Three of the four walls in my room are patched over with different shades of faded yellow, but the doors have a fresh coat of paint. Makes perfect sense.

"I'm sorry," I repeat. "All is good in here."

More knocking rattles the cheap door in the frame.

I jerk the chain out of the lock and fling the door open. "I told you I won't cause any more trouble. Go on back to—"

The words die on my lips when I look up into the very last face I ever expected to see.

"I want to believe you, but I'm afraid you're nothing but trouble, Viviana."

Trofim Novikov smiles, his face curving into vengeance incarnate.

Then he pushes me inside my room and kicks the door closed behind him.

TO BE CONTINUED

Mikhail and Viviana's story concludes in Book 2 of the Novikov Bratva duet, IVORY OATH.
Get it now!

Printed in Great Britain
by Amazon